THE HAYSTACK

A Novel

by

James J. Mulligan

This book is a work of fiction. There is reference to numerous historical characters. Insofar as possible they have been placed in the book in the same context in which they were at the same time historically. However, their interaction with the fictional characters is clearly non-historical. Beyond that, any resemblance between the characters in the book and real persons living or dead is purely coincidental.

All rights reserved. No part of this book may be reproduced or transmitted in any form by any means, electronic, mechanical, photocopying, recording or otherwise without the prior written permission of the author.

Copyright © 2012, James J. Mulligan

To find a needle in a haystack may seem a daunting challenge; yet, with a modicum of patience and the employment of a good magnet, it is barely a challenge at all. The real sense of accomplishment comes upon being able, with only your wits and your persistence to guide you, to find one specific piece of hay in a haystack.

        Carl Gustavus Brownson, M.D. (1799-1878)
        Science of the Autopsy (1863)

Galen 1

The delicate grace of the lachrymal bistoury disguises a strength out of all proportion to its seeming fragility. This one was just over seven inches long, not quite three-eighths of an inch thick at the widest point of the rosewood shaft which constituted its central portion. Through that shaft ran the flawless steel rod, one extremity a probe with a tiny bulbous end and the other a gently curved blade sharper than a razor with a point as acute as that of a needle. It was meant for the painstaking task of surgery upon the delicate tear duct of the human eye, but this one had just served quite another purpose. It had made the incision with ease, slipping in and out with little resistance and leaving almost no evidence of its passage, apart from the scarlet thread of blood that he had just dabbed from the patient's left nostril.

He wiped the bistoury clean with his linen handkerchief, replaced it carefully into the fitted slot of the pocket case, and snapped shut the lid. This attention to detail served to restore his composure. He looked again at the corpse.

This was not the first time he had killed, but, to his surprise, this one had left him shaken, almost on the verge of panic. The eyes had done it. Purely a nervous reflex, of course. The chloroform had done its work, but as he inserted the bistoury the eyes had opened — wide, staring, full of shock and disbelief. An involuntary reaction, the dying spasm of a cut nerve, but unsettling nonetheless.

He pulled a straight-backed chair out from the table, its loose joints creaking as he sat. He looked about, determining that he had left no trace of his presence. No one knew he was here. Even the old hag downstairs hadn't seen him come in, and he would be careful not to draw her attention when he left.

His breathing returned to normal. He got up, went to the small table next to the bed and opened its drawers one by one. They held the usual odds and ends one tosses into drawers, thinking they will be of use later but never really are. But it was the tablet that drew his attention. He opened it and his own *nom de querre* stared back at him. Three pages, all about him. Who would have thought the man had known so much?

He tore the pages from the tablet, flipped through it to be certain that there was nothing more, and dropped it onto the tabletop. What could he use? His eye fell on the glazed washbowl. He took a match from his pocket, held the sheets by one corner, struck the match on the sole of his boot, and set fire to the pages. He watched them blacken and curl up until the flame almost reached his fingers. He dropped them into the washbowl and waited until the final corner was gone. He stirred the charred remains with the end of the matchstick until there was no clue to what the paper had once held. He dropped the spent match into the bowl and brushed the traces of ash from his fingers.

There now remained the body. Should he simply leave it? He could hardly carry it away with him. Yet if it were found here in the room it might create enough of a mystery to encourage investigation. Why had a young man in normal health suddenly died in his room without a mark on the body? Better to supply a solution to satisfy their curiosity. But what? He discarded one idea after another, none of them satisfactory. He got up and went to the window. He stood to one side, opened the threadbare curtain a crack, and peeked out carefully, not wanting to be seen by anyone below, unlikely as that was, since he was four flights above the narrow street. A few children were at play, but they would not be there long. The sky had grown threatening and the temperature was dropping sharply. The wind was picking up and the first random flakes of snow had already started to fall. He would wait. The street would be deserted before long. He sat again, took a book from his pocket and began to read as he waited.

Chapter I: Pay Attention, Young Sir

Training is everything. The peach was once
a bitter almond; cauliflower is nothing but
cabbage with a college education.
   Mark Twain (1835-1910)
   Pudd'nhead Wilson. Pudd'nhead Wilson's Calendar (1874)

[December, 1860]

"Now let us look more closely," said Doctor Brownson.

The snow had ended but the bleak December day continued bitterly cold. The young man thus addressed had his chapped fists buried deep in his coat pockets, his vision obscured by the cloud of vapor that rose before his face each time he exhaled. Intermittent bursts of wind whistled through the canyon of tall buildings on either side of the street and stirred up loose snow from the rooftops, its icy pinpricks blowing sharp against his cold-reddened cheeks. None of this was of any concern to the object of their attentions, who lay against the wall behind the weathered wooden crates. They peered at him, but he ignored them, staring instead at a point far up in the gray, winter sky. Snowflakes had settled on the lashes of the wide open eyes and accumulated in the gaping mouth.

This corpse was not the first the young man had seen. It was the first whose death was attributable to other than natural causes, whose demise an inquest might lay at the feet of some mysterious "person or persons unknown."

Not so for the older man who stood in silence watching him so intently, waiting to see what he would do next. It was the young man's first encounter with Doctor Carl Gustavus Brownson outside the classroom. It was also his first year as a medical student, having come to Philadelphia from his home town of Beaver Meadow.

James Dougherty's education had begun under the tutelage of Miss Lydia Bidlack in the little schoolhouse on Penrose Street. Father Hugh McMahon, pastor of Saint Mary's Church, taught him to serve at Mass and, pleased at the lad's curiosity, allowed him the use of his seminary books to learn the Latin of the church and even some of the classics.

Rensselaer Leonard, a contract physician with the Beaver Meadow mines, also noted Dougherty's interest in learning, and, when he later moved his practice to the county seat at Mauch Chunk, took him on as general factotum and apprentice. That led to his two years of study at the Jefferson Medical College.

Each morning since September he'd walked the three-quarters of a mile from Mrs. Kiley's house to Tenth Street, where, between the residence to its south and Mr. James Keenan's boot shop to the north, Jefferson Medical College stood like Gulliver among the Lilliputians — a fitting image for an institution whose faculty were giants in their fields: Doctors Samuel D. Gross, Robley Dunglison, Charles D. Miegs, John Hill Brinton, and Carl Gustavus Brownson.

Almost before he'd realized it, the leaves fell, the days shortened, and on the coldest day of the month of December, he was wending his way home under a slate colored sky, the sun an all but indiscernible shrouded silver disk. The morning had begun warm enough to melt the surface of the muddy streets, but before ten-thirty it suddenly turned cold and everything froze solid. Brisk flurries in late morning and early afternoon, had put down an inch or two of snow, making the walking treacherous. He shuffled along Walnut Street, his thoughts on the warm fire at the end of those seven long blocks. He would do his chores, enjoy a bowl of Mrs. Kiley's mutton stew, report to her on the news of the day, then retire to his room to read by the light of the lard-oil lamp until bedtime.

With eyes focused on his footing, chin tucked into the greatcoat's collar around which was wrapped the blue woolen scarf his mother had made, his cap pulled down to his eyebrows, he was lost in his own little world; and so took some moments to realize that a cab had slowed down to accommodate to his shuffling pace and that someone was calling from within.

"You there! Young Dougherty! Wake up! Pay attention! Look over here!"

A face peered out from the cab of a single-horse, two-passenger brougham of the type available as a public conveyance. As Dougherty stopped, so did the carriage. The man inside removed his wide-brimmed top hat and Dougherty saw, to his surprise, that it was none other than Doctor Carl Gustavus Brownson.

Brownson was then about sixty, paunchy, with graying hair that ran into side-whiskers cut to the level of his jaw line, his upper lip and chin shaved clean. Bushy black brows shaded the dark eyes which missed little of what any student did, said, or even thought. He favored black suits, as did so many doctors. His had a rusty look, the trousers baggy, the sleeves smudged with chalk dust, the vest front decorated with the cigar ashes that dropped as he lectured on the wonders of anatomy and physiology. He had, upon occasion, favored Dougherty with some small sign that he was pleased with his work — or at least that he was not overly displeased.

"Come here, young man," he said, as he opened the carriage door. "Get in here out of the cold. I want to talk to you."

Without a moment's hesitation Dougherty climbed in, his daydreams now totally replaced by curiosity.

"I've had my eye on you these past months," the Doctor said. "You seem a young man willing to learn. Am I mistaken in that estimate?"

"I suppose not, sir. At least, I hope not."

"Good," he said, "because I am offering you the chance to learn your art in a way seldom available to a young man. I assist the police from time to time in explaining questionable deaths. I am required to perform post-mortem examinations with a view to revealing the cause of death and on occasion a great deal more besides. There is much to learn from this, even at my age, and you have both youth and the capacity to profit from this opportunity. Are you interested?"

"Yes, sir."

The answer was immediate. The very thought of participating in Brownson's unusual work appealed to him.

It was not yet three o'clock, but streets were crowded as the bad weather and early winter darkness encouraged market closings on

High Street. The homeward bound shoppers, the pushcarts of hucksters, and the drays of merchants overflowed into all the streets round about, the cobblestones fast becoming slippery, making everyone eager to get home. With the driver taking great care to avoid an icy accident in the press of vehicular traffic moving in both directions, as the pedestrians, with little apparent regard for their own lives, slipped and slid between conveyances as they worked their way across the street, their carriage continued its progress in precisely the direction in which Dougherty had already been going.

They were nearly opposite Mrs. Kiley's house when they turned right, following the incline of Dock Street toward the waterfront. The street meandered as though laid out by a planner who had imbibed a little too freely. They passed by Naylor's Hotel, a ramshackle affair with peeling paint and a second story entrance nailed shut since its steps had been removed. Its evening clientele was a boisterous lot, sometimes breaking out into loud arguments and fights. It was a neighborhood of contradictions. Where Mrs. Kiley lived, it was full of bustle all day long, but peaceful enough at night. In these few blocks nearer the river, the once genteel houses gave way to the establishments of shipping wholesalers, crowded boarding houses, eateries catering to laborers and seamen, and hotels, like Naylor's, engaged in the simple struggle to hold on.

South of Prune Street, but before Spruce, they turned left to stay on Dock Street. Once beyond Front Street they turned again left onto Water Street. There, in its narrow confines, they halted near a still unlighted street lamp.

"Here we are," said Brownson. The driver was already down from his bench and opening the doctor's door. The horse snorted, expelling a billow of steamy breath, and the driver, having seen to his passengers, tossed a faded red blanket across its back, patted its neck, and slipped over its ears the strap of a nosebag half full of oats. The animal munched contentedly and ignored them all.

Two uniformed constables armed with billy clubs and pistols, ceased stomping their feet and chafing their hands and came toward them. Doctor Brownson introduced them as Constables Delaney and Thompson. Delaney was stocky, bow-legged, with chest and shoulders heavily developed for a man so short. Thompson was tall, thin, blond haired, clean shaven, with a seemingly perpetual smile.

"Let us show ye what we've got, sir. It'll be right over here, if ye'll be so good as to folly me," said Delaney.

The buildings on the west side of the street were all four or five stories high. Their façades on Front Street had entrances a whole story higher than those on Water Street, so most people entered the buildings from that side and went up or down as they desired, leaving this part of Water Street more deserted than the number of residences might have suggested.

The darkening sky and towering buildings shrouded the street in gloom. The new fallen snow and the freezing temperature conspired to suppress both sight and aroma of the refuse that people threw from their windows into the street, where it was eaten by the dogs or the pigs that still roamed this part of the city. The Constable led them to a building where three weathered wooden crates stood side by side, a few feet out from the wall. They were not especially large, no more than two feet in width and the same in height, apparently untouched in the last few hours, the snow upon them undisturbed. As they drew closer, Dougherty saw protruding from behind them a pair of feet in shabby boots with rundown heels.

"It's a man," said Delaney, "Dead as a doornail, he is. Not been here long, I'd say. There's this afternoon's snow on him, but no more than that."

"How did you discover him?" Brownson asked.

"Thompson here was walking his beat. He was over near Front and Pine, not far from Ned Thornton's place. He can tell ye what happened." Edward Thornton was the proprietor of a basement drinking establishment which he called the Great Ale Vault.

"Well, sir, it was like this," said Thompson, with a barely perceptible movement back to a range from which their noses could not detect what he may have been drinking to stave off the chill. "I was coming back up along Front, headed in this direction, when I sees a young lad come tearing outa Dock Street up from the waterfront like Old Nick himself was after him. He stops and looks round and sees me only a block away. It looked like he was running away from something or somebody. I thought for sure he'd been up to no good and that he'd take off in the other direction once he seen me. Instead he heads for me fast as his feet can carry him. 'Help!' he's calling and he gets to me so out of breath he can't even say what's wrong. He's just pointing and sputtering. Then he finally tells me he seen a dead man and he takes me here. He waited at the corner and I come up here to see the body."

"Where's the boy now?" asked Brownson.

"He didn't seem much use to us right now," said Thompson. "He didn't see nothing but the body. I sent him home and told him to find Delaney on his way. Once he seen what we had, he sent a messenger to fetch you."

"Fine," said Brownson, "You did well."

Dougherty turned toward the body, but Brownson's arm shot out in front of him before he took even the first step.

"You're about to begin the next phase of your education, young Dougherty, so do nothing. Stand still and look before you do anything else."

The officers smiled. They'd heard it all before when they had first worked with Brownson and learned to attend to him once they saw the results he so often achieved.

Dougherty looked. This part of the street had been little used for the past few hours and the snow was not much disturbed, save for the immediate vicinity of the body, where he saw two sets of footprints. Those of the child rambled in from Walnut Street to the north. They turned toward the crates, then headed due south with steps so widely spaced that there was no mistaking that the boy had been running. The other, larger set came from Dock to the crates and back again to the spot where they had met the constables.

"There are the boy's prints and the constable's, but not the dead man's," Dougherty asked.

"Why not?" said Brownson.

"There is snow on top of the man's legs. He must have been there before it snowed."

Brownson said nothing. He moved toward the crates and, after a moment's hesitation, Dougherty followed. The snow on the crates was not so undisturbed as he had thought. There were the youngster's small hand prints. They leaned over to see the dead man.

He lay on his back, eyes wide open. There was snow the length of the body, but what was on top of it was not nearly so deep as the snow around it. Flakes had settled on his face, but not enough to hide his features.

"The snow stopped somewhat before three o'clock, did it not?" Doctor Brownson said. "I would suspect that this man has not been here since much before two. Well, young Dougherty, what else can you tell me? Pay attention, young sir, and take notes."

With that he poked around in a coat pocket, extracted a clean note pad and pencil, and put them into Dougherty's hands. Dougherty waited, but Brownson said nothing.

The dead man was of medium height, in his early thirties, wearing a suit once expensive but long since out of style. The frayed cuffs had been cut and resewn. The knees and elbows were shiny and worn thin. It had probably come from a used clothing dealer, of which there were many in the area. He wore no outer coat, no scarf, no gloves, and there was no hat anywhere in sight. His boots, were scuffed and worn, but serviceable. His hair was long, unkempt, slightly greasy. He had a full beard and moustache, and he stared upward with wide open, glazed-over eyes and mouth agape, the lips pulled back from tobacco-stained teeth. The snowflakes lined his eyelashes and had even settled into the open mouth, unmelted in the frigid air. His arms and legs were twisted, his head on a brick, one of half a dozen or so scattered about. The snow on the body and all around it was white, clean, and apparently untouched. All of this Dougherty jotted down in the shorthand that he had developed for himself in class. He turned to Brownson and summarized what he had seen.

"Good," he said, "Now, what can you tell me about how he died?"

"I see no wounds. There may be some underneath, but I can't see what killed him."

Brownson looked for a few more minutes without touching anything, then asked the two constables to turn the body over. As they did so, the head flopped to the side and Dougherty saw an indentation in the skull.

"Examine that," Brownson said, "with your fingers as well as your eyes."

Under the soft hair he felt a pyramidal shaped concavity, the bone pushed inward about an inch behind the left ear, at the lambdoidal suture of the left temporal and parietal bones. Soft tissue from the wound stuck to his fingers. Bits of brain, he thought. It was cold. He started to wipe it on the shoulder of the dead man's jacket, knowing he would offer no objections, but Doctor Brownson did, offering him a cloth instead. The damage had been caused by the corner of the brick, whose shape was readily discernible. The cause of death seemed all too obvious. The left arm, just above the wrist, was also fractured through both radius and ulna, but there was no sign of a bruise. He saw no other injury.

It was fast becoming darker and colder and soon it would not be possible to continue the examination of the body without taking it to some other location where there would be both warmth and light.

"Where did he come from?" Brownson asked.

"I have no idea," Dougherty said, "I have never seen him before."

"No," Brownson said, "What I want to know is how this body came to be precisely *here*. Observe and tell me."

There were no footprints apart from those of the boy, the police, and now their own. Had he come there under his own power before the snow began or just after? Had he been attacked and killed? Not likely. Out in this weather without hat or gloves or scarf or overcoat? It made more sense to think that the dead man had been placed there. But how was he put there forcefully enough to push that brick into his head and kill him?

"Think, young Dougherty," the Doctor said.

If someone had carried the body there before the snow, there would have been no prints, yet the relatively small amount of snow on top of the body pointed to its having been placed there some time after the snow had begun and not long before it had ended. But in that case there should have been some visible footprints. It made no sense.

Did he just fall from the sky? And that ridiculous thought showed him what Brownson had seen almost immediately. He looked up. Near the top of the building he saw a row of contributionship plates, the shield-shaped iron emblems of the Philadelphia fire insurance company founded by Ben Franklin. Just below one of them was a wide open window.

"There," said Dougherty, pointing upward, "No one carried him here! He fell from that window and hit his head on this brick." But even as he spoke he doubted. The window was hardly large enough for a grown man to fall through by accident.

"I agree that he almost certainly came from that window," Brownson said, "But did he jump? Did he fall? Was he pushed? Is it suicide or accident or murder?"

"Maybe we can tell by going up to the room," Dougherty answered.

"Oh, we shall certainly do that," said Brownson, "but these questions can be answered right here and now. Pay attention, young sir, to what you do not see."

What did he *not* see? He did not see the dead man's footprints. What else was missing but should have been there? He was at a loss, and said so.

"Ah, well... you'll learn in time. You've not done badly for a first outing. But you have before you the answer to my question. Think of William Harvey."

"William Harvey? The one who discovered blood circulation."

Suddenly it was clear as could be. The head was crushed in back, the injury due to the brick — a brick surrounded by snow and upon that snow hardly a drop of blood. When Dougherty had touched the fracture earlier, his fingers came away with bits of brain on them, but there was no sign of the quantities of blood that such a wound should have caused and there was no dried blood in the hair.

"The man was already dead when he fell from the window! The blood had stopped circulating, so of course there was none on the snow. The blow to his head was delivered after death, not before. He did not commit suicide and he did not simply fall by accident. Someone must have pushed him through the window."

"So! You see it!" Brownson actually seemed pleased. "We cannot yet say that he was murdered, but it is most likely. Why else push a dead body through a fourth floor window? Of course, even before we saw the wound we knew he'd been dead for some time before he landed here. Otherwise his body would still have been warm and the snow in his open mouth and eyes would have melted. We'll learn more when we take him to the infirmary and look inside."

Thus far, to Dougherty's surprise, they had attracted the attention of no one who lived along Water Street. Perhaps the cold kept them all indoors. There was no response when Doctor Brownson dispatched Thompson to pound on the door of the residence from which the dead man had been dropped, so he sent him around to the Front Street side and they waited in the cold until, finally, the door opened and Thompson emerged with an old crone in tow. Huddled against the cold and pulling up a threadbare shawl to cover her stringy, matted gray hair, she was a walking rag bag in layers of castoffs, and not even the chill wind could dispel the sour odor of unwashed humanity that emerged with her.

"That's him," she said, directing a gnarled finger and a cursory look at the dead man, her tone expressionless, as though one body more or less was all in the day's work for her.

"This is Maggie Warden," Thompson said, "She's the landlady of this establishment. Says the corpse is Joe Fuller. Lived in the room with the open window."

Doctor Brownson questioned her, but she was hardly a font of knowledge. Fuller had moved in about six months earlier, paid his rent on time, kept to himself, was usually out all day and back late at night. As to friends, he might have had some in from time to time, but she really "din't know nothing about it" — and that was her monotonous refrain to all further questions.

With obvious ill will she led them to the top floor, while Delaney stayed to keep the dead man company until the police wagon arrived. Every step of every flight of stairs was accompanied by the sound of creaking woodwork and crackling knees, punctuated with muttered curses and complaints — as though her tenant had gotten himself killed just to spite her.

His room was a far cry from what Dougherty enjoyed at Mrs. Kiley's house. Its walls were faded, dingy, drab, their peeling paper stained with mildew, but its occupant had tried to keep it clean. There was a table with two straight-backed chairs, their paint worn thin. The narrow bed was neatly made. The chamber set was old, its glaze crazed and stained, but it was washed and both pitcher and bowl were placed neatly upon the stand. In the bottom of the bowl were a matchstick, ashes, and burnt paper. A hat and scarf and long overcoat hung on a hook behind the door.

Doctor Brownson went to the open window, carefully examined the sill, and slammed the window shut against the frigid air.

"Nothing there," he said.

He struck a match and lit the lamp on the table next to the bed, where also lay a tablet and pencil. A chest of drawers against the opposite wall revealed no more than a few changes of clothes of a quality in keeping with what the dead man wore.

Brownson picked up the tablet and flipped through it, its pages held at an angle to the lamp. About half the pages had been torn out, and all the rest were blank. He lay the tablet down next to the lamp and gently rubbed the pencil back and forth across the uppermost page to reveal an impression of writing.

"What do you make of that, Dougherty?" he asked.

It was not easy to make it out. Dougherty turned it back and forth in the light of the lamp, until at last he deciphered it. "...is his real name, but most here know him only as G, as I told you before. He was at the anticoercionist rally and he was friendly, but I don't trust him. I think he suspects me. I will take care. What do you suggest I do? J.F."

"It looks like the end of a letter," Dougherty said.

"Probably so. Do you know the anticoercionists?" he asked.

"I've heard of them, but I don't know much about them."

"You'll hear more of them," he said. "They think that if a state secedes from the Union, it should not be forced to come back. With Lincoln elected and the South ready to leave, it's no longer a theoretical discussion. Philadelphia has its share of southern agents who want us to take the lead in getting Pennsylvania to join a southern secessionist movement."

It was not a farfetched idea. This city was strongly Democratic and pro-slavery. There was a lot of talk about breaking away from the radical New England abolitionists.

"I wonder," said Brownson, "if 'G' is one of the southern instigators we've been hearing about."

He looked around the room once more, then said, "That's it. There's nothing else here for us. The rest will be done in the post-mortem."

Back on the street, the lamp at the corner had been lighted and a wagon had come to remove the body. It was dark when the cab driver dropped Dougherty off at Mrs. Kiley's. On the way back Brownson spoke hardly a word, and Dougherty began to fear that he had in some manner disappointed him; but his spirits soared when, as he was about to descend from the carriage, Brownson said, "And so, young Dougherty, shall I expect you at the infirmary tomorrow morning? The post-mortem will begin promptly at seven o'clock."

Dougherty could not believe his good fortune. He was not yet through the first semester of his two years of medical college and he was already working with Carl Gustavus Brownson. He had come a long way from Beaver Meadow. Beaver Meadow... the name conjures up images of babbling brooks and broad-tailed, buck-toothed, thick-furred mammals busily building dams and waiting in patient docility to be skinned and fashioned into stylish hats. Not so the reality. The meadows had long since disappeared, as had the beavers. The town's only industry was anthracite mining and Beaver Creek had a bed of sulphurous coal dust that killed the fish and left the water undrinkable.

He had arrived in Philadelphia in September, leaving the train west of the Schuylkill and going by horse drawn trolley to the Front Street terminus. It was a glorious day, but he felt quite the country bumpkin as he gawked and gaped along the market stalls. The pushing crowds and the din of traffic and hucksters and news hawkers were music to his ears. Even the aromas changed with each step he took: fruits, vegetables, garbage, flowers, sweat, fried fish, manure, boiled potatoes, horse stale, and roasted pork prepared over charcoal burners and sold in cone-twisted sheets of yesterday's newspaper. He basked in the novelty of it all, and it was evening when he had finally arrived at the house of Mrs. Martha Kiley.

"So you are young Mister Dougherty," she had said as she opened the door in response to his timid knock. "Come in! You are welcome to be sure. Set down your bag and come with me."

Mrs. Kiley was a physician's widow near sixty years of age, a friend of a friend of Doctor Leonard. She had inherited enough to eke out a fairly comfortable existence, but still enjoyed taking in a properly recommended medical student willing to earn his keep by helping with the chores.

"Sit down," she said as they entered the kitchen, "I've saved you some supper."

She was small, apple cheeked, cheerful, bouncy as a sparrow. Her blue eyes were full of humor and she brushed aside his apology at being late, caring only that he was well fed. They spoke as he ate, until a stifled yawn revealed his exhaustion and she showed him to his room.

She entered first and lit the lamp that sat on a pie-crust table next to an upholstered wing chair. There was a tall window overlooking Dock Street, a pigeon-holed writing desk with a wooden chair, a small bookcase, a narrow wardrobe and a bed covered with immaculate linen and a colorful quilt.

"It looks wonderful," he said and was rewarded with a pleased sigh and a smile so radiant that he realized that she had been as nervous as he about this first meeting. So had begun his medical career and he imagined that he could not have been happier. But all of that paled into insignificance before the wonder of assisting Doctor Brownson.

He was that night like a child on Christmas Eve — unable to fall asleep and then finding himself wide awake long before it was time to leave for the infirmary. Doctor Brownson, true to his word, began promptly at seven.

The examination was far more painstaking than an ordinary anatomical dissection in which one merely observes and studies structures. The post-mortem looks for the anomalous, generally with no way to predict precisely what should be sought. Doctor Brownson taught as he cut, and Dougherty marveled at his knowledge. In the organs of the trunk they found no cause of death, but he drew Dougherty's attention to a number of items and told him to make notes: The abdominal viscera and pulmonary tissue were unusually congested, the bronchi exhibited spots of bloody froth, and the blood in general was quite fluid and darker in color than one should have expected.

"H'mm," he said, and, "Aha!" Dougherty did not enter those comments into his notebook, but it was obvious that Brownson was seeing more than he.

Finally they had only the head to consider. After laying back the scalp, he used a conical trephine to cut out four circles of bone at intervals around the skull. With a Hey's saw he cut into the skull, moving from circle to circle like a child connecting dots to form a picture and thus removed the top of the skull like a cap.

Removal of the brain from the cranial cavity revealed beneath the frontal lobe a pool of thickening blood. He pointed to where the anterior cerebral artery had been cut. He wiped away the blood and peered intently into the now empty skull.

"Look there, Dougherty, and tell me what you see." He waited.

At first Dougherty saw nothing untoward and then, as Brownson had done, he bent over to peer intently at the interior surface and saw a small hole where no hole should have been. Between the eyes is the cubical ethmoid bone, its sides forming a portion of the ocular orbits and its central portion, the cribriform plate, making a sort of floor for the anterior part of the brain and allowing the olfactory nerves to pass through. It is a light, spongy sort of structure and in it there was a hole less than a sixteenth inch in diameter.

"What is it, sir" Dougherty asked.

"A puncture wound," Brownson said. "Small as it is, it is undoubtedly the cause of death as evidenced by the amount of blood. It is hardly the result of an accident. The killer knew his anatomy."

"How do you think it was made?"

"There is only one way it could have happened," Brownson said. "Someone pushed a long, relatively thin implement — perhaps an icepick — up the left nostril, through the ethmoid, and into the brain. It would cause death quite rapidly and would leave little external trace — as we have already seen."

"How would it be done, sir? Surely no one would sit still and allow it to happen."

"True," he said, "but this man put up no fight. The items I earlier asked you to note are typical of a heavy dose of chloroform. When you get back to the college, look in Taylor's *Medical Jurisprudence* and study what he has to say about ether and chloroform. Our killer knows his anatomy and the use of chloroform. Bothersome facts, indeed, young Dougherty."

"Can we conclude that he is a physician?" Dougherty asked.

"Conclude? Perhaps not, but it is a reasonable conjecture."

The case was to be left full of conjectures. The man had been killed, but only later dropped from the window, after his body had begun to cool. Why? Perhaps because the killer wanted to disguise the real cause of death, and had no earlier opportunity to push it through the window. Were there too many people about? Did he have some other reason? They simply did not know, but Dougherty was certain that Doctor Brownson would discover the truth.

As it happened, he did not. The solution would come eventually, but in a way they could not then have predicted. They did learn that the dead man had spent many evenings at Naylor's hotel, and Dougherty should have seen him had his powers of observation been better honed. But now it was too late. Any hope of resolving the matter slowly waned.

For the next year and a half Dougherty pursued his studies and spent as much time as he could assisting Doctor Brownson. Not every case was one of murder, but each was a source of knowledge. He examined bodies that had been shot, stabbed, poisoned, bludgeoned, run over by railway cars or carriages, or, in one way or another, had succumbed to deaths that were sudden, mysterious, suspicious, or simply needed explanation.

The work would have appeared gruesome to some and so at first he had told Mrs. Kiley only that he was working for one of the doctors at the college. But there came a night when two men were found dead near the docks, and Mrs. Kiley came to tap at his door.

"Mister Dougherty, there is a policeman at the front door. He says that he has come for you and that Doctor Brownson sent him. Is something wrong? Are you in some difficulty? Can something have happened to the doctor?"

Dougherty assured her there was no need for worry. She was still up when he came back and he told her the sort of work that he did for Doctor Brownson. As he expected, she wondered aloud just what sort of person this Doctor Brownson must be to lead a young man in such a direction. Then, much to his surprise, after all the sounds of horror and disgust proper to any gentlewoman, she insisted on hearing much more than he had originally intended to impart. With each new case after that, she not only wanted to hear about it, but even made suggestions and observations that revealed a mind capable of quick and accurate insights, and a temperament not really given to foolish squeamishness.

It was not long before the opportunity presented itself for Dougherty to introduce her to Doctor Brownson, and she suggested that he might like to come to dinner. His obvious pleasure in both her company and her cooking could not help but charm her. It was a side of Brownson that Dougherty had not suspected.

He learned much from Doctor Carl Gustavus Brownson and in later years would often hear that voice saying, "Use your eyes! Use your mind! Observe and learn. Pay attention, young sir. Let the dead speak to you, for no one else will listen to them!" Brownson taught Dougherty their language and trained him to overlook nothing — not even the seemingly inconsequential. In the end, it made him a better doctor for both living and dead, and would also immerse him in a mystery whose solution was, when all was said and done, far more painful than satisfying.

Chapter II: Tenting on the Old Campground

All I have to say is what the girl said
when she stuck her foot into the stocking.
It strikes me there's something in it.
    Abraham Lincoln (1809-1865)
    Comment on a model ironclad, September 13, 1861

[September 12, 1862]

"Ye'll no doubt be watching yer step, sir!"

Sean McBrien's booming voice turned the passing remark into a public announcement that made every officer within twenty yards do a hop, a skip, and a jump for fear that he was about to put his foot into something noxious. His voice suited his stature — over six feet tall, bright red hair and beard, broad shouldered, well muscled, with enormous hands as much at home on the reins of the mules as they were in the kindlier tasks of his duties each day at sick call. Although currently replacing the unfortunate ambulance driver who a few days earlier had lost his footing while dismounting and broken his leg, McBrien would be returning to his usual duties as medical steward now that they had arrived near Frederick.

"Of course I'll watch my step," Dougherty grunted, still full of the first flush of self-importance at being an officer, his demeanor reminding McBrien to save his advice until it was sought. He sprang lightly to the ground and almost fell as his foot landed in something slippery. His nostrils were assailed by an odor already too familiar. His few days at sick call had quickly rid him of the romantic notions of a constant round of life-saving surgery and had opened his eyes to the reality of combating diarrhea by dispensing daily doses of sulphate of magnesia, castor oil, and rhubarb pills.

"Ah, I see ye've found it, sir. That's what I was by way o' referring to." McBrien nodded toward the distasteful mess now decorating the sole of Dougherty's left boot. "I'll do me best in future to give me warning a little louder." His face was serious, no hint of a smile. "Bad as things might be in our own army, sir, the rebs do even more o' the back door trot than we do. A diet too heavy on the green corn and apples, wouldn't ye think, sir? Seeing as how we're using their campground, I suppose the dear boyos didn't want us to think they'd left us nothing but dead grass... Course, the grass is handy fer wiping things off yer boots, ain't it, sir?"

Dougherty glared as he rubbed his boot in the grass, his face reddening under McBrien's seemingly solicitous gaze. Steward McBrien had long since mastered the skill of needling young officers in the most respectful manner.

Riding the ambulance the past few days, Dougherty had heard all about Sean McBrien. In 1845, seventeen and all alone, he'd arrived in New York, hoping for a job but finding that "No Irish need apply." The army was less selective, so he enlisted. He was in the Mexican war and then spent ten years chasing or being chased by Indians in the Southwest. He left the army as a sergeant in 1859 and headed for Philadelphia intending to open a tavern near the waterfront. He found two partners and prepared to enjoy the prosperous life.

"I wish ye coulda met them, sir," he'd said. "They loved a profit as much as meself, and I can't fault them fer that. The problem was they decided to make it from me and they took off with all me savings and the absent minded buggers forgot to leave a forwarding address."

For two years he worked on the docks. Then war broke out and he joined the largely Irish Sixty-ninth Pennsylvania regiment as a medical steward — the pay was the same as a sergeant's, so he was satisfied.

To Dougherty it was no mystery why McBrien was in the army. What amazed him was how he himself had gotten there. By the Spring of 1862, he was a bonafide doctor of medicine, but lacked a few of the essentials — gray hair to simulate wisdom, experience to inspire confidence, and money to set up a practice. By then the country was at war, but still optimistic. Then the real fighting started and initial flamboyance soon gave way to a struggle in deadly earnest. Like a family split asunder by some disagreement that should never have happened in the first place, words turned to blows, argument became acrimony, and both sides fell into a bitterness harsh enough to spawn generations of estrangement long after the original causes of conflict ceased to exist.

In February of 1861, on Washington's birthday, before a shot was ever fired, Abraham Lincoln, on his way to his inauguration, stopped in Philadelphia to raise a flag in honor of Kansas, the newest addition to the Union. The day was crisp, clear, invigorating and Dougherty, like so many others, walked over to State House to see for himself this new president. Both police and militia were much in evidence, fearful of the hard feelings this visit might reveal.

A platform, erected before the door of the State House, some six feet above street level, was draped in bunting that snapped like a pistol shot each time the wind caught it. A double rank of militia stood before it, their eyes on the stage, their backs to the audience.

The band struck up a patriotic air and from the State House came some thirty or forty of the great, the near-great, and the more-than-willing-to-be-thought-great, crowding onto the stage. Head and shoulders above all, came a man, gaunt and gangly, his frock coat loose on his frame, his demeanor that of the typical country lawyer. He stood as Mayor Alexander Henry and others made welcoming speeches, and was, at long last, introduced. The cheers fell to an expectant hush. He doffed his stovepipe hat, raised a hand in greeting, and spoke in a clear, high-pitched voice accustomed to addressing crowds.

"It was not the mere matter of the separation of the colonies from the mother land," he said, "but something in that Declaration giving liberty, not alone to the people of this country, but hope to the world for all future times. It was that which gave promise that in due time the weights should be lifted from the shoulders of all men, and that *all* should have an equal chance."

A great cheer arose. Most may not have realized they were acclaiming a sentiment which might soon push them to fight for ideals not clearly understood and on behalf of a race whose presence among them they generally either ignored or disdained. He proclaimed his dedication to the principle of liberty and, with unwitting prophecy, said, "I would rather be assassinated on this spot than to surrender it."

Now, more than a year later, Dougherty was in the Army of the Potomac in his spanking new lieutenant's uniform, with a pocket surgical kit given to him by Doctor Brownson, a .36 caliber revolver from the gun manufactory of John Krider purchased for him by the usually pacific Mrs. Kiley, and a copy of Smith's new *Handbook of Surgical Operations*, a *vademecum* for the military surgeon which he'd purchased for $3.00. His commission had come from Governor Curtin upon completion of the qualifying examination and through the influence of Doctor Leonard. His orders were to report with all possible alacrity to the regimental surgeon of the Sixty-ninth Pennsylvania.

Alacrity, alas, proved impossible. For three weeks in Washington he lodged in a run-down boarding house and made the rounds of the offices looking for his regiment. All he found were functionaries intent on demonstrating their importance, but leaving him feeling they had somehow misplaced the whole army and were surreptitiously searching for it while they kept him and others like him in perpetual motion, like balls controlled by a juggler afraid to allow a single one to halt, lest the whole come crashing to the ground. It was the first week of September, just a few days after the debacle of Second Bull Run, when he was finally told where to join his regiment, now about to begin its march into Maryland. General McClellan was back in command of the Army of the Potomac and General John Pope was off in disgrace.

Progress from Washington to Frederick was a round of endless dust as tens of thousands of booted feet and horses' hoofs and iron-rimmed wheels of loaded wagons and heavy guns created a constant cloud, ground finer and finer and flung incessantly back into the air in a haze that floated above the miles-long line and then drifted back down to cover clothes and fill mouths and nostrils and ears and eyes with endless irritation. It chafed where the sweat trickled down inside the woolen uniforms and left an all but unquenchable thirst with each mouthful of water tasting more of mud than refreshment. But of enemies, not one was to be seen.

In Urbana, near Frederick, they halted temporarily near where an old man on a stoop surveyed the passing troops and kept an eye on two young lads playing at "soldiers." He had the tanned, leathery hide of a life in the sun, pale blue eyes, red-rimmed and watery, shaded by the broad brim of an ancient straw hat. His white beard was stained at the corners of his mouth by years, of dribbled tobacco juice. His bare feet, stretched out in front of him, their soles tough as boot leather. From time to time, more from force of habit than from need, he'd say, "Johnny? Joey? What're ye up to?" They took it in their stride, no hindrance to their marches and maneuvers. Dougherty walked over to him.

"Were the rebs here?" Dougherty asked.

"Sho' was. Jes pulled out yeste'day. Jeb Stuart's cavalry, it were. Threw a helluva a party las' Mond'y! Invited ever'body. Kind of a grand ball ye might say, up t' th' Academy on the hill. Had they own band and invited ever'body in, secesh or not. We was high society that night, lemme tell ye," he said as he expertly spat a long stream of tobacco juice into the already sizeable puddle just beyond the tips of his toes.

"What were they like?"

"Not bad fellers. Polite, like. Little shabby, mebbe, but nice fellers."

At another stop he got a second opinion. "Never seen such a mangy pack in all my days," one citizen said. "During the day ye'd see them sitting and pickin' the vermin out o' their clothes. They'd scratch and poke and come up with somethin' to snap between two fingernails, then they'd get right back t' diggin' fer more. They was the great unwashed and had a powerful offensive odor. It was a mortification jes' t' be near them, especially indoors. I wouldn't call them the villains some might, but I don't know if I've ever in my life seen a gang of men hungrier or more piratical lookin'."

Their odor, Dougherty thought, could not have been more offensive than his own at the moment, as he rubbed the sole of his boot through a patch of dead grass. Nothing, he thought, could be worse than this — until a familiar voice reminded him that it could.

"Lieutenant Dougherty, when you're done with that two step, I would be obliged if you could give me some of your precious time."

It was the voice of Major Jeremiah Briggs, regimental surgeon of the Sixty-ninth Pennsylvania, Dougherty's immediate superior. He was some forty years of age, balding, with a prodigious growth of black beard, as though slippage had denuded his scalp and made everything come to rest on his chin. He had a squint — possibly due to a mild myopia combined with too much vanity to accept the regular use of spectacles, but he put it to use, creating in his subordinates an uneasy sense of critical inspection, a fear of being accused without being sure of what. Like so many army surgeons, he was conservative in his medical philosophy and practice, full of suspicion at anything new in the field of medical education, especially recent graduates of medical colleges.

He seemed to dislike Dougherty on sight. Nor did Dougherty much like him. He was sarcastic. Unpleasant. McBrien had known Briggs in Mexico and the southwest. Their contacts there had been few and far between, but McBrien was wary of him, careful not to overstep himself. Briggs had also left the army in 1859, not to return to his native Maryland, but to join a practice with a friend in Philadelphia's Eighth Ward, not far from Dougherty's residence, although the two had never met.

"Yes, sir," he said, "What can I do for you?"

"Tomorrow I want you to go to the military hospital in Frederick. I've heard that all of their medical supplies were either taken by the rebs or destroyed by our forces to keep them out of the hands of the enemy. Our own supplies are so damnably slow in catching up to us that I want to know if we can count on anything getting to us by way of Frederick, and, if so, what."

"Yes, sir. What about transportation?"

"Tell McBrien to see to some horses, and take him with you. I don't want you stumbling around by yourself and getting lost before you've even been in a fight. He'll keep you out of mischief... help you not to stick your foot into anything beyond you."

Where McBrien was going to get horses, Dougherty had no idea; but before long he would realize that McBrien was capable of a great many unexpected things. He had been in the army long enough to be an expert at making it work for him as much as he worked for it... maybe even more than he worked for it.

"Take a look at their facilities, too. You might learn something. We'll be sending them our share of casualties in the next few days."

"Do you think a battle is that close, sir?"

"Of course it is," he snapped. "Exactly when depends on our Young Napoleon. It's a blessing he didn't follow in his father's footsteps and become a surgeon. He'd have spent hours sharpening his knives and conducting consultations while the poor patient lapsed into senescence before it came to the operation. This time he won't have a choice. Bobby Lee will decide the matter for him. He won't be chased back to Virginia with nothing to show for his efforts, trotting back to Jeff Davis with his tail between his legs like a whipped puppy. He'll fight. You can count on it."

Briggs's comments surprised him. Even when the press had taken to calling McClellan "Mac the Unready," his popularity with the army had never waned. So popular was he, that his reinstatement had restored the army's morale even after Pope's fiasco at Second Bull Run. But there was something in Briggs's tone other than exasperation at McClellan. It bothered Dougherty. In fact, the Major sounded as though he might be pleased if McClellan failed. Why? Was he that eager to be rid of him?

"In any case, Lieutenant, strategy is for generals. You worry about the wounded. Let McClellan delay all he wants, but don't you tarry. Get to Frederick early, get the information, and be back before noon. You can leave after sick call." He stalked off to the medical wagon.

McBrien was a short distance away, near the ambulance. Dougherty called to him, happy for the chance to exercise a little authority of his own. He should have known better. Before he could open his mouth, McBrien said, "I suppose, sir, ye'll be wanting them horses right after sick call? I'll see to it first thing in the morning, then, sir." No wonder he had escaped the Indians, Dougherty thought. The man had the auditory faculties of a cat.

At last the day came to its end. Dougherty sat by the campfire reading a two-day old Baltimore newspaper, full of information and misinformation in almost equal proportions. When the dusk was too far gone for reading, he set the paper aside, lit a cigar and watched as the sky changed from deep crimson to indigo and then to the ebony of night. Here he was, twenty years old, a doctor, an officer, and vastly pleased with himself.

Stars twinkled from a safe distance as dying campfires winked back at them and the smells of smoke and coffee and bad cooking wafted on the breeze. The bustle of camp yielded at last to the temporary peace that came at this time each evening. He savored the cigar, watching the bright glow of its tip as he drew upon it and the smoke curled up into the dark. It was hard to believe he was in the midst of a great war. He drew a final puff, threw the stub into the embers of the dying campfire and betook himself to his canvas mattress. He drifted into oblivion, dreaming of being in his bed at home in Beaver Meadow, and quite unaware of the lesson that experience was teaching him: As hunger is the best appetizer, so the most effective soporific is the simple prescription of honest exhaustion.

Chapter III: The Hospital

I took early in the morning a good dose of elixir,
and hung three spiders about my neck,
and they drove my ague away — *Deo gratias.*
    Elias Ashmole (1617-1692)
    Diary, April 11, 1681

[September 13, 1862]

The aroma of brewing coffee and the muffled sounds of movement insinuated themselves slowly into his consciousness, until he expected at any moment to hear his mother calling up the stairs, "Jimmy! Time to get up!" Then reality thrust itself upon him in the brassy blare of a bugle and not the voice of his mother. The aroma of coffee was bitter, strong, and mixed with the smells of horses and human waste and firewood still damp and smoldering.

Fifteen minutes later they were gathering in ragged formation — men tugging on blouses or hopping on one foot and then the other as they struggled to come forward and pull on their shoes at the same time, responding to the call of duty with varying degrees of enthusiasm. In one company after another, sergeants called the roll and shouted out tallies. Once there was a semblance of order, Dougherty headed for the blackened coffeepot at the fire in front of the officers' tents and cradled in his hands a steaming cup of the strong black liquid that at home would have been more like his mother's stove polish than her coffee. But for now the elixir worked its magic upon his body, allowing it to ignore its stiffness and begin to move.

The bugle blared again after breakfast, this time for sick call, and Dougherty reported for duty, greeted by an unsmiling Major Briggs. One company at a time the orderly sergeants paraded the sick past the medical tent, where Briggs and Dougherty carried out the daily routine of peering at tongues, enduring blasts of foul breath, feeling pulses, and listening to a litany of complaints presented with all the faith-filled fervor of prayer to a deity who might prove sufficiently beneficent to grant the minor miracle of "light duty" inscribed on the Holy Writ of the day's work roster. It was, in the end, the normal round of foot blisters, dysentery, and diarrhea. McBrien filled the prescriptions, dispensed the doses, and then went to see to their transportation.

"Remember, Dougherty," Briggs said, "I want you back here by noon and I want that information. And one more thing. You're the officer and the gentleman, but McBrien is the one who knows what he's doing, so pay attention to him."

McBrien was back in no time with two horses, saddled and ready. Dougherty was secretly happy to see that his was a docile beast unlikely to call attention to his hesitant horsemanship. He mounted, totally unaware of the direction in which this day's events were about to propel him.

The highway into town was no mean road, but on this day any effort to travel by wagon or ambulance was doomed to be a struggle in the endless stream of fully loaded wagons, each drawn by a team of six mules taking up forty feet of road; and the Army of the Potomac required hundreds of wagons to maintain it in the field. The result was a flood of noise and confusion such as the city of Frederick had never witnessed before, and would not wish to witness ever again. It got progressively worse as the sluggish stream flowed into the bottleneck of city streets and followed twists and turns never meant to deal with this overwhelming congestion. Mule drivers cracked their whips and demonstrated the prodigious capacity of their lungs in the language apparently demanded by human to mule communication, a barrage of invectives impugning their ancestry and proclaiming their stubbornness and stupidity in terms that would have made a Philadelphia dockworker blush. The dust thickened by the minute as the boots and hoofs and wheels continued their incessant churning, a high rising column visible for miles, beneath which, like the Chosen People on their way to the Promised Land, the Army of the Potomac marched under its pillar of cloud by day.

They had gone but a mile and a half when they found themselves on Market Street.

"The hospital's at a place called the Hessian Barracks," McBrien said, "It's on Market Street, to be sure, but it's me own opinion, sir, that we'd best make a detour and come at it from another direction. To get away from the wagons, don't ye see? Maybe breathe air instead of dust fer a bit?"

It was sound advice. The dust and din decreased and they progressed more peacefully until at South Street they turned again toward the stomping feet, squeaking wheels, jangling harnesses and the raucous shouts of the muleteers.

The barracks had been built to house troops of George Washington's Continental Army, but became instead a prison for British and Hessian troops captured at Trenton, Saratoga, and Yorktown. They were now over eighty years old and in deplorable condition when they were reopened as a hospital.

Two L-shaped stone buildings formed the oldest part of the complex, their longer sides placed end to end along South Street, the shorter wings at east and west enclosing the parade ground. The larger two-storied buildings were now surrounded by smaller, more recent wooden structures, sprung up like mushrooms after a summer damp.

Bleak stone walls pierced by small, broken-paned windows formed the outer face of the barracks. Inside, fronting on the common, were two tiers of white railed galleries the length of each wing. The upper was filled with officers and well dressed civilians, the ladies in colorful gowns, sipping lemonade and shaded by parasols as they cheered the troops passing on Market Street.

A sentry slouched at the main door of the first building. He watched as they hitched their horses to the rail, his salute a half-hearted gesture of supreme indifference.

"I am Assistant Surgeon Dougherty of the Sixty-ninth Pennsylvania. I wish to see the Surgeon in charge." He spoke harshly, annoyed at the man's slovenliness.

"Reckon that'd be Surgeon Goldsborough, sir. He's officer of the day. He's inside, up on the second floor. G'wan up, if you want... sir." The half mumbled drawl was as careless as the salute.

McBrien stayed with the sentry, while Dougherty went up the stairs and out onto the gallery. An officer with the green sash of the medical corps, a dark haired man in his forties, saw him emerge from the doorway and left the couple to whom he had been speaking.

This was Surgeon Goldsborough; but for the moment, he was not the focus of Dougherty's attention, whose eyes were riveted on the couple. The man was tall, broad shouldered, exuding self-assurance. His back was toward Dougherty, so he could not see his face; but the dark hair beneath the narrow brim of the smoothly brushed gray top hat said he was not old. His dark blue frock coat and pearl gray trousers were cut to perfection, his boots polished to a sheen.

Yet it was not upon him that Dougherty's attention rested, but upon the woman facing him (and, therefore, facing Dougherty as well). She, too, was dressed in the height of fashion and almost as tall as her companion. Even in the day's warmth she seemed as cool as if in a refreshing breeze. Not a speck of the otherwise omnipresent dust had dared settle upon her person. She stood self-possessed, aloof, her attention fixed on the man as though he spoke words of great import.

Her dress was of deep green silk, but to call it merely green was to do it an injustice. As she moved, it shimmered, its highlights emerald, its shadows deep and dark. The wide skirt was edged with black lace, the high collar buttoned close to her throat, the long sleeves finished at the cuffs with black lace and tiny black buttons like those which fastened the collar. Upon her head was a delicate, feminine parody of the gray top hat worn by the gentleman. A wide band of some gauzy black material formed a large bow at its back, the ends trailing airily down to her shoulders. But all her finery paled in comparison to the jet black hair and the almost violet eyes that were her most arresting features. Her attention remained fixed on the gentleman and her eyes, focused on his face, did not, Dougherty was certain, even register his own presence as more than a blur at the edge of her vision.

"Good day, Lieutenant," said the medical officer, "I am Surgeon Charles Goldsborough. May I help you?"

He smiled in greeting — and in mild amusement. Dougherty realized that he had been staring and that Goldsborough knew precisely where. With a trace of embarrassment he forced his mind back to the business at hand.

"Lieutenant James Dougherty, at your service, sir, Assistant Surgeon of the Sixty-ninth Pennsylvania. I've been sent by Regimental Surgeon Briggs to request your help."

"Come inside, Doctor Dougherty," he said, "where we won't have to shout to make ourselves heard... or have any other distractions."

Dougherty followed him into a cramped, stuffy office. Its single window overlooking the parade ground was closed, the panes dirty enough to dull the brightness of the sunshine. The desk was piled with papers and books, as were two small tables that stood along one wall, and a bookshelf along another. Goldsborough took a seat on a squeaking swivel chair behind the desk and pointed Dougherty to the straight-backed chair that stood before it.

"Now," he began, "what can I do for you?"

"What I need most of all," Dougherty said, "is information."

"Well, I'm glad that's all you need, because until we get some supplies, that's about all we have."

That, Dougherty thought, took care of his errand, and he was certain that Major Briggs would somehow find a way to blame him for the lack of supplies.

"We had more than enough of everything before the rebs came, but we had to destroy most of it. Look at this," he said, digging into a pile of papers and extracting from it a single sheet of paper with a terse message:

> Harpers Ferry, Virginia, 11:17 P.M., September 5, 1862.
>
> Lee's army will enter Frederick tomorrow. Any property that you do not want to fall into the hands of the enemy had better be destroyed. Our communications will soon be destroyed.
>
> > Miles
> > Commanding

"I was at the telegraph when that came in. We assembled the patients who could be moved — almost four hundred of them — and sent them off to Gettysburg. They took two wagons of medical supplies, and most of the remainder we burned. I stayed here with Surgeon Heany and a few stewards and nurses to tend the patients too weak to be moved.

"Next morning Pat Heany was officer of the day and we were on the lower gallery when a reb cavalryman on a worn out horse reined up and asked who was in charge. Pat said that he was, and the trooper demanded immediate surrender 'in the name of Gen'l Rob't E. Lee an' the Confed'et States of Am'e'ca.' Pat was inclined to argue the point, but gave in to the logic of a carbine pointed at his belly... a powerful debating technique."

"They left without taking any of you prisoner?"

"That they did, Lieutenant. They weren't likely to want our sick or wounded and they were delighted to leave some of their own with us. The medical staff they left here in the interests of common humanity."

He drew a large gold watch from his vest pocket, opened it and snapped it shut again.

"I have no wish, Lieutenant, to keep you from your other duties. I can offer you one small ray of hope. Come back about mid-afternoon. I'm expecting a telegram from Baltimore about supplies and maybe I can offer you some information by then. In the meantime you may wish to see the hospital. You're new at this, aren't you?"

"Yes, sir," Dougherty said, disappointed that he was so obviously a greenhorn. "I was commissioned last month, but caught up to my regiment just a week ago."

"Ask the sentry downstairs to direct you to Sister Elizabeth. She'll show you around. You'll see what you'll be facing before long, I fear. The patients here are some of the most sorely afflicted."

Dougherty knew he was dismissed. No offer of lemonade, no mingling with the guests. Any lingering hope of meeting the woman in green evaporated. Dougherty would move on and she would be a pleasant memory.

McBrien and the sentry were getting along like old friends. McBrien was telling him hair-raising stories of the Indians in the West. Gone was the young man's boredom, as he hung on every word. He snapped to attention when he saw Dougherty and the request for directions to get to Sister Elizabeth was answered with courtesy.

"You'll find her in the east wing, sir, just across the parade ground. Enter by the door near the end of the building. She'll likely be with the patients."

"And ye'll do us the favor, Johnny, of keepin' a close eye on our horses?" said McBrien.

"Sure will, Steward," said the sentry.

"Not a bad sort, sir" said McBrien as they crossed the common, "Once ye show him how to stand up proper and give him a bit of a lesson in some soldiering. Like some others I could name, he'll be growing up fast once he sees his first battle."

The parade ground, once a grassy plot, was now bare earth dotted with clumps of dried vegetation, parched and sere. It held a line of carriages belonging to the guests on the upper gallery. Dougherty walked across the area, proud of the self-control that kept him moving forward instead of looking back to seek a glimpse of green. Most of all, he had no desire to draw a knowing glance from McBrien.

In the east wing, at a rickety desk, concentrating on what lay before him, was a medical steward, a hurried, harried little man, much occupied with a stack of papers. He looked up with eyes as weary as those of an old beagle foiled by an overly agile rabbit, saw that Dougherty was a lieutenant, and came reluctantly to his feet, not overjoyed at the prospect of yet one more officer to add to the burdens of his day.

"What can I do for you, sir?" His was the voice of perpetual exhaustion, tempered only with the hope (which he must have thought vain) that Dougherty had perhaps come here by accident and didn't actually want anything. He was a too little man in a too large uniform, further lost in the folds of cares that fitted him just as badly.

When Dougherty inquired after Sister Elizabeth, he could barely conceal his relief that they were but a passing annoyance after all and no responsibility of his.

"I'll get her for you, sir, if you don't mind waiting here a moment." Then, with no least trace of compunction at making them wait, he scurried down the corridor and was back a few minutes later with Sister Elizabeth.

She was a Sister of Charity from Emmitsburg, some 20 miles or so north of Frederick City, about thirty years of age, small, delicate, seeming too frail for the work in which she was engaged.

She wore a habit of dark blue with a wide white collar and a headdress whose starched flaps stood out like wings — something unfamiliar to Dougherty, but already known and revered by many of the wounded on both sides.

"Do you wish to see the wards, Doctor?" she said in a quiet, cultured voice, with a trace of the South, reminding Dougherty of his classmates from Virginia. "The men are always happy to see a new face when they are so far from home. Those with us now are not many, but they have suffered a great deal and are still too ill to be moved."

As she spoke, she set out along the corridor, the two of them in her wake, and up the stairs, where they were assailed by an odor, unpleasant but not unfamiliar, compounded of medications, infections, soap, sweat, putrefaction, chamber pots, and pus. The smell of a hospital.

She opened the door to the first of the wards, where, in narrow hospital cots, lay a dozen or more of the wounded. It was Dougherty's first sight of real Confederates, those men in butternut and gray who made such formidable foes. But not these. These were, for the most part, boys in their teens, all the fight gone out of them and replaced with exhaustion. Even fed and cleaned, they kept their unkempt shagginess, a hungry look, watchful and suspicious.

With the opening of the door had come the unmistakable stench of necrotic infection. Someone in the ward was far gone in the gangrene that kills an inch at a time, leaving limbs dead and blackened even before the victim is fully convinced that he is gravely ill. He was the first to whom Sister Elizabeth took them, a young man whose emaciated countenance could have been that of a man in his forties or fifties, though he was barely into his twenties. He smiled at Sister

Elizabeth and she introduced him as Corporal Jonathan Darby from the state of Virginia. It was hard to think of him as "the enemy." He was a young man like any other, quiet and respectful, brought here a few weeks earlier from the Shenandoah Valley. Dougherty had not the least doubt that he was dying.

"Doctor Dougherty and Steward McBrien are here to visit," she said.

"Pleased t' meet yah, doctah," he said, "Maybe y'all could take anotha' look at this heah leg o' mine? I think maybe it's gettin' bettah. Some a' the pain seems t' be goin' out of it."

Sister Elizabeth caught Dougherty's eye and nodded ever so slightly. She pulled back the blanket from his leg as Dougherty checked his too rapid and shallow pulse.

He unwrapped the outer dressing and set it aside. Beneath it was the wet dressing, stained with dark blood and the foul exudate of gangrene. Under that, the leg was swollen and marred by the blistering of the gaseous infection that works its way to the surface from deep within. The foot and ankle looked almost healthy, but halfway up the calf the skin turned cherry red. The swelling extended about three-fourths of the way along the thigh, with the infection centered at the knee, where the skin was broken in a piteous wound from which the brown, foul-smelling liquid seeped. The skin was swollen to the point of bursting, and Darby winced as Dougherty barely touched the area just above the greatest discoloration. He felt beneath the skin the crepitation, that crackling sensation that is indicative of gas bubbles that form at an alarming rate as the infection pursues its inevitable course.

The ball had struck above the knee. Someone had tried to repair the damage and save the leg; but it had not healed properly. Gangrene had set in, and now it was beyond repair. It was a typical instance of the physician doing his best to conserve all he can for the patient, and then finding to his sorrow that he would have been better advised to amputate in the first instance — it was to be one of the saddest lessons of the war.

Dougherty carefully replaced the bandages and tried to avoid communicating to the young man by word or expression the hopelessness of his situation. He spoke some words of encouragement, but he knew the end was not far off. Even the lessening of pain was itself a sign of just how far the necrotizing effect had progressed.

They went through the wards, smelling the odor of present pain mingled with the lingering odors of the pain of those already gone. For some there was real hope, for most there was only the waiting for the end.

They had taken enough of Sister Elizabeth's time, although neither word nor gesture of hers would have indicated that. She accompanied them back down the stairs and out the door to the parade ground, as she asked them about their backgrounds. Dougherty was amused to see McBrien, the old campaigner intimidated by neither officer nor fellow soldier, as he answered her questions with all the attentiveness of a schoolboy responding to his teacher.

It was noon as they crossed the parade ground. Under the guise of straightening the brim of his hat against the sun, Dougherty glanced up at the guests still gathered on the gallery. To his profound regret, there was no hint of green.

It was still too early to return to Surgeon Goldsborough, so they went in search of food instead. Not far from the hospital they had seen a weather-worn brick building with a faded sign proclaiming that one G. Dietrich was willing to supply fine food and drink at modest price. It was there that they went. There were few customers. Eyes turned as they entered. There was a sudden silence, then conversation resumed and the landlord stepped forward.

"Gerhard Dietrich at your service. Dinner is it, gentlemen?" he said, with a look capable of measuring the depth of their pocketbooks without opening them. He pointed to a table and got each a mug of ale to tide them over until the food came. Service was prompt, the stew was plentiful and good, the bread was fresh and crusty. Dietrich withdrew to a table where there lay open a large ledger.

They were eating when a man came in and looked around, apparently in search of someone. He took the cigar from his mouth, approached the tavern keeper, and said in a Scots burr modified by some time in America, "I'm Allen. I understand ye ha' a private room for me. I'll be expecting someone to join me. Be so kind as to direct him to me as soon as he arrives."

He was of average height with all the cockiness of a street tough. His brown suit had seen some service. The pantaloons were worn shiny on the seat and inners of the thighs, a sure sign of time in the saddle. He had a belligerent mien, his beard close cut, his brows dark and scowling. The narrow brimmed hat was pulled down in front, but from beneath it hostile eyes scanned the room, pausing for a second on McBrien and Dougherty. The landlord showed him to another room.

"Do you know him?" Dougherty asked.

"Never seen him in me life, sir," said McBrien. "But I caught the look he gave us. Sure I thought it must be you he was eying. Maybe he just don't like military types?"

"Could be. But there's something about him that does not attract me."

"Nor me, sir."

Not ten minutes later, a second man arrived, another sort entirely. He was tall and quite thin, clad in a respectable suit of black broadcloth, a vest of the same color, and a flat-topped broad-brimmed hat. His boots were polished, his vest front spanned by a gold watch chain. His hair was long but well groomed, his beard and moustache neatly trimmed. He might have been considered handsome had his nose not been so prominent. He had an air of utter respectability, unlike the belligerence of the other man. He went directly to the landlord and spoke in a low voice.

"Come with me," the landlord said and led him through the same door. The newcomer gave Dougherty and McBrien not so much as a glance.

When they got back to the hospital, the same sentry was on duty. He saw them and headed straight for them, pulling from his jacket pocket an envelope. Upon it was Dougherty's name, and inside was a single sheet of paper. Doctor Goldsborough had received his telegram and no additional supplies were forthcoming. The bridge across the Monocacy had been destroyed by the rebs and trains could not cross it, so supplies would have to be unloaded there and everything brought by wagon.

So now they were late returning to Briggs and had no more news for him than if they had gone back earlier. He would not be pleased and Dougherty knew that he would bear the blame.

The civilian carriages were pulling out from the common. One especially handsome enclosed brougham caught Dougherty's attention. Its maroon surface was highly polished and its liveried driver, a very tall Negro, sat proudly at the reins of the beautifully groomed and matched pair of black horses that trotted just as proudly. Inside was a single passenger sitting back far enough so that her face could not be seen, but the glimpse of a sleeve, rich green with deep shadows, left no doubt whose arm it was. The coach turned onto South Street and was gone.

It was late afternoon when Dougherty reported to Briggs on the disappointing outcome of his first official army mission. As expected, he was reprimanded for being late, just as he would have been reprimanded for not waiting had he returned earlier.

Of the two men in the tavern, Dougherty thought not at all. The horrors of what he had seen in the wards outweighed any idle curiosity about two strangers in a tavern. In any case, if he was inclined to speculate on any event of the day, it would have been that flash of sunlight on a green sleeve.

Galen 2

General George B. McClellan reveled in the fact that he was once again in charge of the Army of the Potomac. He had never really doubted that Lincoln — that "original gorilla," as he delighted to call him — would be begging him to resume command once he saw that John Pope hadn't the talent for it. Second Bull Run had made that painfully clear. And now Lee had made the fateful move. He had crossed into Maryland and it was up to the Young Napoleon to save Washington and drive the invader from northern soil — and he felt up to it.

It was hot for a September evening and perspiration glistened on his forehead. The room was stuffy, overcrowded, uncomfortable. But the minor inconvenience of a little heat was nothing compared to what was about to happen, all of it due to a simple accident, a stroke of luck, but a stroke that the General was sure he could transform into a stroke of genius. And that was something George Brinton McClellan never for a moment doubted — his own genius.

For Galen, this was the first time he had been this close to McClellan, and it had taken some doing to get himself there. There was much to be said for having friends in high places. He'd been here for the last half hour and had taken no real part in the discussions that went on all around him, discussions of strategy, complaints about the slowness of supplies, speculation about the next few days, conjectures about just where Lee was at the moment and whether he would stand and fight or cross the Potomac back into Virginia. Knowing Lee's reputation, Galen doubted he would walk away from a fight, especially a fight with McClellan who had already faced him and been forced to retreat.

"Gentlemen, I have an announcement to make."

The General's voice was not especially loud, but it had a quality of command that made it carry over the other voices, silencing them.

He paused, like a stage actor striving for effect and then held up a wrinkled piece of paper, waving it like a flag.

"You see this? This simple piece of paper? If I cannot whip Bobby Lee with this piece of paper, then I will pack up and go home!"

He had the attention of everyone in the room and most especially the attention of Galen. This promised to be worth hearing, well worth the risk entailed in conveying it to the right people, provided, of course, that it was not just one more piece of McClellan bravado. But what came next removed that doubt. What McClellan held in his hand must be reported and reported quickly, no matter how difficult. And it would be difficult. The direct channels that had existed in the Philadelphia days were no longer available, but he had other ways.

"I hold in my hand a piece of information that came to me within the hour. It was found by two Indiana infantrymen who had the great good sense to recognize it for what it was and to bring it to their commanding general. It was wrapped around three cigars and left in a field that the rebs occupied just a few days ago. Its authenticity has been vouched for by members of my staff who recognize the handwriting as that of Lee's adjutant. What I hold here is a copy of Lee's Special Orders Number 191, that specifies everything we need to know about the present disposition of his troops."

There was a stunned silence as they took in the implications and then a murmur of conversation, which McClellan silenced as he continued.

"Lee has divided his army into three parts and sent them in different directions. We are in the position of being able to take on all three, one at a time, and defeat them in detail. He has made the biggest mistake of his career, and I intend to take full advantage of it. We must prepare for immediate action, swift and certain, and to that purpose orders will be issued immediately to set this army in motion at first dawn. Gentlemen, we have him just where we want him!"

Letting the orders be found may have been Lee's big mistake, thought Galen, but George McClellan had just made his. He couldn't keep it to himself. He had to crow about it, and do it in front of so many people, civilians as well as officers.

The meeting ended so that orders could be drawn up and dispatched. There was no time to be lost. The end of the meeting was just what Galen needed as well, because he too could not afford to lose any time and he knew that his own record for using time far outstripped that of George B. McClellan.

Chapter IV: No Sunday Rest

δός μοι ποῦ στῶ καὶ κινῶ τὴν γῆν.
Archimedes (287-212 B.C.)

[September 14, 1862]

It was Sunday morning and Dougherty hoped to find a Catholic Mass. It was not to be. During the night orders came to be ready to march by dawn. On Saturday General Pleasonton's cavalry had fought a short engagement with the Confederate rear guard a few miles west of Frederick, and the Kanawha Division of the Ninth Corps had marched off in that same direction. By evening almost the whole Ninth Corps had crossed Catoctin Mountain and camped near Middletown in front of South Mountain. Now the rest were to follow. In spite of Major Briggs's dismal prediction of McClellan's dallying, it seemed that the army was on the move.

They were up at 3:00 A.M. By 5:00 A.M. sick call was long since over, camp was struck, the men had their three days' supply of cooked rations and forty rounds of ammunition, and still the order to move had not come. An hour after that Dougherty was told to report to Major Briggs without delay and to bring McBrien with him. They found Briggs seated on a camp stool near the medical wagon tending to paperwork. He noted their arrival, but chose to ignore them. His hat brim hid his face, but not the rigid, ominous posture. At last he very deliberately set aside his work and looked up.

"Well, Dougherty, just what do you have to say for yourself?"

"Sir?"

"Don't try to play the innocent with me, Lieutenant! I know what you were up to yesterday. Did you think that I wouldn't find out? No wonder you weren't back by noon. You had your own private business to attend to, didn't you?"

"No, sir, I did not." He sounded as angry as Briggs and realized that was not a good idea. He forced himself to calm down. He took a breath and lowered his voice. "Sir, I don't know what you mean."

"You know damned well what I mean," Briggs said. "You are an ambitious young man trying to feather his own nest. Seeking out influential friendships. Here a week and already seeking promotion. Are you here just to get ahead? Don't you care at all about your regimental duties?"

"No, sir!" He glared at the Major. "I mean, yes, sir. I do care about my regimental duties and no, sir, I am not trying to get ahead."

"Of course that's what I'd expect you to say. Damnation! There's no use pursuing the matter, is there? Here are your orders."

He handed over an envelope.

"You've got your wish. You are assigned to temporary duty on Major Letterman's staff. But let me tell you this, Lieutenant, I'm not done with you. I'm sending McBrien with you and I want you to keep in mind that these orders are temporary. That's the key word. Temporary. Unless you pull some more of your political shenanigans, you'll be back here. You are, in the end, still attached to this regiment and I'll see you again. Then we'll get things in order. Is that clear?"

"Yes, sir," Dougherty said, although it was not clear at all. He saluted and made a move to withdraw, but Briggs stopped him with a gesture.

"One more thing. You have a letter. Apparently it has been following you for the past few weeks. Take it and go. It's old news by now anyway. You can read it later."

Dougherty stuffed the letter in the pocket with his cigars. He was too angry to do anything else. Briggs's remarks had been unwarranted and he was even angrier that they had been made in McBrien's presence... McBrien, who had stood there in silence, his expression revealing nothing.

Dougherty got his belongings, which were few enough since his best uniform was still somewhere with the supply wagons. McBrien reappeared with the horses of the day before. Dougherty packed the saddlebags (including his revolver), rolled his blanket and tied it to the saddle and they were on their way.

"What's it all about then, sir?" McBrien said.

What a pleasant surprise! Something McBrien did not already know! It was Dougherty's chance to impress him, but all he could say was, "Your guess is as good as mine, Steward McBrien." So much for clever repartée...

This time the road into Frederick City was all infantry and batteries of artillery. Something had lit a fire under General McClellan, and Dougherty wondered what.

But his mind was on Major Jonathan Letterman. How could the Medical Director of the Army of the Potomac even know of James Dougherty? It was only four months since William Hammond had been appointed Surgeon General, determined to bring the Medical Service up to date. He, in turn, appointed Letterman. Archimedes had found his place to stand and had discovered his lever. They were ready to move the world of military medicine.

Almost immediately things began to change. Major Letterman, in the withdrawal from the Peninsula, so impressed McClellan that he now allowed him great latitude in his care of the health of the army. It probably did no harm either that Letterman was a graduate of Jefferson Medical College, schooled in the tradition of the General's own father, the school's founder.

Much as Dougherty would have preferred to forget it, Briggs's attitude still rankled, and he found himself doing something he would not ordinarily have done — he spoke to McBrien about it.

"The Major seemed more than ordinarily... preoccupied today," he said.

"Ye might say so, sir," McBrien said. They rode a while in silence, then he spoke again. "Sir, ye'll not take it amiss if I was to say somethin'?" He paused, "Sir, the Major is a most argumentative sort... always has been. I'd not take him all too seriously were I you. He sometimes seems dead set about a thing and then ye find out he ain't. It's like when we were in Texas... he was a great states' rights man, full of reasons why the South was right if secession was the choice, always talking about his Maryland 'heritage.' Ye'd have been certain he was a dyed in the wool secesh. Most of his friends from the old army are on the other side now. But ye see where he is. Never brings up that topic anymore. When it come right down to it, I'd guess, he decided where his loyalties really lay, and here he is in blue just like you and me. He was even called to McClellan's headquarters last night for a meeting. I was checking on supplies for this morning's sick call when he come in all het up about something'." And that was it. They talked about other things and Dougherty gradually felt better.

This time at the Hessian Barracks there was no cheering crowd. At the hitching rail were fifteen cavalry horses, their owners gathered at the far end of the porch, talking and laughing, but keeping an expectant eye on the barracks door. No green gown today. The sentry — not the same one as the day before — told Dougherty that he would find Major Letterman in Surgeon Goldsborough's office, so there he went.

The officer was seated at the desk, so absorbed in the papers propped against a canvas document case that he did not realize anyone was there, until Dougherty tapped on the door frame. He looked up, startled, took his watch from his pocket, checked the time, and snapped it shut. "Yes?" he said. He stood up, obviously ready to depart.

Major Jonathan Letterman was about two inches shy of six feet. He was then in his thirty-eighth year, energetic, but a man of action. The dusty uniform coat hung open over a shabby tan vest. Blue trousers were stuffed into the tops of well worn riding boots. His thin nose was framed by the triangle of a broad forehead and narrow chin with pointed beard. Dougherty announced himself.

"Dougherty?" he said.

"Yes, sir. I was told to report to you from the Sixty-ninth Pennsylvania. It is my understanding that I am temporarily assigned to your command."

"Ah, yes! Dougherty!" He reached across the desk and shook his hand. "You will assist me for a few days. We are on the verge of a considerable fight and we have all too little time to prepare. I suppose you are wondering how you came by this assignment."

Dougherty hung on his every word. What special talents had he (surely talents in the plural, not just a single one)?

"When Surgeon Goldsborough heard that I needed additional help, he mentioned you. He said that you're as green as grass, but, being the most inexperienced surgeon in the area, you are probably the one most easily spared without loss to your regiment."

Those were his talents? Inexperience and expendability?

Letterman must have read his expression. Without much conviction he added, "Of course, he must also have seen *some* brightness in you or he would not have recommended you at all."

The balloon of personal pride that Dougherty had inflated with hot air and sent soaring so bravely aloft, now began its humble descent under the weight of truth's ballast.

"Yes, sir. Er... thank you, sir," he stammered, feeling all the more foolish, as he realized what he was thanking him for. Letterman got on with business.

"We're going to need every facility we can find to use as hospitals. It is not yet generally known, but you should be aware that General McClellan has information that makes immediate action imperative."

The major, bag in one hand and papers under his arm, walked as he talked. He clapped the forage cap onto his head, pulled its brim down almost to the level of his eyebrows, and finished stuffing papers into his worn canvas bag.

Downstairs, he burst through the door, catching the young sentry so off guard that he almost tripped over his rifle as he snapped to attention and tried to salute. Letterman never even noticed. The troopers headed for their horses. Their young captain saluted and took the canvas case. He was about to turn away when Letterman stopped him.

"Lieutenant James Dougherty. Captain George Sandrow," he introduced them. "We will be working closely together for a few days. Right now, we must be off. You can become acquainted later."

McBrien was astride his horse, holding the reins of Dougherty's. He mounted as Sandrow put the canvas document case in Letterman's saddlebag and they were off. They passed through town and onto the National Pike with its endless lines of infantry — the First Corps and those of the Ninth who had not headed for Middletown the day before.

The army's trail was a mass of assorted litter — books, pots, letters, shirts, rags, hats, shoes — almost anything you might imagine, much of it still usable. All the debris of new recruits, sent off from home with things which grew heavier with each step, until at last the burden of the gift outweighed the gratitude due the giver and it was deposited in the dust.

The debris became gradually more sinister — great gouges in the earth where shells had ricocheted off to explode elsewhere, dead horses ripped asunder, their bowels stretched out in the dust, their legs stiff in the air. One of them, its body bloated and flies thick on the jagged hole in its neck, lay upon the road, the pool of its dried blood staining the whitish crushed limestone with which the pike was paved, and Dougherty thought of the toll that so harsh a surface must have taken on the shoeless Confederates who had marched here from Virginia.

It was past 9:00 A.M. when they crossed the ridge of Catoctin Mountain, where a body of civilians stood viewing the spectacle on the slopes of South Mountain. To the left, hung a haze of smoke from which came the rumble of cannons. Directly ahead, below Turner's Gap, troops deployed in line of battle, prepared for their ascent.

They descended to Middletown and began a process with which Dougherty would soon become familiar. They assigned regimental surgeons to buildings designated by Major Letterman — churches, houses, and, best of all, barns with a good supply of clean straw and water.

By late afternoon they were done with that and the wounded had begun to come from South Mountain, many walking, helping each other as best they could. The worst came in ambulances, jostled and jolted, groaning or screaming as their suffering was magnified with each bump and rut in the road. Dougherty and McBrien were put to the task of triage, deciding those who needed surgery immediately, those who could wait, and those for whom treatment was a waste.

More and more wounded arrived in waves, dozens at a time and then a lull, only to be followed by more. It was during a lull that they heard a dull, distant rumble that slowly grew in volume, changing from an ill defined murmur to the clear sounds of cheering.

"Ah!" said McBrien, "That'll be the hero himself... the Young Napoleon on his way to the front. Have ye ever seen him, sir?"

"No," said Dougherty, surprised at the bitterness in the steward's voice.

"Maybe, sir, ye'd like t' go out front and take a look?" They had been working behind the church, now a hospital.

On the main street, as they had all day, troops moved toward South Mountain. The cheers gained in volume, the troops separated to the sides of the road, forming an aisle. McClellan came, standing upright in his stirrups, handsome, consciously striking a heroic pose. The speed of the canter ruffled his hair. His brows were lowered, his lips unsmiling. The moustache was dark, the beard no more than the merest wisp below the center of the lower lip. He accepted the cheers as his due, like a Caesar passing through the Forum in triumph. He went by and the roar, like the wind rushing through the treetops of a great forest, went by with him and was gone. The march went on, men moving forward to replenish the ranks of those being carried back to the tender mercies of the surgeons.

The fighting at South Mountain went on until dark, until the stream of wounded fell to a trickle. Together with Major Letterman and Captain Sandrow, Dougherty enjoyed a meal in the kitchen of a kindly woman named Birmensen. By the time they retired, a heavy mist had settled over South Mountain, a combination of smoke and fog, the red-orange flashes of cannon fire and shells grew less frequent, until at last they stopped.

Chapter V: In Pursuit of Armageddon

By a sudden and adroit movement
I placed my left eye agin the Secesher's fist.

Artemus Ward (Charles Farrar Browne) (1824-1867)
Thrilling Scenes in Dixie

[September 15, 1862]

Dougherty quickly learned that the quartering of officers is among the perquisites of rank, but that such amenities do not always reach down to the rung of the hierarchical ladder upon which perches the lowly lieutenant. Major Letterman and Captain Sandrow lodged in the house where they had supped. Dougherty was relegated to the barn along with McBrien and the troopers, although, in deference to his rank, he had his own stall.

It was about 3:30 A.M. when he felt McBrien shake his shoulder, completely undeterred by any efforts to shrug him off. Dougherty had been in a deep sleep and now felt sluggish, his mind disturbed. It took him a moment before he remembered that he had been lost in dreams of the horrors of the wounded he had tended the day before. The nightmare was perhaps as bad as the reality.

"Good morning to ye, sir! Sure, ain't it grand to be up and about at this lovely hour? Ye'll be pleased to learn that the Major's already stirring and we're all to be off at first light. Ah! Do ye smell the coffee? Don't it bring cheer to yer heart and a smile to yer lips!"

Dougherty grunted to let him know he was awake, and McBrien left with a chuckle. He pulled on boots and jacket, and put the slouch hat on as he groped his way outside. By the light of a cooking fire he found the trough and splashed cool water on his face, feeling the crispness in the breeze that brought the smell of coffee. A cup of it revitalized him, and McBrien handed him a tin plate of "hash" — hot water metamorphosed into nourishment with some salt pork and hardtack. It was hot — its one virtue.

By four o'clock they were ready to move. But where to go? The previous day had ended with smoke and mist hiding the mountain's summit. The thunder of cannons had given way to a rattle of musketry that became increasingly sporadic and then faded entirely. The rest of the night passed in silence, save for the constant movement of troops.

First light came and there was no firing. Neither was there an order to move. Dougherty reached into his pocket for a cigar and felt the envelope Major Briggs had given him. With his cigar lighted, he sat against a tree and tore open the envelope. It was from Doctor Brownson.

Dear Dougherty,
You will no doubt soon be with your regiment. We hear that while McClellan has the title of commander, it is Pope who leads. Wherever you are, I hope you are well.

The letter was a few weeks old, clearly written before Second Bull Run. By now he would have heard of the defeat and would know that the army was back in Maryland.

I have news that will interest you. You will recall the first case in which we collaborated, and our conjecture that Joseph Fuller's murder may have been the work of a doctor.

Last week I was called to examine a young man who had collapsed in the street and died almost instantly. The autopsy revealed a natural death — an aortic aneurysm. He was identified and his family notified. Three days later I was approached by a detective from Washington. The dead man, George Stevens, was also a detective in search of a Southern agent known only as "Galen." The detective wanted to be certain that Stevens' death had been natural and I assured him of that.

I then questioned him about Fuller. He was unwilling to speak, but I bargained with information he did not have, namely that fragment of a letter referring to "G." He was astounded that Fuller had succeeded in learning Galen's identity. In return I learned that if Galen had killed Fuller, it was not his first killing, and may not have been his last. Thus far three deaths have occurred — deaths of men who had come too close to Galen.

I cannot say Galen is still in Philadelphia. I have no evidence that he is — and the man from Washington offered me none. I know there is nothing you can do, but I knew you would want to hear about it. Have you any further ideas?

I shall look forward to hearing from you and I pray you will continue in safety. Your obd't servant.

Brownson

The letter brought back in vivid clarity the details of that first case, and the twinge of disappointment that it still remained unresolved.

It was 6:00 A.M. before word came that the battle for South Mountain was over. Under cover of mist and darkness, Lee had slipped away — an astounding feat in the face of a force so large, left in total ignorance of his departure. The rebs were now on the other side of South Mountain, headed for Hagerstown or Sharpsburg. They mounted and rode the mile to the slopes of South Mountain, where the way became increasingly steep as they approached the summit, almost three miles from where they had slept the night.

Letterman urged them on, but progress was fitful. Ammunition wagons came empty down the mountainside as fully laden ones worked their way up. Ambulances came up empty and went down full. Troops who had slept on their arms were pulled back, to be replaced by fresh men for this day's pursuit. All along the road lines of the wounded went to the hospitals or sat exhausted at the edge of the road. But even the wounded were buoyant — for the first time the Army of the Potomac was in pursuit of a rebel army scurrying to escape. Rumors abounded that Lee was in full rout, but that was doubtful. This withdrawal was not the disorganized flight of men in terror.

Near the summit Dougherty saw his first rebels in their "native habitat," neither sick nor seriously wounded. Some of the prisoners were barefoot and must have suffered at each step on the road's sharp shards, but they gave no sign of it. They carried nothing but haversack, canteen, and a rolled blanket over their shoulders. These were seasoned veterans, many in their early twenties or less. They were proud, defiant in defeat, but utterly exhausted — not with the dark-eyed drowsiness of a missed night's sleep, but the bone weariness of never enough time to recover from days too full of superhuman effort. Their skin was sallow, their cheeks sunken, their hair down to their shoulders, and their beards a tangled mess. Without thinking, as though by second nature, they scratched at hair, armpits, or groin, the nesting places of the vermin who marched with them.

During a pause, while Letterman and Sandrow conferred over a map, Dougherty spoke to one of them in tattered gray trousers patched at knees and seat, a dilapidated forage cap, and a threadbare jacket with the faded chevrons of a sergeant.

"Where are you from?"

"No'th Ca'lan," he answered, "'n y'all? Weh y'all fum?"

"Pennsylvania," he answered. The Virginians at Jefferson had attuned his ear to their soft, slightly drawling, rather refined speech. This was far more difficult to understand.

"Do you need anything? Food? Water?"

"Don' need nuthin', yank. Come ra'ht wail supplah'd n' afixin' fer a faht. Mebbe y'all'd lahk summa mah vittles?"

From a black painted haversack he offered a piece of ramrod bread — corn meal and pork fat fried into a lump, then wrapped around a ramrod and baked over a fire. It was coated with wood ash and the fuzz and dirt from the bottom of the haversack. Dougherty declined the offer.

They resumed their ride. Sentries, polite but firm, turned back citizens from Middletown. A flood of civilians onto a battlefield was an invitation to confusion and looting.

Artillery shells had blown holes in the earth, torn limbs from trees, left jagged stumps, and set grass fires now reduced to charred patches. Whole stretches of forest were grotesque, as though some furious monster had torn them apart in a rage. Bodies lay in the shapes of the agony in which they had died, their stiffened limbs frozen in feeble efforts at escape. Some were bloated, as if a pin prick might make them explode with a rush of some noxious, miasmic gas. Dougherty smelled the odor of incipient putrefaction, the stench of rotting meat. Burial details were building neatly stacked rows of corpses, as if for one final, ghastly inspection.

There were Confederate dead, left as they had fallen, sad forms bereft even of the defiant dignity of prisoners. They lay alone or in heaps, waiting to be hauled away by their enemies. Some, in spite of all, wore the smile of final peace; others lay with glaring eyes and lips pulled back in rictus, as if to roar in mute defiance for eternity.

Among the corpses, the wounded, too badly hurt to retreat, waited to be cared for by those who had done this. Some lay in patient endurance; others sobbed or groaned in pain. Union ambulances, now done with the evacuation of their own wounded, began to do the same for the enemy. Whatever the ideals which had led them here, no one seemed the better for it. All the wounded were equally appalling in their pain, and all the slain of both sides equally dead.

They passed through open fields and patches of woods until they came to the highest point of Turner's Gap, a flat stretch some three or four hundred feet above their starting point. On the left was the Mountain House, some officers' horses hitched outside. At the end of the flat, the road descended into the valley where lay the town of Boonsborough.

This was the van of the army, and prudence dictated caution. Captain Sandrow held up his arm to signal a halt.

"Major Letterman," he said, "I suggest that I take a few men toward the valley and see what lies ahead. It would not do, sir, for the Medical Director of the Army of the Potomac to be captured before the battle has even begun."

"Very well, Captain," Letterman answered, "Take a look, but as quickly as possible. If there are no hostiles in front of us, I want to continue at all deliberate speed."

"Yes, sir," said Sandrow. He turned in the saddle. "Williams! Gormley! You come with me. The rest stay here."

They set off at a canter, rounded a bend and the thud of hoofs was abruptly muffled by the forest. Dust hung still in the air for a moment, then slowly settled onto the road. The morning haze was gone; it would be a fine day. They sat in silence, the only sound the chirping of the birds.

A quarter of an hour passed and Letterman was visibly impatient, when at last they heard the approach of a single horseman. It was Captain Sandrow.

"Enemy cavalry, sir," he said, "about a mile and a half away, between us and Boonsborough and headed this way. Williams and Gormley are watching to see how close they intend to come. There are too many for us to handle, but our cavalry will be up shortly to clear the way."

"Let's go on," said the Major, "at least to where Williams and Gormley are. We can see for ourselves, and we can always withdraw if we have to."

Sandrow hesitated, concerned about Letterman's safety, but the Major's determination brooked no opposition and his rank precluded argument. They walked the horses into the shadow of the trees overhanging the road. Apart from the fact of their uniforms, they might have been on a pleasant ride in the country on a magnificent late summer's day. They rounded a bend and broke into the clear.

Ahead was the valley, with Boonsborough off in the distance. The white, sunlit pike curved down the slopes, a silver ribbon among emerald pastures and golden fields ripe for harvest, parts hidden by patches of woods. Gormley and Williams sat their mounts, facing straight ahead. In the distance was the dust cloud of the enemy.

There are rules of thumb for estimating distance. Troops between fifteen hundred and twelve hundred yards away can be readily distinguished as infantry or cavalry. These were already closer than that. They disappeared into one of the wooded areas, and emerged considerably closer, perhaps a thousand yards, thirty or forty of them, moving steadily without apparent hurry or concern.

Dougherty was next to Letterman, with Sandrow at his other side. The Captain raised a pair of field glasses and looked. Without a word he handed them to Major Letterman, who, with what seemed the utmost lack of concern, put them to his eyes.

"Well, Lieutenant Dougherty," he said, "here is your first view of some people who would be delighted to make our acquaintance and either leave us dead on the road or lead us off to a prison camp for the duration of the war. Would you care for a closer look?"

Dougherty accepted the glasses and was startled when he put them to his eyes. The Confederates were over a half mile distant, but the glasses brought them to less than one-third that. The foreshortening effect of the powerful lenses made them seem to move all the more rapidly forward. The Major took back the glasses and handed them to Captain Sandrow, who looked again.

"They are intent on coming up to us, sir. Shall we withdraw and come back with reinforcements?"

"We can afford to wait," the Major responded. "We are still out of range of accurate fire, and we are not so very far in front of our own cavalry. Their arrival will give our visitors something to think about before they come much nearer."

Behind them they could already hear the clop of hoofs, the squeak of leather, the jangle of harness, spurs, and sabers. The Confederates were less than five hundred yards away, when again Dougherty was handed the glasses. He put them to his eyes and saw not the faces of monsters but of young men no different than himself. They paused and one, an officer, pointed. From the woods behind Dougherty came the head of a column of cavalry, the signal for the enemy to turn tail and head for Boonsborough.

Dougherty saw one young man, his long fair hair poking from beneath his hat, his beard white from the sun and road dust. He reached down and drew his carbine from its thimble, and laughed as he raised it to his shoulder, took aim, and pulled the trigger. It was a silly act of bravado at so extreme a range. There was little fear of damage, apart from the most outrageous bit of luck. And Johnny Reb almost had the luck that day. Through the glasses, Dougherty saw the puff of smoke before he heard the report. At almost the same instant as the flat crack of the carbine, he heard a whizzing so loud as to be uncomfortable. The hat flew from his head, and he thought someone had struck him a sharp blow with a small hammer just above his left ear. Major Letterman caught the glasses as they dropped. Dougherty's eyes lost focus. He slumped forward and it was all he could do to stay in the saddle. His horse sensed his pain and shuffled nervously, but did not bolt. In an instant McBrien was at his side grasping his left arm at the elbow, enabling him to retain his balance. For a moment he was ill; it grew dark, and then as quickly came light. He touched the side of his head and regretted it as he felt the pain, but his fingers came away with only a trace of blood upon them.

One of the troopers came up and handed him his hat. At the left side, just where brim meets crown, was a gash in the felt. The Minié ball had barely missed doing him serious harm. A hair nearer, and he would have had one of the shortest medical careers on record. The enemy cavalry retreated. The young man who had fired took off his hat, made a comic opera bow, and rode off after the others, leaving Dougherty with a headache that would last for hours.

The Union cavalry swept by and took up pursuit. Dougherty thought of the young cavalryman's smile as he pulled the trigger, the wave of his hat, the laugh as he departed. Had he killed him, he would have slapped his thigh with surprised joy at his accuracy; and he would have done so in all good humor, with no trace of rancor. Dougherty had little doubt that, had they met under other circumstances, they might have enjoyed each other's company. Death can be casual.

The pursuing troopers were six companies of the Eighth Illinois Cavalry under Colonel John Farnsworth, and they were followed by infantry. Captain Sandrow was ready to follow, but insisted that they keep their distance, and Major Letterman accepted the prudence of that. Within a mile of Boonsborough, Farnsworth's men faced dismounted cavalry deployed on either side of the road. A fight ensued, and the Confederate cavalry slowly pulled back to uncover a battery of artillery that promptly opened fire. Farnsworth's cavalry charged down the pike and the enemy artillery and cavalry dashed back through town and out along the Sharpsburg Pike. They were headed, not for Hagerstown, but for Sharpsburg and the crossing into Virginia.

Cavalrymen appeared with prisoners, many of them the wounded who had been left in barns and houses along the way. The infantry turned onto the Sharpsburg Pike in pursuit of General Lee, who seemed more and more not to be in rout, not driven by events so much as proceeding in accord with plans of his own.

They spent some hours in Boonsborough divided again into parties to examine locations for hospitals, many already occupied by Confederate wounded. It was afternoon by the time they completed their work and turned their thoughts to their appointment with General Lee, now waiting for them across the Antietam.

Chapter VI: Wait Again

I began to fear he was playing false—
that he did not want to hurt the enemy.
> Abraham Lincoln (1809-1865)
> Comment on McClellan at Antietam, September 25, 1864

[September 15-16, 1862]

They met in the center of Boonsborough not far from the Lutheran church, now a hospital. Troops trudged through town and onto the Sharpsburg Road. General McClellan had sailed through not long before, borne on a flood tide of cheers, although Dougherty was not there to see him. The army was in full motion, converging on the rebs; but, according to Major Letterman, Jackson was still at Harper's Ferry, so speed could result in considerable advantage.

Captain Sandrow and Sean McBrien appeared with their troopers just as Major Letterman and his came from the opposite direction. With the Major was a civilian, introduced as Oliver Naylor, a local physician. The troopers, McBrien with them, were sent to wait just outside town, while Major Letterman took Captain Sandrow, Doctor Naylor, and Dougherty into the U.S. Hotel to make their reports. The landlady had nothing to offer but some weak and tepid lemonade.

Dougherty made his report and, as Captain Sandrow made his, he studied the newcomer. Doctor Naylor was tall, somewhat over six feet, of athletic build, clean shaven, with dark, wavy hair, his gray eyes attentive to all around him, a smile stayed on his lips as he listened to the reports.

He was not the typical country doctor. His dark suit was well tailored, expensive, the hat carefully brushed. The well polished boots and finely stitched riding gloves were not rustic. He set hat and gloves on the table and leaned back in his chair, so thoroughly at his ease that it was hard to imagine he had not been with them all along.

"Doctor Naylor is from Keedysville, just this side of Sharpsburg. I had the pleasure of making his acquaintance on Saturday in

Frederick. He will be riding with us," Letterman said, "He has offered his services as a contract physician and has already been most helpful in suggesting hospital sites. We may benefit greatly from his knowledge of the area."

"You're very kind, sir," said Doctor Naylor, "It is no more than my patriotic duty."

The accent was difficult to place. A trace of the South? Or the local speech refined by a time of study in some large city?

"Although," he went on, "since early yesterday I've been looking after the wounded of the other side. When General D.H. Hill learned that there was a doctor in Keedysville, he summoned me to Boonsborough. It was all politely done, no hint of threat or coercion. Of course, I came willingly, as either of you or any doctor would have done in the same situation, so I had no occasion to learn what would have happened had I refused."

"Well done, sir," Major Letterman responded. "Once the wounded are out of combat they are no longer enemies. A contradiction of a fallen human nature, but at least this one inclines toward mercy."

They heard the rumble and jangle of a passing artillery battery. Each of its four guns was drawn by six horses, with six more drawing the limbered caisson. Then came battery wagons, traveling forges, and more caissons, all of it taking up a quarter mile of road. The rumble went on and on.

The reports were finished, the lemonade was gone, and Major Letterman was ready to move. McBrien and the troopers saw them coming, gulped their coffee, stomped out their fire, and were ready to move as they reached them. Major Letterman was in conversation with Captain Sandrow. McBrien rode with the troopers. That left Doctor Naylor beside Dougherty.

"Where are you from, Lieutenant?" he asked.

He turned out to be a good listener, an asset to a doctor, and Dougherty enjoyed telling him all about Beaver Meadow, his parents, his apprenticeship, his education, and his time in the Army of the Potomac.

"So you are new to all of this?" he asked. "How did you come to be a member of Major Letterman's staff so soon in your military career?"

Without listing the "talents" that had brought him there, Dougherty explained the circumstances. Naylor laughed and said, "On to the highest levels of the medical staff before you have barely learned to march? Lieutenant, you are to be commended! The Major spoke highly of you and I assumed that you must have been on his staff for some time. What have your duties been since Frederick?"

He explained the rush to establish hospitals and the push to engage Lee in battle, but did not mention the lost orders — information still confidential. He talked about South Mountain.

"Were the casualties heavy?" Naylor asked.

"I thought so," he answered, "but those more experienced say they were not — less than two hundred dead and a thousand wounded at Turner's Gap. The cost seems high enough to me."

"So it is," he said, "but the fighting yesterday was minimal compared to what may yet be in the offing. Do you think the battle will take place tomorrow?"

"I'd not be surprised," Dougherty answered, "Major Letterman seems to think so. It may begin before this day is over. It all depends on General McClellan."

Again Naylor laughed. "The Major General, if the newspapers are to be believed, is not well known for breakneck speed. Your medical talents will be sorely needed. I was horrified at the extent of some of the wounds I was called upon to treat yesterday and today."

The time passed quickly and as they approached Keedysville, Naylor called Dougherty's attention to a narrow road leading north.

"My home is there," he said. "If opportunity allows, you must be my guest. My wife loves to entertain and would welcome a party of distinguished Union officers."

"Most kind of you," Dougherty said, flattered. "I would be honored. Has the home been in your family for a long time?"

He thought it a question that might draw out Doctor Naylor a bit. To this point, Dougherty realized, he had monopolized the conversation and Naylor had said little about himself.

"No," he said. "I was not born here. My family originated in New York City and I settled here with my wife a few years ago after both our parents had died. It has proven a good choice. The State of Maryland has become home to both of us."

"Have you any family in Philadelphia?" Dougherty asked, "When I lived there, I resided not far from a hotel named Naylor's."

"I hope it was an elegant establishment if that was its name," he said, "but I doubt it was a relative of mine; at least none that I am aware of. In fact, I have never been in Philadelphia."

Letterman turned and called Dougherty forward, saving him the embarrassment of describing Naylor's Hotel. In Keedysville they were set again to search for hospitals and it was late afternoon when they came together and Doctor Naylor took his leave.

Within another mile they were on the ridge above the Antietam where the army was coming to rest for the night. Dougherty's own Second Corps was closest to the pike, its regiments still in motion to their assigned places. The hospital search was probably over. It was too late to do more this day and by the next they would surely be in battle.

In the distance, across the creek, the smoke of early campfires drifted upward — Confederate campfires spread out in a line right and left to a distance of two miles. They were through running. Now they sat and waited.

Major Letterman was ready to find General McClellan and submit his report, so he dispatched Captain Sandrow to find headquarters. He was back surprisingly soon with the news that they were to go to the house of a man named Philip Pry.

The house lay at the end of a narrow farm lane rutted into two deep tracks by years of passing wheels. The sun was far down in the sky as they emerged from the tree shaded lane into an open field, its gentle slope leading up to the house. It was a handsome brick structure with a picket fence around a sizeable garden. It was simple in design, two stories high, with a peaked roof and four tall, symmetrical chimneys. A portico, little more than a high and narrow porch, rose above the door. The late sun gave the rusty bricks a warm glow, turned the windows to bright mirrors, and painted their white frames golden.

All around was the ordered chaos of headquarters. Urgent messengers with solemn faces came and went on sweaty mounts as tired as their owners. Outside the picket fence were cavalry horses hitched to ropes strung between stakes. Inside were the horses of the more important, the corps and division commanders in search of orders, hoping to be included in any council of war.

There was an apple orchard behind the house, its fruit almost ripe, and outbuildings with hogs and a few goats. Dougherty felt compassion for the owner, who may not yet have realized that when the army left nothing edible would remain. The plague of locusts called down upon Egypt could not have stripped a land more frightfully bare than can a hungry army.

They hitched their horses while a young man in a gray duster stared at them as though trying to recall who they were. Letterman told them to find a place to settle for the night. He went to the house in search of the General and was long in returning.

They ate with some troopers who were boiling hardtack, onions, and a chicken — part of the burden to be borne by Mr. Pry.

This was Dougherty's first chance to speak to Sean McBrien since he had kept him from falling off his horse. He still had a headache when he moved too quickly, but it would be gone by morning. The chicken soup took his mind off everything else, and it was only when they were nearly finished that they turned to conversation.

"And how would ye be feeling, sir?" he asked.

"Not too much the worse for wear," Dougherty answered, " but I'll be glad for a night's sleep. And I'll not complain about having a headache, when I might have had no head at all."

McBrien laughed his booming laugh. "Well, sir, ain't there a lesson to be learned in just about everything? I remember when first I come back from the West, how I found meself with no excessive apprehension about going bald considering that at least I still had me scalp."

It was the first time McBrien had spoken to him with such ease. The guardedness between commissioned and non-commissioned ranks would remain, but perhaps the bridge to friendship was under construction.

"I wonder now," he said, "whether Little Mac is going to take advantage of this opportunity and try to polish off Lee. Were ye by any chance there today when he rode through Boonsborough?"

"I heard it," Dougherty said, "but I wasn't close enough to see anything."

"Well, an interesting experience it was. He looked all military and heroic. He loves to be the man with the burdens of the world on his back... providing, of course, that everyone acknowledges his heroism. He does relish the sound of the crowds. He even sent someone ahead to get the crowd prepared fer a rousing cheer — like an advance man fer a medicine show."

Dougherty laughed and then realized that McBrien was less amused than bothered. He began to understand the steward's doubts about their commander. McClellan was a great organizer and as a promoter of himself he was unrivaled. But could he lead his men in battle and trust them to do their duty? That was where he had hesitated before. Would he do so again?

"Excuse me, Doctor," said a voice from the shadows.

Into the firelight stepped the young man they had seen at the hitching rail, his duster now draped over his arm. Dougherty thought at first that he was in uniform. The sky blue trousers were stuffed into the tops of cavalry boots, but the dark blue jacket was devoid of piping, insignia, or regulation buttons. The close cropped ginger beard and moustache matched the hair, topped with a flat, black straw hat.

"Frank Schell," he said, offering his hand, "special artist and field correspondent for *Frank Leslie's Illustrated Newspaper*. And your name, Doctor?"

Dougherty wondered how he recognized him as a doctor, but then remembered the medical service "MS" on his shoulder straps and McBrien's steward's chevrons.

Leslie's Illustrated was as popular as *Harper's Weekly*, and both had experienced a boom in sales as their artists traveled with the armies, rushed their drawings to other artists who produced almost instant woodcuts, and, within no more than two weeks, had the pictures in the hands of readers throughout the east coast, all of them eager for news from the front.

"I'm Doctor Dougherty and this is Steward McBrien. How may we serve you?"

"Did I not see you arrive in the company of the Medical Director?" he inquired. "Have you heard anything of plans for battle tomorrow?"

"We were with Doctor Letterman," Dougherty admitted, "but I fear I am not informed of the battle plans of the Army of the Potomac. You could probably tell me more than I could tell you in that regard."

"Maybe so," he laughed, "but it can't hurt to ask. You never know when the right question will get the most unexpected answers. Do you mind if I take a cup of coffee?"

"Not at all. Help yourself."

From his coat pocket he took a collapsible cup, a telescoping affair made of tin rings, and filled it from the pot at the fire. Hanging from his left shoulder was a largish bag made of black oil cloth, about a foot and a half by two feet in size and a few inches thick. This he lowered to the ground as he sat down, stretched out his legs, and sipped the coffee with a great sigh of satisfaction.

"It's been a long day," he said, "but, then, aren't they all? Were you at South Mountain yesterday?"

Had it really been only yesterday, Dougherty thought. Schell spoke of what he had seen, and Dougherty realized that he must have been very near the front. In no time he had them talking about the search for hospital sites and the Confederate casualties in Boonsborough. As they spoke he opened his bag and took out a small pad and some pencils. He sketched as he talked. When he was done, he took out a bottle of colorless liquid and a thin metal tube hinged in the middle, inserted one end into the bottle and blew through the other, spraying the page with a light mist. He tore it from the pad and handed it to McBrien. He had sketched by the flickering firelight, more attentive to the conversation than to his hands, yet he had produced a thoroughly lifelike rendition of McBrien, down to the mischievous gleam in his eye.

"Keep it as a memento," he said, "I must get back to Keedysville. It was a pleasure meeting you and I thank you for the coffee. Who knows? We may meet again before this is over. I wish you both luck."

It was much later when Major Letterman returned, his expression hard to read, but not full of satisfaction. General McClellan was having second thoughts, certain that Lee had him outnumbered, and his own Secret Service assured him that the Confederates had enormous reserves at hand.

"You'll oblige me by not returning to your regiment tonight, Lieutenant," the Major told Dougherty. "If we fight in the morning, you will have ample time to find them. They are camped very near here. But it appears that we may not be fighting and will have other things to do."

They camped in the fields near the house and awoke to an early morning fog, soon burned off by a hazy sun. Enemy positions lay in panorama on the far side of the Antietam. Couriers rushed about and the activity of headquarters never slowed; yet no orders came. At midmorning McClellan emerged from the house, mounted his horse, Dan Webster, and rode off with an entourage, acknowledging the plaudits of the men with no more than a wave of his hand. He already envisioned himself an equestrian monument — a noble ambition, Dougherty supposed, provided one pays no mind to the pigeons.

He was not back until 1:30 and by 2:00 the flurry of messengers increased. What McClellan did not yet know was that Harper's Ferry had fallen and Jackson — doing what McClellan could never have done — had led his men by forced march to Sharpsburg to rejoin Lee. The only clue was the faint strains of bands playing "Dixie," carried on the rising and falling breeze. McClellan had delayed too long.

There was scattered artillery fire from the Union side of the creek, answered by the screams of approaching shells and the delayed, far off thuds of the rebel guns. In the meantime, the Federals were being issued rations and 80 rounds of ammunition instead of the usual 40. The First and Twelfth Corps were ordered to cross the Antietam at the Upper Bridge and make their way to a position at Lee's far left. Major Letterman decided to go with them.

It was past 3:00 when they arrived at the Upper Bridge. The road crossed its three graceful stone arches, followed the bank of the Antietam for about a hundred yards or so, then turned left into the woods. General Meade was there, his exopthalmic eyes more pronounced than ever, his face red as a beet, his voice raised in loud and profane complaint. He had been there since 4:00 A.M. and was sick and tired of waiting for the orders that would allow him to cross the creek.

In a cloud of dust a courier arrived, trying to cut a dashing figure as he reined his horse to a halt, letting it prance in a circle. With a smart salute he handed the general a message. Meade was unimpressed. He signed for the order and dismissed him with a gesture. The youngster left in another dust storm, but only after a salute so energetic that, had his aim not been accurate, he might have put out his eye.

"This is it," Meade said, as he examined the single page. "This division is to go first, just after the cavalry. Now where the hell is the damned cavalry?"

"Ready to move, sir," said a lieutenant with perfect equanimity, and pointed to where men of the Third Pennsylvania Cavalry were already beginning to mount. They set off at a trot, swept right, crossed the bridge and rounded the turn into the woods.

Meade was friendly enough as Letterman made himself known and told him they would be going with him for a time. The spate of temper was not aimed at them.

It was dark by the time they made their way back to headquarters, the search for hospital sites now ended. To the south were the isolated pops of musket fire as nervous sentries shot at shadows. Men of the Twelfth Corps continued to pour across the bridge to find their places near the end of the line — where the dawn's fighting would begin. Their canteens and pots and tin cups were muffled, they marched in silence, and would be allowed no fires for hot food that night — all meaningless effort to keep their movements from the enemy, after two days of allowing Lee to examine the positions and become as familiar with them as McClellan was.

It was after ten o'clock when they reached the Pry farm and Major Letterman, before he went to make his report, thanked them and released them to return to their regiment. Under the rapidly clouding sky, now partly hiding the third quarter moon, McBrien somehow got them unerringly to their destination.

Here there was no prohibition of campfires, no command of silence, yet there was very little noise. Men sat in groups playing cards, talking, or singing quietly. Others stayed apart, thinking, praying, or writing letters which might be their last. They would pass them on to others to mail, in case the sender himself did not survive the next day. Some prepared pieces of paper with their names and addresses to pin to the backs of their jackets so that, should the worst happen, their bodies would not go unidentified.

Major Briggs was with some officers near a fire. McBrien went off with the horses, while Dougherty went to report their return.

"Back at last, are you, Lieutenant? The prodigal come seeking forgiveness?" he said, "None too soon, I'd say. Tomorrow we'll have some work for you. Have you some other plans to amuse yourself, or do you intend to stay with us for a while this time?"

"I have been released from the temporary duty, sir, as has Steward McBrien, and we are fully at your disposal."

"How noble of you! Then I suggest that you get some rest. Tomorrow there will be no time to relax. We expect orders to move before the sun is up — provided that the General commanding has not decided to take still another day to get ready. By the way, you have some post."

"Thank you, sir," Dougherty said, as he handed him three letters. From the pot at the fireside, he poured himself a cup of coffee and went off to sit alone and use the light from the campfire to do some reading.

Two letters from Philadelphia and one from Beaver Meadow, all written a week earlier. He read the one from his mother first.

> Our dear Son,
>
> May this letter find you in good health we are all well. Your Brothers send kind wishes and both tell me they will be with you if this war lasts long enough for them to grow up old enough I hope it will not. Your Sister is well and sends her regards. Your father burned his leg at the forge but is all better now he says it is nothing that many boys in the army would be glad if that was all happened to them. We red in the papers that the boys are coming back from Virginia I hope it is not a step back for our army. Do your best to stay out of danger if anybody is shooting at you. We await the return of our Son and we are proud that he will use his Medical Skill to help the wounded and to bring this horrible war to its end. With Prayers we remain your proud and loving family.
>
> Your loving Mother
> Rose Dougherty

Dougherty worried about his father. His burn was serious, else his mother would not have mentioned it. He worked for the mines, but not underground. He was a blacksmith, shoeing mules, making tools of all sorts, all consigned to the oblivion of the dark underground. In his own time, which was far too little, he made household implements for people in town and that extra bit of income had helped make Dougherty a surgeon. His parents wished for all their children more than they themselves ever had, and Dougherty appreciated that.

The second letter was from Mrs. Kiley, and he smiled as he recalled her initial reaction to Doctor Brownson and his forensic forays. Buried in among her good wishes and fond recollections of Dougherty's years of boarding with her, was this significant passage:

> The good Doctor Brownson was here yesterday. He is a dear gentleman and goes out of his way to insure that he is pleased to be of service to me whenever the occasion arises. He is such a good and gentle soul! Sometimes I think that, save when he comes here, he must not have had a decent meal since his dear wife died ten years ago. I have invited him for this Sunday and I wish you might be here to share in the roast chicken which I know you like so well.

The final letter was from "the good and gentle soul" himself, short and to the point:

Dear Dougherty,

    Just a note to wish you well. News of the return of the army from the Peninsula does not sound promising. I suspect that by the time you get this there may be another battle in the offing. May God protect you if you are in it, and may your medical skills be of service to the Union and to its heroic soldiers. I happened to run into Mrs. Kiley. She is keeping well and I may find the occasion to visit her. I have no more word on Galen. May this war soon end and may a kindly Providence allow you speedy and healthful return to your friends. Your ob'dt servant,

                              Brownson

    Dougherty smiled. Since Doctor Brownson spent most of his time in the lecture halls of Jefferson Medical College and the morgues of the City of Philadelphia, how ever had he just "happened" to run into Mrs. Kiley, who tended to frequent neither? And what of Galen? Would they ever learn more? But none of those thoughts could fully occupy him this night. His mind was on other things. He lit a cigar and sat smoking, taking no part in the conversations all around him, his mind full of apprehension about the morning.

    He finally left the fire and went to the tent, where he found already in place the items that he had carried on horseback as well as those left behind when they had departed. Sean McBrien had been at work. He lay down to sleep. A short time later, at the edge of consciousness, he heard the first light raindrops plop upon the tent. It was midnight, the first moment of the most frightening day of his life.

Chapter VII: The Bloodiest Day

> War is at best barbarism... Its glory is all moonshine. It is only those who have neither fired a shot nor heard the shrieks and groans of the wounded who cry for blood, more vengeance, more desolation. War is hell.
> General William Tecumseh Sherman (1820-1891)
> Address at Michigan Military Academy (June 9, 1879)

[September 17-18, 1862]

Three and a half hours later Dougherty was awake, the anticipation of battle driving out all sense of exhaustion. The light drizzle was now a steady rain, not heavy, but enough to make everyone wet, and would ultimately prove deadly when the resultant scratchy throats and congested noses caused the wounded to develop pneumonia.

They made ready what they would need for the wounded, as rain dripped into collars and boot tops, and cascaded from hat brims each time they tilted their heads; but as the first traces of light appeared, the rain ended, leaving behind a low lying ground fog, which the early morning sunlight began almost immediately to burn away. By then they had for some time been hearing the pop, pop, pop of small arms fire from across the creek, at first scattered and muffled by the fog, but then the individual shots melded into loud, concerted volleys. They waited.

They were still in the same position, when, at 6:00 A.M., from the south there came the deep roar of artillery thunder as a whole string of batteries on the Federal side of the creek unleashed their fire in unison. The echoing rumble went on, going silent only when, by coincidence, a number of guns all reloaded at the same time. The Confederate lines were distant, but the Union's elevated position lengthened the range of their guns and their shells began to rain down on Lee's far left. They waited.

At 6:30 General Sumner, his patience sorely strained, went to McClellan's headquarters to find the cause for the delay. He learned nothing, and was back grim faced with the Corps when at last there came the command to move. It was almost 7:30 and the temperature was rising. The sky cleared, the gray gave way to blue, and the breeze was no more than infrequent, mild puffs. The lingering humidity left the wool of the uniforms damp and uncomfortable.

The Second Corps was the largest of all the Corps, with more than 18,000 men, comprised of three divisions under Generals Richardson, Sedgwick, and French. Sedgwick's Division was to lead the way, and so Dougherty was among the first to cross that morning. French came next. Richardson should have been with them, but headquarters blundered. Brigades of the Fifth Corps that should have moved into place as the Second Corps left the east side of the Antietam had not been informed and Richardson was ordered to remain in place until they arrived. When Richardson finally did cross the creek an hour later, he had no idea where to find French and Sedgwick, nor could he find his Corps Commander. General Sumner had gone across the creek first, marching boldly at the head of his troops. The whole day would be like that, with lack of coordination and piecemeal commitment of troops.

Strategy was not foremost in Dougherty's mind. His heart pounded, his mouth was parched, and he wondered how he would do under fire. He might have looked brave enough on Monday, but that was one random shot with little chance of success, done so quickly that there was no time for reflection. Today he could be the target of more firearms than he had ever seen, all of them at more realistic range, and any of them glad to have him in its sights.

They marched through open fields and patches of brush, ever downward, to the level of the stream, emerging from a strip of woods at a ford, its sluggish water just knee deep. They splashed straight through, resoaking their boots and trousers, turning the stream into a churned up mess of muddy yellow from which minute bits of gravel got into their boots, remaining to irritate for the rest of the day.

Beside him was McBrien in quiet conversation with Dick Sheridan, the other Steward in the regiment. Dougherty felt all the worse when he saw that they were both so unperturbed! Major Briggs rode ahead with Doctor Bernard McNeill, another assistant surgeon. Behind the surgeons and stewards were the regimental musicians, not to play music, but as stretcher bearers. There were but eight of them, led by Principal Musician Paddy Moran. At the head of the regiment rode Colonel Owen, Lieutenant Colonel O'Kane, and Major Devereux. These were all names and faces by now familiar to Dougherty, but today all looked new, as though he saw them for the first time, and he wondered if he would see them tomorrow — or if they would see him. Was he the only one with sweaty palms and jellied knees? Or did he look as calm to them as they did to him?

The upward slope was gentle, but the walking difficult. The ground was littered with jagged limestone outcroppings, as though some ancient race of Titans had taken enormous slabs and jammed them upright into the earth. The maps made their course due west, but nothing is ever so easy as it seems. To get to where they wanted to go, they first turned north and then northwest, always steadily upward. Dougherty expected the sounds of firing to intensify with each step, but they did not. They waxed and waned, now and again fading out almost entirely, whether due to terrain or to variations in their intensity or to movements of the opposing forces, he had no way to tell. What he did know was that each time the sounds became clearer, they were closer.

From a ridge he saw, some two or three hundred yards to the north, a house they had the day before designated a hospital, owned by a family named Line. Ambulances came and went and near one of them was a great commotion, but what it was they were too far away to tell. A rider left the house, headed toward the gunfire, but then turned in the saddle, took off his floppy-brimmed straw hat, held it up to shade his eyes against the sun and peered in their direction. He paused, his posture indecisive, and then made up his mind. He clapped the hat upon his head, tapped the horse's flanks with his heels, and came toward them at a trot.

The division must have been a most impressive sight, the three brigades, marching steadily westward in parallel columns, four men abreast. To the north was the Sixty-ninth, part of Howard's

Philadelphia Brigade, flags flying, officers' horses prancing, men moving steadily at common time, ninety paces per minute, toward the raging conflict. South of them was Dana's brigade, and south of that Gorman's, 5000 men in all, yet only a fraction of this gigantic army. At the head, every inch the warrior, "Bull" Sumner sat straight in the saddle, proud of his forty-three years as a cavalry officer. Although the breeze was feeble, his white hair and beard fluttered as his mount moved steadily forward. Next to him was General John Sedgwick — "Uncle John" — one of the best liked of all the officers, a kind and generous man, a talented and brave officer.

The temperature was not excessive, but the day was humid and perspiration ran down to sting Dougherty's eyes. He puffed as they climbed and his calves ached as he hoped for a stretch of level ground. The sun steamed the damp from boots and uniforms, overpowering the pleasant odor of cut corn stalks and freshly plowed earth with that of wet wool and leather.

The mounted man from the Line house drew near. It was Frank Schell, his wide hat and flowing duster seeming more the uniform of the artist. Attached to his saddle were two oilcloth bags, both bulging at the seams with all his paraphernalia. He headed directly toward Dougherty, dismounted, and walked along, holding the reins of his horse.

"So, Lieutenant Dougherty, we meet again. Good morning, to you."

"And to you, Mr. Schell," he said. "Have you been at the front? Have you any news?"

"Please call me Frank... I've been in a number of places today, but the front is not yet one of them. Maybe I'll come along with you and see what is happening. Did you know Williams has the Twelfth now? Mansfield was hit in the belly as he was coming into the fight. You may have seen them just now bringing him to the house over there. I doubt he'll survive."

"Are casualties heavy?" Dougherty asked.

"I fear so," he said. "The surgeons are busy. There's a pile of arms and legs outside the kitchen window already. I'd seen enough and I was leaving just as I saw you coming up."

"Where's Hooker? Have you seen him?"

"I haven't," he answered. "He's up where the fighting is, but I haven't been there yet. I was at Pry's house this morning when General Sumner came to get his orders and left mad as a hornet without them. Obviously he's finally gotten them."

Dougherty did not comment on the slowness of McClellan's orders.

"There was already a crowd of spectators on the hill to watch the day's activities," he went on. "I didn't talk to McClellan, but I wanted to. He had no time for reporters, but I'm sure he'll be more than happy to see us if there is a victory. When I saw him, he was with Porter and some other loyal followers. Curiosity gave me an attentive ear. He was perfectly satisfied, so far as I could tell. He considers this a magnificent field for a fight, and says that a victory here would cover over all previous errors and misfortunes forever. An interesting remark... I have no doubt that he meant the errors of others and the misfortunes which he always considers uniquely his own.

"While I was there I saw some of what was happening at the far right, the place you're headed for. Troops were pouring into a thirty or forty acre cornfield surrounded on three sides by woods. It was full of troops — rebs. I saw two of our batteries come out of the north woods and fire into the field to clear it. The corn went down as if it were being mowed, and then in the smoke both sides tangled in such a mass that it was impossible to see who was winning. That's where all the musketry's coming from. I decided to try to get closer, so here I am."

By now the acrid odor of powder smoke was unmistakable. A light breeze now and again from the west brought both smell and sounds of battle, but they were fading, and there was no way to know whether that signified victory or defeat. Dougherty felt more than ever the dryness in his mouth as the sulphur and saltpeter of the expended gunpowder made the breathing more uncomfortable.

The columns passed through another wood and into fields of corn not yet harvested. On they went, now veering to the left so as to head more southwesterly. Beneath their feet the cornfields and the grass gave way to fresh earth, recently plowed for a crop of winter wheat, the wet softness making the going harder. Schell said that the buildings there belonged to a family named Poffenberger. They came into fields of corn side by side with pasturage and were ordered to the double quick. Frank Schell mounted his horse, but made no effort to keep up, allowing them to go ahead of him. Behind was French's Division turning so as to face more southerly, probably to form line of battle on the left.

The smoke made Dougherty's eyes water, the humid, dead air holding the brownish haze close to the ground, irritating the throat, making him cough. Voices of command rang out. The regiment halted and was set into the evolutions necessary to turn column of march into line of battle. Suddenly everyone was more sober, more alert, more aware of the proximity of danger.

The line ran north to south, parallel to a road just in front of them beyond which was still another wood. To the right, to the north, red flags flapped at intervals, pointing the way to medical help — an ambulance station or field hospital. The wood, a stand of tall trees, was badly damaged where shells had lopped off high branches and dumped them on the ground. Even with its sparse underbrush, the forest was thick enough to afford cover. The Second Division now faced west, its three brigades one behind the other, Gorman's at the edge of the forest, Dana's forty paces behind that, and Howard's (Dougherty's own) another forty paces to their rear. All were ordered forward.

Just as Gorman's men entered the forest, shells began to fall on it, not an aimed fire that had found the range, but a random attack on the off chance that the wood was populated. More branches crashed to the ground. Troops sought cover, but the sergeants kept telling them to stay in line and to fill the gaps where some had already fallen. Then the shelling ended as abruptly as it had begun and the guns were silent. From the forest came men who had been hiding there — not men of Dougherty's division, but remnants of an earlier attack who had not wanted to go forward and were yet unwilling to be seen retreating. They now decided to withdraw, no matter how it looked. There were some wounded, but none seriously enough to prevent them from walking away, being supported by men themselves not hurt at all, but hoping to look useful as they headed for the rear.

These were the skedaddlers, and everyone in the lines of battle shouted ridicule and struck them if they passed close enough. They didn't stop. They had chosen shame instead of shot and shell. Dougherty hoped he would not do the same.

Sumner was with Gorman's line, mounted, even though it made him a better target. As Dougherty watched, he entered the wood, signaling the line to follow.

Dana's line went next, still forty paces behind. Dougherty was no tactician, but he knew that lines that close to each other were at risk. Enemy fire at the first line had a tendency to pass over their heads as troops in the heat of action fired too high. That was why officers constantly shouted to the men to aim low, aim low, aim low. Lines should be separated by as much as three hundred yards, so that overshot Minié balls and shells would drop into open space and there was room to maneuver without colliding lines. The third line, Dougherty's, was as close to the second as the second had been to the first. As they penetrated the wood he could see what lay on the other side. Major Briggs called a halt to the movement of the medical personnel and they watched as the rest of the line stepped out into the open area beyond the wood in which they now set up the dressing stations, just out of musket shot of the enemy. The wounded would pass through their hands and then be met by ambulances somewhere just behind their position to take them back to the field hospitals out of range even of artillery fire.

There was at first no firing in front of them. The cannons were silent and so, too, were the muskets that had been so loud just minutes before. It was eerie, almost as though they had suddenly gone deaf to all but the commands that kept reminding the long lines to maintain formation and close up. Since General Sumner had not assessed the terrain before the battle, and since he had made no contact with the forces of either Hooker or Mansfield, he did not know their situation. The battle was being joined blindly, and blindness can lead to disaster on a battlefield. The three lines moved across the open field at common time — the stately progress of an exercise on a parade ground.

This was no parade ground. What lay beneath the steadily marching feet was not a cut lawn for practice maneuvers. It was the very scene that Frank Schell had described — a large cornfield. Next to the wood were still some stands of high corn, but further out there were almost none, apart from a few stalks which had, as if by miracle, been spared. Cannon fire and the struggle of thousands of troops had flattened the field into a tangled, trampled mass of broken stalks. But that was not the real horror. The ground was littered with bodies, hundreds and hundreds of them, some dead, some wounded. They lay in dreadful distortion, wounded limbs punctured by shattered bones. Some feebly lifted heads or fluttered ineffectual hands. Some struggled to rise and then slid back again, their strength tested beyond endurance. No one stopped to help them. No one offered them water or solace or volunteered to take them to safety. The march went inexorably on, a parade of zombies in a pit of hell. Blue and gray were intermingled underfoot, the debris of a fight that had gone in one direction and then the other, always leaving behind that ever growing pile of destroyed humanity. Hands snatched at the legs of the marchers, but no one was allowed to stop. Even the bandsmen and stretcher bearers passed by, doing nothing, realizing that at any moment they might be required to exert their effort for the men of their own regiments.

Beyond the groans and cries of the wounded, there was an eerie absence of battle sounds. Gun smoke drifted low in patches like the morning fog, its stillness set in lazy swirls by the passage of the men. Dougherty could see from one end of the line to the other, and in that was yet another portent of disaster. Both ends of the line were visible, which meant that neither was anchored to some protective feature of the landscape nor to an adjoining force of their own. Both flanks were "in the air," open to attack. Where was French? Sumner's command was thoroughly divided — Richardson not yet here and French gone off in some other direction. Only Sedgwick's division was in sight.

Dougherty prayed that the silence might not be deceptive, that there be no enemy force simply waiting for the opportunity to pounce on the unsuspecting regiments.

Across from them and to the south, at the edge of the other woods, was a small white building, a school or a church, with some Union troops pinned down nearby. The left end of Gorman's brigade, a whole regiment, began to veer in that direction as though to go to their aid. It picked up its pace to the double quick.

Gorman's line was well across the field, about to enter the west woods. Dana was behind, even closer than the original forty paces. It was just past nine o'clock and the battle seemed all but ended.

Then came the cannon fire, this time well aimed, and men began to fall. "Close up! Close up! Keep moving! Don't stop!" The voices came back clear and strong. The first line was at the west wood, moving at the double quick, the troops no doubt thinking it safer to enter the woods than to remain in the open or try to retreat with the rebel artillery at their backs. All lines picked up their pace and crowded even closer together.

Meantime, Major Briggs got ready to receive casualties. He dismounted, placed the saddlebags on the ground, and instructed an orderly to take his horse further back, where it would be safer until they had to move to the rear. Other regiments stationed their medical personnel throughout the wood, considerable space between stations, each placing its red flags to guide the stretcher bearers. Dougherty was stationed with McBrien, behind the flimsy cover of a few trees rather close together. He opened the field medical kit brought up by one of the orderlies. In it were surgical instruments, containers of pharmaceuticals and medicines, and roller bandages and lint to care for bleeding wounds. There would be no serious surgery here, just a quick examination to see what was wrong, enough medical care to stop bleeding or the immediate loss of life, and the rush of the patient to the rear. The ambulances had followed and would be somewhere, perhaps a hundred yards back along the road they had crossed, waiting for their passengers to be brought to them. They waited.

The wood swallowed up Gorman's and Dana's Brigades. Howard's was still in sight but moving determinedly after the other two. Scattered sounds of skirmish fire came from the woods. Gorman had found the enemy. At the same time there was renewed fire at the far left, near the church. The sounds of musketry increased and then were overwhelmed by the rolling thunder of artillery, those same batteries which had earlier fired the random shots into this wood.

Now their aim was altered, and Dougherty saw shells explode in the wood across from them, tearing tree tops, bringing down a rain of leaves and branches on the troops hidden within. At almost the same time, overhead, came the scream of shells which passed by and continued on toward those guns behind the woods. The crews of the big twenty pounders on the east side of the Antietam must have seen the clouds of smoke coming from the Confederate artillery and were answering in kind. The din increased with each passing minute.

The lines ceased moving forward, leaving Howard's brigade out in the cornfield, still in the open. From the woods opposite came the now familiar pop, pop, pop of musketry, which almost immediately accelerated into the steady tearing sound of repeated volleys. The shouts and cheers of men on both sides added to the din as rising wisps of gun smoke rapidly became clouds, still further obscuring the view of what was once a peaceful, shaded country wood. Suddenly from among the trees men appeared flowing back toward where Dougherty was, men who had been wounded and were holding onto bleeding parts of their bodies as they pushed past Howard's line. Along with them were some who, in panic, ran away, not because they were hurt, but because they had no desire to be hurt. Officers shouted angrily, pushing them back into the fray, hitting them with the flats of their swords when they did not immediately obey. From the smoke and confusion stretcher bearers emerged, rushing toward the dressing station.

The casualties crossed that field of dead and wounded into the east wood, some of them able to continue through without help, although their wounds were serious. Others faltered, dazed. They stopped, not knowing what to do. The stretcher bearers unceremoniously dumped their loads, retrieved the stretchers, and ran back across hell's field for more. There was now no silence, just constant, deafening uproar. The deceptive lack of opposition had ended and the calm had been succeeded by the storm.

Before Dougherty there suddenly appeared Solomon Aarons and Tim Carr, two musicians, bearing a stretcher upon which lay a young man, his face covered in blood. They slid him to the ground and, without a word, rushed off for more. His raspy breath did not bode well. He tried to speak, but no words came, just sounds of painful exhalation. The blood on his face was from a gash across his forehead which had laid bare the bone beneath. Dougherty pulled together the trailing flaps of skin, as McBrien placed into his hand the strips of adhesive plaster to hold them in place. A hasty bandage was enough, he hoped, to staunch the flow of blood. All this before he realized that his efforts were in vain; the torn scalp was the least of the lad's wounds, in spite of its profuse bleeding. As soon as Dougherty touched his side he felt the wetness and his hand came away all scarlet. The man's jacket was wet with blood, but its dark blue wool had made the blood seem black and so disguised the extent of the hemorrhage. Dougherty used the scissors to cut open the cloth, revealing a hole just below the right nipple, its shape roughly circular, its purplish edges torn and pushed inward. Embedded in the wound were bits of cloth, which he removed as best he could, knowing that their presence would almost certainly bring on infection. With each rale came spurts of bright red, frothy blood, the sad sign of a punctured lung about which nothing could be done, although he tried to close it with lint and adhesive. Two ambulance men appeared and at his signal took the patient away. Dougherty's first casualty and he had done him no good. No comfort, no cure, no use. He felt immersed in futility, wanting nothing so much as to be out of there. It was, like so many desires, impossible of fulfillment. The first man's place had been taken by two more and this was but the beginning.

The first had a strip of cloth on his arm as a tourniquet. Dougherty knew the face, but not the name — a young man recently arrived from Ireland and proudly fighting for his new country. He had seen him at sick call a few days earlier, hoping to be freed of his diarrhea so that he could fight. He would fight no longer. His right arm was shattered below the elbow, the broken ends of radius and ulna protruding from the jaggedly torn ends of the musculature, bone splinters driven into the flesh. The tourniquet was just below the elbow, and Dougherty left it there. The arm would be amputated at the elbow as soon as the surgeons at the field hospital could get to him. In the meantime, removal of the tourniquet could only lead to renewed bleeding and possibly to loss of life. Had the tourniquet been higher on the arm, he might have moved it downward, so as not to lose more of the arm through mortification from lack of blood. As it was, any change would be foolish. Again he had done nothing — except to insure that at least this one did not die here and would have some chance at continued life, even if crippled. An ambulance crew took him away.

The next, another familiar face, came to his attention, as at least three more were placed beside him. Dougherty looked over his shoulder. Still more were being brought across the field. McBrien and he worked together with a wonderful unity of purpose, and he was truly thankful for McBrien's experience, his steadiness, his strength as he did his duty with such disregard for the danger, his amazing gentleness toward the wounded. That he said almost nothing to Dougherty was a confirmation of his growing confidence; if his actions were not what they should have been, McBrien would have told him so.

Dougherty never looked at the face of the next man. There was no time to think of identity. There was only time to examine the damage, do what he could, and go on to the next. He realized how unfeeling he seemed to be, but that was not really the case. These were patients to be cared for, but the attention must be first to their wounds if life was to be preserved. This one's right leg was bloody and he groaned in agony. McBrien administered laudanum as Dougherty cut away the leg of the uniform. On the inside of the man's thigh, midway between knee and hip, was the entry point of a musket ball, a hole large, bruised, but bleeding not nearly so much as might be expected. With a finger, Dougherty gently probed the open wound until his fingernail touched something solid. A round object at the side of the femur where no such object should have been — a musket ball. He took the bullet extractor from the medical kit, inserted it gently along the path he had felt with his fingers and removed the ball, hoping he would not damage the artery. No blood spurted. Again he probed for bits of bone, but found only the softness of external damage to the femur. This man was fortunate. He had been hit by an old-fashioned musket ball and not by the Minié, which would not have been stopped by the bulk of the femur until it had driven itself in and split the bone in all directions. He had escaped bleeding to death, and might even escape amputation. Dougherty packed the wound with lint, covered it with a length of roller bandage, and signaled a returning crew to take him away.

So it went, men passing by one after the other, too fast to keep track of time. And then they were rudely brought back to the vision of what was happening out on the field. There was a crescendo of musketry beyond any they had heard thus far, and from the woods on the other side Dougherty heard for the first time a noise he would hear all too many times. Soldiers in action tend to shout or cheer, but this was something else. How to describe it? It was the high pitched, tremulous "yip, yip, yip" of the fox hunter closing in for the kill, combined with a persistent, steady shout, a roar, a scream from a thousand throats at once, the sound of approaching fury. It was Dougherty's first experience of the rebel yell, and he felt no shame to admit that it terrified him.

Near the little white church the firing was now severe. The Federals began to give ground and fall back toward the east woods. From the woods behind the church, rebel troops pushed forward to overrun them. They could not do it. From the south end of the wood in which Dougherty was at work, two batteries of Union artillery had appeared and prepared to wreak havoc among the men in gray. However, between them and their intended targets was that retreating line of men in blue. The artillerists finished loading as the fleeing lines approached, followed closely by the rebels. Gunners waved a signal and the men in blue fell to the earth as though they had been shot. Lanyards were pulled, streams of smoke and flame belched forth, and canister screamed above the now prone Union troops and tore into the men in gray. They stopped, held their ground for only seconds, then most began to pull back into their own protective woods, out of the range of the hail of canister now mowing men down in droves. Some, instead of going back to the wood, went north to press the left end of the divison's line. The Federal troops continued to fall back, some coming toward the woods, others northward into the cornfield.

General Sumner appeared from the wood across the way, rushing to the left end of Howard's brigade, waving his arms, and trying to communicate an order that could not be heard no matter how loudly he shouted. He wanted Howard's men to turn and face south to fire on the rebels who were driving a retreating regiment before them. It was all in vain. The retreating Federals rushed by, leaving the advancing Confederates to attack the unprotected flank of the Philadelphia Brigade. The men of the Seventy-second, lost in the confusion of changing facing, were caught totally off guard. Their line crumbled. Beyond them the Sixty-ninth did the same, and then all of Howard's brigade was in flight back to the east woods or toward the woods north of the cornfield. The onslaught was too much even for these tried veterans. They broke and ran.

From the west woods the rebel yell increased as their number was suddenly expanded by reinforcements. Cannon fire from the Confederate batteries continued unabated and then, around the northern edge of the west wood appeared still more of the gray clad horde. Federal troops in those woods were in a trap almost impossible of escape. The rebels who had pushed back the Philadelphia Brigade now slammed into the woods just as those from the northern end of the same wood began to fire into the massed lines of Union troops. The men in blue had no room to maneuver, their lines irregular, no more than twenty paces apart, no room to face about and return the fire coming now from their rear. Men fell on all sides, gray and blue. Finally, some of the men in blue began to emerge from the wood, then more and more, all of them attempting to pull back across the cornfield or to head for the wood at the north end of the field.

It was Confederate exhaustion that saved them. Sumner's assault was at least the third they had driven off since sunrise. They could go no further — and they knew that at the end of that field there were Union batteries waiting to welcome them as soon as their own men were out of the way. The gray flood slowed, stopped, then pulled back to the west wood, fully aware that they could do no more.

It was not yet 10:00 A.M.

All around him Dougherty could see destruction beyond imagining. General Sedgwick had suffered three wounds and would be out of action for some time. His dead and wounded numbered more than 2,200, and these in less than an hour — most of them in only twenty minutes.

Dougherty and McBrien stayed there, tending the steady stream of wounded. Both sides were too tired to do more than hold their ground with threats of further fire and hope that the other could not regain the strength to make another assault. The gain of territory? None at all! Like two great beasts, too exhausted to do anything else, the armies lay facing each other, panting and, now and again, snarling, neither willing to concede defeat and neither able to achieve victory.

Dougherty wasn't sure how long they stayed there, but at last the wounded were removed and they gathered their equipment and fell back to assist at the hospitals behind the lines. Those unfortunates still lying wounded among the scattered stalks of corn and the mangled limbs of the dead would there remain until Thursday or even Friday.

"That's it, sir," Dougherty heard McBrien say, "Ye've had yer baptism o' fire today and, thank the Dear Lord, yer still here to tell about it. But, sure, we're not done yet. It's back to the hospitals now and begin on the ones we sent there before and are still waiting their turn fer the rest of the help. Ye done well, Doctor Dougherty, and need feel no shyness about this day's work."

"Thank you," Dougherty said, and meant it. Sean McBrien's steadiness had kept him moving, never letting him falter or fall to the temptation to spend his time in sympathetic horror instead of the constant effort, vain or not, to save what could be saved.

They worked far into the night. Dougherty was still new, not assigned to perform major operations, but Major Briggs put him to work assisting and on that one day he observed and learned as much as could have any new surgeon in years of normal peacetime practice. His theoretical knowledge of the use of chloroform was put to the test and it was not long before he knew just what to do and how to do it.

They went on operating by candle light until all their actions were but rote repetition and their minds struggled to remain attentive. Tubs of arms and legs were emptied, groggy patients were revived and sent off to pray for a successful healing, and the next man was brought forward. It was morning before they stopped. Dougherty slept on the ground behind the barn which was the hospital, and the hard earth did not obstruct a deep and blessedly dreamless sleep.

Late in the morning he was recalled to duty. It was Thursday and they waited for the battle to resume. It had passed yesterday from the right end of the Union line all the way to Burnside's left end, and had raged on until dark. It had been the bloodiest day in the nation's history, and they waited for it to begin again. It did not.

McClellan also waited. Was he right to do so? Dougherty could not have said, but it seemed that his refusal to attack, even with his fresh Fifth Corps and more of the Sixth now come to the field, was, in the end, one more sad blunder. All Thursday the armies waited to see who would strike the next blow. The wounded lay on the field groaning and calling for help. There was no truce, but men of both sides gradually took tentative steps onto the bloody field and started to retrieve the wounded. Daylight came and went, and still nothing happened. They went on with their work and wondered what the next day would bring. They were almost used to the sight of the blood and the sounds of suffering, and Dougherty began to realize just how easy it was to become inured to horror.

He had been in the army a mere two weeks!

Chapter VIII: *E Pluribus Unum*

Nothing except a battle lost can be half
so melancholy as a battle won.
    Arthur Wellesly, Duke of Wellington (1769-1852)
    Dispatch from Waterloo (June 1815)

[September 19, 1862]

Lee's rebels pulled out with a panache to be envied. There was no special effort to go silently. Their departure bordered on the contemptuous, as they held their lines for a full day in the face of an army that should have overrun them, had its commander not been governed by excessive caution and overblown estimates of the enemy's strength.

The enlisted men, always heretofore McClellan's strong support, had begun to murmur at his failure to act decisively and his lack of appreciation for their fighting abilities. Once they had been grateful for his efforts to avoid needless waste of life; now they grew restive at his hesitance to run even well founded risks to achieve final victory.

The most ominous portent of all was a rumor later proved true. During the battle a group of officers, disgusted with McClellan's uncoordinated attacks, wanted to replace him. One of them prevailed upon George Smalley, correspondent of the New York *Herald*, to approach General Hooker about taking command. Hooker had been wounded early in the fight and was then at headquarters. His wounded foot might be an obstacle to field command, but need not prevent his taking full command of the army.

Smalley knew Hooker and got on well with him. He broached the topic; but Hooker knew mutiny when he saw it. He went on with the conversation as though he had not heard the suggestion, and that was the end of it.

By Friday none of that mattered and Dougherty was back at the cornfield by sunrise with McBrien to assist in the care of the wounded of both sides who were still waiting for help. Early as was the start of their day, Briggs must have begun even earlier, for they passed him on the road near the east wood. His presence surprised Dougherty. He thought Briggs was at Pry's mill; but he may have come out to get an idea of what to expect later. He was alone in a commandeered and rather decrepit carriage. He gave them a perfunctory nod in the early half-light, but spoke not a word, almost as though he wished he had not seen them at all. Ah, well... Dougherty was by then reconciled to not being one of his favorites.

They came to the edge of the cornfield and stared. The once well tended farmland was a furious jumble of broken stalks, gouged earth, scorched vegetation — the whole bestrewn with bodies living and dead. Those few acres had been so hotly contested by the two armies without being decisively claimed by either; now one side had walked away and the other was left in full possession of what was, when all was said and done, still no more than a cornfield.

It was mid-afternoon when they finished. All day long the ambulances had carried full loads of wounded, fortified with whiskey or laudanum, enduring the jolting agony of being taken at last to a hospital. There were still wounded gathered near the little white church, so Dougherty and McBrien waited for ambulances to return with fresh crews, after which they would be free to leave. The next day would be spent at the hospital. It would be a relief to leave the staring eyes and gaping mouths of the dead, the headless and disemboweled victims of artillery, the pathetic bodies stripped of weapons, shoes, and even of jackets or shirts or trousers — all gone to clothe an army in dire need, but leaving no shred of dignity for the dead.

They were at the end of the field where the Smoketown Road rounds the East Woods and swings west toward the Dunkard Church, now a far too small temporary hospital, its simplicity marred by broken caissons, dead horses, and human remains which lay all round.

Dougherty looked east, awaiting the return of the ambulances, when there came around the bend, instead, a wagon pulled by two tired horses, a vehicle totally enclosed with roofed over wooden panels, like a woodcut Dougherty had once seen of a gypsy caravan in some European country. Its two occupants looked about, until something caught the attention of the passenger on the right. He pointed, tapped the shoulder of his companion, and called a halt. The wagon was pulled off the road, and turned so that Dougherty could see its rear. They took out a heavy tripod and a bulky photographic camera like one he had seen in a studio window in Philadelphia. They set it up to begin their complex preparations. A black shroud covered the photographer's head as he gazed through his lens and aimed his camera — at a dead horse!

"Shall we go look, sir?" said McBrien. "I've never had the chance to see this done."

"Of course," Dougherty said, with an air of worldly wisdom, although all he knew about photography was a smattering of general ideas and the camera he had seen in the studio window.

Why, he wondered, when they were surrounded with examples of war's devastation, had they chosen a dead horse? The answer soon became evident. This was a dead horse unlike any other. It looked posed, as though in anticipation of this very moment. Dougherty thought of the horses near the Dunkard church — bellies bloated, legs stuck out as straight as sticks, eyes staring, teeth bared. This horse lay on its stomach, legs pulled up underneath in seeming repose. Its neck was upright, turned gracefully toward them, as though it had heard them coming and looked over its shoulder, about to stand and amble over to beg an apple or a carrot.

They sat their horses at a distance and watched the work. The photographers finished and the elder of the two came to greet them.

"Alexander Gardner at yer sairvice, gentlemen," he said with a tip of his hat, reaching up to shake their hands, "and this is my associate, Mister Jamie Gibson. Allow me tae congratulate ye on so grand a victory. I see that ye gentlemen are members o' the medical profession and I ha' nae doot yer work is far from doon. They're already refairin' tae Wednesday as the bludiest day of all that ha'thus far occurred, and all the saddest part o' the mess is left fer ye surgeons tae straighten up."

Mr. Gardner was a businesslike Scotsman, with a wild head of hair and a thick bush of brown beard. His eyes scanned the scene with a view to capturing it all on a photographic plate. Under his travel sullied duster Dougherty saw a crooked tie, a partly buttoned vest, and the heavy chain of a watch, all of them stained by splashed chemicals.

He was a friendly sort, a good quality for a photographer who must put his subjects at their ease so as to avoid the awkward pose and stiff stare of so many of the portraits Dougherty had seen. Of course, the subjects he was dealing with this day were expected to have those qualities and were as much at their ease as they were ever going to be.

His partner bobbed his head in acknowledgment of Gardner's introduction. He was a thin, wiry fellow, his attention on his work, with no time for socializing. His movements were abrupt, almost jerky. He wore spectacles all smudged with finger marks, for he had the nervous habit of constantly pressing the first two fingers of his right hand against the lenses so as to push them back up the bridge of his nose.

The wagon bore the name of Mathew Brady painted on its side, but Mr. Brady was not generally inclined to visit the battlefields himself, being more concerned with selecting at his studio the most salable pictures captured by his subordinates.

"Shall we be doing any more just now?" Gibson asked.

"I dare say not," Gardner replied with a glance at the western sky. The best light of the sun would soon be gone, and, considering the time it took to set everything up, the production of photographs would have to wait until the next day.

"The scene is appalling," Gardner remarked. "Ne'er ha' I seen a sight t' compare wi' it. I suppose ye gentlemen were somewhere behind the lines when it all took place?"

"I'd not say exactly that, sir," McBrien answered, "Sure, we were just over in those woods," and he pointed.

"Ah! It's my intent to examine that part of the field tomorrow," Gardner told them. Turning to Gibson, he added, "What think ye, Mr.

Gibson? I'd say that we begin in the morn with yon wee kirk when we ha' the eastern sun and then get back to the cornfield and the east wood i' the afternoon when we ha' the sun agin at our backs."

"Sounds fine, Mr. Gardner." He had everything back in the wagon by now, and they climbed aboard.

"Perhaps we'll see ye tomorrow, gentlemen," said Gardner. "I wish ye both well."

Gibson clucked his tongue, snapped the reins lightly, and set the horses plodding toward the white church, while McBrien and Dougherty moved slowly in the other direction, still looking for the ambulances. Their path took them nearer to that strange, dead beast and, as if by mutual consent, they dismounted and went to take a closer look.

Beyond the horse was the tip of the East Woods, with the slanting rays of the sun now painting the leaves green-gold. Both at almost the same instant caught sight of a patch of white beneath some fallen branches. McBrien moved toward it, while Dougherty stopped to look again for the ambulances, which ought at any moment to come around the end of the wood.

"Sir, come take a look at this, would ye? It strikes me as a bit of a strange thing, and t'would interest me to know what ye make of it."

Dougherty went over and saw beneath the fallen boughs a pair of unshod feet, their white soles rosy in the lowering afternoon sun. They protruded from a pair of butternut trousers, their edges torn and frayed, their color blending in with the already wilting leaves of the broken branches. Had the sun been higher in the sky and not shone so directly upon those feet, they might never have noticed the dead man. One more body. No surprise with more than a thousand in and around the cornfield. He felt callous at the thought, but he could not imagine what possible interest one more corpse could hold for McBrien or him.

"Can I safely presume that he's dead," Dougherty said. "What else would you like me to see?" Even as he said it, he knew that his tone was condescending. Anyone else might have dropped the matter right there, but this was Sean McBrien and that was not his way.

"Look at the poor devil, will ye, sir," he said, "Do ye not see the oddity of it?"

He had been looking, but McBrien's irritation recalled his attention, and he saw what he meant. In the back of his mind, he could hear Doctor Brownson saying, "Pay attention, young Dougherty, pay attention. Observe and learn!" He felt his cheeks grow hot with embarrassment and was relieved that Doctor Brownson was not there to reprimand him for his lack of attention — and of courtesy.

"Steward McBrien, you are right. It is an oddity, and I should have seen it for myself. I am thankful for the sharpness of your eyes. This merits a closer look." McBrien looked at him, perhaps suspecting sarcasm, then saw that he was serious.

Dougherty felt he deserved to be embarrassed The oddity was glaring. How had he missed it? Almost without thinking he reached for his notebook and pencil. He had seen many feet these last few days, shod and unshod. He had seen them plodding wearily along country roads as they stirred up clouds of dust. He had seen them at sick call. He had seen them protruding from beneath almost identical butternut trousers. He had seen them both living and dead. And he had seen in every instance that they were dirty, dusty, blistered, and usually callused as hard as shoe leather. They were feet which had seen hard use, which had felt pain, which had marched on harsh northern roads and fought in fields across the sharp stalks and stubble of corn. These feet were another matter. These were clean feet, soft skinned, accustomed to wearing boots that fit properly and left neither corn nor callus nor blister.

There was one ready answer. Many of those who had shoes or boots had been promptly relieved of them once they were dead, simply because so many were in dire need and shoes were at a premium. That simple solution did not seem appropriate here. The legs of the trousers were tattered and torn, and did not lead one to expect that the feet below them would have been well shod. More significant was the fact that these feet were so clean. Even a fastidious man under the circumstances of marching and fighting would have had feet far dirtier than these, shod or unshod.

McBrien was about to pull away the fallen branches for a closer look, when Dougherty recalled Doctor Brownson's first lesson.

"Wait!" he warned. "Look carefully at everything before we change the scene. We don't want to destroy the very things that may tell us something significant."

"Right ye are, sir," McBrien replied, a dubious tone in his voice, "I should have thought of it meself... What do ye think we'll see?"

"I don't know," Dougherty had to admit, "but it can do no harm to be careful. There may be nothing to find. On the other hand, the contrast between the feet and the uniform is too glaring to ignore. Bear with me, while we look at everything and make some notes on what we see."

The body lay prone under the branches, their leaves dried by the hot sun, but they were somehow out of place. There was no large branch in sight, just these smaller ones, all piled on the corpse as though by intent. In the woods, both east and west, branches had fallen everywhere, torn from the trees by artillery shells, both North and South. Dougherty had seen enough of them to know what they looked like. They were rudely broken, as if ripped angrily from the trees and cast carelessly aside. The ends of these were cleanly sliced as if by a sharp blade. Had they been purposely cut to hide the body? Not to hide it so well as never to be found, but enough to conceal it for a time. Why? Dougherty told McBrien what was he thinking.

"Yer right, sir. As ye say, the branches was cut apurpose and not shot off the trees. Do ye see just there them short stumps?" He pointed into the wood, where some yards from their position, were the upright ends of saplings cut off clean and smooth. "That's where these branches come from, sir, and t'was no artillery that done it."

Dougherty added this to his notes and then suggested a closer look at the body. They carefully set the branches to one side. The corpse lay face down, its head turned a trifle to the right, but not enough to allow a view of the face. Above the butternut trousers was a shabby frock coat of gray with the blue collar tabs and cuffs of the infantry. On each sleeve was a single braid wrapped in decorative loops reaching almost to the elbow. The collar tabs bore two plain bars.

"Lieutenant of infantry, sir," McBrien said.

The jacket was clearly of better quality than the trousers, but with the usual signs of wear and accumulated dirt. Dougherty saw no belt, no haversack, no sign of pistol, musket, or sword.

"Well, it's clear enough what killed the poor soul," McBrien said.

Not much room for doubt there, Dougherty thought. The back of the jacket was a mass of blood from the top of the left shoulder down the inside of the left sleeve and along the left side of the torso to the waist. It was caked hard in the cloth in an abundance that led Dougherty to expect beneath the armpit quite a large wound, possibly from shell or shrapnel rather than pistol or musket ball. From it blood of heart and lung had gushed forth in scarlet profusion. There was a jagged hole in the cloth, its edges puckered together and sealed shut by the thick clots, hiding the wound.

The left arm was flung upward, the elbow bent, the hand palm down and partly under the head, where it was held in place. The right arm was parallel to the side, the elbow almost straight and the back of the hand on the ground, palm turned upward. It was an interesting hand, under the circumstances. The muscles of the fingers were stiff, but the skin of the palm in life had been soft. Dougherty much doubted it had belonged to a soldier, at least to a soldier who had been one for any length of time. The shabby uniform pointed to considerable service — a service in which even an officer did not long retain the softness of an earlier profession — yet these hands might have belonged to a doctor or a lawyer or a priest. The clean fingernails were clipped neatly, neither bitten nor broken.

The light brown hair was long enough to touch the collar of the coat, but not unkempt. It was clean. Dougherty touched it, and the tips of his fingers came away with bits of dark, almost black, earth. There was not much of it, yet he saw no spot nearby which would account for soil of that particular type. He tore a page from his notebook, folded it into a small envelope, and, with the tips of his fingers, brushed the rest of the dark granules into it. The notebook was bound in thin leather, with both front and back cover having folding flaps. He placed the makeshift envelope within the flap of the back cover, after first marking on it a record of contents, date, and place. The body was not bloated. Quite unusual, if it had been here for two days. Dougherty completed his notes and asked McBrien for any additional impressions.

"Well, now ye've surely got me curiosity aroused," he said, "Fer instance, does it not strike ye as odd that with all the blood on that uniform ye see none a'tall on the ground? Do ye think it means anythin'?"

"It might." McBrien was learning quickly. "Maybe we'll find blood once we move the body, but I doubt it."

From his pocket kit he extracted the razor sharp folding bistoury and cut the back seam of the jacket from collar to hem. So much blood should have congealed and attached jacket to flesh like glue. The cloth was stiff with blood, but was not stuck to the body. Dougherty folded it back to examine the wound. There was no wound!

The skin, unblemished by wounds, was much discolored. On shoulders and back, from the nape of the neck to below the inferior angle of the scapulae, the skin was almost purple, with an irregular webbing of pale wrinkles. Dougherty grasped the waistband, intending to cut open the seat of the trousers and realized that they were far too large for the man, though there was neither belt nor string to keep them up. Had he fought with weapon in one hand and holding up his trousers with the other? A missing weapon was no real mystery; anyone could have taken it. The missing belt was. Why would anyone bother with it? Dougherty slid the trousers down without having to cut them. Across the buttocks were the same cyanosis and wrinkling he had observed on the upper back.

"Take a look at this," he said to McBrien, "and tell me what you think."

McBrien had been looking quizzically at Dougherty, wondering, Dougherty supposed, if he was losing his senses. Nonetheless he gave his attention to the back and buttocks of the dead man, then rendered his verdict.

"Well, they're the same sorts o' marks I've seen on more than one poor dead soul when I helped clean up after battle on the Peninsula and in Mexico, too. Something happens to a body after it's dead fer a while and it changes color like this. It's not a' tall unusual, so far as I know."

"But," Dougherty said, "does it tell you nothing else? Look again. Pay strict attention and consider what you have seen in the past. Be attentive to those buttocks. Meditate upon them. Let them speak to you and listen carefully to what they say, then tell me what you learn."

Dougherty had hoped to seem as erudite to McBrien as Doctor Brownson had to him when he set out to make him an intelligent observer. Yet even as he made the statement in faithful imitation of Brownson's pedagogic method, he knew just how ridiculous it sounded.

"What do I learn from listening to his buttocks? That's what ye ask, sir?"

He favored Dougherty with a characteristic McBrien look full of outward respect for his rank, while just beneath the surface lay a humor that a few days earlier would have nettled him. Instead, Dougherty found himself smiling.

"Well, sir, to the best of me recollection, this is the very first time I've ever been required to converse with or meditate upon that particular portion of anyone's anatomy. But, let me think... Ye know, there is something that might be out of the ordinary. Would ye not expect to find that blue color underneath the body? I mean, here it is on his back, and him face down in the dirt. It seems to me that any time I've seen it, it's always been on that part of the body that was on the ground."

"Well stated!" Dougherty said. "It's a phenomenon known as *livor mortis* in Latin. It means the bruise of death. It comes from what happens to the blood in a dead body, when it obeys the law of gravity and begins to settle. It gathers at the lowest point and is visible as bruises. If the body is lying against something hard, the pressure from the weight of the body stops the blood from flowing into the most compressed parts and that's what causes those whitish wrinkles. That is called blanching."

"What happens if ye move the body?" he asked.

"The blood, if still liquid, just flows again to whatever part is lowest, but it will eventually clot and then not move at all, not even if the body is turned over. That's what these bruises are. It takes hours for that to happen. So what do you think?"

"Seems clear as a bell," he said, "He was brought here from somewhere else. He was flat on his back on a hard surface after death, and he stayed that way fer a good long time before he got dropped here."

"That may be so," Dougherty said cautiously, remembering the care with which Doctor Brownson always came to his conclusions, "but to be strictly accurate, it simply means that for some hours after death the body was in one position and then moved, perhaps just turned over. However, my inclination is to agree with you. Why simply turn it over and then have to hide it? Far more likely it was brought here from somewhere else."

McBrien was caught up in the spirit of the thing, and was turning out to be a more adept student than Dougherty had been. But there was a great deal more to be learned before they should move the body.

"Do you notice," Dougherty said, "the generally clean and healthful appearance of the skin?"

"That I do. It makes ye wonder, don't it? Sure, nobody who'd spent a fair amount of time in that uniform could possibly be so clean. I'd venture another notion as well... Do ye see anywhere about him the signs of the usual inhabitants? The bugs, I mean. These last few days I ain't seen a single Johnny Reb that wasn't busy scratching himself. Of course, the fleas don't stay around once yer dead; no blood left to enjoy, I guess. But I don't see a single sign of bites er scratching. Do you?"

"None at all. And there's another thing about the rebs. Are there any of them who don't have diarrhea? Are there any who don't look hungry? This man is thin, but not unhealthy. He seems well enough fed. The buttocks are blue, but I see no signs of the topical irritation that always comes with a bad case of the Virginia quickstep. Look, and you'll see what I mean."

Dougherty pressed on the buttocks, spreading them slightly. No sign of diarrheal irritation at all. Touching the buttocks, however, had revealed something else. The *glutei maximi* were rigid. He felt lower, and so were the muscles along the backs of the thighs.

"I think we can turn him over now, if you'll give me a hand," and he took hold of the ankles. McBrien grasped the shoulders and together they turned the body face up. It was stiff and hard to manage. Rigor mortis. For the body to have been this stiff, Dougherty would have expected it to have been dead at least twelve hours. And had the man died on the day of battle, rigor would have long since ended.

The jacket was already unbuttoned. The ventral aspect of the body, like the dorsal, was without wounds or flea bites and had a healthy appearance. They brushed the dead leaves and dirt from off the face and saw the slightly less defined look that a face begins to take on after it has been dead for some hours. The little wrinkles, the character lines of the living, begin to fade after death, and there is a blandness, the result of gases already forming under the skin and slightly distending it.

He was a reasonably good looking man, his face clean shaven, but somewhat carelessly. Tiny patches had been missed by the man or his barber and there were some small razor nicks. They were minute, their edges pale, waxy, not sealed shut, no trace of scabs. The pallor of death made it hard to tell, but the lower half of his face seemed lighter than the upper. His eyebrows were thick, his nose mildly bulbous. Dougherty estimated his age at thirty-five or forty.

He pushed up the corpse's sleeves and saw that, while the backs of the hands were fairly well tanned, his arms were not. He was, Dougherty would have said, a man who spent time out of doors, but not a man accustomed to long hours in the sun. The skin had already begun to take on the greenish look of the thoroughly dead. It was cold to the touch, slightly clammy.

Dougherty lifted the eyelids, revealing orbs that had lost their luster and were flattening as the aqueous and vitreous humors dried out. The eyelid had moved easily in response to his touch, so he probed lightly about the jaw and neck, and found their muscles slack. Rigor mortis follows a predictable pattern. The small muscles of face and neck stiffen and it then proceeds to the large muscles, all of it taking place within about twelve hours. It resolves itself in the same order, and even the largest muscles relax within twenty to thirty hours after death. Dougherty felt safe in concluding that he had been dead more than twelve hours and less than twenty — an estimate subject to correction by a few hours in either direction, but certainly showing that he had not died in the battle.

Throughout all this Dougherty had continued assiduously taking notes and pointing out to McBrien whatever seemed of interest. The whole examination had taken some time and the sun would not be long in setting. He had to decide what to do next.

They heard the creak and rumble of approaching wagons and from the other side of the East Woods came the long awaited ambulances. Dougherty mounted, asking McBrien to wait with the dead man and to be prepared to assist in the removal of his body. His brows lifted, but he made no comment beyond the expected, "Yes, sir."

Now what ought he to do? To him this seemed a suspicious death, but he expected no one to be much impressed by his opinions. Who would even want to hear what he had to say? It would sound utterly foolish to claim that among the thousands of bodies on a field of battle, he had discovered the one whose death was suspect — he, whose primary talents were inexperience and expendability! He had little hope that Briggs would concur with his desire for an autopsy. He even wondered whether the ambulance drivers would be willing to haul a corpse when so many wounded remained in dire need of assistance. Yet he remembered Doctor Brownson's dedication to resolving the mysteries of the dead, and he determined to do what he could.

He rode toward the approaching ambulances, then stopped and waited, still thinking. South of him were the charred remains of a house that had been burned by the rebs. Beyond it he knew was a sunken road, where French and Richardson had fought, and where Richardson fell severely wounded.

The stone shell of the building stood forlorn, its chimney a lone sentinel guarding the ruin, looking in envy at the peace of the little family cemetery so near to where Dougherty waited. Between house and cemetery ran a lane that debouched into Smoketown Road almost where he stood. He heard the thump of hoofs and clatter of wheels even before he saw the buckboard. It was the usual battered, country conveyance, its rear seat removed and the space converted to a box for hauling things. It was not, however, the usual horse. This one was far too spirited for the vehicle, but its driver was obviously skilled and quite at his ease as he jolted down the lane straight toward Dougherty. As he drew near, he waved, and it was only then that Dougherty realized that it was Doctor Oliver Naylor.

"Well, if it isn't Lieutenant Dougherty!" He came to a halt, reaching to shake Dougherty's hand. "Are you just now coming onto the field?"

"Just leaving," Dougherty said, "and you?"

"I'm on my way home. I plan to go back to the hospital at the Poffenberger place and then to Keedysville. It has been a long day."

"Where have you been?" Dougherty asked.

"My contract is with the First Division of the Second Corps, so I spent the day at the sunken road south of here. So many killed and wounded men packed into so small a space! I have never seen anything to equal it. I've been there since first light this morning with no time to leave for so much as a moment, and even now the work is not done, so we have been replaced by others."

Dougherty could see the exhaustion in his eyes. His once impeccable tailoring bore witness to his efforts. The knees of the trousers were grass stained, the toes of the shoes scuffed where he had knelt on rough earth to tend the wounded.

"It has been much the same here," Dougherty said. "I'll be going back now to Pry's mill, but there is a problem, and I hope you can help. I hate to impose on your goodness, but at the moment I have no one else to turn to."

"Then what can I say but yes? Could I be so dastardly as to deny a man his last hope?" Dougherty was embarrassed at having forced him to help, but then saw that he was smiling. "I am pleased to help," he said. "What can I do?"

Dougherty explained what they had found. Naylor's face did not much change, so it was difficult to read his reaction; but Dougherty thought that he was perhaps a bit incredulous, a bit skeptical. He realized that he was already inspiring precisely the sort of reaction that he had feared. Or was he reading his own doubts into the other's expression? In any case, Naylor did not object, and when Dougherty pointed to where McBrien waited at the edge of the wood, he simply snapped his reins and headed the buckboard in that direction. Dougherty was relieved that he neither objected to what was asked of him nor attempted to dissuade him from it.

Doctor Naylor greeted McBrien and moved to step down to help them, but Dougherty told him to keep his seat while McBrien and he loaded the body into the back of the buckboard. It was a homely vehicle, such as he would never have associated with Doctor Oliver Naylor. His taste in horses and clothing should have led one to expect something more pretentious, but this was far more suited to hauling the wounded. In the back were a number of folded blankets, and they used them to cover over their gruesome cargo. It was well past 4:00 P.M. as they set out for Pry's mill.

Chapter IX: An Unseasonable Discovery

Curlylocks, Curlylocks,
Wilt thou be mine?
Thou shalt not wash dishes
Nor yet feed the swine,
But sit on a cushion
And sew a fine seam,
And feed upon strawberries,
Sugar and cream.
    Anonymous
    Curlylocks

[September 19, 1862]

    Under the blankets the stiffened body bounced on the hard bed of the buckboard as it encountered the ruts in a road none too smooth to begin with, and now eroded all the more by the flow of military traffic. Doctor Naylor's driving was no longer so spirited. There was too much traffic on this road and there was always the risk that too energetic a bounce might relieve him of his uncomplaining passenger. They stopped briefly at the Poffenberger place. Doctor Naylor went in to report, while McBrien and Dougherty, solicitous to see the body safely to its destination, found a length of rope and tied it securely in place.

    The continued fine weather had been a blessing. The wounded overflowed the buildings and lay out in the open air protected by the most makeshift of tents. Those who could walk helped nurse those who could not, bringing them food and drink and pouring clean water from the farm pond onto their bandages to keep them supple and prevent their sticking to the unhealed wounds or the raw stumps of amputated limbs. The task was overwhelming.

    It was not long before Doctor Naylor reappeared and they set out through Smoketown to the upper bridge — the same bridge they had crossed with General Meade on Tuesday. For a while McBrien and

Dougherty rode behind the buckboard, but once past Smoketown Dougherty drew up alongside to speak to Doctor Naylor.

"Have you had much experience, Doctor, in performing post-mortem examinations?" Dougherty asked.

"None whatsoever, I fear," was the reply. "The last cadaver I operated on was in medical college, and I've never since had to follow the progress of a patient beyond the last breath. What makes you so eager to perform a post-mortem on this one?"

"Simply the facts as I sketched them for you when we loaded the body onto the buckboard." Dougherty knew he had not persuaded him, possibly because his youth made his interest seem more enthusiasm than reason. He told Naylor briefly about his work with Doctor Brownson.

"The problem is that discovery of a dead body here is hardly a surprise to anyone," Naylor said. "I would be amazed if you were granted permission to spend your time examining a corpse found on a battlefield — especially on that part of the field where they are as thick as fleas on a stray dog. I don't want to discourage you, Lieutenant, but I think that you are not likely to be well received when you try to interest your superiors in what you want to do."

"So I expect," Dougherty said, "but, even under the circumstances of war, I believe that a death is important. If this man is not a battle casualty, that is reason enough to justify an investigation."

"I agree with you, Lieutenant, but that will not make it any easier to convince anyone that you should spend time on one death, especially the death of a reb, when there are so many lives to be saved. Perhaps you should consider delaying the investigation until you have completed your other work on behalf of the living."

"That makes sense, Doctor Naylor," he admitted, "but the longer we wait, the less likely we are to learn anything. One thing I learned from my previous experience is that time is of the essence. The longer one waits, the colder the trail, and the more unlikely a solution. Bodies decompose, evidence is obscured, energies of the investigators are diverted, even interest wanes. I think I have little choice but to do what needs to be done, even if I have to do it completely on my own time."

"Do you have any time that is yours? In the army, even if you say that you have found the time, some enterprising superior is certain to find a better use for it. That is the natural inclination of that perverse creature known as the military mind. But I wish you luck, Lieutenant. I admire your intentions, and I hope that you can carry them out."

His words lacked conviction and Dougherty knew that Naylor thought he was simply asking for trouble and should forget the whole thing. Had he seriously contested Dougherty's intention, he might have taken courage from the effort to produce arguments. It was more disheartening to find that he clearly thought the whole thing a waste of time.

The branches darkened the road, but it was not yet twilight as they emerged at the upper bridge. Arriving and departing ambulances, like sand in an hourglass, tried to push through the bottleneck of the stone bridge, but were held to a foreordained pace, no matter the urgency. Finally they crossed and went the quarter of a mile along the east bank of the creek to where the Antietam meets the Little Antietam. It was there that Samuel Pry had his mill.

It was an imposing structure. The road turned along the Little Antietam, curving gradually upward, making the height of the mill all the more impressive. Red hospital flags flapped lazily from the upper windows. The building loomed over them as they drew near, its first story of gray-brown field stone surmounted by a further three stories of red brick. It was a perfect place for a hospital, situated next to the running water of the Little Antietam. It was well ventilated, with wide open doors on each floor — doors used for sacks of grain and flour hoisted and lowered by block and tackle. All about it were hastily erected dog tents, draped over rope stretched between muskets, their bayonets stuck in the ground. Ambulances had turned the grassy area in front of the mill into a mass of dusty clay. Even now there was a string of vehicles from which stretchers were being taken either to the tents or into the operating rooms of the mill, depending on the decisions of the assistant surgeons and stewards who did the triage.

Off to one side, on a piece of level ground, a canvas shelter formed an annex to a ramshackle wooden shed, a sort of roofless porch, hung all around with canvas curtains. Its purpose was no mystery. A large signboard proclaimed to one and all, "J. Wilson Tacket, Fine Furniture, Undertaking, Embalming." It was one more business that, along with the manufacturers of arms and the purveyors of shoddy, had prospered in the war. The place reeked of creosote and the more modern mixture of alcohol and chloride of zinc, explaining the roofless state of the porch. Anyone who worked overly long at this occupation inside a too closed space was liable to feel as though his own lungs had been embalmed. There was something distasteful, in Dougherty's opinion, about the presence of this occupation at the portals of a hospital, but no one could argue with its convenience. Mr. Tacket was doing a booming business.

Dougherty dismounted and announced that he was going in search of Major Briggs. Somewhat to his surprise, Doctor Naylor volunteered to come with him. He said that it would interest him to see the workings of the hospital, but Dougherty suspected that it was because he sensed his apprehension at dealing with Briggs and was offering his moral support, even though he did not truly agree with what Dougherty wanted to do. Whatever the reason, he was glad for the company and appreciated his kindness.

Dougherty was directed to the second floor. Perhaps the words of a Dante or the brush of a Hieronymus Bosch could have done justice to what met them inside, where the denizens of hell or the imagined terrors of a nightmare might have felt at home. Sputtering candles pointed the way without dispelling the gloom. Stretcher bearers, no matter how gentle they tried to be, jostled the wounded who groaned or, beyond power of will to prevent, cried out. Amputated limbs were carried outside, along with their anesthetized owners. The heat, the waste, and the bits of putrefying matter left an odor near unendurable in the close atmosphere.

Major Briggs was in conversation with an officer — a medical officer — whose back was toward Dougherty. They stood next to a makeshift operating table, a door nailed atop two barrels. A medical steward was taking advantage of Major Briggs's preoccupation to clean his instruments in a pan of water already so incarnadine that one could have mistaken it for the vital fluid itself. A smell of chloroform hung in the air, faintly dizzying but not enough to cause anyone but the patients to succumb.

Briggs's collar was open, his sleeves rolled up, and his apron covered in blood. His shoulders drooped in exhaustion, in contrast to the man with whom he spoke. His uniform was neat and clean, his hat well brushed, no apron, no bloodstains, bright oak leaves of a major on new green shoulder straps.

Briggs looked past the stranger's shoulder and his eye fell upon Dougherty. He expected the usual skeptical squint, but, to his amazement, the Major seemed almost happy to see him — not that his countenance exactly lighted up, but it did flicker for a second. Was it perversity on Dougherty's part, or was he right to think that Briggs was up to something?

"Ah, Major," Briggs said, "you are in luck!" Dougherty began to suspect what he was up to. His visitor was the burden and Briggs had been scanning the horizon for a victim, a poor soul upon whom to shunt his annoyance, some unsuspecting fool to assume an unpleasant responsibility. Dougherty was that victim, that poor soul, that eagerly awaited fool.

"Here, Major, is just the man for you. He's familiar with the field and can be a great help to you. Allow me to present Lieutenant James Dougherty. I can assign him to you for the duration of your stay." Dougherty almost expected a drum roll and the flourish of a master of ceremonies presenting the next novelty act, so enthusiastic was he.

The man who turned to face him was in his early thirties, with dark hair cut short at the sides and combed neatly back from a forehead both high and broad, an intellectual countenance. The carefully barbered beard and moustache grew so close to the mouth that when he closed it the lips seemed to disappear. Beneath the straight, moderately full brows, his eyes gazed with an intensity amplified in the shadowy candle light. His uniform was that of a staff officer, not a combatant.

"Dougherty! Well, this is something of a surprise. I had no idea that you had enlisted in the army. I should have thought you would have been in practice back in Carbon County. I am glad to find you here." Dougherty was flattered that he remembered him.

Major John Hill Brinton, was one of those from whom he had learned the art of surgery at Jefferson. He was, at the time of the battle of Antietam, just four months past his thirtieth birthday and had already had a distinguished career as a physician. Like Dougherty, he had been but twenty when he received his doctorate in medicine from the Jefferson Medical College. He, however, had also earned degrees from the University of Pennsylvania and then gone on to study in Europe. It was in Paris, under Doctor Pierre Louis, that he was educated in the identification of disease through post-mortem examination. Dougherty had gained his experience of dealing with the dead from Doctor Brownson and studied the science of medical jurisprudence under Doctor Robley Dunglison. He had been much impressed when Doctor Brinton (as part of his surgical courses) so emphasized the usefulness of the autopsy. Dougherty decided on the spot not to speak of the dead man in Briggs's presence. Brinton would be far more likely to listen to him. His sinking spirits reversed their downward course and began to soar.

"Doctor Brinton! Sir, it is a pleasure to see you again." Dougherty shook the extended hand.

"So, you know each other," said Major Briggs, "Perhaps I should not be surprised at that. Our Lieutenant Dougherty seems to have a great many friends among the distinguished members of the medical corps. It seems there is not a major whose acquaintance he cannot claim."

Dougherty was sure Briggs was having second thoughts about setting him to entertain this unexpected guest. Briggs was still peeved at the duty with Major Letterman and, now that he had found some bothersome task for him, he was annoyed that Dougherty was pleased at it. His youth and lack of experience made him easily expendable, but that obvious disadvantage was becoming his greatest asset. Ironic, perhaps, but it did not improve Briggs's disposition. Had he been able to do so gracefully, Dougherty knew he would have handed Major Brinton on to someone else's care, but it was too late now.

Dougherty's surprise at Major Brinton's presence had made him forget his manners. Only belatedly did he remember to present Doctor Naylor, who seemed not the least put out at the lapse. He had been in conversation with the steward, but now turned to speak to Briggs and Brinton with the same self-assured ease he had with everyone. He could not have failed to see Major Briggs's antagonism toward Dougherty, but diverted his attention with a few questions about the treatment of the wounded. It was a short conversation. Briggs was intent on getting back to work.

"Major Brinton," Briggs said as he ushered them out, "I am sure you will find Lieutenant Dougherty most helpful. You can explain to him better than I the nature of your business here and I will get back to my work. It has been a pleasure to meet you."

He wiped his bloodied hand on the stained apron and held it out for Major Brinton to shake, then sent the orderly for the next patient. They went to the buckboard as Major Brinton explained what he wanted.

"The Surgeon General is establishing a military medical museum in Washington and I am here to gather exhibits," he said.

"Exhibits of what sort?" Dougherty asked.

"All sorts... some perhaps gruesome to the lay mind. Amputated limbs to show the damage done by weapons, bones with bullets embedded, whole skeletons at times. Even exhibits of soft tissue will be preserved in alcohol. All of it for the advancement of medicine and surgery. We will produce detailed reports on typical medical and surgical cases for statistical comparisons, and descriptions, drawings, or photographic exhibits of particular anomalies. In the end, the exhibits will be much more than objects to satisfy curiosity; they will become the source of knowledge to serve the needs of the living. I would be most interested in what you can show me, based upon your own observations of the past few days."

By this time they were at the buckboard. Dougherty introduced McBrien and decided then and there to take the plunge. He untied the rope and pulled back the blanket.

"Sir," he began, "we have here one of those anomalies. One body among so many may seem to be just a piece of hay in a haystack, but this one merits concern. The circumstances under which we discovered this body — its condition, its clothing, and its state of health prior to death — all these things cry out for investigation. I honestly admit that I have little confidence that my superiors would grant permission for me to perform any real examination. I hope I am not being presumptuous in thinking that you may wish to help me. Let me explain."

Briefly he outlined his arguments. Naylor also listened intently, but said nothing either for or against the proposal. Not surprising, since he had never examined the body for himself. What was surprising was McBrien's enthusiasm for the project. Dougherty knew that he was interested, but until this moment had not been aware of just how strong his feelings were. He was circumspect in the presence of the major; but, as opportunity presented and with a deferential, "Begging yer pardon, sirs...," he did all he could to present a mystery in serious need of solution.

In the fading light Major Brinton looked at the hair, the hands, the lack of wounds. Dougherty could see his initially polite attentiveness turn into real curiosity, and that, in turn, give way to interest, and Dougherty knew he was with them. By the time Doctor Naylor left and the body had been moved to the mill, he had made up his mind.

"Well, Dougherty, it seems you will have your autopsy, after all," he said with the trace of a smile.

"So it does, sir, but will this create any difficulty for you? Do you need approval from Major Briggs?"

"I think not. I am here from Washington under direct orders of Surgeon General Hammond. He knows that officers in the field have serious — and, I might add, quite proper — concerns about their immediate tasks and may well be less interested in the sorts of things that are my concern. My written orders take that into account."

He unfolded a piece of paper and handed it to Dougherty.

Washington City, D.C., Sept. 18, 1862

Sir:—

> You will proceed without delay to Frederick, Md., to superintend the selection of specimens for the Pathological Museum, connected with

this office. All medical officers are hereby ordered to give you any aid in their power to further this object.

     Very respectfully yr. obt. Servt.
      By order of the Surgeon General,
       (Signed) JOS. R. SMITH,
        Surgeon, U.S.A.
Dr. J.H. Brinton, Surgeon of Volunteers, etc.

"So now you are under my orders to do an autopsy and that means there will be no repercussions from other quarters, even if they think it a waste of time."

In a room at the back of the mill on another makeshift operating table they placed the dead man on his back, his arms now relaxed enough to be stretched parallel to his sides. On a smaller table they set candles and McBrien suspended a lantern from a hook set into the heavy beam overhead. Dougherty laid out his pocket medical kit, only then realizing that its folding scalpels were too small for the job. McBrien had the same thought.

"If ye'll excuse me fer a bit, sir," he said," I'll see if I can't get ye some more suitable implements. These are a trifle dainty fer some of the work that we'll likely be doing."

In less than ten minutes he was back with a straight rongeur and a sequestrum, both of them pliers-like instruments used for chipping off and removing parts of cut bone. He had also a 15 inch amputating knife, a pair of medium sized catlins, double edged knives about 9 inches in length. That did not surprise Dougherty, but he was surprised, and gratified, to see that he had also produced a gum-elastic bougie — a flexible rod quite useful in probing into narrow spaces. There were also a good sized copper basin, a few large surgeon's needles, a ball of strong twine, and a pannier of clear glass jars with wide mouths and broad corks to secure them.

"Do you wish to perform the autopsy, sir?" Dougherty asked Brinton as a courtesy, hoping he would decline.

"Please proceed, Doctor," he smiled, "I am well aware of your previous experience with Brownson. He was satisfied with your skill, so I am content to observe and to add whatever I can as things progress."

The clothing consisted only of jacket and trousers, nothing else. They were in tatters and offered no information at all. Dougherty laid them aside to package as evidence later.

They examined every inch of the body, front and back, bringing the lantern down close at they did so. The skin was clean and healthy, no marks, no bruises beyond the lividity. The minute facial nicks Dougherty had already noted were the only wounds. Palpation revealed no broken bones. The corpse was that of a perfectly healthy male, clean beneath the ragged uniform, thin but not undernourished. There was no external indication of a cause of death.

"Is it possible he was strangled?" Brinton asked.

"It's not completely out of the question," Dougherty said, "but I doubt it. The throat shows no damage, no bruises from rope or cord or strap, no marks of hands, none of the usual abrasions of strangulation."

Dougherty pressed his fingertips to the throat The thyroid cartilage was unbroken. The autopsy would show any internal bruising or a broken hyoid, but strangulation seemed unlikely. He looked carefully at the eyelids, the sclera, and surrounding tissue. Strangulation often ruptures tiny blood vessels in that area, leaving pinpoint sized splotches of blood — marks known as *petechiae*. They were nowhere to be seen, nor was there any facial cyanosis.

The muscles about the mouth were now relaxed. He opened the jaws, leaned close, and sniffed. There was the odor of incipient putrefaction, but nothing else — no garlicky odor of arsenic, no bitter almond of cyanide, no odor of violets from turpentine, no sign of damage due to acid or caustics. The buccal cavity and fauces were unremarkable. He ruled out strychnine, which left the body in full rigor, but in a convulsive state with spine bent backward, teeth exposed by rictus, and eyes wide open and staring. They were proceeding inexorably to the exclusion of every cause of death imaginable. The only consolation was the realization that there must be a cause and that perseverance would discover it. After, all the most basic diagnosis still held — the man was dead.

Beneath the shoulder blades, they placed a rolled pillow of sacking, slightly arching the back, making it easier to reach the organs once they had laid open the chest and abdominal cavity. With a catlin Dougherty cut an incision in two lines, beginning at the apex of each shoulder and meeting at the sternum, with a third straight cut down to the pubis. They were assailed by the odor of gases already forming in the decaying body.

McBrien, in spite of his experience with the wounded and the dying, had never before attended an autopsy and was unprepared for this. He gagged and averted his face. He said nothing for a moment then shook his head and held up his right hand, palm forward, in a gesture that told Dougherty to go on.

Dougherty's small folding scalpel proved best for peeling back the tissues over the rib cage. With the rongeur, he snipped through the ribs on both sides and lifted away the sternum and attached rib sections, like taking off a lid, to view the lungs and the pericardium. The lungs were normal and relatively healthy, although an incision into one of them showed the darkness one might expect in a frequent cigar smoker, but no sign of fluid from drowning or pneumonia. Pressing produced no crepitation. He removed the lungs from the thorax and placed them in the copper basin. He opened the throat, but found no damage to thyroid cartilage or hyoid.

Opening the pericardium, revealed a normal heart, without the broken or clogged vessels of heart failure, no apparent discoloration, no sign of excess fat, no clotting, no hemorrhaging.

Dougherty removed the heart to the basin, and inserted a finger into the pulmonary artery. If the man had died from heart failure, there might be a clot. There wasn't.

It was when they got to the organs in the abdominal cavity that Major Brinton took a more active part.

"One of my colleagues in the formation of the museum is Surgeon Joseph Woodward," he said. "He is quite an expert in the post-mortem signs of camp diseases. Very adept in the use of microscope and photographic camera in the study of tissue. I wish he were here now, but I've learned from him what to expect in a military corpse."

He commented as each organ was studied. The liver was healthy, without the lardaceous or bacony indication of chronic malaria. The spleen was unremarkable. The outer surface of both large and small intestine was clear of symptoms. Inside the intestines the mucous membrane had no discoloration or ulceration of typho-malarial infection, no thickened membrane of dysentery or enteritis.

Opening the large intestine released an odor that made them all flinch, but it was normal. Brinton looked for what he called "shaven beard" appearances. Dougherty was unfamiliar with the term, and Brinton was delighted to have the chance once again to lecture his former student.

"It comes from chronic diarrhea," he said. "The ileum assumes in the patches of Peyer an appearance of tiny blue-black dots, like the discoloration on the chin of a man with a heavy beard. It is not here, nor is there any green discoloration at the ileo-coecal valve."

The contents of the tract were healthy, neither watery nor frothy, nor excessively hardened. It was, all in all, a thoroughly negative sort of examination, with no signs of acute or chronic illness or disease. Yet this made the case all the more interesting, since the well worn clothing was that of a tired rebel and not of the perfect specimen that this one seemed to be. No one could have come through the recent campaign so totally unscathed by camp diseases, wounds, or parasites — and without even soiling his feet! Dougherty began to wonder if the man had simply succumbed to the rigors of remaining so robust.

The stomach was likewise unremarkable. The inner lining was whitish, with none of the inflamed redness of disease or corrosive or irritant effects of certain poisons. The contents, however, offered another mystery.

Under the watchful eye of Doctor Brownson, Dougherty had studied Beaumont's *Experiments and Observations on the Gastric Juice and the Physiology of Digestion*. William Beaumont was an army surgeon in the Michigan Territory in 1822, where he met Alexis St. Martin, a Canadian *voyageur* who had been shot in the stomach, leaving a wound which never healed. For years Beaumont took advantage of this to insert food into St. Martin's stomach cavity and remove it later to examine the state of its digestion. He wrote a treatise to explain digestion, but it was enormously useful for forensic medicine. In death the digestive action ceases, so examination of the stomach contents of a corpse can give a fair idea of the time elapsed between the dead person's last meal and the time of death. Whoever this fellow was, he had eaten a good meal probably less than an hour before his death.

Ignoring the odor of vomitus, Dougherty used his small forceps to withdraw and place in a jar the stomach contents. This man had not been fed on hardtack, salt pork, green apples, or parched corn. He had eaten a meal of beef or lamb, probably in a stew with carrots and potatoes and onions. He had partaken of cheese and bread. There were other bits not so readily identifiable, probably the more perishable items, and the gastric juices had affected them more quickly than they had the meat and vegetables. There were numerous little lumps, whitish with touches of brown like wilting plants, reddish material speckled with small, dark spots. What it was, Dougherty had no idea, but it struck a familiar note in memory. In any case, the man had not lived long after that last meal, a point that might later prove useful in a court.

They sealed the jar with a broad cork. Over this, with a length of the twine, McBrien tied a piece of cloth made from a bandage, upon which both Brinton and Dougherty wrote their names and the date. They took the candle, dripped the melting wax over the cloth, and tied still another piece of bandage over that, where they inscribed a statement of the contents and covered it with another thin layer of wax. The result was a proper sample of stomach contents that would remain for a long time relatively moist. Dougherty would have preferred some tightly tied sheet-caoutchouc in place of the waxed cloth, but this would do. It was sufficiently protected to serve later as evidence.

They turned last to the kidneys. There was no enlargement, as from typho-malarial fever. There was neither paleness nor the soft, yellow cortical discoloration of fatty degeneration. It was precisely as they had expected: Not helpful.

There still remained the skull. Had he perhaps succumbed to an apoplectic seizure? Dougherty thought of sending McBrien for a trephine and a Hey's saw, but first he asked him to help slide the folded sacking from beneath the back and place it under the corpse's head. This would bring it a little forward, and make the next stage of the operation easier. Dougherty lifted the corpse's shoulders as McBrien grasped the sacking and slid it upward.

"Ouch! What the hell..." said McBrien, "begging yer pardon, sirs. Look at that, would ye now."

The fleshy pad at the base of his left thumb had blood on it. He wiped it with a piece of sacking, and revealed a cut about an inch in length. It was not deep, but like most cuts about the hands it bled more than its size should warrant. He wrapped a strip of bandage around it and asked for a candle.

Dougherty took hold of the corpse's shoulders and held it in a sitting position, while McBrien, by the light of the candle, looked beneath the long hair near the base of the skull. The light reflected from a sharp metal point, small and so hidden by the hair as to have escaped earlier notice. They turned the body on its side. The hair had none but the faintest trace of dried blood and minute bits of the same black dirt they had noted earlier. The point projected so slightly from the skin that it could not be grasped with the fingers.

Dougherty took up the sequestrum, a small one, no more than six inches in length, with arms thinner and lighter than those of the rongeur, but its toothed ends gave good purchase on small objects. With the addition of a small pad formed of a folded bit of sacking, that purchase was increased and he grasped the projecting point of metal. He patiently and gently worked it back and forth until it loosened. Once it began to move, he got a better grip on it, and it slid into view. A small quantity of pinkish liquid seeped out, a mixture of spinal fluid and blood.

He placed the object on the palm of his left hand and touched it with the index finger of the right. It was a round, slightly curved piece of steel, about two and one half inches long and a bit less than a sixteenth of an inch in diameter. It resembled a portion of a much magnified surgical needle. The pointed end, however, was not needle-like. It was triangular in cross section rather than round like the rest of the length of the implement. The other end, that which had protruded from the back of the head and whose jagged tip had cut McBrien's hand, was obviously broken off from what had been a longer piece. One would not have expected steel of that quality and thickness to have broken easily, but closer inspection revealed that its quality was not consistent. It would seem that there had been a fault in the metal. An air bubble or some impurity trapped within it during its manufacture had made it hollow at its breaking point. It would have served quite easily the purpose of penetrating soft tissue without much risk of breaking, but not so when it lodged in bone.

Dougherty reached for the gum-elastic bougie. It was thin enough to pass into the hole at the base of the skull, curving inward and upward, meeting no resistance. He pushed it in no further than the two and one half inch length of the broken piece of metal. Leaving it in place, he employed the small bistoury from his medical kit to incise the muscles and tendons at the base of the skull, carefully following a path parallel to that of the bougie.

The weapon had been pushed in at the level of the articulation between atlas and axis, passed along the left side of the spinous process of the axis, entered at the jointure of axis and atlas, and traced a path along the odontoid process. This caused it to sever the spinal cord and push up into the lower extremity of the medulla oblongata. It would have caused a rapid death. The weapon had then broken off *in situ* and the wielder had either been unable to grasp it and take it out, or had simply decided to leave it in place, probably thinking that it would never be found in any case. After all, who would bother to examine one more battlefield casualty? Whichever had been the motive, the result was the same. It had caused death with wonderful efficiency and the tightness of its containment in the bony structures had prevented any severe bleeding. Whatever small amount of blood there had been, someone had wiped almost completely away. They really had no need to proceed further with the autopsy. It was best at this point to do no more damage to the body itself. They still wanted to preserve the facial features until a photographic image could be made. They had found the cause of death, and it could not be explained away as accidental or unsuspicious.

The metal piece which had come from the wound had another sinister implication, one that created great uneasiness in Dougherty's mind. All three of them recognized it for what it was: Part of the curved shaft of a trocar — a medical tool. The whole implement would have consisted of a curved steel shank and polished wood handle, all of it six to eight inches in length. It was used to puncture soft tissue so as to draw off fluids such as pus. The mystery now had a dimension that disturbed Dougherty greatly. Another cleverly hidden cause of death, pointing once again to a killer who might be a doctor. Had Galen somehow come from Philadelphia to Maryland?

They returned the organs to the cavity, keeping portions of each for further examination and to serve as evidence, and sewed it shut with cord. The samples they placed in the glass containers, one for each organ, corked and sealed with melted wax as before, each container as full as possible, so as to allow no room for the air to dry the samples and encourage their deterioration. Again Brinton and Dougherty affixed their signatures and the date.

McBrien returned the implements to the orderly who had lent them to him, and came back in short order with news that solved one problem: What to do with the body. He had found out there was an ice house just behind the mill with still enough ice to protect the corpse for the time being. Assuming that the dead man had not been one of the rebels, then he may have been a Federal or even a local civilian. For identification they needed likenesses to show to people. Two names came to mind: Frank Schell and Alexander Gardner. They already knew where Gardner would be on the next day and it should be easy enough to find Frank Schell. In the meantime Dougherty wanted to transcribe his notes while they were fresh in his mind. Major Brinton returned to Keedysville, where he had a room at the inn and a comfortable bed waiting for him. McBrien and Dougherty would remain at the mill.

McBrien, with his usual efficiency, directed Dougherty to a small room near where they had performed the autopsy. It was far into the night by the time he had completed his written record, but he took advantage of the remaining stump of the candle to write to Doctor Brownson. He recounted, in as much detail as he could manage in his tiredness, the events of the day and outlined the conclusions they had reached, asking that Brownson forward his thoughts on the matter.

What he would be able to do, Dougherty was not certain; but he had confidence that, if he had missed something, Brownson would pick it up. He also hoped for any further word on the elusive Galen. In the end, he was so tired that he did not finish the letter. The morning would be time enough.

He blew out the candle. His eyes closed and in seconds he began to drift off. Suddenly he was wide awake again as in his half dreaming state he saw the open stomach. He relit the candle and held it up to the bottle with the partly digested contents of the man's last meal. In it were those bits they had not been able to identify. They were wilted where the gastric juices had done their work, but what they were was so obvious he was surprised they had not seen it immediately. The reason, of course, was simple enough. It was September. They had not expected to see what was right before their eyes. Small lumps, whitish with pink and darker red traces. The small, dark specks were obviously seeds. It was nothing more exotic than partly digested strawberries. In September! But even that was not enough to keep him awake by then, and moments after he had extinguished the candle he was sound asleep, too exhausted even to dream.

Chapter X: The Unstrange Stranger

There was an Old Man with a beard,
Who said, "It is just as I feared!
    Two owls and a hen,
    Four larks and a wren
Have all built their nests in my beard."
    Edward Lear (1812-1888)
    Book of Nonsense (1846)

[September 20, 1862]

Saturday began with that same clement September weather to which they were growing accustomed. The object of their concern was safely stored in the ice house, but even there he could not keep much longer. It was time to find Alexander Gardner or his partner and prevail upon them to make the photographic records they needed.

Dougherty also had another idea, but to turn thought to deed required knowing the whereabouts of Mr. Frank Schell. He had a proposal for Schell that might seem unusual, if not downright macabre. Still, he was a reporter, and so just likely to get caught up in the oddity of it all. Of course, everything depended on Major Brinton's willingness, and that was something Dougherty might be well advised not to take for granted.

The first hint of pre-dawn gray had barely touched the sky when Dougherty awoke, his mind immediately active. He must post his letter to Doctor Brownson and he should at least send a note to his parents and to Mrs. Kiley to assure them of his safety. They would have heard of the great battle and would be worried. He wrote the notes, put them in his pocket, and left the mill.

Once outside, like iron to a magnet, he was drawn to the fire and its steaming coffee. There was real bread — stale, but still better than the petrified lumps of hardtack. He was dipping the bread into the hot bacon grease at the bottom of a frying pan, when out of the darkness, a trooper rode up, all businesslike and purposeful. He dismounted, used his hat to slap the dust off his uniform, then headed for the mill.

He was about to open the door, when someone else did it for him. It was McBrien, tin cup in hand. The trooper passed him by with barely a nod. McBrien paused, spotted Dougherty, and made a beeline in his direction.

"Good morning to ye, sir. How are ye this fine day?" In a lower voice, he added, "Sir, I think I need to talk to ye before ye decide what we're to do today."

They filled their cups and stepped some little distance from the fire. Even in its flickering light Dougherty could see the steward's discomfort. His curiosity was piqued; but he waited for McBrien to speak first.

"Sir, last night after we finished the post-mortem, something come to me attention, and I was of a mind to tell ye of it then, but it seemed not quite the right thing to do without some further thought, if ye know what I mean. Well, sir, I've now had the time to think and the time to do just a bit more investigating on me own, and I'd appreciate yer thoughts on what's bothering me. Last night it didn't seem proper fer me to say what I'm about to, but now I think I have reason."

Dougherty wondered where this was leading but he didn't interrupt. McBrien would tell it in his own way.

"Last night, Lieutenant Dougherty, sir, after we finished, ye'll remember that I took all the instruments back to where they come from?"

"Indeed, I do."

"Well, they were given to me by Solomon Aarons. Ye'll know him... He was one of the musicians, a stretcher bearer. He was working here yesterday as orderly and assisting Major Briggs all day long. The tools we used all come from the surgical kit that Doctor Briggs uses. Now, Aarons didn't ask the Major if we could use them, he just let me take them, if ye know what I mean, knowing that they wouldn't be needed fer a while by the Major — and I knew we didn't want to disturb him. I told him that, when we were done, I'd see that everything got cleaned and back to its proper place. And that's just what I done."

That was the problem? They were in the Major's bad graces for using his instruments? Dougherty was not overly concerned. He never had been in Briggs's good graces. Being in his bad graces for one more day should be no grave inconvenience, provided it did not interfere with the search for an answer to the mystery. Or was it McBrien who was in trouble? Dougherty hoped not, but that could be resolved. After all, McBrien had only acted on orders.

His mind had begun to wander, until McBrien's words broke into his reverie and caught his full attention.

"And so, ye see," he was saying, "it wasn't there."

"It wasn't there?" Dougherty asked, "What wasn't there?"

"Why, sure, sir, what I just told ye! It wasn't in the medical kit. Ye know how the Tiemann cases are all laid out, everything in its place?"

Dougherty knew exactly what he meant. They were beautifully produced: Polished wood cases, brass hinges and locks, with drawers that lifted out, each lined in red or green plush with slots the exact size and shape of the implements they held. They were wonderful instruments, precisely made and beautifully balanced. He looked forward to the day when he would be able to afford such a set.

"Well, sir," he said, "I replaced all the instruments in their proper places in the case that Doctor Briggs uses, and there was an empty space stood out like a sore thumb. The size and shape of the slot told me what was missing. It was the trocar!"

Dougherty felt ill. His stomach churned in dread. He wanted not to jump to conclusions — something that Doctor Brownson had drummed into him. Perhaps the trocar had been long missing? But McBrien dispelled that hope.

"Lieutenant, sir, I said not a thing last night because I was sure that it'd turn up. I knew fer certain that there was a trocar in the box, because it's more than once that I've had the task of cleaning and sharpening the tools meself. I just seen it Wednesday morning when we was preparing fer the battle. I decided to go back this morning and find it. Well, I've been looking fer the blamed thing fer the last hour or more, and it just ain't there. I thought ye ought to know."

Dougherty hardly knew what to say. In spite of Briggs's antagonism, he found it all but impossible to think that he could be connected to the death of this man. Even the suspicion was distasteful. Yet, to be objective, his knowledge of Major Briggs was limited to a few weeks and the little he had heard of his reputation as a doctor. None of which inclined Dougherty to think him capable of murder. But none of it ruled it out either. And there was the fact that he had been in Philadelphia at the time of Joseph Fuller's death. And they had seen him near the cornfield the same day that they had found the body there.

"We must be prudent," Dougherty said. "The absence of the trocar raises a serious question, but there are too many possible explanations. It could simply have been misplaced. I doubt it would have been needed these last few days, so its absence would not have been noted. Who knows how many people had access to it. In any case, it does not seem prudent to question him yet."

He nodded. "Yer right, sir, of course. Best we let it go fer the time being."

"Good. We will look, but we will say nothing yet." Dougherty was glad they were not working at cross purposes. There was also the fact that an overt effort to investigate his own superior officer, whether he was guilty or not, was almost bound to result in his being forced to abandon the investigation entirely. He had to be careful.

For now he was content to put off the question, but he knew that, before all was done, it would have to be resolved. Dougherty had still not told McBrien about Fuller.

"We need to have either Gardner or Gibson come here," Dougherty told McBrien, "while we can still get a recognizable photograph of the body. It won't be long before the features begin to lose their clarity of definition."

"If ye want, sir, I can go and try to fetch one of them," he said.

He went to get the horses, hitched Dougherty's near the door of the mill and set off for the Dunkard Church. He would have to prevail upon one or the other to come to Pry's mill and make the photographs. Most likely, both would come. Dougherty relied on their curiosity and their desire for saleable pictures. He also had great confidence in the persuasive powers of Steward Sean McBrien.

He reopened the letter to Doctor Brownson, added news of the missing trocar and asked him to learn what he could about Major Briggs. He began to wonder if Briggs's earlier arguments in favor of secession were as theoretical as McBrien had thought. He found an orderly who promised to post the letters that same day.

Dougherty had not yet heard from Major Brinton, but that was soon resolved. The cavalry trooper, the one he had seen earlier, came out of the mill looking like a man in search of someone. He spoke to the orderly Dougherty had given the letters to and headed in his direction.

"Lieutenant Dougherty?" he asked. He was about Dougherty's age, but his mix of self-assurance and properly measured deference to authority pointed to more military experience.

"Yes. What can I do for you?"

He held out a folded sheet torn from a tablet. "Major Brinton's compliments. He said that he would not require an answer, but that I should give you this personally."

Dougherty opened the note, read it, thanked him, and let him go his way. Surgeon General Hammond had arrived in Keedysville with a British medical officer named Muir and Brinton would be occupied with them for the morning. He suggested that Dougherty go on with the investigation, and that they meet at the mill about noon. By far the best sort of orders — to do what he wanted to do.

But where would he find Frank Schell? No doubt, like a bloodhound on the trail, he would be sniffing out the day's news, and that was best done at headquarters. Dougherty set off for the Pry house.

The sun was well up by the time he turned off the pike and onto Mr. Pry's property. The lane was now a rutted mess. The picket fence that had set off the house so attractively was a dilapidated relic of its former self, with dangling pickets, the few that were not already gone for firewood. The garden was stripped; the orchard behind the house bore no more fruit and its clumsy harvest had left broken branches drooping down to wither and die. No cannon shot had reached this area, but it looked as though it had. This was not the work of the enemy; it had been done by an army here on behalf of the citizenry, including Mr. Pry.

The perpetrators of the debacle were all about. They came and went, they stirred up their campfires, they boiled their ever present coffee, they talked and laughed and breathed in the relief of a battle that had ended with the sparing of their own lives; and, at least for now, they set aside their grief for companions lost or their concern for the damage that they saw as no more than a mild by-product of the struggle in which they were engaged. Dougherty, foolishly thinking himself above all that, hitched his horse to the remnants of another man's fence, placed his booted feet upon that man's property, and sought the whereabouts of Frank Schell.

"He was here a while ago... don't know where he is now," a trooper told him over his shoulder, as he strode off — the questions of a lieutenant not quite enough to bother with. Finally, a more cooperative sort sent him to the hill behind the house, where he said he had seen Schell just a half hour earlier.

Dougherty walked up through the orchard and out into the morning brightness beyond. Frank Schell was seated on a rock, tablet on his lap, pencil moving rapidly across it, as he sketched one more scene of the activity across the creek. Squads of men, like an army of ants scurrying about in apparent aimlessness, were burying the dead of both sides.

"Ah, Lieutenant Dougherty," he said. "To what do I owe the unexpected pleasure of your company? Or are you here to survey the results of the week's work?"

"No, sir," Dougherty responded, "I was looking for you. I find myself in need of your help in a matter that I hope will interest you."

He explained most of what he wanted him to do and was not disappointed. His initial curiosity, mixed with a trace of incredulity, turned gradually to real interest. He sprayed his drawing, packed his tools into the black oilcloth bag, and was ready to go.

The day was growing warm and the movement of troops and vehicles went on as before, with one essential difference. The occupants of the ambulances and wagons no longer groaned or moaned as the rumbling wheels slipped into ruts or bounced over rocks. They lay haphazardly, limbs poking out like sticks from their bloated bodies or flapping loosely across the corpses of their fellows. These were the casualties who had been recognized and whose bodies might eventually be shipped home to grieving families. The rest would be buried in shallow common graves near where they had fallen, their lives spent anonymously as part of the cost of the cause they had espoused; this was the butcher's bill the older troops spoke of so lightly, glad themselves not to have been part of the expense.

When they arrived at the mill, Gardner's gypsy wagon was already there. They were greeted by a sight that, under other circumstances, would have been grotesque enough to shock any passerby. On this day it drew but scant attention, only a few still curious enough to stop and gawk. Most went on unconcerned.

An inch thick pine plank, almost two feet in width and about seven in length, was propped against the wall of the mill. The bright sun shone directly upon it, picking out its burden in stark simplicity. A rope around his chest and under his arms held him upright in near nakedness, his chest and abdomen marred by the rough sewn cord that held closed the incisions made the night before. A ragged scrap of blanket modestly covered the pudenda. His eyes were closed, his features limp and sagging, but he was still well enough preserved so that, had it not been for the ghastly stitches that held his organs in place, he might have been one of the wounded rather than the dead. The camera stood before him on its heavy tripod; partially hidden under the black hood was Gardner himself. Jamie Gibson stood off to one side.

"Ah! There ye are, sir," McBrien said, as he came toward them. "As ye can see, Mister Gardner and Mister Gibson have been most cooperative. They've made photographs of the face, the head, the wound, the feet, and the hands. They'll now do full front and back, and then they'll be done. Ye'll have copies of everything by tomorrow. And how are you today, Mister Schell?"

Schell shook his hand, greeted him, and then turned to Dougherty in puzzlement.

"I thought you needed me to draw pictures of the guest of honor," he said. "No matter how hard I try, I doubt that I'll be able to produce a better likeness than the one you're going to get from Alexander Gardner."

"Every picture that Mister Gardner makes may become evidence at a trial. I am counting on you to do what he cannot."

Gardner emerged from under the black curtain, and Gibson took the wet plate into the wagon. Dougherty thanked Gardner for his work.

"I was pleased to be of sairvice to ye, Lieutenant," he said, "but I'm sure that ye'll nae doot realize that I must also ask something of ye in retairn. Although ye may ha need to keep our work private until sooch time as this matter shall come to trial, it is my hope and expectation that ye'll then release to me the right to make use of them for commaircial purposes — only, as ye'll surely realize and, as I'll pairsonally guarantee, in a proper and tasteful manner."

"I would expect no less," Dougherty answered, although he was not certain how one made proper and tasteful use of pictures of a near naked, mutilated corpse. "But their release may well be up to a court. In the meantime I have full confidence in your word to keep them confidential and I will certainly support your claim to use them afterwards."

Taking Schell with him, Dougherty went to look more closely at the body. Its night in the ice house had helped. The decomposition was little more than it had been yesterday. He showed Schell the small cuts on the face and explained what he needed. His face lighted up as he realized precisely how he could do what Gardner could not.

"I think you're right," he said. He looked about and found two hardtack boxes that had not yet been reduced to kindling in the constant search for fuel to boil coffee. He lined up his tools on one of them — pencils, charcoal sticks, sharpening knife, some gray and white chalks, his little bottle, and the spray pipe. He stood before the pine plank, studied his subject, then began to do what the camera could not. He restored a sense of life to the features, opened the eyes, and took away the dead sag of the mouth. Almost immediately, even before he set to work shading in the outline with the charcoal sticks,

Dougherty began to gain some impression of what the man must have looked like in life. Having made his first approximation of the features, Schell seated himself on the second hardtack box with the tablet on his lap and became totally absorbed in his work.

By then Gardner was back under his black hood and Gibson was holding up the head so that it faced straight forward. They had removed even the scrap of blanket, intending to take the remaining pictures of the whole body in all its sadness. It stood stark, its pallor in the bright sun emphasizing the bleakness of death. Back and forth the photographers went between camera and wagon, while Schell looked time and again at the corpse and then at his papers, his hands never idle.

When Gardner left, he promised to send copies of all the pictures but reminded Dougherty he wished to use them later. Meanwhile, Schell was finishing his work and he motioned Dougherty over to see the results.

There were four different portraits. One was simply the face of the dead man, but with eyes open and an animation that made him seem alive. It was not a face Dougherty recognized, but Schell's skill was such that anyone who had known the man in life should be able to recognize him from this picture. On the other hand, he might be even more easily recognized from one of the other three pictures, each of which was different than the rest, according to the suggestion that Dougherty had made to Schell earlier.

The cuts on the face of the corpse had given him the idea, small nicks that showed no sign of bleeding or healing, clean cuts, made with a sharp blade. This man had been shaved after death. Why? For the same reason that he had been clothed in someone else's uniform — to disguise him, to put him among the anonymous dead and so consign him to the oblivion of a shallow pit, filled and soon forgotten. Was he a Confederate? Was he one of their own? Was he a civilian who had taken no part at all in the battle? It seemed safe to say that he was not a Confederate. Almost certainly the rebels had already departed the field before this man had died. The state of his rigor mortis suggested that. Besides, had he been a Confederate he could have been simply abandoned with impunity with no effort to disguise him. After all, who would have been left to identify him; or, even were he identified, who would care? Clearly someone feared that this man, if left in his natural condition, would be recognized and pose a problem.

Dougherty looked at the remaining drawings and was duly impressed at how much the human face could be changed with insignificant variations. The first of the drawings showed a man whose features were the same as those of the corpse, but the addition of a few lines had made him seem another person. He had tousled hair and a beard in need of trimming, a disheveled look that made the eyes take on a wild cast, even though comparison of this face with the unadorned one established clearly that the eyes were not different at all.

The next portrait was milder, more refined, the face partially covered by side whiskers and a well developed moustache. It had about it a look of reality that came home to Dougherty as he stroked, almost unconsciously, his own moustache, still coming to fulfillment at a lackadaisical pace. He'd begun growing it a week earlier, thinking it would make him look older, more military.

The final face had the look of relative prosperity. It was the face of a man careful of his appearance, hair neatly combed, beard properly tended. It was this face which caught Dougherty's attention — not because of the gentlemanly mien, but because he recognized it! The look of utter respectability, the almost handsome face marred only by the largeness of the nose.

"I can't believe this," he said. "I have seen this man just recently — but where?"

He called to McBrien. Without giving away the game, he handed him all four of the drawings and asked him what he thought. One by one he went through them, beginning with the one on which the others had been based. Dougherty held his breath as he came to the last.

"Well, what do ye know," he said. "Sure and it's the same man we saw on... when was it? Saturday, to be sure. Wasn't that when we were at the hospital in Frederick?"

"Surely he wasn't at the hospital," Dougherty said.

"Not at the hospital, sir," McBrien looked at the face once again. "He was at the tavern where we stopped to eat. He come in and met that tough looking mug. Don't ye recall?"

That's who it was! The man, the man who had inquired of the landlord the whereabouts of the Scotsman who had come in earlier, and had been shown into the rear of the tavern.

"When did this happen?" Schell asked, his reporter's instincts suddenly at full alert.

"On Saturday," Dougherty said, "just as McBrien recalls. We went to a tavern to eat before returning to the hospital and it was while we were eating that the man came in. He was looking for someone — another man who had come in earlier."

"And who was that one? The one who came in first? Did you learn that?" Schell asked.

"Let met think," Dougherty said, "I recall that he announced himself to the landlord when he came in. Ah, yes! I recall now. He said his name was Albert."

"Sir, I beg yer pardon," McBrien interrupted, "but surely it wasn't Albert? Wasn't it Allen?"

"Are you sure? He called himself Allen? He was in civilian clothes?" The excitement was almost palpable in Schell's voice. "Can you describe him?"

"He was of medium height — perhaps a bit shorter than I... fairly close cropped, dark beard. He had a touch of Scotland in his speech... smoked a cigar..."

"Wait a moment," Schell said and got his tablet and a pencil. He closed his eyes, tapped the end of the pencil against his teeth a few times, then began to sketch. He turned the pad toward them and said, "Is that the man?"

"The very one!" said McBrien, and Dougherty had to agree with him.

"Who is he?" he asked.

"That," said Schell, "is Major E.J. Allen. Let me tell you about him."

He sat on his box and it was clear he was about to enjoy spinning his yarn, as if it were to be read in his paper.

"It was at the end of last year, late November or, more likely, early December, when a dispute erupted in the *Washington Star*. There was a man in Washington who had taken upon himself the job of looking into the running of the local jails. He was most interested in the condition of the Negroes in the city jail, and he was dissatisfied with what he found. His investigation became the basis of a report that Senator Henry Wilson submitted to the Senate and it caused something of a stink. That was what aroused the ire of the editor of the *Star*, who has little sympathy with abolition.

"He lambasted the perpetrator in an editorial and named him a Major E.J. Allen. He denounced Allen and his associates — all of whom he derided as nothing but a bunch of trouble making abolitionists — and accused them of being a gang intent on undermining the internal peace of the Nation's capital.

"As you can imagine, that did not sit well with Major Allen. When his friends continued the dispute, trying to stand in support of him, the same editor decided to go a step further. But, before he got too far, Major Allen brought some political and military pressure to bear and the dispute ended. The upshot was that the editorials ceased, while the Major got out of the political matters in which he had become embroiled and went back to the military activities which constituted the real bulk of his duties."

"You think this is the same Major Allen?" Dougherty asked.

"Oh, I have no doubt of it," Schell said.

"How can we find him? He might be the man to tell us the identity of our corpse."

"You can find him, I am sure," said Schell, "but you may not want to once you know who he is."

"We already know *who* he is," Dougherty answered, "We need to learn *where* he is."

"Well," said Schell, with a grin to show that he'd saved the best for last, "There is one other piece of information. When the last editorial appeared in the *Star* — the one that really riled up our Major

Allen — it contained a statement that may give you a new insight into the whole affair. Having said all he had wanted to say about the nefarious Major E.J. Allen, the editor finally wrote, 'E.J. Allen means Pinkerton.' That was the straw that broke the camel's back and ended the editorials. Pinkerton complained to McClellan and, I suspect, even to Halleck and the dispute ended. It never got much publicity after that, so Pinkerton went right on using his *nom de guerre*, Major E.J. Allen."

It dawned on Dougherty that they might be involved in something much deeper than they had suspected. Allan Pinkerton was McClellan's advisor on military intelligence, the man who controlled the spies, the director of the Secret Service of the Army of the Potomac.

Pinkerton was then about forty-five years of age. He had come from Scotland about ten years before the war. He went to Chicago and became a police detective in Cook County. Before long he left the county police and started a force of his own: The Pinkerton National Detective Agency. His location in Illinois made for some interesting contacts. He found himself employed by a wide variety of clients, including the railroads and through that he became acquainted with a lawyer, a man with some political aspirations, a Mr. Abraham Lincoln. He also did police work for the Illinois Central Railroad and got to know its vice-president, George Brinton McClellan. When Mr. Lincoln was elected President, Pinkerton came east with him to see to his safe arrival in the Capital for the inauguration. Events made Pinkerton the logical choice when he offered his talents to set up a Secret Service to discover and coordinate information about the movements and forces of the enemy.

Dougherty was pleased at what Frank Schell had done, but he had one more favor to ask of him. Schell wanted to take with him the drawing they had recognized for possible use in *Leslie's Illustrated*, once they had a story to go with it. In the meantime, Dougherty requested that he make a few smaller versions that they could use to show people.

He took one more sheet of paper and divided it into quarters. On each, with impressive economy of line, he produced replicas of the face. Dougherty gave one to McBrien and put the other three inside his notebook.

Dougherty's mind was a jumble of thoughts, all of them thoroughly disconcerting. He did not share Schell's glee at the way things were going. He smelled trouble where Schell sniffed only the first scent of a good story.

Chapter XI: Haha Horror

I used to be glad to prepare private soldiers.
They were worth a five-dollar bill apiece.
But, Lord bless you, a colonel pays a hundred,
and a brigadier general two hundred...
I might, as a great favor, do a captain,
but he must pay a major's price... Such
windfalls don't come every day. There
won't be another such killing for a century.
    Embalmer's comment, made to
    George Alfred Townsend
    June 1862

[September 20, 1862]

Allan Pinkerton was a paradox, best known for remaining unknown. He was not anonymous, but those who knew his name seldom recognized his face. He was an enigma, and he preferred it that way, reveling in secrecy that he would break only when he wrote his memoirs. His intrusion into the mystery of the dead man was equally enigmatic. If he held the key to the mystery, then the solution might be permanently beyond their grasp.

Who was the dead man? Why had he met Allan Pinkerton in the back room of an obscure tavern in Frederick City? Was he a part of the army? Was he a Pinkerton operative? Or was he the object of one of Pinkerton's own investigations? Dougherty feared he was about to step into something more distasteful than the mess McBrien had tried to warn him of at Frederick.

He had another concern. Now that the dead man had spent the morning in the hot sun, it took no olfactory hypersensitivity to know it was time to find him a resting place. He would almost certainly be the object of a legal case, and it would not do to consign him to an unmarked grave. The best course was to embalm him or at least to ensure that he was buried in a proper coffin and in a location duly marked.

Higher authority than Dougherty's would have to approve the embalming. That, Dougherty feared, might have to be Major Briggs, and he did not look forward to approaching him. The missing trocar had added a new dimension. As he tried to work up the gumption to act, a horse clattered up to the mill and Major Brinton dismounted, a smile on his face, his hand outstretched in greeting. Dougherty would one day have quite a large debt to discharge to him, because for the second time in twenty-four hours he was about to ask of him another favor.

He explained his problem, but said nothing about his suspicions of Briggs, not wanting to violate McBrien's confidence. He found he had no need to. Major Brinton had already seen how Briggs and Dougherty got along — or failed to — and was only too willing to help.

He wrote out an order for the body to be embalmed or otherwise preserved and kept safe until released for trial or for use in the new medical museum. He stipulated that it be done at a reasonable rate to be paid by the medical department — a rate low enough to enrage the selected embalmer, who wouldn't be able to refuse without becoming *persona non grata* in the future. That did not sadden Dougherty. He had already heard of their sharp practices and inflated rates.

"Now, Lieutenant," the Major said, "You're familiar with the battlefield, and I want to see it, so I would be obliged to have you and McBrien as my guides."

They were soon mounted and on their way. Every farm they passed was now a hospital, and Major Brinton wanted to see them all, but not this day. For now, he was more intent on the battlefield itself before it was fully cleaned up.

As they rounded the end of the East Woods, they were confronted again with the scene that McBrien and Dougherty had almost begun to take for granted, but which was all new to Major Brinton. His startled gaze moved slowly left to right, from the Dunkard Church to the ruin of the cornfield, where the dead lay everywhere, the landscape dotted with wagons and ambulances, among which moved not only soldiers but civilians, both men and women. Burial crews mingled with grieving relatives who had converged on the field in the now all but futile hope of discovering a loved one left for dead but still by some miracle holding to the thread of life — or, once that hope had been crushed, reclaiming the remains of a departed husband, brother, son, or sweetheart, before he was lost to a nameless grave. The dead who had someone to care would cease to be a burden to the burial squad and would become instead a bonanza to the embalmers.

At his request, they showed him the horse and where they had found the body. The site revealed nothing new. In fact, apart from their testimony, the body might never have been there.

"Where do you suggest we go now?" the Major said.

Dougherty pointed toward the Mumma farm. "Down there is a part of the battlefield I have not yet seen. All I know is that there is a sunken road that the Confederates used as a fortification. That was where Richardson and French were."

"Why don't we go there first?" Brinton said.

They turned south onto the farm lane. On the left was the Mumma family cemetery, a fenced-off, grassy knoll with tall shade trees, in the midst of a field just plowed. The broken windows of the roofless house were like the empty eye sockets of a skull. Beyond the house the lane ran between a cornfield on the left and a meadow to the right, both now trampled by the passage of troops.

"I was sorry to get so late a start today," Brinton said, "but I had to entertain General William Muir. He is Her Majesty's Deputy Inspector General, an office much like that of our Surgeon General. He has been all over the world — China most recently. He is quite the character. This morning he almost had us on the verge of an international crisis."

He laughed as he recalled the incident.

"Muir is like a schoolboy in his love of military parades. This morning we were at the inn, speaking to the innkeeper and his wife, an exceedingly attractive little woman, when a regiment with a band went by. Muir leaned out the window to watch, but he also put his arm around the landlady's waist and pulled her over to join him. She turned scarlet and her husband was ready to fight — but the old boy was so thrilled at the parade and so clearly not trying to offend, that we passed it off as a result of his being a foreigner who forgot that a landlord's wife is not a barmaid. In any case, I think Surgeon General Hammond will have his hands full with this observer."

For a while they were the only ones in the lane and rode three abreast looking at the devastation on all sides. It was probably McBrien's riding ease and Dougherty's still obvious lack of equestrian skill that drew Brinton's attention to their horses.

"Quite good mounts you have," he said, "Are they both yours?" He would not have expected a steward to have his own horse, but a surgeon, even such a novice as Dougherty, if he were affluent enough, might have owned both.

"Neither, I am sorry to say. Steward McBrien procured them for both of us."

"Well, Steward, I congratulate you on your choice," he said. "How were you able to get them?"

For the first time since Dougherty had met him, he saw Sean McBrien at a loss for words.

"Ah, sir..." he said,"Ye see, sir... It was like this, don't ye know... That is to say... It was after the nature of a favor returned, ye might say..."

He suddenly acquired an unwonted interest in the scenery. Without really seeming to, he held back his horse just enough to fall a little behind. A speechless Sean McBrien was a new and rather enjoyable experience for Dougherty.

"Of course, of course," the Major said with a smile, and he asked no further questions. Instead, he spoke to Dougherty, but just loudly enough for McBrien to hear.

"Did I tell you," he said, "how I came to have this horse? It has to do with a method of preservation somewhat different than embalming.

"We preserve specimens for the Medical Museum with quantities of alcohol. Now alcohol is best not made readily available to men on active duty, so the Provost Marshal confiscates a great quantity of that precious liquid. The Secretary of War told him to turn over to us all that he had, and before long it was being shipped to us from all directions. We had jugs, bottles, barrels, and containers as novel as hollow wooden legs full of wine, rum, whisky, and even champagne. Some of it we used and the rest we distilled to concentrate the alcohol.

"In the meantime, I am often in the field to conduct just this sort of mission. I usually travel by train and need a horse once at my destination. I borrow mounts from the cavalry.

"The horses should be supplied by the quartermasters, but they are never as obliging as one might hope, so I came to a practical understanding with the cavalry officers.

"Whenever I am sent anywhere, I arrange to have a trooper at the depot with a horse for me and another for my luggage. That luggage has, by custom, come to consist partly of a small barrel of some preservative — cherry brandy seems to be preferred."

He laughed, as did Dougherty, but McBrien had the look of the cat who swallowed the canary — or, perhaps, more the look of the canary. In any case, it aroused in Dougherty no small curiosity about the level of their current regimental supply of medicinal spirits.

The road swung south again and then east to the end of a lane once nameless but now known as the Sunken Road or Bloody Lane. Even before it came into sight, they knew it was at hand. The breeze brought with it an odor not easily forgotten — the smell of the autopsy, but magnified a thousand times over. The scent of bowels and bladders suddenly emptied by death, the sick-smell of spilled blood that drew every fly for miles, their buzzing as loud as some endlessly whirring machine. It was what Dougherty would come always to associate with the aftermath of battle, the harsh reality unknown to those who speak so glowingly of the military glories it has never been their lot to witness.

They topped a small rise and were confronted with a scene whose horror would never completely leave their minds. It was an ordinary country lane. Generations of use had worn it deeper and deeper, until it lay four feet or so below the level of the surrounding fields. Atop the banks at either side were rail fences, now knocked apart by shot and shell and human hands. Within this natural barricade the

Confederates had lain in wait. They stayed low, firing from behind the bottom rails of the fences as waves of Union troops rolled toward them like surf breaking on an implacable shore.

Richardson's men had pressed harder and harder until suddenly the solid shore was eroded and its eastern end flooded. Union troops poured into the lane, firing down its length with dreadful effect. The men in the sunken road had no way to return the fire in any adequate measure and withdrew, leaving behind the scene that now lay before them.

Dougherty had once read of a European device called a haha, a sunken fence placed in a trench, so that it separated properties without obstructing the view. This was a haha composed not of wood or mortar but of a row of corpses so dense that one might have walked from one end of the lane to the other without laying foot upon bare earth, yet they did not obstruct the view.

Men in uniform moved through the fields, searching for survivors, but finding few. Along the length of the sunken road, on the banks just above it, were carriages and wagons belonging to the military and to civilians in search of loved ones who could no longer be helped but could at least be decently buried.

In the sunken road men worked at the grisly occupation of removing the dead. One of the soldiers braced his foot against a body, while his comrade tugged to pull another loose from its rigorous embrace. It was gruesome, yet it was not done from disrespect but simply out of necessity.

They dismounted and led the horses along the upper edge of the sunken road. The bodies had also been visited by scavengers. Foxes, stray dogs, possums — in the intervening nights they all had done their bit. Even as they watched, crows brazenly alighted just out of reach of the burial squads and took their share of the spoils. The buzzards, more cautious despite their size, circled overhead waiting their chance.

"Look there," Brinton said.

It was a body seemingly still in the midst of some action. Brinton called it the "rigor of instantaneous death." He stopped to describe it in his notebook.

The body was turned away from them, its face leaning against the slope of the bank, one foot squarely on the ground, the other leg slightly bent at the knee, as though he were about to stand. His arm reached out to the bottom fence rail. Beside him was his musket, its ramrod halfway down the barrel. He had been about to fire at the oncoming troops, when he raised his head for a look and it had been his last. A Minié ball had hit him square in the forehead and emerged through the back of his skull. His last act was frozen solid, on display for all to see, until the burial detail took him to his unmarked grave.

They went at Brinton's pace, searching for anything odd enough to merit a place in the medical museum. It was a sad labor, made sadder by the fact that the men who lay before them would be lost in a common pit unless they achieved anonymous fame in an exhibition case.

"Lieutenant Dougherty! How are you? I am so glad you are alive and well. I have prayed for you and Steward McBrien all week. I'm so thankful you have been spared."

He knew the voice even before he turned. Sister Elizabeth was with another Sister, both walking but accompanied by a Negro driver in an old buggy, its once slickly painted surface now a dust-covered, faded shadow of its pristine glory. The horse that pulled it was old and tired. As the two Sisters moved forward, the gray-haired driver clucked his tongue and slapped the reins lightly against the old nag's rump. It looked over its shoulder to see if the command was in earnest and complied with the few steps required, then promptly came to a halt and closed its eyes. This was an animal experienced in having its own way, even while it did what was required in order to humor its taskmasters and lull them into the illusion that they were still in charge. It was, Dougherty concluded, a horse of military disposition, a McBrien of its species.

Her companion was Sister Mary Agnes and they had arrived at Sharpsburg on Thursday and were finishing a now vain search for the living among these stiffened bodies. Major Brinton was most interested in their experiences at the hospital in Frederick and what had happened to them since their arrival at the scene of the battle.

Sister Mary Agnes was younger than Sister Elizabeth, but taller, darker, with quiet brown eyes. As Sister Elizabeth spoke to Brinton, Sister Mary Agnes followed the conversation, but spoke no more than a few words.

"The hospital at Frederick already overflows into every church, barn, and public building where there is space. The people of the city prove their goodness. They are a wonderful example to us. In fact," Sister Elizabeth said with a smile, "they have even begun to like the Sisters!"

Boonsborough and Middletown, she said, were just as crowded, as thousands of wounded were evacuated to hospitals farther from the front.

"I find," she said, "that the wounded who have no place inside the buildings may be the most fortunate, at least in this good weather. The buildings have poor ventilation at the best of times. They are dreadful when filled with the wounded and the oppressive odors of sickness and gangrene. The only consolation is the speed with which the wounded are being tended."

Once she had answered all the Major's questions, she turned to Dougherty.

"How have you found your first experience of battle, Lieutenant?"

He tried to respond, but words failed him. But he realized that what he said was enough. He was not speaking to someone ignorant of war's aftermath. Sister Elizabeth and Sister Mary Agnes had seen as much as he had and more, and had dealt with it for far longer. Perhaps for them it was worse. They were not there when spirits were high and patriotic sentiment held sway. They always faced the bloody result. Dougherty suddenly realized that her inquiry was not out of curiosity. It was a kind effort to let him try to put into words the feelings that are so often buried deep and never truly faced.

He told her about the dead man and took the drawing from his pocket. She showed no recognition, but Sister Mary Agnes, who was looking over her shoulder, drew a quick breath and said, "My goodness! I have seen him before."

"Who is he?" Dougherty asked.

"I don't know his name," she said, "but he was at the hospital in Frederick about a week ago. Saturday it was. He came looking for someone and he spoke to Steward Gilbert."

"You'll remember Steward Gilbert," said Sister Elizabeth. "You asked him to get me to show you the hospital. He is the little man who scurries like a chipmunk, harmless but scared of predators, with its heart beating so fast it seems it may collapse... Well, I don't want to seem unkind, but I think you know who I mean."

Dougherty smiled at the description. She was right. Gilbert was the philosophical personification of the essence of chimpmunkness.

"The man in the picture was there near the end of the morning," Sister Mary Agnes continued. "I heard him ask for a Major he wished to see. The Steward was unable to help him, but the man said he knew where to look next."

"Near the end of the morning?" I said, "Then Steward McBrien and I must have been there at almost the same time. I think we saw him at his next destination, which was a tavern not far from the hospital. You say you don't know him, but had you ever seen him before?"

"No, Lieutenant," she said, "Never. I only recall him because he seemed somehow so distinguished with his black suit and his upright posture and his authoritative bearing. I remember that at the time I thought that he was one of the civilian doctors who had come to help the wounded, but I did not know him."

Dougherty recalled his first impression of the stiff corpse with its soft hands — the hands of a priest or a doctor, he had thought. He was, perhaps, not so far off after all, but the body still had no identity. All he had to go on was the link to Major Allen — Pinkerton . Like it or not, he knew he would have to see him.

Chapter XII: High Society

Never scratch your head, pick your teeth, clean your nails, or worse than all, pick your nose in company; all these things are disgusting. Spit as little as possible, and never upon the floor.
The Art of Good Behaviour (ca. 1845)

[September 21, 1862]

Introibo ad altare Dei... Ad Deum, qui laetificat juventutem meam...

The familiar words comforted Dougherty as they had since childhood, even before he knew their meaning. Now they rang out loud and clear for the men whose lives God's grace had spared, summoning them to approach the altar of the God who brought joy to their youth — at least the joy of life preserved against a panoply of pain and suffering and death. Life... the simplest gift of all but quite beyond compare.

Hoc est enim corpus meum... Hic est calix sanguinis mei...

The words were both incongruous and appropriate on this field of bodies and blood, a reminder that even death has meaning.

Ite missa est. Deo gratias.

The Mass, in stately progress, concluded and all were dismissed with thanks to God. The unselfconscious awe of the past hour, was suddenly awkward, as men slipped back into the humdrum, their faces sliding from grave solemnity to sheepish reverence. They tugged on their hats, took up their weapons, and resumed their normal occupations. Two enlisted men dismantled the altar and packed away the vestments. The canvas apse was now another army tent and the sacred moment faded into normality, like the briefly resurrected shade of an earlier life.

The priest who said the Mass and to whom Dougherty had gone to confession before taking the Sacrament, had his hair and beard been white, would have been the image of an Old Testament prophet. Father William Corby, chaplain of the 88th New York Volunteers, was not large in stature, but full of strength. His high forehead led to the thinning hair on top, long at sides and back. He wore no moustache, but a full beard down to his chest. He had heard confessions in a tent at the end of a cleared field. Afterwards the tent flaps were opened, an altar of plain boards was set up in its opening, and the canvas pyramid became an apse whose nave was circumscribed not by buttresses but by the reverence of the participants. The altar was covered with a white linen cloth, on which rested the missal, the veiled chalice, the crucifix, and two tin cans (relics of someone's taste for evaporated milk) filled with wild flowers.

His sermon called them to duty, to God, and to country — the constant theme for Irish immigrants faced with American prejudice that held them in contempt for their poverty and in suspicion for their allegiance to the Pope of Rome. Yet those same sons of Erin came in their thousands, struggling and dying for a Union reluctant to accept them.

It was McBrien who had found out the time and place of the Mass, and it was with him that Dougherty had come. The morning was still young when they said their *Deo gratias* and made their way back to the mill.

Major Brinton was at Keedysville writing a preliminary report on his visit. That left Dougherty and McBrien free for normal duties. They passed the morning and early afternoon tending to the wounded who lay under cover of the dog tents strung everywhere around the mill.

It was mid-afternoon when an orderly approached.

"Major Briggs presents his compliments, sir, and asks that you report to him at your earliest convenience."

Briggs was in the mill, not in surgery but tending to the most serious cases — the fortunates who had undergone surgery and now took their first halting steps to complete recovery, or the unfortunates who would develop the complications that signaled the quick downhill slide to eventual demise. No one could distinguish the one from the other and only time would sort them out. He was clearly exhausted. Had he been Dougherty's patient, he would have advised rest and proper nourishment, but he knew that his advice would not be asked.

"Lieutenant Dougherty, I have some news for you. You are to betake yourself to Keedysville and there report to the surgeon in charge. That will be Surgeon Houston, the divisional medical director. You will find him at the church."

Dougherty opened his mouth to speak, but Briggs held up a hand to forestall him.

"You are still under the orders of Major Brinton whenever he needs you; but when he does not, you will go on with normal duties just as you do now. Is that clear enough for you?"

"Yes, sir," Dougherty said, and would have turned away, but Briggs stopped him.

"Lieutenant, what have you been up to?" He paused, but not long enough for Dougherty to respond. "I've heard about the foolishness with the body. You were assigned to assist Major Brinton. That means doing what he wants you to do and not finding ways to draw him into some idiotic scheme of your own. Just what are you up to?"

"I am not 'up to' anything," Dougherty said. "On Friday McBrien and I found a dead man near the corn field, and..."

"About as exciting as finding a leaf in a forest," he said. "In a war, people die. Their deaths are violent. Anywhere else they would be criminal. It is ridiculous to examine each with a view to determining the cause of death. They have been stabbed, shot, bludgeoned and blown apart, and it was all done in the line of duty."

"Sir," Dougherty said, "the condition of this body tells a different story. It tells me he did not belong where he was found. He was not killed on that field. He was not a casualty of war."

"Nonsense," Briggs said. "Your are a young man, rich in imagination, but poverty stricken in experience. All around you are men who need your help — living men — and you waste time on a dead one. You are not a policeman. You are an army surgeon. The body was found on a battlefield and there it belongs. Have the sense to let it go."

"Even an army surgeon ought to have the brains to recognize the truth when it stares him in the face," Dougherty said, regretting the words almost as soon as they left his mouth.

"Be careful, Lieutenant. You go too far." Briggs's face had turned scarlet. "You are new to all of this, new to taking orders, so I will not hold you insubordinate — not this time. But have a care. Don't think one of your pet Majors can protect you."

"Yes sir," Dougherty said, tight jawed but prudent enough to know when to stop.

"And what has your investigation produced?" The question surprised Dougherty. Why should Briggs care about that, if he thought the whole thing a waste of time? Or did he have some other concern?

"I have little to report," Dougherty said, "beyond the fact that the cause of death was certainly not natural and not the result of a battlefield wound. He was stabbed at the base of the skull and there is evidence that he was no Confederate officer, in spite of the uniform."

He did not mention the weapon and did not intend to. Instead, he asked Briggs a question.

"Did you have the opportunity to examine the body?"

"I did not," Briggs said. "Should I have? I'm afraid I was far too busy dealing with the living and doing what I could to see to it that as few as possible would join him."

"Perhaps you might like to see what he looked like," Dougherty said, and handed him the drawing.

Briggs took it to a window, where he held it up to the light. Dougherty watched for any glimmer of recognition. A foolish hope, actually. If Briggs already knew the identity of the dead man, he would not be surprised to see the face in the drawing. If he did not know him, then there would certainly be no recognition. In short, the presentation of the picture and Dougherty's astute observation were but an amateurish exercise in detection.

"Never saw him before," he said and handed back the picture. "Is it really the same man? I thought that the corpse had no beard."

If Dougherty had been a hunting dog he would have had ears perked up and his tail all aquiver. He was catching the scent of something interesting here. But Briggs's next words threw him right back into the old uncertainty.

"Or do you now have two bodies to tend to? Did I not yesterday morning see Alexander Gardner here? He had a body propped up against the wall outside, and that one had no beard. I saw it when I looked out the window. I imagined it must be your corpse. Gardner would not be taking so much interest in one particular body, unless someone had asked him to."

So there it was. He had not examined the body, but merely seen it, as everyone had. So Dougherty had learned nothing, apart from the fact that he was now on his way to Keedysville.

"By the way," he said, "you'll be taking McBrien with you. I've no doubt you'll find some new patron to get you nearer to the seats of power once you get to Keedysville. You'd best be on your way."

Dougherty saluted and had turned to go, when Briggs said, "Oh, yes... One more thing. A message came for you earlier today. You are to call on a surgeon at the Smith farm near Keedysville. What was his name?... Oh, yes... Surgeon Anson Hurd, H-U-R-D, with the Fourteenth Indiana Volunteers. He says that he has something for you. I wouldn't be surprised if it was a gift left by General McClellan himself as a token of his appreciation for all the care you have shown his friends and relatives these past few days."

A half hour later McBrien and Dougherty were on their way. The corpse was embalmed and buried in a shallow grave, in a wooden coffin lined with a cheap layer of tin. It would be available should it be necessary to produce it later. The evidence, still sealed and marked, including the clothes and the broken trocar, had been retrieved from the place where Dougherty had hidden them for safekeeping, and would be placed in some other safe site once they were settled in Keedysville.

Their inquiries after the Smith farm and Surgeon Hurd led at first to some confusion even among the natives of the area, since the name of Smith was not unique. Of course, in this area neither were names such as Poffenberger or Rohrback or Pry. In any case, they soon had things sorted out and went to the farm of Doctor Otho Smith on the west bank of the Antietam, not far from Pry's mill.

Again they crossed the Upper Bridge, but, instead of going toward Smoketown, turned left. The road entered a wood and almost immediately was no more than a narrow farm lane. The overarching trees offered a pleasant serenity, filtering the sunlight to a sleepy glow. No shot or shell had fallen here. No men had died in agony. No hovering clouds of smoke had irritated throats and made eyes water. Above them birds chirped and squirrels chattered their annoyance at being distracted from their task of storing acorns and chestnuts against the stress of winter. They rode in companionable silence, lost in their own reveries, until reality intruded. The leaves fluttered, their movement all but imperceptible — a breeze so mild it might have gone by unremarked but for the odor. The smell of death and pain, the smell of a hospital.

They rounded a bend and emerged onto a wide expanse of farmland, once well tended but now caught in war's harsh embrace. A prosperous farm, judging from the number and state of its buildings. The large white house was in good repair, although its vegetable garden and nearby orchard had been stripped bare. There were as yet no large hospital tents in the area, but smaller wall tents, probably those of the surgeons and officers, were erected near the house. Everywhere else were low slung dog tents and stretched sheets of canvas, beneath which lay the wounded of French's division, almost 1400 of them. Near the house was the barn, a long, low structure, its wide doors open, filled with prostrate figures. They looked there first for Hurd.

They were directed to the field of dog tents. There they found him, his medical kit slung from his shoulder. He was pleasant, but obviously exhausted, his dark hair and beard in pronounced contrast to his grayish, sweaty complexion, even though the heat of the day was more pleasant than oppressive. He had clearly not been well.

"Lieutenant Dougherty! I am pleased to meet you," he said in his flat mid-western accent. "I hope my message did not take you much out of your way. I have a package for you. It was described as important, so I hesitated to entrust it to a courier who might leave it for you, without seeing that it was placed directly into your hands. In all the confusion of these days, I simply could not be sure that you would see it at all."

"I am most appreciative," Dougherty said, "You have done me a kindness, not created an inconvenience. I am indebted to you." His curiosity was piqued, but he didn't want to appear impatient as Hurd spoke of the scene that surrounded them.

Finally they they went to the barn, with its odor of suppuration, and Doctor Hurd retrieved a package about nine by twelve inches, and less than an inch thick, wrapped in newspaper and tied with a stout white cord.

"This was left here by James Gibson, Mr. Gardner's partner. They were here early this morning to make photographs of this area before they went to the other end of the battlefield. He asked me to deliver this and placed particular emphasis upon its importance."

They left the exhausted Hurd to his work and were on their way. Dougherty opened the package. Gardner, true to his word, had used his delicate glass negatives to produce positive images on treated paper. They were almost startling in their clarity, and Dougherty was surprised to see that in many instances the reduction of living colors to the starkness of black and white had actually emphasized details. Even the difference in tone between the jaw and the rest of the face, slight as it was, could be discerned. He had produced quite good likenesses both in frontal view and in profile. He had even made some close pictures of the wound at the base of the skull. Someone, probably Jamie Gibson, had held back the hair so as to show the gaping hole. His fingers could be clearly seen. The incision that Dougherty had made parallel to the length of the wound was also visible, now sewn shut. The finger and thumb in the photograph supplied a scale of comparison that might later help in court. Dougherty carefully rewrapped the photographs and placed them in his saddlebag with the other evidence.

With pictures of the body and medical exhibits and a start to identifying the victim, they had material dear to the heart of any prosecutor. There were autopsy results and expert opinion of time and cause of death. All the elements of a fine legal case, but for one small detail — a defendant. It reminded Dougherty of when he and his brothers played at being red Indians in the woods near town. They found trails to pull them first in one direction and then in another, only to have them peter out before, within a few feet, there would be another false trail. Efforts to follow them led in circles. McBrien and Dougherty discussed what they knew, and found themselves going in circles just as aimless.

Keedysville consisted of so few houses that Beaver Meadow seemed sizeable by comparison, except for the enormous influx of medical personnel and patients. Directly ahead was the Dutch Reformed Church, now the site of the central hospital. It was an attractive structure set back from the road upon a small rise with just enough height to give it some sense of importance. It was brick with a modest, graceful bell tower surmounted by a domed roof. Five wide steps led up to the doors flanked by tall, narrow windows.

They hitched the horses to the white fence that still stood unharmed (spared, perhaps, because it was the church's fence), and went in search of Surgeon Houston. He was a pleasant sort, but with the same hurried and harried aspect that was just then the hallmark of every member of the medical services.

He showed them the church — not that there was much to show. Like any church, it was one large room, with side rooms too small to be of much use for patients, although they could serve as places for the doctors to find some rest for their weary bones. Of the patients, there were none whose wounds were slight or whose condition was less than serious. Doctor Houston wanted to impress upon them that their services were sorely needed.

The rest of the day they changed bandages, looked for signs of infection, and removed proud flesh or maggots from wounds, some smelling of laudable pus and others with that first faint tinge of gangrenous putrefaction.

It was late in the evening when they finished. They ate supper in the churchyard back of the church and sat there, before its dying embers, watching the stars emerge on this moonless night. Their lantern flame was set low. Dougherty offered McBrien a cigar and lit one for himself. They sat, each lost in his own thoughts.

"I've enjoyed working with ye, sir," McBrien suddenly said, and Dougherty was more pleased at those words than he wished to show. "I hope ye'll not take it amiss if I say that ye've the makin's of a real army doctor."

"Thank you," Dougherty responded. He did not know what else to say.

"Well, then, sir, where do ye think we go next with the dead man? Do ye think we can find our fer sure just who he is?"

"I think we have the perfect way to discover that," Dougherty said, "We know who to ask... Allan Pinkerton. The problem will be to get to him."

"Sir, that may be less of problem than ye think. In me own estimation, the real problem will be to get him to talk once we've found him."

"What do you mean?"

"Why, sir, ye've still got yer friend Major Brinton at hand, and I'd suggest that ye see him in the morning and find out if ye can't get him to help us to get General McClellan's permission to speak to Pinkerton. After, that, of course, ye've still got the final obstacle... getting Pinkerton to tell ye what he knows. There's the real puzzler, as far as I'm concerned."

"You may well be right," Dougherty said, "Tomorrow we'll see if the Major can get us into the good graces of his exalted cousin. It will be an adventure in itself just to have a chance to see the Young Napoleon."

Most of those who had been near the fire had already departed shortly after the food had been eaten. Now a figure came around the church, unidentifiable in the dark. He called out, "Lieutenant Dougherty? Are you there, sir?"

"Right here," Dougherty said, and stood up, showing him the way more clearly as he took a puff on the cigar, making its tip glow in the dark.

"Sir," said the young enlisted man, "Surgeon Houston asked me to deliver this message to you. He said it just arrived from Pry's mill,"

He handed over an envelope of rich, ivory paper, Dougherty's name inscribed in an elegant hand. Written across that was a smudged note in pencil telling the bearer that he would find Dougherty at the church in Keedysville and signed by Major Briggs. He took it, thanked him, and turned up the lantern.

The note, to his surprise, was a formal invitation, written in the same elegant hand that had addressed the envelope. It read:

> Doctor and Mrs. Oliver Naylor present their compliments to Assistant Surgeon James V. Dougherty, M.D., Pa. V., and are honored to request the pleasure of his company on Monday, the 22nd of September inst., at half past six O'clock, for dinner at seven.
> Willowbrook Hall, September 20th, 1862   R.S.V.P.

It was Dougherty's first formal invitation and filled him with both elation and trepidation. Naylor seemed a prosperous physician, a gentleman, much at ease with men of higher rank than Dougherty's. Hence the elation. But that was also the source of the trepidation. Dougherty had learned his etiquette from his parents and teachers, but had never "put it to the test," so to speak, in the company of members of "society." He'd even, on occasion, looked into a book of etiquette that had come his way. But most of it, he thought, could be reduced to a simple enough notion. "The true gentleman is the one who chooses not to offend and who always treats others as ladies and gentlemen." But that did not reveal the intricacies of deportment at a formal dinner, with its likely plethora of forks, spoons, and other implements. However, those mysteries could probably be solved by paying attention to the others at table and not being first to dig into any dish or make the mistake of drinking from the finger bowl. Simple rules, but, he hoped, reasonably effective ones.

The next item was apparel. His uniform, although as new to the service as he was, now had a pungency that might not go unobserved in a dining room; and the dark stains that marred the coat might interfere with the appetites of the other diners, once they recalled his profession and realized what those stains might be. His good uniform was still with the regimental baggage, and he had no idea how to find it. But he had no doubt he could rely on McBrien in that regard.

He handed him the note.

"I'd suggest, sir, that ye'll be needing a few things. Have ye another uniform with the baggage?" Dougherty nodded. "That's to the good, then. I'll find out where it is and have someone fetch it. The boots'll need some spit and polish. The hat we can treat with a good, stiff brush and the little hole in it, will be no detriment a'tall. Sure, if the ladies see it, yer explanation can be nothing other than a reason fer added interest. In fact, I'd suggest that ye take some opportunity to draw attention to it under the proper circumstances."

Dougherty smiled. McBrien might have a point. It could do no harm to have something to say to the ladies. Until then his experience in that regard had been so limited as be non-existent. He hoped self-consciousness would not render him mute. Better to discuss a hole in his hat than to leave them thinking he had one in his head.

It would be quite a day between the effort to find a way to Pinkerton, the demands of their patients, and the visit to Willowbrook Hall.

Galen 3

That damned trocar and that doubly damned Dougherty! Why in the name of all that was holy would anyone take the time to perform an autopsy on a body found in the worst area of a battlefield the size of this one? Any normal person would have seen that he was dead and gone on to the next. What sort of fool was this Dougherty? Galen could not fathom his persistence.

The trocar was already taken care of. That had been no problem at all. It would be replaced and that would be the end of that. Just one more implement temporarily misplaced in the chaos of the hospital and then found again. It happened all the time. Some steward would get the blame and, in spite of protests to the contrary, would be reprimanded for carelessness and no one hurt by the whole thing.

Dougherty was another matter. He didn't seem likely to go away — thinks of himself as a detective, the damned fool. The trouble is that he might go on until he found something important. He might have to be taken care of, too, before this was all over.

Galen regretted what he had been compelled to do about Arthur, but it was, after all, his own fault. He had chosen the wrong side to begin with and then he tried to play the hero and let his feelings get in the way of common sense. That was something Galen would never have done. Well, he had made his choice and had paid the price. At least his death had been merciful. Galen never saw himself as a cruel man — just an objective one, capable of carrying out the proper decision even when it was hard to do so. Even when it meant having to deal with someone who had once been a friend. The cause was always bigger than the individual.

But it all kept coming back to that damnable Dougherty. Galen would have to keep a close watch on that young man, but he had no doubt that, if the time came when something drastic had to be done, he would do it. Even military surgeons were prone to the fortunes of war in and out of battles. Accidents happen all the time.

Chapter XIII: Willowbrook Hall

All human history attests
That happiness for man — the hungry sinner! —
Since Eve ate apples, much depends on dinner.
George Noel Gordon, Lord Byron (1788-1824)
Don Juan, canto xiii, st. 99 (1823)

[September 22, 1862]

McBrien was as good as his word. By noon he had located the regimental baggage, and Dougherty had his new frock coat and the green medical service sash which he had not yet worn, apart from the few times that he had self-consciously tried it on before the cracked mirror in the bleak rented room he occupied while searching out the whereabouts of the Sixty-ninth Pennsylvania. He now had a clean shirt, a vest devoid of food (or blood) stains, and the other apparel he required to replace the items that he was only too glad to remand to the attention of a willing washerwoman. He found time for a quick bath in water that was cold, but no colder than the pump water that the miners in Beaver Meadow washed in when they came from work each day. He cleaned his boots and applied the spit and polish whose lack McBrien had been pleased to call to his attention.

Surgeon Houston excused him for the evening, so Dougherty was able to pen a response to the invitation's *Répondez s'il vous plait*.

> Lieutenant Dougherty presents his compliments to Doctor and Mrs. Naylor and will be both pleased and honored to accept their kind invitation to dinner on this day, September 22nd, Inst. He regrets that the invitation did not reach him until last evening, and thus begs to be excused for the tardiness of his response, and hopes that this will occasion no inconvenience.
> Keedysville, September 22nd, 1862.

He had time, too, to find Major Brinton, and show him the photographs, copies of which he wanted for his museum. He agreed that the only way to get to Pinkerton was through McClellan, and he offered to help — and soon, because he was returning to Washington shortly.

The rest of the day sped by so far as work was concerned, but was endless as Dougherty anticipated his departure for Willowbrook Hall. By 5:00 P.M., he was spruced up and ready to leave, but it would be awkward to arrive too early, so once more he examined his uniform. As expected, it looked no different than it had ten minutes earlier. He brushed his hat, enjoying a moment of silly pride as he touched the bullet hole (his closest brush with heroism, involuntary as it may have been). He wiped imaginary imperfections from his boots. He patted his pocket, assuring himself that he had his notebook and a few cigars. McBrien, along with his uniform, had retrieved his box of cigars, better than the long nines Dougherty usually smoked (which made up in length what they lacked in quality). McBrien was delighted when he gave him two for himself.

Finally it was 6:00 P.M. and he could go. The weather was so fine, the air cooler than it had been, that he could not help but be pleased as he went his way. He found the narrow road that Naylor had pointed out the week before. The entrance to Willowbrook Hall was not far from there. It would have been hard to miss. Two stone pillars supported a wrought iron arch, upon which, in iron letters, was spelled out "Willowbrook Hall," and beneath that, in smaller letters: *Ut languores curarent*. "That they might cure illnesses." A phrase from the gospel of Luke, himself a physician according to tradition.

The road wound through a stand of trees, their natural wild state coerced into the sort of orderly disorder that one associates with the great estates of Europe. The house was by any standard large enough to be styled a "hall." It could have been a plantation home in the deep South. Doctor Oliver Naylor was a man of means. Again Dougherty wondered how he had come to be invited. A lieutenant on whose commission the ink was barely dry was usually not much sought after.

The house stood three stories high, constructed of the gray-brown stone native to the area. The walls of the uppermost level sloped slightly inward with peaked projections enclosing dormer windows. The wide façade was pierced by no less than six large windows on the second level, indicating a goodly number of rooms. At the extremities two double chimneys projected above the slate roof. On both first and second levels were spacious porches with narrow, white-painted wooden pillars, delicately fluted to suggest a Greek influence, and between them a railing supported by gracefully turned balusters. The windows on the first floor ran full height from floor to ceiling, so they could be left open to allow easy access to the porch, although on this evening, with its touch of chill in the air, they remained closed.

As he hesitated, from behind the house came a little Negro boy no more than eight or nine years old, skipping along until he saw Dougherty. His eyes opened wide. He stopped short. But the surprise was momentary and a wide smile blossomed on his face. He made an imitation salute and addressed Dougherty with an air of confidence.

"Evenin', gen'l," he said, knowing he could hardly go wrong if he gave everyone an immediate promotion.

"Suh," he said, "y'all kin go raht on in, if y'all please. Dey's waitin' fo' yah. Ah kin take de hoss 'roun de back."

Behind the house lay other buildings, hidden by a line of trees and shrubbery. Dougherty dismounted and his greeter, with another salute (and a broad, white-toothed grin and a hearty, "Thank yah, suh, thank yah," at the coin Dougherty handed him), led the horse around the house and out of sight. Dougherty suffered a sudden indecision. He took off his hat, clapped it against his other hand to free it of dust, replaced it on his head, gave a cursory brush at his coat, tugged at its hem to adjust its lines, squared his shoulders, and started up the steps to the broad porch. To the casual observer, had there been one, he was the picture of self-confidence, but inside he felt more like a man headed for some dreadful trial than one invited to the pleasures of a good meal.

He had just set foot on the topmost step, when the door opened and a Negro man, tall and erect, with grizzled white hair, and a countenance wrinkled by age, greeted him. He wore the livery of the servant and Dougherty wondered if he were a freedman or a slave.

"Good evenin', L'tenant, suh. Is you L'tenant Doc'ty? Kin I take yo' hat, suh?" suiting action to words. "The doctah is 'spectin' ya in the drawin' room, if y'all could jes folla me."

The entry was on the east side of the house and, this late in the day, received little illumination from without. The servant held an unlighted taper, as if he had just been preparing to light the lamps at either side of the entrance. The hall was narrow, with two doors on the left and two more on the right, and a double door straight ahead. Two straight-backed, cane-seated chairs on each side constituted the only furniture. The floor was polished satiny by years of use.

He went directly to the double doors, opened them and stood aside, motioning Dougherty to enter, as he announced: "Doctah Naylah, suh, L'tenant Doc'ty is heah."

The room was large, simply furnished in the style of some years back, not the more cluttered look that was rapidly becoming the fashion. The windows faced west, their drapes still open, so the light of the sinking sun bathed everything in a warm, golden glow, even though some lamps had already been lighted in anticipation of the gathering dusk. Dougherty faced a company, all of whom, for a moment at least, were unrecognizable to him, since some faced away from the door and, of those who did not, he knew no one. Then his eye was drawn to one configuration of persons whose presence gave him a start.

Now and again almost everyone experiences a feeling that a present event is a repetition of one that occurred in the past. Dougherty saw himself again on the upper gallery of the Hessian Barracks in Frederick City. People stood in animated conversation. An army officer spoke with a man and woman, the man with his back toward Dougherty, she facing him. The man, a civilian, was broad-shouldered, dark-haired, in finely tailored frock coat and trousers, boots highly polished, the picture of self-assurance. For a moment, Dougherty's mind's eye beheld the dark blue coat and gray trousers, but reality immediately intervened and he saw that the man wore the darker shades of evening dress. Precisely as on the last occasion, Dougherty's eyes went past him to the woman — but this time the announcement by the butler had caused her to take note of him — something that she had not done the last time.

She was not in the green gown she had worn at the hospital, but there was no doubt that it was the same woman. There was the same aura of aloofness, the jet black hair drawn back and gathered into a chignon, a mass of curls at the back. The violet eyes came to rest upon Dougherty and, to his considerable surprise, her lips curved into a smile, their redness enhanced by skin as pale as roseate marble. The frock this time was royal blue, its short sleeves accentuating the beauty of her arms, the smoothness of neck and shoulders revealed by the scoop of the neckline. It was accented with delicate black lace. Narrow velvet ribbons the shade of the dress were woven into the dark curls of the chignon. She wore little jewelry, yet seemed almost regal. Her companion turned to face Dougherty. It was Doctor Oliver Naylor!

"Lieutenant Dougherty! How good of you to come. Althea, my dear, allow me to present Lieutenant Dougherty, one of the talented surgeons of the Army of the Potomac. Lieutenant, this is my wife, Mrs. Naylor."

Mrs. Naylor... Dougherty's feelings were an indescribable hodgepodge The joy of meeting her filled him as he touched, for a moment, the slender, graceful fingers of the hand she extended in greeting. Her cool, dry skin would not, he hoped, be offended by contact with a hand roughened by the week's work and now suddenly become damp with nervousness.

"Ma'am. Most pleased to make your acquaintance. An honor indeed." He wanted to sound witty, urbane, but he felt his cheeks flush as he mumbled his unimpressive inanity, all cleverness driven from his mind. Even over words so uninspired, his tongue went not trippingly, but merely tripped.

Perhaps she was accustomed to besmitten males offering that sort of initial response, or perhaps she was supremely kind, but in any case she merely smiled and said, "Welcome to our home, Lieutenant Dougherty. We are honored to have you with us. You are perhaps not acquainted with all of our guests? Allow to me to make you known."

There were not so very many, in spite of his initial impression. The first she introduced was the next surprise. It was the uniformed man with whom she and her husband had been speaking.

"You may already be acquainted, I think, with Major Briggs?"

They'd been accustomed to seeing each other daily, but the Major shook his hand and said, "Well, Lieutenant, you never cease to amaze me. Not only do you number the military hierarchy among your acquaintance, but it now seems that you find time to grace the civilian social circle as well. I am gratified that you found the time to be with us."

He was dressed formally, as was Dougherty. The frock coat, the sash, the polished boots made him seem a different man. Yet there was still the squint, intent as ever, and the same sarcasm in the voice. Before Dougherty could respond — perhaps with a comment he might later regret — under the mild pressure of the hand his hostess had (to his secret delight) placed upon his arm, Dougherty was gently but firmly moved on to the next person. Mrs. Naylor's quick redirection of his attention and her slightly bemused expression told him that she had sensed the strain in their relationship.

"I am sure, Lieutenant, that we are all appreciate your presence in our army and your kind attendance upon us this evening. My husband has spoken so highly of you." Her words thawed the self-protective iciness that Major Briggs so readily produced in him.

With the sun now all but fully set, the light of the candles was more necessary, but the next guest was a source of illumination unto himself. He was a tall, gray-haired man, stout as a barrel, clothed in a uniform Dougherty had never seen before, but whose origin he recognized. From the mountainous chest of his scarlet tunic and cascading down toward the sloping foothills of his more than ample middle, was a veritable avalanche of decorations, its lower borders marked by a wide leather belt as spotlessly white as were the trousers above the perfectly polished black boots. His epaulettes shone like gold. His impressive mustache and bushy brows graced a face whose nose was as rubicund as his coat. This was General William Muir, Deputy Inspector General of the British army. He and Surgeon General Hammond had both been invited this evening, but duties prevented Hammond's attendance. General Muir had not been thus encumbered and, Dougherty suspected, would never have been guilty of reckless rejection of a dinner invitation. He was a veteran of foreign service, but, if looks did not deceive, had never been forced to undertake a campaign which threatened starvation.

"My dear Lieutenant," he said, although he pronounced it *Leftenant*, "an honor to make your acquaintance, I'm sure. May I ask, sir, have you been here throughout the recent campaign?"

At Dougherty's response, his eyes, already glowing, absolutely beamed, and he said, "Quite so... quite so. I hope we shall have some moments of conversation before the evening is over. I should very much like to hear of it."

Dougherty wasn't sure what he could tell him. The one thing he could say was that in the midst of a battle the individual sees little but the backs of the men in front of him, the enormous confusion of conflict all but lost in clouds of powder smoke, and, when all clears, the dreadful heaps of wounded and dead.

He recalled Major Brinton's laughter at the story of the innkeeper's wife, and he resolved to be alert and to intervene should General Muir seem disposed to repeat that with their hostess, although it defied imagination that he should ever confuse the elegant Mrs. Naylor with an innkeeper's wife or a barmaid. Still, Dougherty would not have been displeased to be in the position of rendering some small service to her, to be in any manner her protector.

Their circuit of the drawing room led next to three people, obviously parents and daughter — Mr. and Mrs. Collingwood and Genevieve. He was tall, thin, stern, a taciturn gentleman in his early fifties, who looked as though he had recently swallowed a very sour pickle and was wondering just why he had. Yet even with his graying temples and thinning hair, he retained something of the good looks that would have made him attractive to the wife who seemed his antithesis in personality.

Mrs. Collingwood had all the good spirits her husband had not. She was a few years younger than he, of medium height, quite pretty, with twinkling eyes, and rosy cheeks. Her simple lavender evening frock was like her personality — bright, pleasant, in need of no additional frills. Where her husband said no more than a quietly polite, "Pleased, I am sure...," she welcomed Dougherty with an acknowledgment of the heroism of their brave soldiery, implying his inclusion among those noble patriots.

Genevieve was quite another matter. She was pretty, but without the mature beauty of Mrs. Naylor. Yet, she made a good first impression. The last bits of daylight and first glow of the candles created highlights in her chestnut hair that sparkled as she moved — and she seemed always to be moving. Not that she was graceless or unseemly; she was simply too vivacious ever to be totally at rest. Her brown-yellow dress put Dougherty in mind of a September sun shining on Autumn leaves. Her hair was in ringlets. She wore no jewelry, only a narrow ribbon of velvet tied in a bow at her wrist — a ribbon of that same brown-yellow. She could not have been more than nineteen. Of course, Dougherty had been nineteen only a few months ago, but that did not occur to him.

"Most pleased to meet you, Miss Collingwood," Dougherty said. To his embarrassment, he sounded even to himself like an adult greeting a child who has been invited into grown-up company. She must have thought he was going to pat her head and send her off to play.

"Not nearly, Lieutenant, so charmed as I am to make the acquaintance of a genuine, authentic hero." Her words may have echoed her mother's, but they were contradicted by the mischievous gleam in her green eyes. "How wonderful it must be to have achieved so noble a status at so tender an age." Her lips curved into a smile — a pleasant smile, but it annoyed him nonetheless, and that must have shown in his face, for her mother said, "Jen!" Just that one word; she lowered her eyes, but could not quite suppress the smile.

"I am sure that you and Miss Collingwood will have ample opportunity to continue your conversation and further your acquaintance," Mrs. Naylor said, "I know you will enjoy each other's company."

Dougherty had his doubts. Miss Collingwood's smile was becoming, but there was a sting in her humor. She took too lightly the dignity that Dougherty was still new enough to consider his due. He did not appreciate being readily dismissed by a mere slip of a girl!

There remained four more guests. Doctor and Mrs. Holbrun, were gray haired, sedate, old fashioned, but quite pleasant. His shoes were the old Alberts, with the cloth tops, patent leather toe-caps, and side laces. His suit and waistcoat were rusty with age, and he wore the high collar and wide cravat of a decade or so ago. His wife's hair was smoothed out from its central part, leading to ringlets over the ears and a bun low on the back of the head. The sleeves of the plain gray dress fell in tiers and the bodice had a modest V neckline. She smiled at the introduction, apparently her habitual expression.

"Doctor Holbrun," said his hostess, "has not long since come from Richmond. He may perhaps be pleased to tell you some of what he experienced while there."

"Ah, yes, I should be most pleased to speak of it," he said, and he proceeded to inform Dougherty of some of the salient features of his personal history. Dougherty soon realized that here was a man who never settled for the abridged version if a fully amplified one were at hand. He spoke of Richmond, but only after situating his recent life within the context of its whole. Dougherty was grateful that he had not chosen to begin by situating his life within the context of the full history of the nation. He had been born in Richmond, studied medicine, and then settled in Baltimore, where he built up a flourishing medical practice and taught medicine and surgery to a number of private students. It was in 1858, past his sixtieth year, when he met a group of physicians who wanted to establish a medical college in Richmond. The doctor sold his practice in Baltimore and he and his wife and their two daughters moved south to begin a new phase in their lives. It proved unsuccessful. When the war broke out, they decided that their sympathies lay with the North and they returned to Maryland (which was as far north as they were inclined to go), purchased a modest property just west of Smoketown, and there retired.

The last guests were their two daughters, in their middle years, both single and living with their parents. Miss Caroline and Miss Benedicta, were as dour as their parents were pleasant. Their gowns were not merely modest; they were foreboding. One a lackluster gray and the other a drab green. Their eyes flitted among the guests as though they were suspicious of the whole lot. They were thin, almost gaunt, with cheeks as pale as if drained of all blood. Their pinched nostrils flared, as though at some faintly noxious odor. Dougherty was happy he had worn his best uniform, or he might have thought himself the offender. They pursed their lips, ready at a moment's notice to "tut-tut" at whatever ran counter to their aesthetic susceptibilities. He said a silent prayer that he would not be seated between them at the dinner table.

Having met everyone, Dougherty looked forward to a few minutes with Althea Naylor, but just then the door opened and the Negro butler entered to catch her eye.

"Please excuse me, for a moment," she said, "while I see to some of the final preparations, I will leave you with Miss Caroline and Miss Benedicta. I am sure you will have much to discuss." Was there a smile in her eyes? He wasn't sure.

The Holbruns listened to his vapid comments, pursed their lips, and nodded in a non-committal fashion, but his mind was elsewhere. Mrs. Naylor's departure had left him as foolishly pained as if she had been his lady love going to a foreign land instead of his hostess going to the kitchen. Objective considerations, had he been sensible enough to have had objective considerations, would have told him that they were nothing to each other, that she was older than he, that she was married to his host, and that he was acting the fool. But at that moment he had no least interest in objective considerations. He simply wanted to savor the undefined fantasy inspired by the beauty of Mrs. Naylor — Althea, as in his thoughts alone he dared to address her. A talent of youth — to cause itself pain in actions and decisions that it thinks the source of deep satisfaction.

Long as it seemed, it was not more than five minutes before Mrs. Naylor returned, spoke briefly to her husband, and announced that they might proceed to the dining room. With the smooth efficiency of experience, they sorted their guests into pairs as smoothly as if the careful orchestration had been mere coincidence. It was Genevieve Collingwood whom Dougherty escorted, and he took a sly delight at seeing that Major Briggs escorted one of the Misses Holbrun and the Deputy Inspector General the other.

Above the long oval table the crystal pendants of the chandelier reflected the flames of its candles, bathing the room in soft, warm light. Snow white linen hung almost to the floor; dishes and silverware sparkled. Cut flowers splashed color among silver candelabra. Above the polished cherry of the sideboard, the whole room was reflected in a gilt-framed mirror. The whole scene was as far removed as possible from the tents and barns and the rooms of mills and churches that Dougherty had dwelt in since the battle.

But the treats were more than visual — wonderful aromas emanated from the kitchen. This meal would not be hardtack, salt pork, and bitter boiled coffee. His stomach growled, bringing a smile and a sidelong glance from Miss Collingwood and a blush to Dougherty's cheeks.

As host and hostess guided them to their places, Dougherty's disappointment at escorting Miss Collingwood was replaced by relief as he was shown his seat. Doctor Naylor took his place at the head of the table, his wife at his right. To Dougherty's surprise he was situated just between Mrs. Naylor and Miss Collingwood.

Beside his plate was an array of cutlery more daunting than the contents of a surgical kit, recalling his resolve not to be first to consume any course, and to follow the example of the others. When in Rome...

The spicy fish chowder that appeared before them was better than anything Dougherty had eaten in weeks. And that was only the beginning. There was roast beef, a cured ham baked with brown sugar, roast stuffed duck, boiled potatoes seasoned with butter and salt and finely sliced onions, and sweet potatoes boiled, then cut into slices and fried. There was corn baked in cream and eggs, squash mashed fine and seasoned with nutmeg and brown sugar. It was a meal such as Dougherty had never experienced. Only later would he sense an embarrassment at the thought of such opulence in the midst of the pain of war.

At first his mind was not on conversation, although he was aware of the voices on all sides. Miss Caroline Holbrun was telling General

Muir of her birth in Virginia, her childhood in Baltimore, and her recent return from Richmond. It seemed also that, although the Holbruns had only recently come to Smoketown, Doctor Holbrun had been acquainted with Doctor Naylor's parents many years ago, prior to his leaving Virginia to study in Philadelphia. They were both now dead, but Doctor Holbrun, upon arriving in Smoketown, had heard Doctor Naylor's name mentioned by the local inhabitants, and had made it a point to seek him out. Their common vocation to medicine had helped rekindle a friendship. Meanwhile, the courses of the meal passed by in endless succession, and Dougherty alternately chewed and listened.

At the same time, he was required to participate in some conversation of his own. Miss Collingwood, in spite of her tendency to smile at what Dougherty considered inappropriate moments, was genuinely interested in what the army was doing and was quite attentive as Dougherty spoke of what had happened to him in the past few days — his description abridged in some respects, for fear of offending the feelings of so young a lady with things distasteful.

He said nothing of the discovery of the dead man or the subsequent examination of the body. None of that was fitting conversation, especially during the carving of the roast and the slicing of the ham and the dismembering of the duck, all done with a surgical flourish by Doctor Naylor himself. With what he considered befitting humility, Dougherty recounted the incident of the hat being shot from his head. Her reaction surprised him. He had almost regretted telling the story, expecting another smile and a mildly scathing reference to his heroism. Instead, she said, "Oh, Lieutenant Dougherty, I hope that you were not injured. It must have been most distressing to come so close to death." Her eyes were wide and her concern — to his gratification — quite genuine.

"Distressing? I suppose it might have been distressing, had I been given an opportunity to reflect upon it at the time. It was all over in a few seconds and we were on our way without another word about it." For a moment he regretted letting the butler get away with his hat. Still, he could hardly have kept it on or held it in his hand while he ate dinner, on the off chance that the topic might come up. He couldn't even show her the wound, since it was concealed by his hair and besides it was healed by now. — and, even if it hadn't been, it would not have been quite the thing to display at table. Maybe at another time he would have the hat handy.

"Of course," he added, "to a soldier risks such as these are a part of daily life and one must learn to take them in one's stride."

"My, what constant courage you do exhibit, sir," she said, but her eyes had again that annoying twinkle and there was humor in her voice. This time Dougherty was not so very irritated; he had sounded a bit pompous even to himself and he was amused as well. That made her smile all the more, but it was quite a friendly smile indeed.

"I have seen a great deal of courage in these past few days," she said. "My mother and I have been able to help with the nursing of the wounded both in Keedysville and in Boonsborough. So, too, have the Misses Holbrun and the Doctor, their father, although their labor has been for the most part in the farm buildings out past Smoketown."

Dougherty was caught completely off guard. She seemed far too young to be allowed to take part in work of that sort. On the other hand, he supposed that having her mother with her made a considerable difference. Still, it was not easy to picture someone such as Miss Collingwood being either willing or able to carry out nursing duties that are frequently difficult and almost always distressful and distasteful. His respect for her grew.

"Are you enjoying your meal, Lieutenant?" said the voice from his other side, the throaty, more mature voice of Mrs. Naylor. "I suspect that it may be a change from the usual army fare."

"That it is, ma'am," he said, "and a most pleasant change indeed. Not only is the food superb, but its service is wonderful. I marvel at the beauty of the table itself — the flowers are so very impressive."

"I thank you for your kindness in mentioning them," she said.

"Do you not know, Lieutenant, that it is Mrs. Naylor herself who arranges them so cunningly? They are all fresh — she grows them herself." The words of Miss Caroline Holbrun had about them a sense of distaste, even though they were said politely enough.

"Yes, indeed," said Miss Benedicta Holbrun, "our hostess is really quite artistic. You must ask her to allow you to see some of her painting and calligraphy. You may have noticed one example in the invitation that you received." Like her sister, the words were polite, the tone was not. There was a cutting edge that Dougherty found offensive.

Mrs. Naylor showed no offense. She smiled her wonderful smile and said, "How kind of you both to remark upon it. It would be an honor to show Lieutenant Dougherty some of my efforts, should he ever desire to see them."

"Oh, I would indeed," he was quick to say. "Perhaps you might have some of them at hand this evening." He blushed at his own brashness.

"I would be most happy to oblige you," she said. "At least, I can show you some of the drawings and calligraphy. The flowers will have to wait until another time. They are best seen in sunlight. Surely you can come back to see them. We are quite proud of them."

The meal ended with hypocrite's pie, a delightful concoction of pastry crust, custard, and dried peaches restored to their original vigor with the addition of brandy. As the last of the dishes were cleared away, Mrs. Naylor arose, suggesting that the ladies might enjoy withdrawing and so leave the gentlemen to their brandy and cigars.

The brandy was excellent and Dougherty smoked not one of his own cigars, but a far better one from the polished walnut box passed around by their host. Talk was, as ever, of the war and there was general agreement that the Union had achieved a signal victory on the banks of the Antietam. There was not the same unanimity in regard to the subsequent failure to press the attack on Thursday and McClellan's continued lack of forward movement since then. No one even hinted at disloyalty, although even that would be conjectured in the days that followed.

Since all the men present, with the exception of Mr. Collingwood, were involved in the practice of medicine, it was inevitable that talk should move to the treatment of the wounded. At some point the conversation turned in Dougherty's direction as someone — Briggs or Naylor, Dougherty was not sure which — referred to the oddity of anyone's finding something suspicious in regard to a body discovered on a battlefield.

"Aha!" said the Deputy Inspector General, "so that's it! I thought the name of Dougherty was familiar. Was not Major Brinton with you just lately? I am sure it was he who spoke of the incident of the body. Can you tell us more about it, Leftenant?"

Since almost all in the assembly were medical men, Dougherty knew that the topic would not meet with the distaste that might be expected elsewhere. Briggs, he noticed, said very little, but attended carefully to every word. He had not heard the whole account, and Dougherty was surprised that as he spoke the Major had no comment, not even the critical lifting of an eyebrow. He simply listened, his expression unreadable. Doctor Naylor lamented the probable failure of investigation under present circumstances, but had little else to say. Dougherty did not reveal the cause of death, beyond saying that it was a stab wound at the base of the skull. He wondered at Briggs's continued silence.

It was late by the time the gentlemen rejoined the ladies in the drawing room and the guests began the preliminaries to departure, speaking of the fine evening, how quickly the time had passed, and the earliness of the morrow's labors. Dougherty's own departure, to his secret satisfaction, was delayed beyond that of the others. Mrs. Naylor reminded him of his earlier interest in seeing the results of her artistic endeavors, and thought that he might also like to see her husband's medical office. Dougherty had to admit to himself that, had she suggested that they examine the doorknobs or contemplate the pattern of the grain in the wood of the floors, he would have happily accepted the invitation, provided only that she were there to examine them with him.

They went first to the doctor's office. Dougherty was impressed by the care that he had lavished upon it. The tools and equipment were of the finest, including the expected Tiemann surgical kit with its polished wood and plush-lined trays to hold the scientifically designed tools. It was an exact replica of the kit used by Doctor Briggs, but in this kit there was no unoccupied spot; the trocar was in its proper place. Its shaft was the twin of the one in the back of the dead man's head; an exact copy of the one no longer in Major Briggs's possession.

On a table next to the cot for patients, were two bistouries and a forceps which had yet to be cleaned, as well as some soiled rags. He must have been tending a patient not long before their arrival.

The walls were lined with glass enclosed cases, some for medical equipment and the rest containing an impressive medical library. It was clear that Naylor was no simple, self-taught physician, but a learned man. Both French and German texts stood side by side with English, as well as some works in Greek and Latin.

"I hope, Doctor Dougherty, that you find these quarters up to date. I am always pleased to get the opinion of someone who has just completed his medical education. It is an opportunity to hear of the most recent methods and theories, and to see just how my practice has kept up."

"There is nothing lacking that I can see," Dougherty said, "including the authorities in your medical library. It leaves little to be desired."

"I am glad that it meets with your approval," he said, with not the least trace of the condescension that Dougherty had begun to grow used to in dealing with Briggs. He seemed genuinely pleased at his comments.

"Perhaps you would now like to see my wife's 'office.' I shall be with you in a few minutes, after I clean and replace these instruments. I don't like them to remain uncleaned. It mars the surface. But this evening I was pressed for time. A young man, a neighbor, suffered a slight accident and I finished dressing his cut just as our guests began to arrive."

"Come along," Mrs. Naylor said, and led Dougherty out of the office and along a short corridor to another room. She must have spoken to the butler about their intended visit to her domain, for the lamps were already lighted when they entered. The room was about the size of the office they had just left, but intended for a totally different purpose. The shelves here were filled with boxes of watercolors, chalks, charcoal, pencils, pens, penknives, gum rubber erasers, ink scrapers, and all the odds and ends of the artist. On one table, with a top that tilted at an angle, there was a partially completed drawing of a little girl, done in chalk with colors as lifelike as one could imagine. She looked radiantly happy, dressed in the clothes that any child her age would play in. Her face expressed a surprised pleasure, as though something had just happened to delight her. On her lap was a kitten looking expectantly at her, ignoring the ball of yarn that had fallen to the floor. Dougherty was much impressed and said so.

"You are very kind, Lieutenant," she said. "I have a great deal to learn, but I do so enjoy trying. The girl was a wonderful model, very patient and so pleased to have her portrait taken. I told her that it could be hers once it is finished, so she comes by quite often to see to its progress."

On a small desk off to one side were more containers with pens and pencils, and sheets covered with writing rather than drawings. There were intricately designed calligraphic studies of proverbs and inspirational adages. There were what seemed to be practice sheets, with the same letters or groups of letters written over and over again in a variety of styles. One page in particular caught his eye. It was a verse of Scripture, whose words seemed somehow appropriate to the days that had just passed.

> The words of his mouth were smoother than butter,
> but war was in his heart:
> his words were softer than oil, yet they were drawn swords.
> Ps. 55, v. 21

It was done with a very fine pen on a sheet of vellum-like paper little more than six inches square. It was undecorated, its beauty in the letters themselves.

"Oh," she said, as she saw him looking at it, "that is nothing but a practice sheet. Rather plain, I fear."

"I don't find it the least bit plain," he said.

"If it catches your fancy," she said, "please take it with you as a small memento of this evening. I am gratified that you like it."

"Indeed, Lieutenant, please do accept it. My wife is quite talented, even though she is embarrassed when I point it out to anyone."

Doctor Naylor had entered the room so quietly that Dougherty jumped, not knowing he was there.

"I am honored to have it," Dougherty said, and knew that the evening had reached its end, although, as he looked at Mrs. Naylor's violet eyes and raven hair in the flickering light of the lamps, he hoped that it would not be the last. Yet he also felt the discomfort of being so attracted to a woman who was the wife of a man who had given him no reason to feel about him in any way but that of admiration.

His confusion increased when Naylor said, "We have been honored to have had you with us, Doctor Dougherty. I believe I earlier heard you express an interest in my wife's efforts at horticulture. You must visit again in daylight and I am sure that she would be pleased were you to prevail upon her to show you what she has done."

It was an invitation that, for a moment, Dougherty knew would be wiser to forego, but he knew that he would not. On that note he took his leave, the last to go, and so found his way back alone in the dark, fortunate that the night was cloudless and that there was starlight to show him the way.

Chapter XIV: The Young Napoleon

"And everybody praised the Duke,
Who this great fight did win."
"But what good came of it at last?"
Quoth little Peterkin.
"Why that I cannot tell," said he,
"But t'was a famous victory"
    Robert Southey (1774-1843)
    The Battle of Blenheim (1798)

[September 23-25, 1862]

Dougherty that night dreamed wonderful dreams, but, as is always the case, even the most vivid of dreams disappears when reality dips its coarse brush into the pigments of the day and splashes their garish hues across the delicately painted canvas of blissful recollection. He packed away his good uniform and the little piece of vellum, his remembrance of Althea. (The name came so easily to his mind, but he would not have dared to so address her had she been present!)

The washerwoman brought back his laundry. At last, his clothes felt and — above all — smelt like real clothes. That wouldn't last long, but it was nice while it did. By sunup he was at the church, where he found McBrien already about his tasks.

"A good morning to ye, sir," he said, "Did ye have a pleasant evening then?"

"Pleasant, indeed," he said. He talked a bit about the house and the food, but said little of Mrs. Naylor. He had no desire to arouse McBrien's curiosity.

For some hours there was time for nothing but the wounded. Some were improving. Their pain and fever had begun to abate. Others had hospital gangrene, with wounds needing constant attention. It was a painful process. He used nitric acid to break down the slough and then removed it with forceps. A bromine solution cleaned the open wound and it was dressed with dry lint, then with lint soaked in the bromine, and finally covered in lint soaked in cerate. This painful process would be repeated until the condition changed. For some, treatment might be more drastic, with further amputation higher on the afflicted limb. But when not enough tissue was left to amputate, nothing could be offered but the effort to make the last days easier.

The rain the night before the battle had left some with a cattarh that now turned into pneumonia. They had fever, dry cough, dyspnoea, dry and brownish tongue, dull chest pain, and frequent and feeble pulse. Next would come lung congestion and copious expectoration of thick mucous tinged with brownish stains of blood. On treatment there was nothing but disagreement. The traditionalists offered blood-letting, strong purgatives, and the more rigorous antimonials and mercurials. A more enlightened treatment, and the one Dougherty preferred, avoided heroic agents, in favor of saline diaphoretics, muriate of ammonia, mixed with either digitalis, aconite, or veratrum viride in a tincture. In every instance, the results were unpredictable.

It was well into the afternoon when Dougherty received a hastily scribbled note from Major Brinton.

> Major Allen not available. Has gone to Washington to consult with President. Will contact the General Commanding later this day and will advise you of results.
> September 23, 1862   Major J.H. Brinton

He stood near the window with the note in his left hand and wondered. He was so lost in thought that his first notion of her presence was when she spoke.

"Good day, Lieutenant. I hope it is not distressful news that you have received?"

It was Miss Genevieve Collingwood, dressed in costume quite unlike the finery of last evening. The dress was brown with small white dots, and no further decoration. The apron was white, or had been white when the day began. It was now stained with spots of blood and pus and the waste one acquires in the course of duty in a hospital. Her lustrous hair was pulled back into a bun that could have been severe were it not for wisps that had come undone and whose disorder made her seem all the younger. There was her usual inner vitality, but her eyes betrayed her exhaustion.

"Miss Collingwood! What a pleasant surprise! Thank you for your concern, but, no, it is not very bad, just a minor disappointment. When did you arrive? Have you been here all day?"

"No," she said, "I arrived just a few moments ago with my mother. Most of the day we assisted with the wounded in the houses here in town. We came to see if there was anything we could do before we leave for Boonsborough."

"You'll not be disappointed if work is what you want," Dougherty said, "We never run out of the need for help. There are wounds to be cleaned and rebandaged, if you're up to it."

"Of course I'm up to it! That's why I asked. Good heavens, what do you think I've been doing all day? And the days before! I'm not a child, after all!" Her response took him aback. It was not loud, but there was an undercurrent of offended feeling that surprised him.

"I apologize if I have offended you," he said. "I had truly no intention of doing so. I had no wish to imply any lack of ability. I only meant that you looked as though you have had a long day, and you know as well as I just how taxing this work can be."

She lowered her eyes and took a deep breath, then looked straight at him.

"No, Lieutenant, I should apologize for jumping to conclusions. It is just that there are times when I do so tire of having everyone looking out for my welfare and treating me as though I were still a child. Perhaps not even a child, but 'just a weak woman.' Some don't even make the distinction! You cannot imagine how vexing it is to be constantly protected from reality, when reality is something from which no one should be forced to retreat. Why try to push people into a world of make-believe, when there is far too much to be done in this?"

"Shall we start anew?" Dougherty asked. "We can truthfully agree that we are both tired, but that we can give still a few more hours. I will do my best to overlook your wrongly imputed feminine weakness, if you, in return, will kindly agree to ignore my sadly misplaced masculine superiority." He spoke with such seriousness that she first lowered her eyes and then began to smile.

She had made her point and he would remember it. In the meantime, he was glad for the help and soon found himself working with her more smoothly than he would have thought possible. She had learned a lot in the past few days and was most efficient. Moreover, she evoked from the patients a courage which he could not so easily inspire. He remembered a professor in Philadelphia who had spoken of the days in which all surgery was done with no anaesthesia. He said that he had seen men so strong they could not have been held down by three powerful assistants, and yet a slip of a girl had influence sufficient to cause them to lie still for an operation with hardly a groan or a whimper. He supposed that it was due to the hesitance that most men have of showing any weakness in the presence of the "weaker" sex. In any case, her presence was not only a help, it was also a gift to the suffering soldiers so eager to have her notice them.

The rest of the time flew by and he was surprised when her mother appeared to say that their carriage was leaving for Boonsborough. Her apron was as stained as that of her daughter, her eyes as tired, and yet she, too, retained her lively, spirited manner, and even a sparkle in eyes that had seen so much suffering.

"I hope that our efforts have been of some assistance, Doctor Dougherty," said Mrs. Collingwood. "I thank you for being so attentive to Jen."

"It was no chore, Mrs. Collingwood. I was privileged to have Miss Collingwood's help, and she has done much for the wounded that I should have never been able to accomplish alone. May we expect to see you both tomorrow?"

"Why, yes, I expect so. Perhaps we shall come directly here since you have so many wounded. Of course, we must go where we are told. Shall we be on our way, Jen?"

"Yes, Mama," she said. "Thank you, Lieutenant, for your 'attentiveness.' Perhaps you will have the time to be equally attentive tomorrow." Her emphasis on the "attentiveness" and her smile both had that same impish quality that had so annoyed him the evening before. Today it did not. He was sorry to see her go.

He went back to work and caught McBrien watching him with a smile that was too knowing.

"Have you run out of things to do, Steward McBrien?" he asked, trying to sound authoritative, but seeming even to himself merely peevish.

"Ah, not at'all, sir. And have ye had a busy afternoon yerself, sir, in spite of the need to be teaching a novice the tricks of the trade, as it were?"

Never had Dougherty met a man with McBrien's talent for needling a person without saying a single word that one could reasonably take as disrespectful!

"Oh, it was not so much of a burden. She is a pleasant enough child and truly helpful with the patients," Dougherty said. As he spoke the words, he almost looked over his shoulder to be sure that she wasn't there. A comment so unfairly condescending would have lit up in those green eyes a fire bright enough to cauterize his tongue.

"Child, sir? Well, indeed, I suppose she is such. Sure, she must be much younger than yer ownself... Why, at least six months or even a year, I'd be willing to wager. A significant difference to be sure, then. Careless of me not to have noticed."

It doesn't seem so significant a difference when one speaks of a year, Dougherty thought. It seems much more so when one has been in battle and then compares himself to a girl who has never been away from home and who is still young enough to require that her excursions, even to assist the sick, must, for propriety's sake, be done in the company of her mother. Or so he told himself.

It was not until late on Wednesday that he heard again from Major Brinton, when he stopped at the church.

"Lieutenant, I must apologize," he said. A magnanimous gesture, since it is a rare day indeed when a major must excuse himself to a lieutenant. "I had expected to communicate with you before this, but duties have intervened."

"Please, sir," Dougherty said, "think nothing of it. We are all taxed to our limit and I am gratified that you have been able to think of it at all."

"I wanted you to know that I contacted General McClellan, and he will speak with you tomorrow at his headquarters promptly at 10:00 o'clock in the morning. I suggest that you take the photographs with you, and that you be prepared to offer a succinct explanation of the circumstances of the death, the questions it raises, and your need for his assistance."

"If you don't mind my asking, sir," Dougherty said, "do you think that he is disposed to help?"

"I wish I could offer you greater assurance," he answered, "but the fact is that I saw him so very briefly that I had no clear impression of his intentions. However, I would certainly not think it hopeless, if only for the simple fact that he is willing to see you. He was much distracted today by the news from Washington."

The news was momentous. It was McBrien who had first told Dougherty of it, and then the papers had been full of it. The President had issued a proclamation emancipating the slaves. It was to go into effect in January of 1863.

"Old Abe never made a secret of the fact that he'd no use fer slavery. But still it's an odd sort of proclamation, wouldn't ye say? It don't free them in the North where he's President and it declares them free in the South where he isn't President. He says that states that return to the fold before January can keep their slaves, but, sure, don't it seem that Jeff Davis could tell them to keep their slaves and leave the Union anyway?"

He had a point. Still Lincoln was not fully inconsistent. For the states not in rebellion he called upon congress to give "pecuniary aid" to enable them to free the slaves voluntarily over the next few years. The South might scoff at Lincoln's proclamation, but, if it lost the war, its way of life would be forever changed. Many in the North who might not have fought to end slavery were willing to support the proclamation as a punitive measure against rebellion.

While people were attempting to digest that bit of news, there came another to some even more disturbing. On September 24 word came by telegraph that the President had also issued a proclamation suspending the writ of *habeas corpus*. Earlier in the year, he had called for volunteers to fill the depleted ranks of the armies. When the number forthcoming was insufficient, he called up the militia of the States, drafting them into national service. That met with resistance in some States, even with forceful ejection of persons assigned to enroll men for the conscription lists. The proclamation suspended the writ of *habeas corpus* for those who were rebels and insurgents, and included those who aided and abetted disloyalty by interfering with the process of the draft.

Discussion of both proclamations was heard on all sides, and the disagreements were passionate. In the army there was military authority to prevent discussion from turning into violence, but most expected to hear about conflicts at home when next they received their mail.

However, Dougherty's mind was not on thoughts patriotic. He was caught up in what to do about the dead man, and even after Major Brinton had left, he continued to mull over the same question: Would McClellan be willing to help? But, to his surprise, he also found himself wondering if Miss Genevieve Collingwood and her mother would return.

True to their word, they had come back early on Wednesday and spent the whole day occupied in the care of the wounded. Miss Collingwood proved a capable student with a natural kindness and an air of sympathy that of itself would have been a boon to anyone whom she served. Beyond that, however, she had a quickness of intellect, a calmness of judgement, and a clarity of purpose that Dougherty had not seen even in some physicians. One particular incident stood out.

Private William Dolan, nineteen years of age, had joined the Sixty-third New York, a part of General Meagher's Irish Brigade, and was already a seasoned veteran when he arrived at the banks of the Antietam. He had survived the Peninsular campaign and might well have survived the Maryland campaign as well, had he not made a very foolish mistake. His regiment was in line of battle and had begun to move forward into the maelstrom of the Sunken Road. A cannon ball, a twelve pounder, an iron sphere about four inches in diameter, hit the earth some distance in front of him. Like a stone some child had skipped across a pond, it bounced a few times and then rolled steadily toward him. It looked harmless enough, and he swung out his foot to deflect it. It went on in its original straight line, shearing off his leg just at the ankle. Both tibia and fibula split like dried twigs, not cut cleanly but splintered for some few inches longitudinally. He was rushed back to a field station, where a surgeon quickly amputated the shattered section of bone, forming a good stump some three inches or so below the knee; but, in spite of the careful surgery, it was clear that there was a problem. He was feverish and there was the first hint of an odor that might signal gangrene.

Miss Collingwood was changing his bandage, when she saw not only the foul smelling exudate of gangrene, but also a seepage of blood that should not have been there. It came from the hole in the stump from which protruded the strands of silk suture that had been used to ligate the ends of the artery. It was along this suture that the laudable pus should have come. Dougherty was nearby and Miss Collingwood, with hardly a trace of upset in her voice, said, "Doctor Dougherty, could you help me please?"

He saw the bright red of arterial blood, now flowing freely and, he knew, flowing even more profusely within the leg. He applied pressure to the femoral artery at the groin even before Private Dolan realized that something had gone wrong.

"Please get me a tourniquet, Miss Collingwood," he said. Without a word or a moment's hesitation, she did as he asked and applied it as he instructed, while he continued the pressure. Private Dolan was suddenly too frightened even to move, and could do no more than repeat, "What happened? What happened?"

What had happened was obvious enough. The ligated ends of the artery had undergone necrosis and broken. Private Dolan was fortunate that it had happened just as Miss Collingwood was unwrapping the bandage. He was also fortunate that she had acted so swiftly and so calmly. McBrien and another of the stewards took him out of the church to a building in the rear, where the table and tools were laid out for just such an emergency. Dougherty sent for Doctor Houston, and assisted him with the surgery.

Houston handed him a clean napkin, which he rolled into a hollow cone, pouring into it about a fluidrachm of chloroform, which he had tested for purity by allowing a drop to fall upon the back of his hand, assuring himself that it evaporated almost immediately, leaving behind neither odor nor moisture. He inverted the cone over Private Dolan's mouth and nose, bringing it to within two inches of his face. He asked him to blow strongly into it, which, in turn, caused him to inhale just as deeply as Dougherty lowered the cone to within about one-half inch of his nose. After two or three breaths he grew groggy and within less than five minutes had lost consciousness and was ready for the operation to proceed. From that point onward, it was Dougherty's duty to be attentive to his breathing, his color, and his pulse, making sure that he could breathe fresh air and adding chloroform if he began to recover too quickly. At the same time, he had to be prepared to administer artificial respiration, should Dolan show signs of failure.

Doctor Houston was an adept surgeon. The signs of gangrene were centered externally at the tip of the stump where the arterial ligature emerged. The tissue above that was not yet involved. He made a circular incision around the leg, about three inches below the knee, and dissected back to just above the knee. The skin and the fatty tissue beneath (which was quite thin in view of the young man's lack of appetite the last few days and the days of marching which had preceded that) he rolled back to a point above the knee joint, much as one would roll back a tight trouser leg. The muscular tissue beneath the integument looked healthy, assuring that the gangrene had not yet much spread. McBrien held the retracted tissue in place, while Houston flexed the knee and cut deeply into the front of the joint below the patella, much as one might do in cutting a leg of mutton into segments. Before it was totally detached, he slid the blade of the amputating knife between the back of the tibia and the front of the gastrocnemius and sliced downward, cutting that muscle in such a way as to leave a goodly portion of it hanging, so as to be brought forward later and used to form a soft pad for the new stump.

The tissue now revealed was healthy enough. The foul odor of gangrene had grown stronger, but it was contained within the tissue of the old stump which he now cut completely away and dropped into a tub beside the table. With the saw he trimmed flat the condyles of the femur which, when covered with the pad derived from the gastrocnemius, would form a surface conducive to a comfortable prosthetic attachment. He drew forth the popliteal artery with the tenaculum and ligated it with waxed silk surgical thread. He drew the threads just tight enough to cause the soft inner and middle coats of the artery to part, and the much stronger outer coat to be compressed and firmly held together. At his order, Miss Collingwood gradually loosened the tourniquet, allowing the artery to become engorged with blood. It swelled, but the ligature held firm and there was no spurting. He drew the dangling gastrocnemius forward over the end of the femur, allowing the long end of the ligature to protrude from it, and rolled down the retracted skin to form the new integument over all, sewing it into place.

His technique was smooth and flawless, accomplished with the calm self-assurance of frequent practice. There was no unnecessary hesitation, just the constant flow of skilled motion. The whole procedure had taken not much more than fifteen minutes. Before Private Dolan was taken to his bed to recover, Houston took the stump out of the tub and cut it open. The tissue around the old ligature was inflamed, there was the foul pus of gangrene, but it had not spread much before weakening the artery and causing it to rupture. Private Dolan was fortunate that it had happened at that juncture rather than somewhere further along the leg, and even more fortunate that someone had been with him when it had. He would owe a great debt of gratitude to Miss Collingwood.

Much as Dougherty appreciated Houston's skill, he was every bit as much impressed by what she had done. Her calm, her apparent imperturbability, astounded him. They walked back toward the church, and it was only then, after the surgery had been successfully completed, that he saw her eyes fill with tears. She placed both her hands on his forearm as though to steady herself and, for a moment, he feared that she was about to faint. She held tightly and her hands shook, but then the color came gradually back to her face. When she seemed sufficiently composed, he led her back into the church and to a small room behind the sanctuary, where there was a bench, and had her seat herself. He went for water, gave her some and sat beside her until she was herself again.

"Thank you," she said, "I beg your pardon for being so foolish. It is just that I have never before seen anything of that sort, and I was not at all sure what to do."

"What you did was fine," he said, "No one could have asked more, not even from a long experienced nurse. You needn't be ashamed. I was no more calm myself the first time I assisted at surgery, and it never becomes easy to witness someone else's pain. If it did become easy for me, I would think myself heartless, and the physician who does that has begun to lose the sense of who he is. What matters is that you did all that needed to be done, and did it well, before you allowed the experience to overcome you."

She sat for a moment, head bowed, then took a deep breath. She raised her eyes, still red from tears. They were next to each other, and she placed her hand upon his in such a natural gesture that he responded to the gentle pressure of her fingers by grasping them in his. He realized that only a slight inclination of his head would cause their lips to touch. They looked into each other's eyes and, for a second, seemed about to lean toward each other, but it did not happen. The genteel cough, the mild clearing of a throat informed them that someone was present. Although they had not in any way offended against propriety, they looked foolishly self-conscious, embarrassed as their eyes turned toward the door.

"Good day, Lieutenant. Good day, Miss Collingwood. I hope that I do not interrupt your work?"

The comment was made without sarcasm, no indication of anything amiss, no pointed emphasis on "work," all of which made Dougherty wonder why he could feel his cheeks grow warm and why he and Miss Collingwood drew back from each other. He could not see the expression on their visitor's face. The room in which they sat was on the east side of the church, and the light of the afternoon sun came through the west windows. That made the church brighter than the little room, so Dougherty could see only a silhouette framed in the doorway. But voice and outline were both unmistakable. He could not see the raven hair and the violet eyes, but it was Mrs. Naylor. His cheeks grew brighter, and he was thankful for the dimness of the room.

"Mrs. Naylor," he said, "what brings you here?"

His surprise made it sound like a challenge or an impertinence and he wished he could unsay it.

"In fact, Lieutenant, I came to visit the sick, but it also seemed an opportunity to greet you. I had flattered myself to think that you might have been pleased. I hope that I do not intrude."

By this time Dougherty had risen and taken a step toward the door, leaving Miss Collingwood behind, or at least seeming to do so. He glanced at her, and saw that she was looking at him with an expression somewhere between incredulity and annoyance, but he ignored it. His thoughts were in a whirl at seeing Althea Naylor, and nothing else mattered. He was pleased to think that she had come to see him.

"I am truly pleased to see you," he said, "It is just that you seem so out of place here... That is to say, I would not have expected you to come here... That is... I mean..."

"Perhaps you should explain no further," she said with a smile, "Being the wife of a physician, I am truly not a total stranger even to these circumstances, although I must admit that I do not usually have occasion to assist in my husband's profession. I hope, however, that I am not completely out of place. I know that other women come to visit the poor wounded heroes of our army."

"Not only to visit. Some of us have even come here to work," said Miss Collingwood. She sounded angry, although Dougherty could not imagine why.

"I have no doubt at all that your kindness has been most appreciated, Genevieve," she said. "Even at your tender age, there are certainly some things that you must be able to do. Are you here in the company of your mother? I thought that I may have seen her as I came through the church."

"Yes. She is here. I consider it wonderful to think that my mother is still young enough not only to visit but to be able to do such hard work along with me." She turned to Dougherty. "I thank you, Lieutenant Dougherty, for your kindness. I should, perhaps, see if I can be of some help to my mother."

With that she turned and walked out into the church. Marched rather than walked. Her steps were as precise and her back as straight as a soldier's on parade.

"Would it be an inconvenience, Lieutenant, were I to ask you to show me about? Would my visit be of help to the poor patients?" She smiled, softening the formality of the words.

"I can hardly imagine anything that they would enjoy more," he said. "It is good of you to come."

For the next half hour he escorted her from one patient to the next, each flattered by her visit and sorry to see her pass on to the next. Her clothes were not meant for nursing, but that only made her more attractive. She was pleasant and encouraging, and she did not do what some visitors did — holding a kerchief to theirs noses against the smell or averting their eyes at the sight of the damage to broken bones or amputated limbs or distorted features. Some were constantly on the verge of tears, unable to hide their distaste or prevent the upset to their stomachs, all of which brought home to the suffering men that they were the cause of this sadness or disgust. Such visits were hardly a consolation, even though the women who made them left quite pleased with themselves, convinced they had performed a Christian service, a corporal work of mercy. Mrs. Naylor faced each man, looked them in the eye, and spoke kindly, moving from one to the next without hurry and without conveying a sense of relief when she left one and went to the next. Those she visited were genuinely cheered.

All the while they moved about, she was also speaking to Dougherty, asking him about home, about his schooling, about what he had done in the army. She told him that she and her husband had discussed his cleverness in finding the body and his ability to undertake a post-mortem examination. He had even been able to solicit the assistance of Major Brinton, in spite of the fact that Major Briggs had not been enthusiastic about the investigation.

"Have you discovered how the man died? Was it really the result of foul play? Do you know yet what it was that killed him?"

"There is much yet to be ascertained," Dougherty said, using his best diagnostic tone. "I do know that he was stabbed and that it was hardly an accident, nor was it something self-inflicted. Beyond that there is not much more to say."

"Ah! So it was possibly a battle wound after all," she said.

"No, ma'am, I think not. It was not the sort of wound which could be explained in that way. Nor was it caused by a military weapon. No... I fear it was indeed foul play," he said.

They finished their circuit of the church and she prepared to leave. Outside was the same brougham he had seen at the hospital in Frederick, its maroon surface glistening as it had then. Its driver, the same one, must have polished it while Mrs. Naylor was in the church. He opened the carriage door and lowered the steps. As she entered, she turned and extended her hand. Their fingers met for a moment and Dougherty had the desire to kiss her hand, but also had sense enough to realize that doing so would only reveal him as more pathetically adolescent than worldly wise.

"Your visit has been a privilege and a pleasure. It is an honor which I dare to hope may befall us again."

"Thank you, Lieutenant. And I hope that you will be our guest at Willowbrook Hall again before your regiment departs."

For the next hour he worked, but without the assistance of Genevieve Collingwood. She was there, accompanying McBrien as he distributed medications to the patients, but each time that Dougherty came near her she found a need to go elsewhere. It was supremely annoying. When it was time to leave, it was her mother who came to bid him farewell. Miss Collingwood remained at enough of a distance to make any conversation awkward.

"Shall we see you tomorrow?" he asked Mrs. Collingwood.

"I expect so," she said, "I am sure that Genevieve would never forgive me if we had to remain at home when there is so much to be done, she does so enjoy working with you."

Genevieve had certainly heard the comment, but ignored it and seemed perfectly well disposed to forego the enjoyment of working with him. Instead, she turned toward McBrien, who happened to be standing nearer the door, and thanked him for allowing her to help. She swept out with a coolness that would have been a great comfort to the patients if they had been able to bottle and distribute it.

The next morning, Thursday, by 9:00 o'clock Dougherty was ready to leave for headquarters, when McBrien came with a bit of news that he was not pleased to hear.

"Were ye aware, sir, that we've been given our marching orders? The Second Corps is to be on its way tomorrow by morning's first light."

"Where are we going?" Dougherty asked, thinking that perhaps it would be another great battle, perhaps to Virginia. Would McClellan risk that?

"Why, as I heard it, sir, we'll be on our way to somewhere near Harpers Ferry, a place called Bolivar Heights on the Virginia side of the Potomac."

Probably not an invasion, but a defensive maneuver, Dougherty thought. But where would this leave the investigation? He had no illusion that he would be permitted to remain in Keedyville. The army simply did not work that way. In the meantime he expected no problem in being released from his daily duty in order to meet with the commanding general.

He still had not seen Miss Collingwood and her mother that morning, but he was certain that they would come. Unfortunately, he could not wait, and so, armed with his notebook, the photographs, the drawings, and what he hoped was a clear explanation of events as he understood them, he mounted his horse.

It was not yet 10:00 o'clock when he arrived at the Pry farm, now in even sadder condition than before. The sentry at the door told him to wait. For the next half hour he twiddled his thumbs, gawked at the flurry of messengers, and wondered if the general had decided not to see him after all. But a Lieutenant came to the door, invited him in, and told him to take a seat in the hallway where a number of others were already waiting. He disappeared through a door and more time went by.

Finally the same Lieutenant reappeared and took him to a room where the normal furniture had been pushed against the walls and a portable field desk and two chairs stood in the center of the room. He told him to sit and wait, and then he left.

No sooner had he done so, when the door at the other end of the room opened and McClellan entered, causing Dougherty to leap to attention and salute — in the process dropping his photographs and papers. McClellan sat, told Dougherty to do the same, and waited with obvious impatience as he picked up what he had dropped.

The general was not a large man, but his posture, his stance, his way of moving all made him seem to fill the room. At his entrance he had paused to survey the scene, but also, Dougherty thought, to allow his visitor to be duly impressed. He posed with his right hand tucked into the open button of his frock coat — the only button left that way so that he could assume that pose. Apparently he enjoyed the soubriquet of the Young Napoleon.

He was handsome, well proportioned, his dark hair a little shorter than the prevailing fashion, with an arrow-straight part on the left side. The moustache drooped slightly, the wisp of dark beard beneath the lower lip could almost have been mistaken for a shadow in the dim light of the room.

"Major Brinton informs me that you have a request," he said. His voice was clear and pleasant but, like his stance, proclaimed his authority.

"Yes, sir," Dougherty's voice felt as quivery as that of a schoolboy called to task by a teacher. The papers rustled in his hands. "If I may be permitted a brief explanation, sir, perhaps my request will make more sense."

"Very well, but we have only a few minutes."

Dougherty opened his notebook and, without thinking, pulled his chair closer to the desk. McClellan drew back a fraction, but said nothing. Quite shamelessly Dougherty invoked Major Brinton's participation in the autopsy to lend it greater authority. He explained how identification of the corpse had led to the connection with Major Allen, using the *nom de guerre* he had heard Pinkerton use in Frederick.

"Do you imply, Lieutenant, that Major Allen is incriminated in the death of this man?"

"No, sir," Dougherty said. He had thought about this, and had decided that the best approach was to put this into the context of something that Pinkerton would want to know. "My concern is quite the opposite. Major Allen may not even be aware of what has happened and might wish to learn of it. I did think in Frederick that he and the stranger had business with each other and that it was confidential."

There was a knock at the door and the same Lieutenant entered.

"General, sir, you wished to see Colonel Key immediately upon his arrival. He is here."

"Thank you, Lieutenant." He turned to Dougherty, "Lieutenant Dougherty, if you will excuse me for a moment, we will continue our conversation shortly."

"Of course, sir," Dougherty said, and rose to leave.

"No, no. Stay where you are. I shall see Colonel Key elsewhere. Please remain here until I return."

Dougherty was left alone. He had drawn his chair quite near the desk during their conversation. Now he found himself looking at the papers which lay right before him. Reports, letters, maps, telegrams, notes written on scraps of paper and letters on high quality stationery. One of the latter, partially completed, caught his eye. He was so surprised by what he saw that he could not refrain from reading it. It was a letter to a Mr. Aspinwall, and it would certainly have been the source of some embarrassment had it fallen into the wrong hands. In it the general accused the President of treasonous despotism in regard to the military draft. He called the draft legislation "servile war," and the emancipation of the slaves the destruction "of our free institutions." These words coming from the commander of the Army of the Potomac in defiance of his commander-in-chief could hardly be construed as full loyalty.

Dougherty had just leaned back in his chair as the door opened abruptly and a distraught McClellan entered. He walked around the desk as Dougherty jumped to attention. He took his seat and told Dougherty to do the same. His already fierce brow was drawn into an even more foreboding frown, and he sat in fuming silence for what could not have been more than a few seconds, but to Dougherty seemed an eternity. He was sure that the anger was directed at him and that McClellan knew he had read the letter.

"Lieutenant, I hope that you will always be cognizant of the need to avoid associating with fools. Of course, that may prove impossible. They are over us, under us and on all sides. They distort military considerations to accommodate political expediency and subordinate truth to pie in the sky aspirations."

"Yes, sir," Dougherty said, with no notion of what he was agreeing to, but agreement was usually the best policy when dealing with generals.

"Were I a political man, Lieutenant, rather than a simple soldier, I might be tempted to act contrary to the constraints of duty."

In view of the letter Dougherty had just seen on his desk, he could only imagine to what lengths McClellan might go if he did not feel "constraints." Whatever Colonel Key had reported, it had certainly put a bee in the Young Napoleon's bonnet.

"We have achieved a great victory. We have driven the enemy from our territory. We were overwhelmingly outnumbered, but we prevailed. Now some would have us rush forward before we can recoup out losses. Military men are told not to be political. Perhaps someone must tell the politicians to abandon the illusion that they are militarists."

He stopped speaking, perhaps realizing his imprudence.

"Well, Lieutenant, you were speaking of Major Allen. Please continue."

"Yes, sir. I think it quite possible that the death of this man would be of interest to Major Allen. If the dead man is one of his subordinates, then he will wish to know what has happened, and he might be particularly interested to learn that he was not a normal casualty of war."

"Very well, Lieutenant. I shall refer your concerns to Major Allen and he may contact you if he sees fit. In the meantime, please leave one of the drawings of the man and I will see to it that it is delivered to Major Allen."

Dougherty had hoped for something more, but he was in no position to argue with the commanding general. He left the picture, thanked him for his kindness, and took his leave. Even before Dougherty left the room, McClellan was back at work on something else and had, Dougherty was certain, already dismissed his request. He would have to find some other way to get the information that he needed.

In Keedysville Dougherty found Miss Collingwood back at the hospital, but just as icy as when she had left the preceding day. Any comment Dougherty made was greeted with an evenly voiced, "Yes, Lieutenant," and a prompt response in action, but there were no more smiles — at least not for him. Of Althea Naylor there was no sign, nor did anyone speak of her. Dougherty could not keep his mind off his failure with McClellan. Should he have approached him in another manner? Had he failed to present his arguments strongly enough? What else could he have said? And all the while, in the back of his mind, lurked the deepest disappointment — the frustrating thought that on the morrow they would depart for Harpers Ferry and the investigation, in spite of all his desires, would almost certainly fail. All in all, it had not been a pleasant day.

Chapter XV: The Truth?

Merely corroborative detail, intended
to give artistic verisimilitude to an
otherwise bald and unconvincing narrative.
    W.S. Gilbert (1836-1911)
    The Mikado, Act II (1885)

[September 26, 1862]

    The brisk morning was without frost, but carried the crisp reminder that Fall was conducting tentative skirmishes against a Summer not yet suspecting its own inevitable retreat. The air was clean, the light wonderfully bright, and the leaves of some of the oaks and maples were just beginning the shift to the paler green that presages the advent of the glorious golds and flaming scarlets yet to come. Under other circumstances it would have been a day to delight Dougherty's heart. But for now it was not. They were to remove to Harpers Ferry. It was no great distance geographically, but it meant a world of difference, with new responsibilities, and no way, so far as he could see, to solve the mystery.

    In the hospital, in spite of departure preparations, they still had normal duties to complete before tending to anything else. Most of those who had begun to heal were on the road to final recovery, which might yet prove a long, difficult journey for most of them. Those who had fallen into decline moved inexorably to their end. Private Dolan showed signs of improvement. He was at first sorely disappointed at the further amputation, but youthful resilience stood him in good stead. Where many might have dwelt on their misfortune, Dolan was speaking of recovery, intent on accomplishing it by sheer force of will if nothing else

    Dougherty kept an eye open for the arrival of Miss Collingwood, which he expected, and for the arrival of Mrs. Naylor, which he did not. It was ten o'clock before the expected arrival occurred. Mother and daughter arrived in simple dresses and clean white aprons, ready for the day's work. The coolness of the day before had vanished. She entered the church and came straight toward Dougherty.

"Lieutenant Dougherty, how pleased I am to see you. I am informed that the Second Corps is departing today, and I was fearful that I might not have the opportunity to thank you again for your kindness toward me these last few days. I apologize if I have seemed less than grateful, and I hope you will forgive me. I am so appreciative of the confidence you placed in me and the instruction you gave me. I truly hope that we will meet again."

With unselfconscious directness, she extended her hand to shake his. He was beginning to realize how much he had come to enjoy her company and how much he was going to miss her.

"Oh, Miss Collingwood, you have no need to apologize. I could not begin to thank you for all you have done and I will never forget how wonderful you were with Private Dolan. No one could have done more. You are a talented nurse and these men will always remember you — as will I." Surprised at the strength of his own feelings, he hoped he had not embarrassed her.

She began to say something, then paused as though her voice had for a moment failed her. Where the conversation would have gone from there, Dougherty never knew. They were interrupted by a voice he knew all too well.

"Well, Doctor Dougherty... how nice to know that you are not too hard pressed to find time for idle chatter. Does this mean that you have solved all your mysteries and have nothing further to do? Do you need employment? If so, I am sure that I can oblige."

Major Briggs had arrived. He would also be going to Harpers Ferry, his work at Pry's mill handed over to others.

"And how are you... Miss Collingwood, is it? I much enjoyed the pleasure of your company at our delightful supper just a few days ago. How are your parents?"

She told him briefly that she and her mother had been working with the wounded, and then she withdrew. Dougherty could see the puzzlement in her eyes at the way Briggs had addressed him.

"You have heard the news, I imagine," he said after she had left. "The Second Corps — most of it, I should say — will be moving to Harpers Ferry today. Some of us, however, will not be so fortunate. We will be remaining here for some time, until more of our patients are sufficiently strong to be removed to the general hospitals. Doctor Houston, of course, will be going with the Corps. I shall remain here in his place, and you will be remaining as well... you and Steward McBrien both. Here is a written copy of your orders."

He placed an envelope into Dougherty's hand, and waited for him to open and read it. He was to remain in Keedysville under the command of Major Briggs for a period of time defined only as "so long as should be required for the wounded currently hospitalized in Keedysville and vicinity to be sufficiently recovered as to be removed to a hospital to be established at Smoketown or to a general hospital well behind the lines." The order was issued by Major Jonathan Letterman.

The possibility of further investigation now remained open, but it would have to be done under the watchful eyes of Major Briggs; and, if past experience were any guide, Dougherty was certain that he could abandon any hope that Briggs would make things easy. In fact, if Dougherty's misgivings about him proved true, he could expect not only lack of cooperation but purposeful obstacles as well. He might even find himself in danger of being the next victim.

There was now no need to prepare for Harpers Ferry, so he continued with his duties, and for the next hour successfully avoided Briggs, who was consulting with Surgeon Houston about the transfer of command.

Miss Collingwood reappeared to assist and, with obvious hesitance, asked if Major Briggs had some reason to dislike him.

"His comments at supper on Monday and the things that he said today concern me. In fact, had I not been present at dinner on Monday I would probably have thought that his words today were directed at me, as though I had been wasting your time. I hope that my presence did not create a problem for you. I would never want that to happen."

"Have no fear of that," he said. "Major Briggs has disliked me ever since I joined this regiment. Perhaps it is just his way of dealing with new surgeons. Please don't be concerned. Your presence has never been a problem to me."

"He is so intent upon exercising his authority," she said.

"That is the way of the army." He smiled. "He is like the man in the Bible who knows what authority is, and who is accustomed to saying to a subordinate, 'Go, and he goeth.' And I am his subordinate."

He said nothing of his deepest concern, since Miss Collingwood had no knowledge of the details of their discovery of the body. In fact, Dougherty reminded himself, he had only some ill-defined suspicions. Perhaps unfair suspicions, since a trocar going missing in a makeshift hospital on a field of battle was nothing unusual. He wanted Briggs to be guilty of nothing, but the doubts still gnawed at him.

It was early afternoon when Steward McBrien came in search of him.

"Lieutenant, ye have a visitor, and he says he wants to see ye outside and that ye're to go with him."

"Go where?" he asked, thoroughly puzzled.

"Ah, sure and he didn't tell me that, sir. Just told me ye're the one he wants to see and I was to send ye to him. He acted, indeed, as though I ought to consider meself lucky to be told even that much... a poor, insignificant type such as meself. He's as tight lipped as a clam and, I'd say, as slippery as an eel. Dressed in civilian clothes and all impressed with his own importance. Do ye want to go see him, sir?"

"Thank you. Please tell him to come in if he wishes to see me," Dougherty said.

"That I shall, Lieutenant." He went off with a smile, obviously pleased that Dougherty had not allowed his military rank to be insulted by yielding to the stranger.

The man who followed McBrien into the church wore his sense of self-importance like a stage costume designed to attract the attention of everyone in the audience. His thumbs were stuck in the band of his trousers, his sack coat opened to display a broad expanse of vest. The watch chain stretched tight from one vest pocket to the other, like a reinforcement for the strain that his bulging belly placed upon the buttons. A sloppily tied green cravat clashed with the checkered shirt surmounted by its detachable collar, once white but now a dingy gray. He did not merely walk. He planted his feet as though each step were a challenge to be met or a battle to be won, daring anyone to get in his way. He carried his head high and looked about, asserting his right to be there, even though no one seemed interested enough to contest it. He had the bulbous nose and vein-crazed cheeks of a man who likes his whiskey. The dark beard was untrimmed, and his piggy eyes swung about, in search of something criminal, some nefarious plot it would be his joy to reveal.

He was of a "type" that Dougherty had seen before and had little trouble recognizing. In Philadelphia he had dealt with policemen of all sorts, and this was a sort that had never appealed to him, one of those hired toughs who enjoys having a way to justify his bullying. He would later learn that the stranger had once been a policeman in Chicago and had left that to take up a job with Mr. Pinkerton's Detective Agency.

"Are you Dougherty?" he asked.

"Do you have a name?" Dougherty asked in turn. "If so, the best way to present yourself would be to announce it and then state your business. Also, feel free to call me either Lieutenant Dougherty or Doctor Dougherty, whichever comes more easily to you, or, if you prefer, you can simply say, 'Sir.'"

Dougherty wondered if he had been foolhardy. This was a man not prone to take kindly to correction. At the same time, he was gratified by the smile that now beamed from McBrien's face. The visitor was a man who persuaded with a cudgel, not allowing logic to make even rudimentary demands upon his mind. His face grew crimson and his lips tightened into a hard, straight line; his fists clenched, their knuckles white with tension. Then common sense overcame him — or the fact that McBrien looked like he would not be averse to dealing with him. When he answered it was with barely concealed anger, yet his words were civil, even if grudgingly spoken.

"My name is Thomas Hanson... *Mister* Hanson, that is. Major Allen would like a word with you... *sir*...," he let the word hang in the air for a moment. "He says you're to come with me now."

"I shall be pleased to consider it," Dougherty said, "I will speak to Major Briggs about the need to leave my post. How long do you expect that I will be gone?"

"That's up to Major Allen," he said.

"And just where is he, Mister Hanson?"

"Sharpsburg."

"Sir," said McBrien, "I'd be pleased to accompany ye, if ye like." Hanson's face darkened still further, but his gaze never left Dougherty.

"I would be glad for it," Dougherty said and went to find Major Briggs. He was in the shed that was their operating room, in process of setting up his surgical tools in the event they should be needed. Doctor Houston had already left and Major Briggs was in full charge. Dougherty told him what he wanted. He was not pleased.

"Excused from your duties again, Lieutenant Dougherty? Do you ever do anything except gallivant around the countryside on private business of your own while everyone else tries to fill in the spaces created by your absence? On whose orders this time?"

Dougherty did not think that was exactly fair. The time he had spent with Major Letterman was certainly all in the line of medical duty. The time he had spent on the puzzle of the dead man was far less than the hours he had spent caring for the sick and wounded. His association with Major Brinton had, after all, been at Major Briggs's orders. Yet, he was not foolish enough to argue. He told him about the arrival of Hanson, and that he was expected to report to Major Allen. He was not in the least mollified.

"Major Allen? Another of your endless line of majors! I'm getting sick and tired of this. What authority does he have to summon you? Where is this Hanson? I want to find out just what this is all about and by whose orders he acts. A civilian you say? What authority has he to come here and demand the presence of one of my officers? I suppose this is still to do with your nonsensical investigation?"

Together they returned to the church, where McBrien and Hanson stood near the front door, neither speaking, each taking the measure of the other. Major Briggs lost no time on civilities, but got right to the point of Hanson's authority. Hanson was as sullen with the Major as he had been with Dougherty, but almost smirked as he reached into a pocket and extracted an envelope. With a show of deliberation that was almost insulting, he withdrew from the envelope a sheet of paper, unfolded it, handed it to the Major and then waited with an air that defied him to contest what he found therein. Briggs looked at it, lifted his eyebrows in surprise, and handed it to Dougherty.

It was a note signed by Major E.J. Allen, written in the form of an order to Dougherty to report to him immediately, giving General McClellan himself as the authority for the order. Major Briggs's displeasure hung heavy in the air.

"Well, Lieutenant Dougherty, it seems that whenever you have something to do, you are promptly removed from it, and each time by higher authority. What do you have planned next? Shall I expect to receive a presidential proclamation on your behalf permanently emancipating you from the control of your superior officers? Go! Go! And as soon as you have completed whatever it is, I expect you back here. Do you understand that? Perhaps then we can discuss your real duties. It would be a novelty, one of these days, to see you do something that resembled the activity of a physician."

He turned on his heel and left. McBrien, without seeking permission, said that he would bring the horses around to the front of the church. Hanson, smug faced, walked out the front door, went down the steps, and mounted a horse that he unhitched from the fence. He said nothing further, but, overflowing with poorly contained impatience, awaited McBrien's return. That did not take as long as Dougherty expected, and they were soon on their way to Sharpsburg.

As it happened, that was not where they went. Dougherty would learn eventually that what the men of the Secret Service said and what they did were not always in total conformity. They followed the

Boonsborough Pike, crossing the Antietam at the Middle Bridge, but turning southward along a narrow road long before they ever reached the town. They had gone perhaps a quarter of a mile, when they turned again, this time west, and followed a road hardly wide enough for a single carriage. This brought them to a house, beyond which a narrow lane curved off into the woods. This they followed until they came at last to a sizeable clearing in which were a number of mid-sized wall tents. Near them a mixed bag of civilians, soldiers, and some who may have been either, were talking, laughing, and enjoying the pipes and cigars whose blue smoke circled gently and then slowly dissipated into the still air.

As they approached, one man caught sight of them, stamped out the butt end of a cigar, and came toward them, a smile upon his face and a hand held out in friendly greeting. He was totally oblivious of their guide, whose glare extended to him as much as to them. That disposed Dougherty almost immediately to like the man.

"Lieutenant Dougherty, is it?" he asked and, without giving him time to do more than nod, he went on, "Thank you for coming. Would you care to dismount here? Major Allen will be with us shortly. May I offer you some coffee?" His tone was more suited to the drawing room than the campfire.

"Yes," Dougherty said, "I am Lieutenant Dougherty and this is Medical Steward McBrien. To whom have we the honor of speaking?" They dismounted and another of the group came and took the horses, hitching them to a rail.

"John C. Babcock, at your service, gentlemen," he said. He led them toward a makeshift table knocked together from scrap lumber (or at least lumber that had become scrap once the army laid its gentle hands upon it) at which were set some folding canvas stools. He sat them down, left them, and was soon back with some battered tin cups of the ubiquitous beverage, the army coffee that could clear the mind, blear the eyes, and melt the enamel off teeth.

John C. Babcock was a young man, quite a dashing figure. Thin, athletic looking, full of energy, he seemed constantly on the alert, as though he were about to be assigned a task of some moment and had no doubt about his capacity to carry it out. Whether he was a civilian or a military man, Dougherty had no way of knowing, but he was part of Pinkerton's Secret Service. His dress was rakish. He wore a light blue jacket with a row of brass buttons stretching from neck to waist, where the jacket ended. Its upright collar gave the impression of a military uniform, but bore no insignia. None of the buttons were buttoned, making him too casual for the army. Beneath the jacket was a tan vest and a bright red shirt. From a wide, black belt with an impressively large brass buckle hung a sword, the real article and not one made for ceremony. His flat-crowned, broad brimmed, black straw hat sat at a jaunty angle. Even as he talked he kept an eye on everything and everyone around him.

He was jovial, easy going, and quite clever in his effort to interrogate them without seeming to do so. However, Dougherty did not intend to speak to Babcock or anyone else, and then find himself being bidden a fond farewell before seeing the elusive Allan Pinkerton. From McBrien, Babcock got nothing either, even though he was as bright and cheerful as ever. McBrien had long since mastered the fine art of speaking endlessly without saying a thing.

They had been there almost an hour when they heard the sound of a horse. It emerged from the narrow lane, its rider apparently having come some distance if one could judge by the dust on both him and his mount. Dougherty remembered him from Frederick, how he had glared at them in Mr. Gerhard Dietrich's establishment. He was no friendlier now. The brim of the derby shaded the eyes, the black cigar was clamped in the corner of the unsmiling mouth. They were about to meet Major Allen.

Or were they? He surely saw them, but simply rode on past, dismounting at a tent some yards away. He tossed his reins to one of the men and entered the tent, its flap falling shut behind him. Babcock excused himself and followed. They waited. Nothing happened; nothing was said. Dougherty decided that this was a ploy designed to impress them with his importance. In that case, they might try a ploy of their own. He caught McBrien's eye and they both headed for their horses. Immediately one of the men headed for Allen's tent and scratched on the flap. Babcock popped his head out, saw them preparing to leave, ducked back inside, and then was out like a shot and headed toward them with a grin. Dougherty didn't know what Major Allen thought of their move, but Babcock obviously enjoyed it.

"Major Allen will see you now," he said, as though they had just arrived and had been put to no inconvenience whatsoever. He turned to the tent, clearly expecting them to follow.

Inside, Major Allen sat at a folding desk, absorbed in the papers which lay upon it — or at least wishing to seem so. There were camp stools available, and he looked up, waved McBrien and Dougherty to take a seat, and said to Babcock, "That'll be all, Johnny." Babcock, the smile still on his face, withdrew, pulling shut the tent flap as he did so. Apart from camp desk and chairs, there was nothing else in the tent. Wherever Major Allen resided, it was not here.

From among the papers on the desk, he recovered a letter and the drawing that Dougherty had given to McClellan. He said nothing, just looked at the sketch and read the letter. This was not the first time he had seen it, and it was only a single page in length, so he hardly needed to review it so closely. He was, Dougherty could see, something of an actor, wanting to keep them in suspense and, perhaps, make them just a bit nervous. At last he looked up, examining first McBrien and then Dougherty as though trying to recall in what rogue's gallery he had seen them before. Dougherty looked at him the same way.

"Ye're Lieutenant Dougherty," he said, "And who's this ye ha' wi' ye?"

He introduced McBrien and waited to see what would come next. Allen looked again at the letter and the drawing. Finally he spoke.

"So ye've discoovered a dead man, eh? Such a discoovery these days must ha' held all the novelty o' findin' a road apple on a racetrack. Why did ye think that I might be interested?"

"Are you?" Dougherty asked.

His eyes narrowed, his face reddened. Dougherty waited. Finally he said, "Aye, I am. But why did ye think of it?"

"Because we saw you with this man less than two weeks ago in a public house in Frederick, not far from the hospital. You met with him there."

Dougherty saw recognition dawn on his face.

"Ah, yes! So ye were. I ken ye now. I remarked yer presence when fairst I arrived there. Wha' de ye expect t' lairn from me, then? Why've ye come here?"

"That, sir," Dougherty said, "is simple enough. I was after the identity of the man. The circumstances surrounding his death tell me he was not a battlefield casualty. Once we have his identity, then perhaps we can find out how and why he died."

"D' ye fancy yerself a detective, then, Lieutenant?" he said with a snort of barely suppressed laughter, his tone all amused condescension.

"In a fashion, I am, sir. I was employed in Philadelphia as a police surgeon and I have learned a thing or two about the techniques of investigation."

"Then tell me just what ye've lairned thus far about this particular death." He spoke the words as though they were a challenge.

Beginning with the discovery of the body, Dougherty told him what they had found and what they had surmised. He explained how their inferences, made from simple observation and from the autopsy, had left them in no doubt of the fact that he was not a Confederate soldier. He told him how they had made use of the talents of Frank Schell and Alexander Gardner and had thus arrived at the present meeting. When he finished, Allen sat in silence until, at last, begrudgingly, he acknowledged that they had been fairly successful — for amateurs!

He questioned them closely, and they told him what they could. They did not refer to their suspicions about Major Briggs, nor to the trocar missing from his surgical kit, but they did tell him that a trocar was the fatal weapon.

"I'll admit I'm impressed by yer ingenuity, but I feel compelled t' warn ye of a difficulty. There are things, Lieutenant," he said, "that ye are in no position to know aboot. Much that we do is of a confidential nature, and ye canna' possibly consider it yer business."

"That may well be Major," Dougherty replied, "but I think you may need my help. I think you would very much like to know how this man died, and I can find an answer — unless you already know and have no need of my services. If so, then I would like to have some answers so that I can resolve the issue and make a report of the matter to Major Brinton for his report to Surgeon General Hammond."

"Hammond, ye say? How does he come into this?"

Dougherty told him of the Major's role in the post-mortem and his interest in the progress of the investigation, leaving him with the impression of a much deeper interest on the part of the medical department than was the case. But, he thought, why not? Major Allen liked intrigue, why not offer him some?

"Perhaps, Lieutenant, ye *can* be of some sairvice t' me," he finally conceded. "We're constantly pressed fer time, and the investigation o' this mon's death would place yet another strain upon our resources. Ye're already embroiled in the thing, and ye may be in a position tae conduct an investigation, the results o' which ye can then report tae me. Let me explain."

It was an interesting tale. The dead man was an agent of the Secret Service, although Allen merely spoke of him as a "friend of the Union." His name was Arthur Elgin. He was a physician, a Virginian, who had been in the regular army from his graduation from medical school until two years before the war began, serving in the southwest and, for a time, in California. After his resignation from the army, he had developed a thriving medical practice in Richmond and was perfectly content in what he did. He had not been active in the political debates prior to the outbreak of hostilities, but when that time came he realized that his sympathies were fully with the Union and he decided to seek a commission as a regimental surgeon in a northern unit. Consulting with no one, he left Richmond for Washington to offer his services. Some former army friends in the capital, however, prevailed upon him to remain where he was and to serve the Union from there. He went back to Virginia and found that his absence had not even been remarked and that he was still considered a loyal Virginian. He did not seek a commission in the Confederate Army, but remained in Richmond, where he took a position as a civilian surgeon in the Chimborazo hospital, where he had contact with men and officers of every part of the army. He proved an astute observer and a capable supplier of military intelligence.

"More recently, just wi'in the last month, he sent word of a suspicion that bothered him. He'd haird reports of a spy, a pairson who was supplying information to the South and false information t' the North, false troop movements and false numbers and the like. When ye saw him in Frederick, he was there t' see me and t' say that he was on the vairge of findin' oot the identity of the spy. He had taken a serious chance in crossin' intae Maryland, but he thought t'was warranted by the seriousness o' the situation. He promised t' report back t' me wi'in a few days. I never saw him again."

"Did he give you no clue to the identity of the person?" Dougherty asked.

"He had his suspicions, or so he said, but he was not of a mind tae reveal them until he had some evidence. I had the impression that the object o' his suspicions may ha' been someone he knew fairly well and that made him hesitate all the mair t' incriminate him. He thought he would be able either t' verify or t' disprove his suspicions wi'in nae mair than a few days."

"And you have learned nothing further?"

"Nothing," he answered, "I did ha' some ideas, but nae mair than what ye might call a conjecture. I'd be not surprised tae lairn that he might ha' suspected some medical acquaintance, possibly from his days in the military. As it happens, we were ourselves, for other reasons, in search of a man who might have a medical connection — a man who seemed a serious danger. In any case, it's all uncertain."

"What can you offer us beyond conjecture?" He was being all too careful in what he said, and Dougherty was sure that there was more that he was holding back. He was also beginning to suspect just where the information given by Doctor Brownson to that Washington detective, had been sent.

Allen did not answer immediately but sat in thought, trying to make a decision. It was obvious that he did know something more, but did not want to reveal it.

"Do ye truly think ye can discover who killed him?" he asked.

"It's possible," Dougherty said, "but not likely if all I have to go on is what we have found so far. There are some thought provoking indications, but without something more I fear that we will proceed no further."

He sat, eyes downcast, elbow propped on the desk, chin cupped in his hand, fingers stroking his beard. Then he made up his mind and picked up a leather dispatch case which had been propped against a leg of the desk. He took out and unfolded a single sheet of paper, and perused it carefully, almost as though he had never seen it before. He handed it over. It made no sense at all. There were five columns of groups of letters.

```
HXWAT  ZHWJW  GRYII  EIIGI  VDEGX
UDJYL  KWIEO  IZTOJ  PTAGN  OXSUO
OZLVS  EINNP  RNTCH  JIXVC  TIUIF
MYMTC  FUHUF  GSKHD  OISVG  OBYTV
TYJEM  KKFRI  TICLC  LDUVX  UZGQW
ZY
```

It was a cipher, or so Dougherty assumed, but of ciphers, he knew precisely nothing. If Allen had any fears about revealing this paper to him, they were, he could have assured him, totally unfounded. He didn't know what the letters meant and had no notion of how to find out.

"What does it mean?"

"We ha' nae yet deciphered it," he said, "but ha' nae fear, we shall... we shall. Have ye seen aught like it before?"

"I have not." He handed it to McBrien. Allen's muscles tensed and he made a move, as though to snatch the paper back, but then thought better of it and relaxed, waiting while the Steward looked at it with no more comprehension than Dougherty.

"It means nothing a'tall t' me, sir," he said and handed it back.

"I'll give ye a copy of it," the Major said, "If ye decipher it, ye can tell me what it says."

He said it with a straight face and a voice that oozed sincerity, but Dougherty had the uncomfortable feeling that it was something of a joke. Without some instruction in ciphers, Dougherty could make nothing of it, and he knew that. But he did not argue. He thanked Allen and promised to do his best. Allen had already given him some interesting information and it could do no harm to have a try at the cipher. At least they now knew who the dead man was, where he had come from, and what he had been doing in the tavern in Frederick. It was possible that on the basis of that much information they could learn a great deal more than Allan Pinkerton was willing to give them credit for.

"I wish ye good cess," he said, "I'll be waitin' t' hear from ye. I'll report to General McClellan that ye've been here and that ye lairned from me what ye wanted t' lairn. Is that so?"

"Yes," Dougherty said, "I will let you know what else I learn."

"Then, if ye'll wait a wee bit, I'll ask Babcock t' make ye a copy o' this bit o' paper and ye can take it wi' ye. My thanks fer comin' t' see me."

They were dismissed. As they left, Allen called Babcock into the tent and in a few minutes he was back with the copy. He handed it over and Hanson appeared with the horses in tow. He took them as far as the Boonsborough Pike, where, without a word, he pointed eastward, turned his horse, and left.

They were sure Pinkerton had held back information. He had given only as much as he thought necessary to satisfy their curiosity and to comply with whatever orders General McClellan may have given him in their regard. Dougherty was fairly certain that the encoded message was authentic, but he was equally convinced that Pinkerton had no intention that they should ever succeed in deciphering it. No doubt he was already laughing at them.

When they arrived at the hospital, Miss Collingwood and her mother had already departed and they were welcomed back by Major

Briggs who reminded them of all that remained to be done before the day ended. Later, Dougherty found time to pen a short note to Major Brinton, telling him in summary of what they had learned and expressing the hope that on the next day they could meet.

It was well after dark by the time they retired for the day, but Dougherty's mind was so active that he knew it would be some time before he would sleep. He sat by the light of a candle, smoked a cigar, and puzzled over the slip of paper. Where would one begin?

```
HXWAT  ZHWJW  GRYII  EIIGI  VDEGX
UDJYL  KWIEO  IZTOJ  PTAGN  OXSUO
OZLVS  EINNP  RNTCH  JIXVC  TIUIF
MYMTC  FUHUF  GSKHD  OISVG  OBYTV
TYJEM  KKFRI  TICLC  LDUVX  UZGQW
ZY
```

He could think of nothing apart from simply substituting one letter for another, one alphabet for another. That thought drew his attention to one particular set of letters — the group in the first position of the fourth column, "EIIGI." What letters could he substitute for those three I's? What if they were to substitute for the letter "D"? He would then have "EDDGD" and that might make "E" a substitute for "A" and "G" a substitute for "E," making "EIIGI" translatable as "added." Of course, that would make the combination of letters at the top of the preceding column (GRYII) a word which had to end in a double "D." He could not think of one.

What if the letter "I" really stood for "E"? Then the combination of "EIIGI" might be a word such as "geese," provided that "E" stands for "G" and "G" stands for "S." Of course, that would make the preceding combination (GRYII) equal the combination "S??EE" and all that he could think of to fill it in was the word "spree." That gave him two words in a row: "spree geese." They were words, but not words that made much sense, unless there was a nefarious plot afoot to steal the geese in the area and smuggle them off to the South. He was getting nowhere. He finished the cigar, blew out the candle and sank into a deep, deep sleep.

Chapter XVI: A Major Difficulty

The atrocious crime of being a young man...
I shall neither attempt to palliate nor deny.
   William Pitt, Earl of Chatham (1708-1778)
   Speech, *Hansard* (March 2, 1741)

[September 27, 1862]

   Dougherty awoke, his mind a jumble of letters, as though a printer had taken trays of fonts and tossed them all in a heap in the middle of a dark room, leaving him to put them to rights again, so that if properly assembled they would spell out a message so urgent to his welfare that he could not afford to abandon his project until it had been completed.

   It was a day of surprises, starting with the arrival of Doctor Naylor. Like so many of the other hospital sites, his, too, had been closed and the patients moved elsewhere. He was reassigned to Keedysville, that being the hospital nearest his home. Dougherty was glad to see him. He had known him less than two weeks, but war accelerates all things, and he already felt as though he had known him for some time.

   "Doctor Dougherty, it is good to see you again. It seems that we will be working together for a few days at least."

   "I look forward to it, Doctor Naylor" Dougherty said, and meant it. He found him pleasant company and appreciated his learning. But there was a touch of guilt, too, in that his welcome was due in part to the hope that his presence would lead to a visit by his wife.

   "Today will be quite busy I have been told," he said. "Major Briggs informs me that some of our patients are leaving, but will be replaced with others whose recovery is uncertain and who cannot bear the rigors of transfer even as far as the hospital at Frederick."

   He proved correct. Much of the morning passed in triage. They sent to Frederick those who were recovering, but who would most likely be discharged from the service or sent home for convalescent leave once their wounds had sufficiently healed. Others — those whose wounds were serious but after recovery should not result in permanent debilitation — were prepared for transfer to Smoketown. Those whose recovery seemed all but impossible would remain and they could expect the arrival of some more before the day was over. The number of patients might decrease; the intensity of the care required for the rest would increase.

The morning was dreadfully busy. Dougherty saw Naylor from time to time in the course of their duties, but with no chance for conversation. Miss Collingwood and her mother, like everyone else, were caught up in attention to the patients. McBrien worked with Dougherty for a while, but then was sent by Briggs to see to the condition of the shed behind the church, since the increased numbers of serious cases would almost certainly lead to further surgery.

The morning brought one great disappointment. A cavalryman arrived with a message from Doctor Brinton:

Dear Dougherty,

Like you, I am subject to orders. My presence is required in Washington. I leave today. I hope that your investigation will proceed apace and will reach a happy conclusion. I am still interested in the results with a view to the inclusion of the case in the museum. If I can assist from afar, do not hesitate to call upon me. I remain

Yr. Obdt. Servant

(Signed) Major J. H. Brinton

Keedysville, Sept. 27, '62

5:30 A.M.

P.S.

Yours of yesterday just arrived. Congratulations. At least he now has a name. Best of luck with the code. Perhaps you might be well advised not to place full and complete confidence in *all* that is told you by E.J.A.? However, judge as you see fit.

J.H.B.

Dougherty's heart sank. With Major Brinton gone, he was left to the tender mercies of Briggs and the influx of patients provided a perfect excuse to curtail his other activities without Briggs's seeming to have any ulterior motive.

By early afternoon, patients had begun to arrive and their condition was all that they had been led to expect. Some might recover, but they were ones whose wounds were most disfiguring and their time in Keedysville was intended to help them come to grips with the despair they must have felt at their condition. Of the others who arrived, almost all would probably, in the end, succumb to their wounds. Dougherty found this the most disheartening aspect of the practice of medicine — the daily proof of mortality, the reminder that the physician's struggle to sustain life may enjoy its victories, but that, in the end, death always wins. It is like being a general who wins one battle after another, but in the depths of his heart knows that he can only lose the war.

The events of the day were for the most part a sad cataloguing of war's horrors. There was, however, one situation that served to open Dougherty's eyes to new medical possibilities and also showed him something of the extent of Doctor Naylor's learning.

Private Carl Wentz of the Seventy-second Pennsylvania had fallen in the cornfield, his first and last battle. Miss Collingwood was changing his bandages when both Naylor and Dougherty happened by. She asked them to look at his wound. He complained of an unusual pain, a burning sensation throughout his left arm, but without sign of rash or inflammation. Wet dressings gave some relief, but the pain continued. Naylor asked him what had happened.

He had been loading his rifle, his left arm extended to hold it, while with his right he was about to slam home the ball with his ramrod. A bullet entered his left arm six inches above the interior condyle of the humerus and exited two and a half inches above that on the postero-internal face of the arm. It nicked the artery and he saw the blood spurt. He turned to go to the rear but was overcome by pain and fainted. Hours later he awoke. The bleeding had ceased. He was taken to a field station. He could not move the arm below the shoulder and from the elbow to the tips of his fingers he had no tactile sensation. By the next day he had a severe neuralgic pain in his hand, the paroxysmal pain that follows the course of a nerve. Within another day he could move the elbow and the thumb, but there had been no further improvement since, and the constant pain was severe.

His hand was congested, purplish in color, with the fingers (all but the thumb) not voluntarily moveable and curled as though into a claw. There was anaesthesia and analgesia in the palm and palmar face of the fingers and on the dorsum of the hand, but not the dorsal face of the fingers. The motion of the arm was normal above the elbow, but flexion of the wrist was severely limited.

The wound had damaged the ulnar and median nerves, but the prognosis was obscure. Most nerve damage was beyond the powers of medicine to control and was always unpredictable.

"What would you suggest, Doctor Dougherty?" Naylor spoke as a colleague, not as a teacher asking a student or as an experienced physician checking on a younger.

"It seems that the damage to the ulnar and median nerves has left an interosseal palsy. If it does not correct itself, there will be permanent damage and distortion of the fingers." Dougherty thought for a moment. "As to treatment, we might use a splint to correct the flexion and prescribe treatment by energetic passive motion."

"What does that mean?" Miss Collingwood asked.

"I'm sorry," Dougherty said. "It means that the bullet damaged the nerves above the elbow, so the effect is felt from there to the tips of the fingers. This caused a paralysis of the muscles which control the motion of the fingers. A splint might stop the fingers from curling. Passive motion means having someone move the paralyzed muscles to help restore their strength. It is a matter of exercise to alternately stretch and relax the muscles. A nurse could do it, or the patient could be taught to do it for himself."

"There is still another possibility," Naylor said. "Are you familiar with the work of Duchenne on the medical use of electricity?"

"I've heard of it," Dougherty said, "but only in general terms."

"You might find him interesting. Do you read French?"

"I do. I studied it on my own, so my pronunciation might reduce a Parisian to tears, but I can read it."

"I have his book, *De l' Électricité Localiseé*. You must visit and look at it. He has obtained excellent results through Faradization of the muscle. Unfortunately, we lack the equipment here, but it can be employed once the patient is taken to a general hospital."

His knowledge was impressive, and Dougherty was flattered to have been treated as an equal. To his own surprise, he found that he was somewhat piqued at Miss Collingwood's obvious admiration for Naylor. Then from behind them he heard the voice of Major Briggs.

"Experimental measures! Bah! Passive motion has proven itself time and again. That is what we will use. The electrical currents we will leave to the telegraphers."

As Dougherty turned to leave, Major Briggs said, "May I have a moment of your time, Doctor Dougherty?"

They moved a few paces, enough to be out of earshot of the others.

"Lieutenant Dougherty, I am aware that you are much occupied with thoughts of that body. A dead man on a battlefield should not cause such preoccupation, but I realize that you are young and you lack experience of warfare. I realize also that your head has perhaps been turned by the attention given to you by Major Letterman and Major Brinton, not to mention the fact that you have breathed in the rarified atmosphere of the Commander of the Army, and that may have gone to your head. You seem to think that you are now independent of the normal chain of command of this army."

"Sir, I certainly do not..."

"Just listen, Lieutenant," he said. "If, when I have finished, I have not made myself clear, you will have ample opportunity to seek fuller elucidation."

"Yes, sir."

"You are a good doctor. I have seen that. You lack maturity, but that is beyond your power to change except through the normal expedient of continuing to live, which I hope you shall make every effort to do.

"Your first duty is to the patients in your charge, and it is to them that you must devote your time. I expect you to do that. I will not go so far as to order you to have nothing further to do with the case of the dead man, but I warn you that your time here is to be spent in your assigned duties. You can get back to your mystery when our work in Keedysville is done. You cannot give the living your full attention if your thoughts are on some other problem. Do I make myself clear?"

"Perfectly clear, sir," he said through clenched teeth.

"Then nothing more need be said. Please be so kind as to continue with your normal duties."

"Yes, sir."

Dougherty was so angry he could hardly think. Young indeed! As though youth were a reason to doubt ability or to ignore facts not admitted by a more seasoned eye. He would do his duty! He had been doing it. But he could and he would find time to pursue the matter of the dead man. Besides, Pinkerton's concern about the death of Arthur Elgin might be a matter of some moment for the progress of the war. In either case, whether the motive for the murder involved matters of state or just human greed or jealousy or perversity, the mystery remained to be solved and the discovery of the perpetrator could not be ignored. Abstract justice means little if never put into practice. It was hard to accept Briggs's orders, when Dougherty was full of misgivings about whether Briggs had violated the most sacred ideals of his profession and had actually taken lives.

"You seem preoccupied, Lieutenant," Miss Collingwood said, appearing suddenly at his side — or perhaps not so suddenly, since he had been lost in thought and she may have been there for some time. "I hope I do not intrude."

"I beg your pardon," he said. "I am afraid my thoughts were occupied with things other than what is immediately before me."

"Is anything wrong? Can I be of help?" Her concern was genuine and it occurred to Dougherty that he might take her into his confidence. He decided not to. She could probably not help with the murder investigation or with the Major. Discussing the matter with her would be a selfish attempt on his part to feel better by sharing a burden that would only be an added concern for her and would still not improve Dougherty's situation.

"It is nothing," he said, "Just a difference of opinion between me and Major Briggs. That is nothing new."

"I am sorry. I think he fails to appreciate all that you do for these poor soldiers. Perhaps I should speak to him about it."

"Oh, please, Miss Collingwood, do not even think of doing such a thing! I truly appreciate your desire to help, but any intervention would be misunderstood and might turn his displeasure toward you as well. It's best to let things run their course and hope that time will heal all."

How platitudinous, he thought. But what else was there to say?

The day went on. Patients were tended to, but there was so little that could be done. Earlier days had been hard, but many recovered. For most of the present patients there was nothing but palliative care and inevitable death.

It was early evening when Dougherty and Naylor left. Dougherty had turned down Miss Collingwood's offer of help, but it occurred to him that Naylor might have some advice to offer.

"Doctor Naylor," he said, "might I have a moment of your time? I know how tired you must be, but it would be deeply appreciated."

"Of course. How can I be of service?"

Suddenly Dougherty was full of misgivings. What if his suspicions about Briggs were unfounded? What evidence did he have? Briggs was a doctor. He was in Philadelphia at the time of another murder. He had access to a trocar. These things proved nothing, now that he thought about them. In fact, each of those points could be made about Dougherty himself. Perhaps he was making a mistake, but he decided to say only part of what he thought.

"I'm sure you have remarked that Doctor Briggs and I are not on good terms. I have no argument with his surgical skills. He is a fine surgeon and I can learn much from him. The problem I'm having now has to do with the body that I asked you to transport to the mill."

"Surely that does not totally surprise you," he said. "In the midst of the chaos of the battle and its aftermath, that one death may very easily seem of small significance to many people, not only to Major Briggs."

"I realize that," Dougherty said, "but what he fails to realize is that we have other obligations as well. This man was brutally killed, and there is an obligation to justice and to society — an obligation to protect the living by finding a killer."

"That is true enough," he said, "but what do you think can be done to fulfill that obligation in the present case?"

"I don't want to disobey the order of a superior officer," Dougherty said. "At the same time, there must be some way in which I can continue this investigation. I think that it is of importance not only to the abstract concept of justice, but perhaps to the welfare of this army. I have some reason to believe that this death is related to disloyalty on the part of the person responsible."

"What in the world has led you to that conclusion?" he said. He was clearly surprised — perhaps even skeptical. Even as Dougherty had said it, he realized that he may have gone further than he intended.

"It was merely a thought that had occurred to me. Perhaps I should not have mentioned it, but I am sure that I can trust your discretion."

"Of course you can," he said, "but perhaps this is neither the time nor the place to discuss this. There is also the fact — and I hope that you are not already weary of hearing it — that you are somewhat new to this and your youth may still need tempering by the discretion of a more experienced officer.

"I am sure this is not an answer which satisfies at present; and, perhaps, you should *not* be satisfied with it. In any case, tomorrow is Sunday and perhaps you can request the Major to allow you some time. If so, would you care to visit me at home? I should be pleased to have your company, and I know that Mrs. Naylor would welcome the opportunity to fulfill her promise to show you her flowers. We can discuss your question at length. Even if we cannot solve your dilemma, we might at least discuss Duchenne's work on electricity, so our time would not be lost."

"I would be honored," Dougherty said.

"Fine, then. I shall expect you in the early afternoon, if that proves satisfactory. If not, you can send me a message."

On the way to his quarters Dougherty was handed two letters that had been delivered earlier in the day. He ate, then lit a candle and prepared to enjoy the letters — one from Mrs. Kiley, the other from his mother.

Mrs. Kiley's told him how thankful she was that he had been spared injury in the fighting and mentioned that she had again enjoyed the company of Doctor Brownson for dinner. Dougherty smiled at the thought of their attraction for each other. A more unlikely pair he would not have imagined. One comment aroused his curiosity.

> By this time I am sure that you will already have heard from Doctor Brownson. He expected to write to you directly from New York. He went there a few days ago, just after he received your recent letter. He hoped to discover something that could help you. But I fear that none of this is news to you, since you have certainly heard from him by now.

What had Brownson hoped to find in New York? He would have to wait for his letter.

His mother's letter held news both unexpected and frightening. It worried Dougherty to realize that the war was now touching much too close to home.

> Our dear Son,
> We are happy you did not get hurt. The news is a horrer for a Mother to read even when her son is not hurt. People here is upset about the conskripshun. There was riots in Mauch Chunk and women was put in jail. Up in Archball there was worse. The enrollers come for names and was chased by women of the town. They come back with two soldiers and a possy, but they got throwed out too. The enroller went to the mine office. The women come for him and he said he would give them the list and not come back. His friends wouldnt let him give the list so the women said they will teach him a lesson and they got holt of him and took his trousers away. Then another enroller come to try again. He had more soldiers and even a priest to talk to the crowd. There was a riot and a soldier shot one poor man dead. Some buckshots in Jeansville and Coleraine and around Hazleton is said to be goin to do something against conskripshun. Any way we are proud

of our son in the army and we think that he is doing right. We pray for you all the time. Your Father and your brothers and sister send love and prayers as does
>Your loving Mother,
>Rose Dougherty

There was no end to the violence. The comedy of the enroller having his trousers threatened became all too easily the tragedy of the man who had been killed.

He was about to end the day and give himself over to sleep, when he heard a knock at the door and a voice saying, "Lieutenant, Dougherty... are ye awake, sir?"

It was McBrien and Dougherty saw immediately that he had something of importance. He came in and closed the door behind him.

"Lieutenant, sir, I've found something that I think ye must know about." Dougherty couldn't tell if it was good news or bad, but there was no doubt of its seriousness.

"Of course ye recall, sir, the fact that the trocar belonging to Major Briggs had gone missing?"

"I do."

"Well, sir, this afternoon I was told to go to the operating area and to inspect everything and to do whatever needed to be done to assure that it was in good order. That's where I spent me time, and that's the reason ye haven't seen hide nor hair of me for the latter part of the day."

As usual, he got at things in his own way. Dougherty couldn't decide whether he did this out of excitement or a desire to give a complete picture or because he was blessed with a natural flair for the dramatic. Perhaps all three. In any case, Dougherty did not interrupt.

"Sir, there in the room, of course, was Major Briggs's own surgical kit, the one he always uses... the one with the missing trocar. Except, sir, the trocar is no longer missing but is back in its usual place!"

What now? Dougherty was relieved to realize that this might remove his suspicions in regard to Briggs. On the other hand, it threw everything right back into mystery.

"You are certain, are you, that it is the same one?"

"Well, sir, I should think so... One trocar looks much like another, of course. Though, now that ye ask, I mind that there was something of a scratch on the handle of the Major's as I've noted when cleaning it in the past. In fact, it was an odd mark, a dent in the wood like a small curve, like somebody'd pressed it with the tip of a thumbnail. T'was not so easy to see, but easy enough to feel. I hate to say it, but I was so surprised to see the thing that I didn't think to look fer the scratch. I don't know why I didn't ask meself the same thing."

"Can you examine it again tomorrow without making your interest seem unusual?" Dougherty asked.

"I'm sure I can, sir. I'll find some reason to do it. I'm sorry I didn't think of looking when I had it in me hand."

He was annoyed at himself, but had no need to be. When you see a thing in its place, you make assumptions. Dougherty had little doubt that it was the same trocar, but he would feel better if that could be verified.

Chapter XVII: The Pleasure of the Company of Ladies

I used your soap two years ago;
since then I have used no other.
    Punch, Vol. 87 (1884)

[September 28, 1862]

The buzz of bullets, the shock of shells, the cries of the wounded, and the need, in the worst of circumstances, to treat men in their last extremity are experiences Dougherty wished upon no one. He had lived through them all and that, one might think, should have confirmed him in his courage, given him the confidence to face any trial. But there are other sorts of crises, and he had come to one of them — he had to confront Major Briggs with the request for permission to visit Doctor Naylor. He steeled himself for the onslaught as, in the early morning light, he approached Briggs in the church where he was already hard at work.

He thought through the most tactful way of stating his request and had marshaled every argument as carefully as a general aligns his ranks for battle. His courage was mustered up and he had the assurance (perhaps unfounded) that even his voice would not betray him by quivering. All wasted effort. Briggs's first salvo took him in a totally different direction

"Lieutenant Dougherty," he said, "how gratifying to see you up and about at this early hour. You slept well, I trust? No sudden calls to join other commands? No messages from the commanding general or the president?"

"Yes, sir."

"From which then? From the commanding general or from the president? Or was it just from some wandering major?"

"No, sir," Dougherty answered, "none of them. I meant merely that I slept well." His carefully marshaled thoughts were about to desert him.

"I'm glad to hear it. You will appreciate that sleep when I tell you that you may not get any this night. I will be occupied this evening and I intend to leave you in charge of the hospital. I think that you can manage that without lasting harm, or is my confidence in you misplaced?"

"Yes, sir," Dougherty said, "I mean, no sir. I mean your confidence is not misplaced."

"Good. In the meantime, Lieutenant, since you will be busy tonight, you may consider yourself excused until five o'clock."

"Thank you, sir," Dougherty said, marveling at how much effort is wasted on plans destined never to be used and mustering up courage that is not needed.

From McBrien he learned that, although the Irish Brigade was now in Harpers Ferry, there would be a Mass not far from Keedysville. A priest, a Jesuit from Frederick, had come the day before. Mass was scheduled for half past eight o'clock.

This priest was an old man, frighteningly frail as he approached the altar, veiled chalice in hand and on his head an overlarge biretta that had slid down almost to the level of his eyebrows. The sermon, unfortunately, was a learned exposition of a doctrinal point, without engaging the interest of a military congregation. Returning to his place after Communion, Dougherty saw coming toward the altar Miss Genevieve Collingwood and her parents. Her eyes were downcast, and her head modestly bowed, so she did not see him. Until then, it had not occurred to Dougherty even to think about her religion, but it gave him great pleasure to realize that they had this in common.

After Mass he did not at first see them, but as the crush of bodies thinned, there, among the civilian carriages, in a black buggy, sat Miss Collingwood between her parents. Motioning McBrien to follow, he made his way through the crowd. They reached the buggy just as Mr. Collingwood was about to turn the horses in the direction of Boonsborough. It was Miss Collingwood who first saw them and called out a greeting.

"Lieutenant Dougherty! Steward McBrien! How are you today? What a pleasant surprise."

Her father leaned back on the reins and brought the horse to a halt, while her mother said, "You will recall Lieutenant Dougherty? And this is Steward McBrien. They have both been so very good to us these past few days."

"Lieutenant, it is a pleasure to see you again. Steward McBrien, I am honored to make your acquaintance." His face took on the proportions of something that might have been a smile — a subdued one, to be sure, but a smile nonetheless. In a man whose countenance was so habitually serious, this might be almost the equivalent of blissful exhilaration. "I have heard much this past week about the good Doctor Dougherty and his medical skills, as I have heard also about the kindness of Steward McBrien."

"I had not expected to see either of you today," said Miss Collingwood, "My mother and I will not be coming to the hospital again until tomorrow."

"How wonderful," Dougherty said.

"It comes as a relief to you then, Doctor Dougherty, not to have my wife and daughter at the hospital for a day?" said her father.

"Oh, no, sir, I did not mean that... It won't be any relief to me at all, because I will not be there today either... Rather, I meant that Miss Collingwood and her mother deserved a day of rest after all they have done."

"Oh, I see," Mr. Collingwood said, and this time there was no mistaking the smile. Miss Collingwood laughed, and Dougherty realized that it was not from her mother that she had inherited her sometimes disconcerting sense of the comical. The Collingwoods had a previous engagement, so they parted with mutual assurances of seeing each other at the hospital. Most surprisingly, there was from Mr. Collingwood the indication of a forthcoming invitation to visit them at their home.

McBrien and Dougherty, both free for the day, went straight to Dougherty's quarters to get back to deciphering the message Pinkerton had given them.

Dougherty placed the message on the table. He had noticed in the past that, when foiled by some problem, it helped to set it aside for a while and when he returned later the solution fairly leaped out at him. This was not one of those occasions. It remained as obscure as ever.

```
HXWAT  ZHWJW  GRYII  EIIGI  VDEGX
UDJYL  KWIEO  IZTOJ  PTAGN  OXSUO
OZLVS  EINNP  RNTCH  JIXVC  TIUIF
MYMTC  FUHUF  GSKHD  OISVG  OBYTV
TYJEM  KKFRI  TICLC  LDUVX  UZGQW
ZY
```

He explained to McBrien what he had tried to do, substituting the letter "E" for the letter "I" and the results it had produced. They tried other combinations, but none helped. Finally, they made a list of all the letters and the number of times that each occurred. By far the most frequent was "I," occurring 14 times, the next "T," occurring 9 times, and then "G," "O," and "U," each occurring 7 times. All of which was a most annoying exercise in eyestrain, since mistakes were so easy to make.

It occurred to Dougherty that it might help to know which letters occurred most frequently in the use of the English language. How could they determine that? Their solution was not very scientific, but it offered some hope. The whole message contained 127 letters. They should find some uncoded texts in English of the same or similar length, and see what letters were most frequent. The only book available was Dougherty's copy of Smith's *Handbook of Surgical Operations*. It was no easy task. The book was filled with medical terminology, and they wanted passages with a greater proportion of frequently used words. They settled on two:

> Blood may be taken from any of the superficial veins, but those of the neck, the bend of the arm, and at the ankle, are generally selected. The patient may be seated...

And:

> The seton may consist of a few threads or a full skein of silk, according to the effects desired; or a piece of tape, or, what is now more frequently used on account...

Again they counted all the letters The original message contained 127 letters; the two samples contained 128 and 129 respectively. They arranged the letters in each according to frequency. In the first passage, the letters most frequent in order of occurrence were: E, T, A, N, H, O. In the second, they were: E, O, T, A, N, S. They also found that many letters occurred infrequently and some did not occur at all. In the first passage, those which did not occur were: J, Q, W, X, Z. In the second, they were: B, J, V, X, Z. In the first text, two letters occurred only once: G and V. In the second text, those which occurred only once were: G and Q. They agreed, then, to take G, J, Q, V, X, and Z as the least frequently used.

Then they hit an unexpected problem. They counted the occurrences of letters in the encoded text and found that there were *no* letters of the alphabet which failed to occur! Every letter was used at least once. Furthermore, although the letter "I" had occurred most frequently, for the most part all of the other letters seemed to occur between 4 and 7 times. This did not seem normal. How likely was it that a message with only 127 letters could have used every letter of the alphabet at least once, and most of them between 4 and 7 times? After a morning of fruitless labor, they arrived at the only possible conclusion. This was not a message in which there was a simple substitution of letters, and so they were on the wrong track entirely. They had eliminated what would have been the easiest of the possible solutions, but were left with no idea where to begin with another.

Not knowing what to do next, they decided to come back to it later. Behind the church they rekindled the fire and ate bread and bacon with good hot coffee. By then it was time for Dougherty to make his visit to Doctor Naylor.

It was just before one o'clock when he turned off the main road in the direction of Willowbrook Hall. The day was beautiful, this side road almost deserted. He allowed the horse to amble along at its own pace. Alternating patches of cool shade and bright sun gave the world a dappled serenity that was totally at odds with the idea of warfare, and for a moment it was possible to think that it was after all a matter of the idealized posturing that the country had once thought was all there was to war. The birds chirped, their flashes of bright color caught the corner of his eye in almost every bush and tree along the way. It was, all in all, a perfect day, its perfection assured by the knowledge that he was about to meet her again.

He looked up from his daydreaming and realized that he had almost passed right by the archway, with its "*Ut languores curarent*" as a reminder that this was a Doctor's estate. Dougherty wondered what the motto of the Doughertys could have been — or if they had ever had a motto. Surely they must have. Every Irish family he knew laid claim to descent from a king or two. Old Ireland must have been a regal nation indeed.

For the first time he saw Willowbrook Hall in the full light of day rather than in the deepening twilight of his first visit. Some imposing structures are like the wonders one sees on a stage; in the subdued light of the theater and at a distance they are impressive, yet are nothing but paint and canvas when seen close up in the glare of the sun. Not so Willowbrook Hall; it was, if anything, even more impressive when held up to scrutiny in the full light of day.

In the drive, off to the side of the house, was a well polished black buggy, hitched to a handsome horse. Another visitor? Or was someone preparing to leave? His heart sank. His appointment was, after all, with Doctor Naylor, and Mrs. Naylor may well have had a previous engagement to keep — although Naylor had given him reason to expect that she would be here.

"Hello de', Gen'l, suh." It was the same boy and the same smile and again he went off with the horse. The butler opened the door and took his hat.

"Good aft'noon, Lieutenant Doc'ty, suh. Doctah Naylah's 'spectin' y'all. Please come with me."

They went, not to the formal parlor he'd seen the last time, but to a smaller one, where Naylor and his wife rose to greet him.

"Ah, Lieutenant, so you were able to come after all. Was Major Briggs overtaken by a moment of kindness... or perhaps I overstep myself with that remark."

"The matter was easier than I expected. The Major had his own reasons for changing my hours, so I am free for at least a portion of the afternoon."

"Good afternoon, Lieutenant," Althea Naylor said.

He bowed over the outstretched hand, thrilled at the coolness of her fingers. But it was the smile that captivated him and the violet eyes, like the depths of a still, dark pond on a moonlit night.

"Lieutenant, I must apologize," the doctor said. "You may have noticed my conveyance in the drive. Just moments ago I received an urgent message that the elderly grandparent of a neighbor has been taken quite ill, and I must attend him. If, as I suspect, it is no more than a case of severe indigestion, I should be back in almost no time at all. Even if it is only that, I must still see him; at his age it could be more serious. In the meantime, I know that you will not be disappointed if Althea entertains you until I return. You may see her flowers."

He left and Mrs. Naylor invited him to sit at the other end of her sofa. It was rather a long sofa (Dougherty was both disappointed and relieved to discover its length), and they sat turned slightly toward each other. The buggy set off down the drive, sounding as loud as if there were two carriages, but Dougherty's attention was all upon his hostess.

"How wonderful that you have been able to visit so soon," she said. "We were so pleased to have had you with us last week. I hope you enjoyed your evening here?"

Of course, he had already sent a brief note of appreciation, but he thought to demonstrate his courtliness with a gentlemanly response.

"Mrs. Naylor, after the dinner at your table, I had no desire to eat another since."

"Oh," she said, "was it then so hard on your digestion?"

"No, ma'am, I did not mean that at all. In any case, not harder than army fare... That is to say, it was not so very hard at all... I mean, it was really quite delightful..."

Her laughter rescued him, but he felt the heat in his cheeks and hoped that he could redeem himself. Unfortunately, he did not have the opportunity. At that moment the door opened and the butler announced that the other guests had arrived. Other guests?

"Thank you, Tully." She turned to Dougherty, "I know you will be pleased to renew some of your acquaintances from our recent dinner."

Tully stepped aside to admit the Misses Caroline and Benedicta Holbrun. Dougherty could not recall which was which, but he hoped to avoid displaying his ignorance by addressing both simply as "Miss Holbrun." Fortunately, as Mrs. Naylor mentioned their names, the direction of her eyes gave him all the clue he needed to sort them out.

"You recall Miss Caroline and Miss Benedicta Holbrun?" Mrs. Naylor said, "Lieutenant Dougherty was kind enough to accept our invitation to spend some time with us this afternoon. Perhaps we can hear something of his adventures in the military."

That, he feared, would not take long. His adventures to date had consisted of one shot fired at him half in jest and the battle itself; and since his experience of the latter was limited to dressing wounds, it seemed that he was doomed to have but little to say that a lady would wish to hear. Miss Caroline and Miss Benedicta sat expectantly, their lips again pursed in mild distaste, as he groped for something to say. Fortunately, salvation arrived in the shape of Tully, who had come to report to Mrs. Naylor that someone named George had finished and they might now see the flowers.

"Thank you, Tully," Mrs. Naylor said. "I recall, Lieutenant, that you had expressed a desire to see the flowers. George, our gardener, was making things more presentable for us. Miss Caroline and Miss Benedicta, I know you are both lovers of horticulture and would enjoy accompanying us."

They went around the house, past the line of trees and shrubs which hid all the outbuildings. Dougherty was surprised to see a rather large conservatory. A rectangular structure with walls of glass panes, those near the top clear, those lower down on the sides either steamed or whitewashed on the inside. His surprise must have shown on his face.

"It is rather large, isn't it," she said.

"I have heard of conservatories," he said, "but I have never seen one before."

"They are certainly not common in this area either," she said. "We built it just a few years ago. I am not aware of any other nearer than Washington or Baltimore. Let us go in, I think you will enjoy it."

They were surrounded by lush greenness. Plants of every description, many with broad, heavy looking leaves, created a sense of the tropics. That impression was accentuated by the heat. The glass let in and retained the heat, accentuating the humidity. The result was an atmosphere that fostered an abundance of flowers not otherwise available in that part of the country. Some of them quite exotic, at least to Dougherty.

"I so much enjoy the flowers," Mrs. Naylor said. "My husband has also become interested and has found me many that I could not have acquired on my own." She showed them any number of colorful blooms whose names she recounted, most of them unfamiliar to Dougherty. Botany — apart from plants with medicinal properties — was not among his talents. No matter. On this occasion his interest was more in the horticulturist than the horticulture.

The place had been laid out with great care. There were shelves upon which stood crockery pots for the plants, all arranged to the best effect for the display of colors and foliage. At the back was a work area, with a long potting table. Next to it were a number of wide, flat, shallow boxes in which were creeping vines, probably for transplant to appropriate locations near the house, their small, erose leaves a pleasant green. There was a large collection of pots of all sizes and the various tools of the gardener's trade, although Mrs. Naylor proudly informed them that she herself did much of the gardening here. It gave her great pleasure, and she was justifiably proud of the beauty she produced — an example of which had graced the center of the table during their recent dinner. There were watering cans, trowels, shears and, against one wall, a large wooden bin of dark, rich potting earth which Mrs. Naylor informed them was mixed with various other elements, depending on the plants being grown.

It was impressive, but Dougherty was glad at last to escape the humidity when Mrs. Naylor suggested that they repair to the house.

Back in the parlor were the refreshments — a pitcher of cool lemonade and an urn of flavorful hot coffee. There were china plates, gleaming silverware, fresh linen napkins. Trays of small sandwiches and cakes had been laid out in a pattern as pleasing as that of the plants in the conservatory.

They sat and talked and, for the first time, Dougherty paid attention to the conversation of the Misses Holbrun. At their last meeting, he had thought that both were as sour as lemons, their conversation critical, their tone condescending. But, then, his attentiveness to them had been minimal, and he had, in all honesty, given them little reason for an exchange of ideas, or even the normal pleasantries. This time, at the prompting of Mrs. Naylor, they began to speak of the things which had occupied them since last he had seen them. They too were caring for the wounded, along with their mother and Doctor Holbrun. They lacked the loquacity of their father and the pleasant countenance of their mother, but there was no doubt that their concern for the wounded was heartfelt, even though their expressions never quite lost that sourness. Miss Benedicta began to recount the sad case of a young Confederate officer for whom she and her sister had cared.

"He is from Richmond," she said. "His family lived quite near our father's medical school, although we had never known them. The young man had been grievously wounded at South Mountain, but his men brought him with them to Sharpsburg. He grew weaker and finally was too weak to go with the army when it withdrew to Virginia."

"He is such a nice young man," Miss Caroline added. "He was engaged to be married to a young woman, but was having second thoughts. He had lost his right arm, and had convinced himself that it was wrong of him to hold her to an engagement made when he was whole.

"When he was wounded, the friend who had helped him knew his fiancée and he got word to her even before the last battle."

"She and her mother," Miss Benedicta said, "gained permission to pass through the lines to see him. She was so persistent in expressing her undying fidelity, that she renewed his hope for their future together. She was obliged to return almost immediately to Richmond, but she left him full of hope and ready to make the best of his condition."

"How wonderful," Dougherty said.

"It was," said Miss Caroline, "but just yesterday he received word that they had gotten to Richmond, but just a short distance from her home their carriage overturned on a steep hill and she was killed."

The eyes of both the Misses Holbrun filled with tears as they finished their tale, and so did Dougherty's. They sat in silence, until at length Mrs. Naylor spoke.

"Lieutenant Dougherty, we were interrupted as you were about to recount for us some of your own adventures in the army. I wonder if you might tell us something now? In fact, my husband has spoken to me of the dead man that you discovered on the battlefield. Perhaps you might tell us something of that?"

He was caught completely off guard. Earlier he had hesitated to speak because he felt that he would have too little to say. Now he hesitated because he was not certain just how much he wanted to reveal. All three of the ladies sat in wide-eyed anticipation of what he would say; he could not disappoint them.

Without speaking of the identity of the dead man or of the actual weapon, he told them the story, omitting all the details that a non-physician, let alone a lady, would be likely to find offensive. To his delight, not only the Misses Holbrun, but Mrs. Naylor as well, paid close attention.

"How was the artist able to produce a lifelike image, if the model was actually dead?" asked Miss Caroline.

"In part, Miss Caroline, he used his imagination and produced more than one image, until he finally produced one that we recognized. It turned out that Medical Steward McBrien and I had indeed once seen the man."

"If you think it not unseemly, Lieutenant, might we at some time see that image?" Mrs. Naylor asked. "Perhaps it is someone local, someone, God forbid, that we may even know."

"I hope not," Dougherty said, "but I do have with me a copy of the drawing and it is not offensive to view. It is no more than a drawing of the man's face, quite lifelike."

He reached into his pocket and withdrew his notebook with its copy of Frank Schell's rendering. He offered it to her.

She took it somewhat warily, but it sparked no sign of recognition. She held it out to Miss Caroline, who accepted it with evident curiosity and then shocked surprise as she turned it around and looked at it.

"Oh, no! This cannot be! It is impossible!" The drawing slipped from her fingers, and Miss Benedicta took it before it could fall to the floor. She, too, looked with the same fright and shock. "Oh, Caroline, this cannot be!"

They were both surprised and grieved, and Dougherty realized that either they knew the man or they had mistaken him for someone else.

"Do you know him?" he asked.

"For a moment I was sure that I did," said Miss Caroline, "and apparently so did my sister. But it cannot be. The man of whom we are thinking could not have been here. He lives in Richmond and is still there, so far as we know. Of course, he could have joined the Rebel army, but I do not think that he did."

"What was his name?"

"I doubt that you would know him," Miss Benedicta said. "He was an acquaintance of my father, a doctor named Arthur Elgin. We came to know him a few years ago when my father was attempting to establish the medical school in Richmond. Much as the resemblance caught us both by surprise, I do think that we must be mistaken."

"Have you not seen him since you left Richmond?" he asked. "Is it possible that he could have come to this area for some reason?"

"Oh, no, he has not been here at all. If he had, I'm sure he would have come to see my father, and we would have known of it. I cannot conceive of his being the victim of a violent death. He is, I think, the most unwarlike of men." Miss Caroline hesitated, her voice filled with emotion. "Oh, how I hope it is not he! Can you discover the truth of the matter?"

"I hope so," Dougherty said, "but there is still much to be learned, and even now you and your sister are not certain of the image being that of Doctor Elgin. If it should turn out to be he, I will let you know."

He did not mention that he already knew the name, because that would mean having to explain how he had come by that knowledge. Nor did he want to pain them. He was also filled with uneasiness at the notion that there might be some connection between the dead man and their father.

"Perhaps it is not he. I am sorry that the likeness caused you such distress."

Clopping hoofs and jangling traces signaled a carriage in the driveway. Minutes later Naylor came in.

"It was as I expected. The gentleman was suffering from nothing more serious than a slight dyspepsia for which I offered him a drachm of bicarbonate of soda, with an additional drachm to be taken later if needed. He would be able to avoid even that, if he were to follow the advice I have often enough given him in regard to adhering to a more bland diet. But then, who follows a physician's advice to prevent an ailment in preference to taking the medication after it has occurred?"

"Oliver," Mrs. Naylor said, "Doctor Dougherty has just shown us a likeness of the man whose death he has been investigating, and Miss Caroline and Miss Benedicta were quite taken aback, when they thought that it might be someone known to them. A doctor from Richmond named... Elgin, was it, my dears?"

"Yes," Miss Caroline said, "Doctor Arthur Elgin, a friend of our father's. But we are not sure that it is he. Doctor Dougherty is going to discover the truth of the matter, and then we will know. Of course, we will discuss it with our father in the event he has had any news of Doctor Elgin."

"I certainly hope that it is not your father's friend," said Naylor. "In any case, I suppose that we shall have to await further information. Under other circumstances, it would have been easy enough to telegraph Richmond, but not now."

To Dougherty he said, "May I see the likeness of the man?"

He took it and studied it with care. "Is it a fair likeness?" he asked.

"Quite good," Dougherty said. "He had been shaved after death, but when I saw this drawing I knew without doubt that I had seen him in Frederick less than a week earlier."

"He has rather a distinguished look," he said. "I had begun to wonder if he might be someone local, but if this image is accurate, then he is not from near Keedysville. Otherwise I think I should recognize him."

The afternoon was passing quickly, and Dougherty wanted to be sure that he was not late by even a minute in relieving Major Briggs. He suggested to Naylor that they take a moment to discuss the matters that had been the original purpose of his coming to visit. Excusing themselves to the ladies, they adjourned to his medical office.

"Doctor," Dougherty said once they were their, "I'd like to see the copy of Duchenne that you mentioned, but I am even more interested in discussing with you the difficulty that I am having with Major Briggs."

"Then let's begin with that," he said.

He appreciated Dougherty's frustration at Briggs's desire to prevent his proceeding any further. On the other hand, he did not see how this investigation could be hopeful of any fruitful results. In fact, if the victim's life and connections were in Richmond, it might prove impossible to contact those who might be able to help. As to Briggs, the most he could counsel was to bear up under it with patience, making use of whatever time he did find, and trying to do his utmost not to provoke the Major into an outright refusal of all permission to continue the investigation.

They talked about Duchenne's book. It was interesting and Dougherty hoped to be able to try some of its ideas, but in Keedysville there was neither time nor equipment. Still it was refreshing to speak with a fellow physician who was not in opposition to everything new.

When they returned to the parlor, the Misses Holbrun were leaving. Dougherty said his own goodbyes and left with the Naylors' kind invitation to honor them with another visit.

Back in Keedysville he changed uniforms and relieved Major Briggs even before the appointed hour, receiving not a word of thanks, but just the admonition to tend to duty.

McBrien was there to help, but they had little time to talk. It was late when McBrien excused himself and said that he would be back in a few minutes. When he returned, it was to say that he had taken advantage of Briggs's absence to examine the trocar. The trocar in the medical kit was totally without blemish, there was no scratch on the polished wood handle. This was *not* the trocar that had been there originally!

Chapter XVIII: The Law of the Letter

You shall see them on a beautiful
quarto page where a rivulet of text
shall meander through a meadow of margin.
   Richard Brinsley Sheridan (1751-1818)
   The School of Scandal, Act I, sc. 1 (1777)

[September 29, 1862]

Occasionally in the newspaper one comes upon an account of a dam that has suddenly collapsed, spewing forth its contents in uncontrolled fury — water that only moments before had been a placid lake is suddenly a lethal force, disdainfully sweeping away all that stands in its path. The survivors never fail to deplore the insidious unpredictability that has overcome them, allowing no opportunity either to prepare for or to avert the disaster. Yet it is a rare instance in which the collapse is truly as sudden as it seems. Most often it begins in a way so subtle as to be at first unremarkable, a tiny trickle that gradually enlarges even as the observer holds it too insignificant to merit concern; then comes the crucial moment when the full weight and force of the water's placid depth is at last brought to bear upon a weakness that cannot withstand its power and the mildly gurgling trickle becomes an elemental force beyond the power of man to dispute. Thus was the downfall of George Brinton McClellan. The trickle had begun, and even though Dougherty was one of its witnesses, he did not predict it and when it came he was as surprised as most.

In spite of his late hours the night before, Dougherty reported for duty early on Monday. Briggs had spent the preceding evening in the company of a group of officers who, before the war, had been stationed together in the West. They reminisced, bemoaned the war that had killed some of their comrades and turned others into enemies. And they gossiped. Two of them had brought back from a recent visit to Washington some information that was supposed to be confidential, but which in an army never is.

Major John J. Key was on General Halleck's staff in Washington. As Briggs told it, Major Key, after the battle of Antietam, was asked why he thought the rebel army had not been bagged completely. He said that such was "not the game." The object, according to him, was that neither side should get any real advantage, but to keep both in the field until they were exhausted and then make a compromise that would preserve slavery.

"Lincoln was informed of the remark," Briggs said, "and had Key in for an interview. The Major did not contest the truth of the report, but said he had not intended to be disloyal to the Union. Lincoln believed him, but considered it unacceptable that a commissioned officer should express such a sentiment. He had him dismissed from the service.

"The most interesting part of the whole story, is who Key's brother is. He is on McClellan's staff."

Dougherty remembered the Lieutenant at the Pry farm telling McClellan that there was a Colonel Key to see him, and how agitated the General had been upon his return. It must have been then that Colonel Key had learned of what was happening to his brother and had come to report it to General McClellan.

"Colonel Thomas Key, I should imagine, is now in some pretty hot water himself," Briggs continued. "No doubt the powers in Washington will surmise that the remarks of Major Key originated with Colonel Key, who must have been repeating the words of the commanding general. I should imagine that the Young Napoleon may be well on his way to Waterloo."

It made sense of McClellan's complaint about fools, and his scathing remark about politicians trying to make themselves militarists. Dougherty thought of the letter he had seen on McClellan's desk. There was also no disguising the fact that Major Briggs was pleased.

Briggs's real purpose in talking to Dougherty, however, was to inform him that his schedule was changed, and that he would now take charge of the hospital during the nights, beginning that very night. He would also begin taking his regular turn as officer of the day. That, Briggs said, should show how desperate was the situation, when even novices were called upon to pretend that they knew what they were doing.

"You'll be working at night," he said, "but, seeing that you are already up and might well find further rest more tedious than refreshing, you may as well carry out your normal duties today, too. After that your presence will be required only at night, barring emergencies."

Naylor's arrival that day was delayed and Dougherty was curious to see how Briggs would greet him when arrived late. But as it turned out, Naylor was quite adept at seizing the initiative. His motto should have been *carpe diem*. Before Briggs could properly fix his gaze, Naylor was speaking of his being summoned to the side of a patient — not the dyspeptic patriarch of yesterday, but a woman truly in need of his ministrations. He diverted the Major's focus from his own dilatory arrival to the medical niceties of a course of treatment. What started out as a reprimand from the Major became an academic discussion between equals. It was adroitly done. Consternation turned into consultation. Naylor's technique was worthy of emulation: Instead of hiding his tardiness, he pointed it out, he involved Briggs in a discussion of it, and he gave the squint something else to squint at. Dougherty decided he could learn more than medicine from Doctor Naylor.

Dougherty did his day's work, but kept an eye open for a chance to speak to Naylor about Doctor Holbrun and his connection to Arthur Elgin. In fact, he had earlier spoken to Miss Collingwood and led the conversation to Doctor Holbrun by way of speaking about the daughters.

"Aren't they a matched pair!" she said with a good natured laugh "I do so enjoy them, even though they sometimes wear such sour expressions. In fact, they are not really so disagreeable; they are at heart quite gentle and sympathetic, but for some reason those are qualities they prefer not to display. I can't imagine why that is. Perhaps they fear that others may take advantage of them. The sad thing is that in their protecting themselves they must also make themselves so unhappy."

"Do you know their father very well?" Dougherty asked. "He seems a pleasant gentleman. Does he still practice medicine, or has he given that up?"

"I don't know him exceedingly well, but I find both him and his wife congenial people. In fact," she said, "sometimes he can be almost too congenial, especially when he begins to tell a story from his past. He can go on at such length, describing events and places and relationships among the people who play a part in his tales, until, finally, one almost forgets what the story was about in the first place." She said it with a smile, clearly finding that foible far more endearing than aggravating. Dougherty recalled his meeting with Doctor Holbrun a week ago, and knew precisely what she meant.

"His wife is a lovely, kindhearted soul. It's a shame she didn't pass on to her daughters something of her own joviality." She paused for a moment. "Sometimes I feel sorry for Caroline and Benedicta. They seem so... lonely. But you asked whether the Doctor still practices medicine. Right now, as you might expect, he is quite active, taking care of the wounded. Apart from that, he has not practiced with any frequency since his return from Richmond, but I know that he has, as a favor, seen some of his old patients from Baltimore from time to time. He seems to have a good deal of contact with them. Actually, he seems to receive many visitors. He must have been quite a popular doctor."

"What brought him to settle here?"

"I'm not certain," she said, "but I think it was simply the fact that, even though his attachments were great in Richmond, he did not adhere to the Confederate cause. I suspect he came to Maryland simply because, although he was in sympathy with the North, he had grown much attached to Maryland through his years in Baltimore. I'm sure the decision to leave Virginia was a difficult one. Sometimes I suspect that he feels a degree of pain that his native state is following a course with which he cannot ally himself. He has no sympathy with slavery and does not favor an armed rebellion, but neither does he like to see the proper rights of the states trampled upon. These are dreadful days for so many people, full of difficult and painful decisions in addition to all the pain of the war."

Dougherty was uncomfortable when she asked, "What brings the Misses Holbrun to mind?" He recalled her reaction to Mrs. Naylor; but he said, "Doctor Naylor invited me to his home and the Misses Holbrun were there when Mrs. Naylor showed me her flowers."

"Mrs. Naylor is quite attractive, isn't she?" Her voice and expression were almost too neutral

"I suppose so," he said, "but it was her husband I went to visit. He showed me the book he had spoken of when we were discussing the case of Private Wentz."

"He is a very learned man, isn't he," she said. "My father, I know, is much impressed by him. He is so well read in so many areas, not only in medicine. He has continued to be a student, and has frequently traveled to academic meetings in New York and Baltimore and Richmond — before the war, of course. He has even been in Philadelphia on occasion."

It was past noon when Dougherty found the chance to speak with Naylor. He wondered how to bring up the topic of Arthur Elgin and his connection with Doctor Holbrun without making his interest seem suspicious. Fortunately, Naylor first broached the matter.

"Lieutenant, I think I may owe you an apology. When you told me you had found a dead man and wanted to investigate, I gave you no encouragement. Indeed, as I recall, I tried to discourage you. I was certain then that the investigation would go nowhere, and that you would find yourself either ridiculed or in trouble. In fact, I was sure you must have been mistaken in even thinking of foul play. Yet you seem to have established it as fact and identified the man, even if only to the extent that you had seen him before. Where was it that you saw him?"

Dougherty was not sure just how to answer, how much to explain, so he told him only that he and McBrien had seen him at a tavern in Frederick, but had not spoken to him.

"It is unfortunate that the Misses Holbrun were not sure of their identification. You might at least have had a name for him. As it is now, I cannot see what else can be done without going to Richmond, and that is out of the question. What do you intend to do next?"

"I think," Dougherty said, "that the Misses Holbrun were right in identifying him as Doctor Arthur Elgin. I did not insist on it yesterday. I could see that they were holding onto the hope that they were wrong. I preferred to spare their feelings until the matter can be fully resolved. But what do you think of a connection between Arthur Elgin and Doctor Holbrun?"

"I have no notion what to make of it. Doctor Holbrun is not the sort of man to ally himself with anything criminal or disloyal. He is a gentleman of the old school, a man of honor."

"I met him only once," Dougherty said, "and cannot pretend to know him, but my first impressions coincide with what you say."

"Doctor Holbrun, as I think you would quickly learn were you to come to know him better, is just what he seems." He paused, choosing his words with some care. "He is a retired medical man who relishes the opportunity of some leisure in his later years. He has been unfortunate enough to find himself at odds with his native state. All of this must be most distressing to him and to Mrs. Holbrun as well, yet both remain in surprisingly good spirits, thanks, I would say, to an innate optimism they both share."

"I am sure it must be hard," Dougherty said, "for a man of his age, retired from the practice of medicine, to be forced back into it, not by an occasional emergency but by as many emergency cases in a single day as some other physicians may see in a whole lifetime."

"Difficult as it is," he said, "he seems to take it in his stride. In Smoketown, his services will be put to full use for some time yet to come."

Smoketown, a tiny village which in the coal regions of Pennsylvania would have been called a "patch," had become the focal point of care for the wounded. It was there that Doctor Letterman had established the hospital to which would come those patients who could be moved no further. Hundreds might remain there for months to come.

"Doctor Holbrun," he said, "has made himself available there as needed — not as a contract physician but as a volunteer, so he works the same long hours we all do, but without even the recompense of a government salary. In my opinion he deserves to be commended."

Dougherty could not disagree. He pursued the matter no further, but made up his mind to talk to Doctor Holbrun. The rest of the day passed quickly, and it was mid-afternoon when he was presented with two letters. One had come by mail and was from Doctor Brownson. The other had been hand delivered to the hospital. Its envelope bore only his name. He put both in his pocket for later, rather than risk the wrath of Major Briggs, who by now was hovering everywhere at once in his efforts to be certain that the tasks of the day had all been completed and that the patients had been made as comfortable as possible. His unrelenting overseeing was as maddening as it was commendable. He also told Dougherty that he might have an hour or two of freedom before it was time for his night duty.

When Dougherty got to his quarters, he opened Doctor Brownson's letter first. His fertile mind had followed a train of thought that had not occurred to Dougherty. Brownson regularly visited New York, where he knew many people in the book stores and the medical supply houses, including the Tiemann Company. He wrote:

> Whoever used the trocar must have been surprised when it broke. Still, it probably made little difference to his plans, since the body was to be so conveniently disposed of. That should have been the end of it, except for the action of some busybody. (Allow me to congratulate you. I rejoice that you are as much a busybody as I.)
>
> It occurred to me that he might seek to replace the trocar, and leave no glaring absence in his surgical kit. He could send the damaged handle back to Tiemann and ask that they send him a trocar with a matching handle.
>
> I spoke to a friend at Tiemann and he was quite surprised because, as it happened a trocar had just been returned. It had an internal fault which had caused it to break. A replacement had been sent to Maryland. The man who filled the order was out of town for a few days. However, my friend said that as soon as he returns he will learn the identity of the person to whom the trocar had been sent, and will telegraph the name to me. I will relay it to you. He may even be able to retrieve the damaged implement itself, provided it has not already been discarded.
>
> I also take this occasion to inform you that the acquisition of this information cost me the price of a rather good meal. Now

that you are at last in honest occupation and making your fortune with the army, I shall expect a return upon my investment by having you repay me in kind when next you deign to visit Philadelphia.

The other envelope held two sheets of cheap paper. There was no signature and the handwriting was not familiar. The contents pointed to someone on Pinkerton's staff, someone who wanted Dougherty's investigation to succeed but was not in a position to act openly. Had Dougherty been pressed to name his benefactor, he would have guessed the name of Mr. John Babcock. He recalled his amusement when he and McBrien had failed to be intimidated by Pinkerton's antics. In any case, what lay before him opened up new avenues of thought.

The first sheet was nothing more than rows and columns of letters. These filled one side of the paper, the other was blank. The rows and columns were as straight and neat as if they had been ruled, the letters carefully printed.

```
  A B C D E F G H I J K L M N O P Q R S T U V W X Y Z
A a b c d e f g h I j k l m n o p q r s t u v w x y z
B b c d e f g h i j k l m n o p q r s t u v w x y z a
C c d e f g h i j k l m n o p q r s t u v w x y z a b
D d e f g h i j k l m n o p q r s t u v w x y z a b c
E e f g h i j k l m n o p q r s t u v w x y z a b c d
F f g h i j k l m n o p q r s t u v w x y z a b c d e
G g h i j k l m n o p q r s t u v w x y z a b c d e f
H h i j k l m n o p q r s t u v w x y z a b c d e f g
I i j k l m n o p q r s t u v w x y z a b c d e f g h
J j k l m n o p q r s t u v w x y z a b c d e f g h i
K k l m n o p q r s t u v w x y z a b c d e f g h i j
L l m n o p q r s t u v w x y z a b c d e f g h i j k
M m n o p q r s t u v w x y z a b c d e f g h i j k l
N n o p q r s t u v w x y z a b c d e f g h i j k l m
O o p q r s t u v w x y z a b c d e f g h i j k l m n
P p q r s t u v w x y z a b c d e f g h i j k l m n o
Q q r s t u v w x y z a b c d e f g h i j k l m n o p
R r s t u v w x y z a b c d e f g h i j k l m n o p q
S s t u v w x y z a b c d e f g h i j k l m n o p q r
T t u v w x y z a b c d e f g h i j k l m n o p q r s
U u v w x y z a b c d e f g h i j k l m n o p q r s t
V v w x y z a b c d e f g h i j k l m n o p q r s t u
W w x y z a b c d e f g h i j k l m n o p q r s t u v
X x y z a b c d e f g h i j k l m n o p q r s t u v w
Y y z a b c d e f g h i j k l m n o p q r s t u v w x
```

The other sheet was covered, both sides, in a careful hand in writing so minute as to indicate that the writer had been intent on saving paper, or on trying to emulate in penmanship the small whisper of clandestine conversation. It contained neither salutation nor valediction, but got directly to its purpose, having accomplished which, it ended.

> The rebs use a code called the Vicksburg Square, an alphabetical sheet and a key. The key is any word or phrase known to both sender and receiver. E.J.A. gave you the coded message, but didn't mention the code. We do not yet have the key.
>
> The code is simple. Suppose you wish to send this message: "The British are coming, the British are coming." Suppose your key is: "Victory now." Above the message, write the key, repeated as often as necessary, until every letter of the message has above it a letter of the key.

```
VIC TORYNOW VIC TORYNO  WVI CTORYNO WVI CTORYN
The British are coming, the British are coming.
OPG UFZRVGD VZG VCDGAU  PCM DKWKGFV WMM EHAZLT
```

> To encode the message, take the first letter (T) and look at the key letter above it (V). Find the T in the left column of the alphabetical chart and find the V in the top row. Trace down from the V and across from the T until you come to where row and column intersect. There you find the letter (O) which is used in the coded message. For the second letter (H), find where the H row and the I column intersect, and you will have the letter P, the second letter of the coded message. Etc., etc.
>
> To decode the message, reverse the process. Above the letters of the coded message, write the letters of the key. For example, take the letters of the first word of the coded message (OPG), and above them place the first three letters of the key (VIC). Trace down the V column to the letter O, then across the left, where you will find the letter T. Trace down the I column to the letter P, then left to the H.
>
> Some messages (such as the one you have) remove all breaks between words and then reinsert breaks at regular intervals. This prevents anyone from guessing even the length of the original words.
>
> There is much that E.J.A. did not tell you about A.E. It is possible that the spy he sought had been in the army, maybe in the West prior to the rebellion. This is not certain, but A.E. knew that information was being sent to a surgeon from North Carolina in D.H. Hill's division. He

> did not tell us the name of that surgeon, but he knew that he had served in the West in the U.S. Army.
> After A.E. met E.J.A. in Frederick, he crossed the lines again and sought out the N.C. surgeon, whom he knew. He told a story to explain his presence and, while with him, found a coded message which he copied. That is the message you have. A.E. thought he knew who had sent the message, so he decided to cross the lines again just after the battle. He sent a copy of the coded message to E.J.A. and promised to prove or disprove his suspicions and to report on it within a short time. We never heard from him again.

That was it. There was no indication of the sender, no key, no notion of the intended recipient. Dougherty had little time to reflect on it, because he had to begin his first night of running the hospital. During the night three patients died. The hours after midnight so often seemed to be the time to die, almost as though letting go of consciousness to fall into the comfort of sleep also makes it easier to relinquish the last grasp on life and so sink into the final sleep of death. For all three, death was a mercy. They were in excruciating pain. It was 4:00 A.M. when Dougherty was at last able to retire, so tired that he did not even think of codes or spies or anything but sleep.

Chapter XIX: The Sadness of Success

If it was so, it might be;
and if it were so, it would be;
but as it isn't, it ain't. That's logic.
   Lewis Carroll (1832-1898)
   Through the Looking Glass (1872)

[September 30, 1862]

The subdued light through the smudged window panes was just enough to bring him back to consciousness. He had the disquieting sensation of something wrong, something forgotten or left undone. Then came the flood of thoughts and questions about the things he had learned the day before. To his surprise, he was already fully dressed, boots and all. He had never undressed the night before. His watch said eight. It was the latest he had slept since joining the army. Unfortunately is was only four hours since he had fallen asleep.

He found some water, completed his morning toilet, and went in search of sustenance. He had, for a few hours at least, the luxury of doing whatever he wanted, provided he was back in time for his appointed rounds.

The first thing on his list was to visit Doctor Holbrun. He hoped to find him at the hospital in Smoketown. If he was not there, then perhaps his home would not be far away. He thought of taking McBrien with him, but decided against it. Why draw him into the sights of Major Briggs? He would go alone and risk only his own reprimand.

Before saddling the horse, he decided, for a reason that he could not have defined, to take his gun. He withdrew the charges (which had been in it for days and might have become damp), reloaded the chambers, and checked to see that the percussion caps were properly seated. Instead of taking the holster, he stuck the gun into the waistband of his trousers, where it was hidden beneath the uniform jacket. He left before Briggs could see him and assign him something to do.

It was bright and clear, the heat of the sun-warmed air perfectly tempered by a refreshing breeze. Military personnel and vehicles were everywhere, but without their former urgency. He enjoyed the alternating sunny warmth and refreshing shade as the road passed through open fields and under groves of trees, their sheltering branches spread wide overhead.

Just past Smoketown was the hospital, an encampment already large and growing larger as tents were set up in long lines beneath the glorious stand of trees, oaks and walnuts reaching up seventy and eighty feet, their overarching branches shading the canvas of the tents from the sun, whose direct rays would otherwise have heated them to a level of acute discomfort for their occupants. In the branches, so far above, birds flitted and chirped and squirrels looked down and chattered, troubled by the activity below them, the interference with their pre-winter occupation of gathering fallen nuts.

Rows of hospital tents had been set up end to end, the back flaps of each facing the front flaps of the next down the length of each line. Between the tents, a distance of about ten feet, flies had been set up so that one could pass from tent to tent under cover, almost as though they formed a corridor, one long peaked canvas roof ten feet or so in height. Each tent was about fourteen feet in width and length, its top sloping down to the four foot high walls. Within, he saw rows of cots, all occupied, as many as eight or nine in tents that would have been far more comfortable with six. An aisle ran down the center, the cots on either side, their heads against the tent walls and their feet facing the central aisle, leaving barely enough room for the staff to work. The crowding explained the flurry of activity as crews hurried to set up more rows of tents. As the temporary hospitals on the farms were emptied of their patients, many would come to Smoketown.

He dismounted, hitched the horse to a low hanging branch, and approached a tent. In front of it, seated on empty hardtack boxes, were four men, all amputees, their crutches lying across their laps or propped against the taut ropes of the tent. They smoked their pipes and spoke quietly together, now and then breaking out into laughter — an unexpected sound in such circumstances. They were in good spirits as they greeted Dougherty, happy to see a visitor even if it was just another surgeon. He asked about Doctor Holbrun, but none of them knew him. They suggested he ask Miss Hall.

Inside was a nurse, a woman of early middle age, who looked up from the patient she was tending, and then looked down again and went about her business, pausing only long enough to say, "I will be with you in a moment, Doctor."

She finished and came to the front of the tent. This was Miss Hall and she did know Doctor Holbrun. He was in Ward F. Seeing his puzzlement, she led him outside and pointed above the open tent flaps to a wreath surrounding a large letter "C."

"Each of the wards is marked," she said, and pointed. "Ward F is three rows that way." She was already back at her work as he headed in the indicated direction.

At Ward F, he passed through three tents before he found Holbrun, completely absorbed in his work. His gray hair was tousled, as though he had more than once run his fingers absent-mindedly through it as he worked. Even here he maintained his old-fashioned air with his old style high collar and tie, but his Alberts had been replaced by a sturdier pair of Wellingtons more suited to standing for long hours on the hard packed ground, and in place of a frock coat, he was garbed in a long, linen medical coat, clean but yellowed from storage, probably a remnant of his former medical practice that had not seen service for some time. However, there was nothing old or feeble about the way in which he worked. He was cleaning a dreadful wound, a gash surrounded by the dying flesh of a burn. His actions were economical, deft, completing a painful task with as little pain as could be managed. As he worked, he talked to the patient, trying to distract him from the intense agony of the process that had as its ultimate intent his healing.

He finished and signaled to a young woman to begin bandaging. He looked up, not seeming at first to know Dougherty and probably thinking he was but one more of the many doctors on duty there. Then he recognized him.

"Well, Lieutenant! Lieutenant... Dougherty, isn't it? Are you to work here? We can certainly use the help. We expect more of the wounded in the next few days. We will be glad to have you with us."

"I regret to say so, Doctor," Dougherty replied, "but I am not assigned here — at least not yet. For the moment, I am still in Keedysville. For now I am here simply to see if I may have a moment of your time. Would there be a better opportunity later on?"

"Lieutenant, if we wait until later, it will be no easier, so we may as well take the time right now. How may I help? Is this about the dead man you found? My daughters told me of their conversation with you, and how they had mistaken the likeness of the dead man for that of a former associate of mine, Doctor Arthur Elgin."

"I regret to tell you, sir," Dougherty said, "but I truly have no doubt at all that the dead man is indeed Doctor Elgin. Allow me to show you his likeness, and see if you do not agree with me."

Again he produced the drawing, unfolded it, and handed it over. He saw the shock in Holbrun's eyes. At first he said nothing, then took a deep breath, and handed it back.

"I can confirm it," he said, "That is Arthur Elgin. It surprises me that my daughters were not certain — they have seen him many times. Of course, I suppose we all tend to see what we want to see, what most corresponds to our hopes or desires."

"I think that is precisely what happened," Dougherty replied. "I was hoping that you could assist me."

"Whatever I can do, I will," he said, "although that is probably little. I am deeply saddened by this turn of events, but cannot begin even to guess how it came about. It is some time since I have seen Arthur — before the war, in fact. I thought he was in sympathy with the Union in spite of his love for his home state. But then, who could have predicted how so many loyalties have gone? When I left Richmond and came north, I truly expected that he would soon follow. To my surprise, he did not, and I later heard that he had become a surgeon at the Chimborazo hospital near Richmond. Why he should appear dead on the battlefield here, I could not possibly explain. Had he gone into a regiment?"

"No, sir, I don't think so. So far as I know, he was still at Chimborazo, but had come here for some other purpose. I never knew him, but I saw him in Frederick just two weeks ago, although I did not speak to him or even know his name. What can you tell me about him?"

Dougherty was hoping that he would want to assist, if, indeed, he knew anything. Of course, he also realized that he was running a risk. What if Doctor Holbrun were himself a spy? It is one of the unpleasant aspects of detecting — that need to suspect even the seemingly innocent.

"He was the son of a friend of mine from Richmond," he said. "His father, Randoloph, was a prosperous cotton and tobacco merchant and Arthur could have entered into the same business, but did not wish it. He was always inclined to a more academic life, and then, before the age of twenty, became enamored of the medical profession. He was apprenticed to a local doctor and later studied in New York. His mother... She was one of the Barstows, a rather wealthy family of planters, with a sizeable estate in the Shenandoah Valley... Her father had come from Georgia years ago, where they made their fortune and decided to invest it in land and businesses in Virginia, where the family has been for two generations now. I don't know what their background was in England, or precisely when they had come to this continent, but we all know that Georgia had been a penal colony in its origin. Of course, I never saw anything in the Barstow family to indicate that there was a criminal element in their past. The whole family always had been, to my knowledge, the very model of virtue... as was Arthur... In some ways I was surprised that Arthur had gone into the army at all... I mean in the West, in the Federal army. He was the least violent of men. Got that quality more from his mother than his father, I should think. The father was quite a brawler in his early days, before he married Lily Barstow — she cured him of that. Well, of course, Arthur was a doctor, so I suppose that even his duties for the army could hardly be considered violent — just the opposite, one should think. I remember hearing him speak of his distaste for inflicting death. On one occasion there was a hanging in Richmond. It was a well known ne'er-do-well, a fellow who had hurt more than one person and had finally killed someone in a fight — a very vicious fight — something everyone had known that he would do sooner or later. Even then, Arthur was forceful in his denunciation of the penalty. He was quite convincing in his arguments that the legal killing of a killer was a way of bringing society to the sad brink of becoming the very sort of miscreant that it wanted to eradicate from its midst. A most non-violent man... Of course, if his own ancestors had been part of a penal colony, that might account for the strength of his opinions in this regard. Yet, as I said, I would not have suspected the Barstows of descent from a violent criminal. If there was a crime involved in their coming to the New World, I should think that the ancestor who had committed it would have been one who had fallen into a crime of weakness rather than anything more unsavory. Of course, that would have been years ago, well before our independence from England. But, in any case, he chose medicine and was quite pleased with his choice."

His words flowed like the Meander from one generation to the next, but Dougherty presumed that he was now back on the topic of Arthur. He could see what Genevieve Collingwood had meant when she spoke of how hard it was to keep track of a story told by Doctor Holbrun. He went on at length, weaving a tale that moved in and out of the present and past, wrapped finally into an intricate tangle, a Gordian knot, whose unraveling, even if it did not lead to the rule of all Asia, should yield at least some tangible reward. At length he did come to the conclusion of his story and Dougherty was left with the task of having to loose from its bonds any kernel of information imprisoned within.

"I much enjoyed my conversation with your daughters on Sunday," Dougherty said. "They are certainly to be commended for their kindness and courage in caring for the wounded. As we are both aware, it is no easy task."

"They are wonderful girls, the both of them." Dougherty could detect the note of parental pride. "They are so tender hearted, a quality which makes this work even harder."

"They seemed much taken with the beautiful flowers in Mrs. Naylor's conservatory. Even though they must have seen them many times, they were kind enough to view them again so that I could see them. I suppose that they have known Mrs. Naylor for some time?"

"Not at all," he said, "just since our return to Maryland. Of course, they had long ago known Oliver, when he was just a lad, some years younger than they. Not that they knew him very well... Actually it was I who knew him best. My mother's family had lived near his. In fact, it was through them that we first met the Barstows. We were, of course, in Baltimore for years, which is where I had my practice — a wonderful practice, not only insofar as patients were concerned, but also in my great good fortune in taking on some fine young men as apprentices. It was that experience, as I believe I may have told you, that led to my desire to establish a medical school in Richmond... We had had almost no contact with Oliver for many years now, ever since before he left for medical school and eventually came to Maryland. Of course, we had more than once visited Richmond over the years and had seen his parents a number of times, but he seemed never to be there when we were, so our paths did not cross. They had both passed away before we went back there to live. Althea's parents I never knew. They came from the Tidewater, as I understand, somewhere near Williamsburg. Plantation owners, I am told, but her parents, too, are dead, if memory serves me correctly."

He went on with a wealth of information on the complexities of genealogies of families far beyond Dougherty's ken, leaving him to rehearse it all later in his mind and glean the few useful nuggets of real information. At length — at *great* length — he reminded himself that duty called. He shook Dougherty's hand with sincere friendliness, and expressed the hope that they would meet again — perhaps, he opined, Dougherty might enjoy some further conversation with the Misses Holbrun (an offer he was not inclined to pursue, coming as it did from the father of two unmarried daughters, either of whom he would wish to see suitably settled).

By the time Dougherty left, he was all but totally convinced that Doctor Holbrun could not possibly be the spy sought by Arthur Elgin. He was not a man of secrets, nor capable of supplying the gist of a thing in a clear, concise way. He would have supplied information so enmeshed in conversational convolutions, that it would have all but ended the war effort while all energy went into decoding his communications, and then trying to uncover the entangled bits of real information — like the disquieting bits about Doctor Naylor. Doctor Holbrun was putting his conversational skills to better use as a soporific for patients in pain.

Dougherty's mind was a morass of conjectures as he rode back, arriving at Keedysville without clear recollection of the scenery on the way, thankful that at least the horse had kept his mind on the task at hand. Naylor's buggy was in front of the church. Even so simple a conveyance, when it belonged to him, was well cared for, its black sides and leather hood cleaned and polished to a sheen that reflected the light of the sun. Another task, Dougherty supposed, for the smiling boy who had taken care of his horse. For a second, the presence of the buggy gave him the surge of foolish hope that Althea Naylor might have come to visit; but that faded quickly enough — she was more likely to come in the brougham. The buggy was more in accord with Doctor Naylor's vocation as a country physician, and it was he who emerged from the church and came to retrieve something that he had left in the buggy. He saw Dougherty, waved, and came to speak.

"Doctor Dougherty, how are you? I thought that you might be resting today after all the work of yesterday, and here you are already returning from an errand." He was pleasant, but distracted — another patient's condition had suddenly turned worse, and he could not last the day. Dougherty could feel his frustration and helplessness.

Dougherty led the horse to the rear of the church, where he hitched it, but did not remove the saddle since he was already thinking of another visit that he might have to make. He was wondering if he should have spoken to Naylor about the incongruity in what Holbrun had said. It would wait until later. He saw McBrien coming from the shed where the operations were performed.

"Ah, Doctor Dougherty, there ye are then! And how are ye this fine day? I've not seen ye fer some time now."

"Steward McBrien! Have you a minute to spare?" It was a perfect opportunity to apprize him of some of the things that he had learned.

"Why, it's pleased I'd be, sir. Ye couldn't have asked at a better time. I've just now finished compounding the prescriptions, and I've a minute or two on me hands before I start me rounds t' serve out the doses."

Once in his quarters, he showed McBrien the anonymous letter. He agreed that Babcock was its probable author. His reaction was much as Dougherty's had been — at first delighted and then disappointed as he realized that it left them still at a loss for a solution.

Dougherty told him of the letter from Doctor Brownson and the importance of the name he would be sending. Dougherty was now on duty at night, so it was quite likely the telegram would be delivered during the hours when he was not there; he knew he could rely on McBrien to be on the lookout for it and to bring it to him, even if it meant waking him at any hour. There was little else to be said and it was time for McBrien to be back with the patients.

What next? Perhaps the best course of action would be to reconsider the evidence and make one more attempt to weave it into a coherent whole. He reviewed his notes, starting with the finding of the body. He placed his notebook on the table, bit the tip from a cigar to assist the cogitational process and lit it. He shook the match to put it out. He should have been more attentive to what he was doing. He hit his elbow on the edge of the table, knocked the notebook to the floor, and groaned at the pain. After much shaking of the affected arm, and muttered and mumbled complaints at his own stupidity, he bent down to retrieve the notebook. There on the floor next to it was a slip of paper, folded into the shape of an envelope. He picked it up, glad that Doctor Brownson was not there to point out his lack of attention to what had been in his own pocket the whole time. Too much suddenly became crystal clear.

What most embarrassed him was the fact that everything had for some time been obvious, and he had managed to overlook it. He even knew (he thought) the key to the encoded message. He went back to his notebook, copied out the coded message onto an empty page, leaving between the lines enough room to insert the key above them and the translation below them. His results were not heartening. He thought of giving up, but finished anyway. Why he did so, he did not know — perhaps his natural stubbornness (which he preferred to call laudable persistence). It seemed useless. As a translation it made no more sense than had the original.

```
NELAG TNISS OPERI NEVNO CSETR
APSUT ICREX EMAUQ ETNAT AGOCM
UILEO RPTUE RANIT SEFTI CIDES
TETIC SONGO CAINM OROIN UINTI
NEVNI SILAI CEPSI SSUIR ALPME
XE
```

For a half hour or more, he sat and stared and wondered and was no nearer a solution than he had been. He folded the paper to put it into the notebook. And then it came to him — a chance realization of a sequence of letters. He examined it again, began to write, and there it was. He had broken the code! But there was more dismay than elation. He realized how useless a great secret can be. So sad a death for something now so utterly valueless.

Chapter XX: The Woman in the Story

> Constant you are,
> But yet a woman: and for secrecy,
> No lady closer; for I will believe
> Thou wilt not utter what thou dost not know;
> And so far will I trust thee, gentle Kate.
> William Shakespeare (1546-1616)
> *Henry IV, Part I*, Act 2, sc. 3 (1598)

[September 30, 1862]

It was already into the afternoon, but Dougherty had one more visit to make. It would take some time, but with good fortune he would be back before his duty hour. By then he would have either disproved what he feared was true or proven what he hoped was not. He looked for McBrien, but he was nowhere to be found, so he scribbled a note and gave it to an orderly with strict instructions to place it directly into McBrien's hands as soon as possible. It seemed prudent that someone should know where he had gone. The notion that he might have solved the mystery made him ill.

The lush, late summer green leaves, the sweet trill of birds, the freshening breeze — all might as well not have existed for all the notice he took. When he looked up and saw the motto above the entry, the words had lost their gentle pretension and had become glaring hypocrisy. He dreaded the short ride to the house, but he could not put it off. His heels tapped the horse's flanks and it resumed its forward movement.

There was no buggy in the drive. It was still at the church in Keedysville. Dougherty had seen it there as he left. The façade of Willowbrook Hall that had so impressed him was now as false as stage scenery after all. It hurt him to think that he was about to bring pain to someone who did not deserve it. The same boy would have led the horse back to the stables, but Dougherty stopped him.

"I will hitch him here," Dougherty said, pointing to the rail near the porch.

"Sho' thing, gen'l," he said, his grin as pleasant as ever. If Dougherty's face showed the dismay that filled his heart, it was not yet enough to cause alarm.

Tully opened the door just moments after Dougherty had used the ornate brass knocker and, like any good butler, showed no sign of surprise at an unexpected visitor.

"De Doctah in't t' home, suh," he said.

"Yes, Tully, I know. I am here to speak to Mrs. Naylor if she is available."

"Suh, if y'all'd like t' come in outta de heat and set fo' a minute, I'll jes go see if Miz Naylah is in."

He sat, dejected, on one of the chairs, hat balanced on a knee, and wondered where to begin with Mrs. Naylor — provided that she was "at home." If she did not wish to receive him so unexpectedly, he would have to insist, as distasteful as that would be. But Tully returned, took his hat, and led him directly to the same small parlor where they had met on Sunday. Althea was seated on the same sofa, beautiful as ever. Her smile was warm, her voice cheerful.

"Lieutenant Dougherty, how kind of you to visit. What a pleasant surprise!"

He should have expected a slight emphasis on the surprise; instead her intonation drew attention to the pleasure, making him feel all the worse. As before, she gestured to the far end of the sofa, but he chose a chair facing her. He wanted to put this off, to begin with the small talk that courtesy demanded. But it would be cruel — like a doctor performing an operation one small step at a time and, through misplaced mercy, protracting the ordeal beyond endurance.

"Mrs. Naylor, on Sunday I showed you a drawing of Arthur Elgin. You said you did not recognize him. The Misses Holbrun had no difficulty recognizing him, even though they wished they hadn't. But their reasons were different than yours. They wanted to hold onto the hope that the dead man was not their friend. But you didn't want to have to explain how you knew him. You didn't want me to know that, on the night before his body was found, Arthur Elgin had eaten a meal in this house."

She sat perfectly still, scarcely breathing. Dougherty paused, hoping that she could prove him wrong. There was a look of seemingly genuine surprise on her lovely face.

"Doctor Dougherty, I really have no idea what to say. Surely you cannot be serious? Why would you say this? I am sure that you are sincere in your belief, but this is simply not true."

"It would be far better, Mrs. Naylor, to admit to the fact, so that we can speak of what happened and what can be done about it. I have no doubt that Doctor Elgin ate here. In the post-mortem, we found something in his stomach that puzzled me for some time. He had eaten fresh strawberries. Where, I thought, could he possibly have gotten them in September? Then on Sunday I visited your conservatory, but it was only later — in fact only this very day — that I realized that among the plants I had seen there were strawberries. I hadn't recognized them at first, because they no longer bore fruit. So I am certain that he ate here. There is no other explanation. You yourself told me there is no other conservatory nearer than Baltimore or Washington."

Her violet eyes shimmered and welled up. A single tear appeared at the inner corner of her left eye and rolled slowly toward her quivering lips. Dougherty hated himself, but he had to see the matter to its end.

"I knew we should have told the truth as soon as we realized that it was Arthur's body that you found. But it just seemed impossible to speak of it to anyone, and we hoped that the murder would be solved without implicating my husband and myself. We had nothing to do with his death, but who was going to believe us? You are right. He was here that evening."

"Tell me about it," Dougherty said, "It seems to me that there is no alternative."

"There may be an alternative," she said, "if you should promise not to tell anyone what you have learned."

Her head was bowed, but she raised her eyes and looked at him through her long lashes. Where he might have expected to find dismay or surrender, he was shocked to see something else — or perhaps he only imagined something else, a trace of seductiveness? Whatever the alternative she was ready to offer, he had no desire to pursue the matter.

"I cannot make such a promise," he said.

"No," she said, "I suppose you cannot. It was foolish of me even to suggest it. Please forgive me. Let me tell you what I know, and then you can decide what must be done about it.

"On the day after the battle, before the Confederate army had withdrawn, I was surprised when Arthur Elgin suddenly presented himself at our door. It was late afternoon. Oliver had been away helping the wounded ever since the night of the battle, and it was not until about five o'clock on Thursday afternoon that he came home to find Arthur here.

"We had known Arthur for some time. He and Oliver had both grown up in Richmond and, in their earliest days, had known each other quite well, although there had been little contact for many years since then. Arthur said that he wanted to discuss with Oliver something of great importance, but at first he did not say what it was. Of course, we asked him to stay with us, and he said that he would.

"We ate our evening meal rather early that night. We talked about common acquaintances and the days before the war... the things people talk about these days. Everything except why he had come. Arthur asked after Doctor Holbrun, wondering where he lived and seemed pleased that it was not so very far away. We finished eating not long after six-thirty. Oliver and Arthur went into Oliver's office and closed the door. They spoke for quite a long time and were still at it when I retired for the night. It was almost ten o'clock."

"What did he come to discuss?" Dougherty asked.

"Oliver told me that it was about someone that Arthur thought was acting as a spy for the Confederacy, and that he was seeking the identity of that person. Oliver was quite surprised to hear this and even more surprised when Arthur told him that he had been working for the Union even while carrying out his duties at Chimborazo."

"Why did he come to your husband?"

"We were never really sure, except that he seemed to hope that we might know something about this spy. His only reason for that notion was that he had somehow concluded that the spy might also be a medical man. In any case, Oliver was not able to help him, and he was quite disappointed. For a long time they discussed the matter, Arthur constantly hoping that Oliver might have some information, even if it was something whose significance he did not grasp. But there was nothing. Finally, somewhat after midnight, Oliver said, Arthur decided not to stay the night after all. Instead, he set out toward Sharpsburg, but never did say just where he intended to go, nor why he would have gone out in that direction, since, so far as we knew, both armies were still there facing each other and it seemed such a foolish risk for him to take. That was the last that either of us saw of him."

"Why did your husband say nothing of this to me when we first showed him the body? Surely he could have explained it."

"Oliver told me that at first, when you asked him to help with the body, he did not realize that it was Arthur. He had no beard and he was in a blood soaked uniform. We had seen him only in civilian clothes. Oliver never even thought that it could be his friend. It was only later, when you removed the body from his buckboard at Pry's mill and he got a real look at the face, that Oliver realized the identity of the dead man. By then he was both shocked and fearful that, were he to say that he knew him, it would seem that he must have had some reason not to admit it in the first place. He came home and told me about it, sick with grief and not knowing what to do without casting suspicion on himself. I can see now that it was a dreadfully mistaken decision, but at the time we both agreed to say nothing. From that point on, it became worse with each passing day. The longer we waited, the more suspect we were likely to appear. It was the most terrifying experience on Sunday when you showed me that drawing. It was all I could do to retain any semblance of composure. I was so amazed at your cleverness in discovering his identity, but I could not possibly admit that I knew him! However would I possibly explain it? It hurt all the more since I found myself wilfully deceiving you, and I had by then become quite fond of you — a fondness that I had begun to think might be reciprocated."

Her head was bowed, but again she lifted those magnificent, violet eyes, looking at him with great sorrow and that same veiled promise she had shown before.

"You say that he remained here until well after midnight?"

Dougherty made no comment on her last remark, afraid that any acknowledgment would take the conversation in a direction in which he had no desire to go.

"That's right," she said.

"So your husband was the one who saw him off? You did not hear him leave?"

"No," she said. "In fact, I did not even speak to Oliver about Arthur the next morning. Arthur had gone, and Tully told me that his room had not been used. But by the time I learned that, it was too late to ask Oliver. He had left before daybreak on his way to help the wounded and he spent the rest of the day on the field, which is how you came to meet him there."

"Mrs. Naylor, it pains me to say this, but I must. If your husband told you that he spoke to Arthur Elgin until late in the night, he was not telling you the truth. You say that you finished eating before seven o'clock, and that the gentlemen then withdrew to have their discussion. That discussion could not possibly have lasted until late in the night. In truth, it could not have lasted more than a very brief time after supper."

"How can you possibly say such a thing?" She was puzzled, perhaps even indignant.

"Much as I hate to speak of something so gruesome," he said, "my statement is based on a quite incontrovertible fact. When we performed the post-mortem examination, we found the strawberries, as I told you. They were easily recognizable as such, even though the oddity of their presence at this time of year prevented us from realizing what we were seeing. The point is that they were recognizable. Strawberries are quite perishable, and the gastric juices would have reduced them to a stage beyond recognition within a very short period of time. The only conclusion one can draw is that Doctor Elgin did not live long enough for that to happen. He could not possibly have been alive at midnight. He was surely dead well before eight o'clock."

"No! That cannot be! You are mistaken! Oliver told me what happened, and I am sure that he did not lie to me. What you are saying is all a dreadful error."

Her weeping was now in earnest, no longer a single tear. He hated the sorrow that he had brought to her, and yet he needed to learn something more.

"Mrs. Naylor, I am sorry, but there is something else I must ask. May I examine your husband's office? His surgical kit?"

At first he thought that she did not even understand what he had asked. She merely looked at him, almost looked through him, her eyes not properly focused. She took a kerchief from her pocket and held it to her eyes.

"Yes," she said, "I suppose you must. I will come with you."

That was when they heard the carriage in the drive. They waited, both knowing who would come through the door. It was only minutes — minutes of the most painful silence — before the door opened and Oliver Naylor entered, his eyes, full of curiosity, moving from Althea to Dougherty and back again.

Chapter XXI: Fact and Fiction

The truth is, the science of Nature has been already too long made only a work of the brain and the fancy: It is now high time that it should return to the plainness and soundness of observations on material and obvious things.

Robert Hooke (1635-1703)
Micrographia (1665)

[September 30, 1862]

"Oliver," she said, "I am so relieved to have you home! I know you can explain to Doctor Dougherty just how mistaken he is. He has gotten it into his head that you are in some manner responsible for the terrible thing that happened to Arthur Elgin. Please help him to understand the truth of the matter."

He looked at her and then at Dougherty, waiting, expecting Dougherty to say something.

"This morning," he began, "I spoke to Doctor Holbrun and what he told me has convinced me that you knew Doctor Arthur Elgin. Your wife confirmed the truth of that, yet, from the beginning you have pretended that it was not so."

Before he could say anything further, Mrs. Naylor began to recount for him what she had already said, but Dougherty interrupted her. He did not want her to speak before he had heard Naylor's version of the events.

"Doctor Naylor, may we please speak alone?" Dougherty asked.

Althea went to Naylor and took his hand, looking into his eyes with a gaze that pleaded with him to offer some explanation, to undo all the fears and misgivings that Dougherty's words had instilled in her.

"My dear," he said, "perhaps you should leave us for a while. Take some time to compose yourself, while I speak to Doctor Dougherty. I will be happy to explain things and put his mind at ease. Everything will be quite all right. You shall see."

He placed his arm around her shoulders and drew her to himself. For a second she rested her head against his shoulder, then he gently turned her toward the door and she left.

"And so, Lieutenant," he said, "where shall we start?"

"Perhaps, sir, we might go to your medical office and have our discussion there? That is where we were about to go when you arrived."

With no more than a shallow nod, he led the way. In the office atop a cabinet sat the medical kit, its polished lid reflecting the light that came through the window. Before Dougherty could examine it more closely, he spoke.

"Now, Lieutenant, perhaps you can explain just what you are up to and why you have so disturbed my wife with your questions and accusations."

He took a seat on the swivel chair at his desk, swung it around to face Dougherty, and gestured for him to take the one in which patients would sit to hear their diagnoses and receive their prescriptions. He tilted the chair back against the desk, brushed a speck of lint from a dark trouser leg, and gave every impression of being at ease and fully in charge of the situation, even though the tension in his voice belied that.

"Let me begin," Dougherty said," with one simple fact. In all the times that we have discussed the dead man, you have never indicated that you knew him. It was only when I spoke with Doctor Holbrun that I realized that you must surely have known him and your wife has confirmed that. Why had you not told me the truth?"

"I'm sure that my wife must have explained that," he said. "When you first told me about the body, I did not actually see it. You and Steward McBrien loaded it into the wagon. Even at the mill I had no idea who it was, until you brought Major Brinton outside and I had my first look at the body. By then I felt that were I to admit knowing him, my failure to speak earlier could only cast suspicion on me. I chose to keep silent — a mistake, as I now realize."

"Doctor Elgin," Dougherty said, "worked for Allan Pinkerton as his agent. He came here looking for a spy."

"I know nothing of that," he said.

"Oh, but you do," Dougherty said. "Your wife told me that you mentioned it to her."

"Surely you must have misunderstood. I said no such thing." He was so calm and so convincing that it almost seemed believable.

"No," Dougherty said, "I did not misunderstand. You knew that he was here, you knew why, and you knew that he was at least connected with Pinkerton, even if you did not know that he was in his employ."

"And precisely how would I know such a thing?" he said. "This is nonsense. I knew Arthur Elgin years ago, but we had had no contact with each other since he first went west with the army. How could I possibly have known what he was doing now?"

"You saw him in Frederick just four days before the battle. He was at the hospital that day just about noon. I am sure that you saw him from the upper gallery of the barracks and that you followed him to his meeting at the tavern. Then, no doubt, you waited until he came out and you saw Pinkerton with him."

"That is ridiculous. I was half the day at the barracks and I left with my wife and we came all the way back to Keedysville that same day. We were never separated for a moment, as she will verify."

"I hope not," Dougherty said, "for I would not be able to believe her. I saw her leaving the barracks, and she was alone in the carriage."

"Again you are in error," he said, "but you seem intent on establishing your point whether it coincides with the facts or not. You must take my word for it."

"I think not. On the first day that I met you, you lied to me, although I did not realize it at the time. You told me that you were from New York. Why you chose to lie to me about that I do not really know. I have noticed that you do not usually lie so baldly. Perhaps it was just part of an effort to acquire whatever information I might be able to supply and you thought that your Virginia ancestry would make me more reticent. Besides, I am sure that you never thought we would be meeting again. Indeed, we may not have, had it not been for the finding of the body. Still, so evident a lie is unlike you. You are much more inclined to flaunt the truth as much as possible, and still explain it away. I've seen you do it."

"And when would that have been?" he said, an eyebrow lifted and an expression of mild amusement on his face.

"The day we met you with the buckboard," Dougherty said. "I remember thinking that it was a conveyance somewhat out of character for you. You actually pointed out its incongruity, explaining that you had been hauling patients — even though it was also you who said that you had never left the Sunken Road the whole day.

"I heard you head off a reprimand from Major Briggs by using your visit to a patient to forestall any negative comments on his part. You easily drew him into quite another discussion without his realizing it, and he soon forgot all about the lateness of your arrival that day. I was amused at the time and even admired the technique.

"And I am sure you will recall that it was you who on more than one occasion all but insisted that I view your wife's flowers, knowing that in the conservatory I would see the strawberry plants. No doubt you knew that we had found strawberries in Doctor Elgin's stomach, and must have considered it almost comical to let me see the bare plants and probably not even realize what they were."

He sat in silence for a time, looking more pensive than disturbed, as though he were trying to make up his mind about something or planning what to say next. At last he looked directly into Dougherty's eyes.

"I think you give me too much credit," he said. "Perhaps I had better tell you the truth, before you use a variety of half-truths to fabricate a scenario that seems so plausible and yet is so far from reality.

"Maybe I should have told you some of this earlier, before you had gone so far, but I felt honor bound to say nothing. Now it makes sense to tell you, so that your effort at solving a crime will not end up interfering with matters essential to the war.

"The truth is that I am an agent of Major E.J. Allen. You say that Elgin was also an agent of Allen's, and had he told me that perhaps much of this would not have happened."

"Of course, you are right. We were friends in Richmond years ago. I saw him in Frederick as you said, and, yes, I did follow him. But I did not see him with Major Allen. He entered the tavern alone and he was still alone when he left, so I never did know what he had been doing there, apart, perhaps, from eating his dinner. My wife did leave the barracks by herself, but I met her shortly after that and we returned to Keedysville. We were able to pass through the Confederate lines with complete ease, since General Lee had issued strict orders not to interfere with civilians. We were able to get through the Union lines for quite another reason. I said that I am an agent of Major Allen, and this should prove it."

He drew from his pocket a slip of paper and unfolded it for Dougherty to read. It was a pass, signed by Major E.J. Allen, authorizing any sentry to pass the bearer and anyone accompanying him. Dougherty handed it back to him and he put it in his pocket.

The lack of credence must have been plain on Dougherty's face.

"You seem to find it difficult to believe," he said. "A secret agent in Keedysville? Who could blame you for not believing? But realize just where Keedysville is located. It has been the scene of nothing significant — at least, until this month. It was a simple matter for our agents to send information here by way of the bridge from Shepherdstown or across the ford. It was placed in a certain location where I could discover it, and then at a location near Boonsborough I passed it on in the same manner to a courier who would take it to Major Allen. That way, neither the agents nor the couriers ever knew my identity, which has been a considerable protection to the whole operation.

"You may not yet believe me, but allow me to go on and explain what happened with Doctor Elgin.

"I was thoroughly surprised when he appeared at our doorstep the day after the battle. I could not imagine how he had come here nor could I think of any reason for his arrival. At first he said nothing to allay my curiosity, although he promised to do so later. We enjoyed a meal together and then Althea withdrew and we came to my office to talk. The story that he told was not especially enlightening. He was vague about his reasons for the information he wanted, but it was information simple enough in itself. He wanted to learn the names of any medical personnel in the area — local doctors or even army doctors that I may have met in the preceding days. To tell the truth, I could see no harm in that sort of information, so I told him first about Dr. Holbrun. Much to my surprise, Arthur said that he knew him quite well and had been associated with him for some months in Richmond just before the outbreak of hostilities. He was very interested in what Holbrun was doing now. I hope you will not too much mind, but I also told him about you and about Dr. Briggs and about a few others whom I had met in the course of that very day. It was information that seemed to be without any real value.

"In the end — at least so far as I could tell — what I told him meant little to him. If anything, he seemed disappointed. We had invited him to stay the night, but he decided not to. It suddenly seemed that he had something much more pressing to attend to. It could not have been much later than nine o'clock when he took his leave. Althea had already retired, so she did not see him off. I returned to my office and sat here deep in thought. I lost track of the time and it must have been after midnight by the time I retired."

"Why," Dougherty asked, "did you tell your wife that he had remained here until after midnight?"

"Again, I think you must have misunderstood what Althea said. However, we can clarify that with her later, I am sure."

If he was not telling the truth, he was certainly one of the most accomplished liars that Dougherty had ever met. Even with his awareness of the small inconsistencies in his story, he was tempted to believe him.

"Do you mind, sir, if I examine your medical kit?" Dougherty asked.

"Be my guest," he said.

"I think you know quite well, that Doctor Elgin was killed with a trocar — a trocar which broke and a part of which remained in the wound."

Dougherty stood and went to the cabinet upon which sat the medical kit. The trocar rested in its proper place. He took it out and looked at it, turning it in his hands as he did so.

"I think," Naylor said, "that you should be able to draw some clear conclusions from what you hold in your hand. I would suggest that you go elsewhere and look for a surgical kit that lacks its trocar or has a damaged one."

"I regret to say it, sir," Dougherty answered, "but I am quite certain that this particular instrument is not yours."

In turning the handle in his hand he had found the small imperfection, the tiny crescent mark as though someone had pressed a thumbnail into the wood, precisely as McBrien had described. This trocar belonged to Major Briggs and the one that McBrien had recently found in his case was not the one that had been there originally. Dougherty could see from his expression that Naylor had realized that there was some way to contradict his claim of ownership. It was the first crack in the façade of self-assurance that was so much part of him. Still, he was not to be so easily deterred.

"Not mine?" He smiled. "To suggest that I should be able to prove that this trocar is mine is ridiculous. One trocar is much like another. This one happens to be mine, but I cannot convince you of that if you do not wish to take my word for it." The slightest hint of uncertainty had crept into his voice. Dougherty pressed on.

"I should probably have suspected long ago that you may have been the one who took the trocar from Major Briggs's medical kit. I am sure it was a spur of the moment decision. You came into Pry's Mill with me when I went in search of Major Briggs. I thought you had done it to lend me your support, but I realize now that you did it simply to learn what I was going to report. I remember that while I spoke with Major Briggs and Major Brinton, you were in conversation with the steward who was cleaning the instruments. That was when you took the trocar, not wanting to leave an empty space in your own surgical kit. You then ordered a replacement from the Tiemann Company, which magically reappeared in Major Briggs's medical kit on the very day that you began to work at the hospital in Keedysville. There is little use denying this, since I am expecting confirmation from the Tiemann Company on the identity of the person who recently replaced a trocar."

Again he said nothing, but simply waited to see what Dougherty would do next.

"Perhaps I should tell you what I think actually happened on the night of September 18," Dougherty said, "Arthur Elgin came here in search of someone disloyal to the Union, and he came not for information but because he was certain that you were his quarry. You had supper and then came almost immediately to this room. He told you why he was here and, I suspect, offered you the chance to escape, knowing that such an action would end your career as an agent of the Confederacy. At some point in the conversation, you were able to stand behind him, put an arm around his head, and push the trocar into the base of his skull. That should have been easy enough to do quickly. That was when the shaft of the instrument broke. Either you were unable to remove it or you simply didn't see the point to doing so. In any case, you left it there. You took the body from here to the conservatory and left it there until morning."

At Dougherty's mention of the conservatory, his surprise was evident.

"You wonder how I know that? It is not difficult to explain. The day that I found Doctor Elgin's body, I realized that in his hair were particles of a dark soil that had not come from anywhere in the vicinity of the body. It was the same rich potting soil that I saw the day I visited the conservatory.

"I am certain that, early in the morning of September 19, you left here in your buckboard, with Doctor Elgin's body in the back under the blankets that I saw there later. It was no difficult matter to pause near the East Wood and move the body from the buckboard. You took the uniform coat of one of the dead in the area and the trousers of another, knowing that their absence would not be noted, since clothing had already been taken from so many. You threw some branches over the body and left, convinced that it was the perfect way to be rid of your problem. Much as it pains me to say so, I must accuse you of being both a murderer and a traitor."

Dougherty could see in his face that he had finally realized that further denial was futile. He looked at Dougherty, a slight smile still upon his lips.

"Lieutenant, allow me to congratulate you. You are more far clever than I gave you credit for. I never expected you to learn quite so much. However, sir, do not call me either a murderer or a traitor. Elgin had the audacity to call me a traitor, but what did he think he was? He was the one disloyal to his native state, not I. It was he who was going to betray me to Pinkerton, leaving me to escape to the South or be hanged here. Neither am I a murderer. Elgin's death was no crime of passion or vengeance. It was a simple act of war. We are in the midst of a war, Lieutenant, and he was my enemy, so I killed him before he could kill me. If you call me anything, at least have the decency to call me a patriot."

"No," Dougherty said, "what you did was no act of war. Elgin did not come here to kill you. Those who knew him could not even imagine him doing something so violent. I suspect that he came here simply intending to let you know that your work for the Confederacy must end and that all he wanted was for you to go back to Virginia and end your spying. Why else would he have sought you out himself and not simply have given your name to Pinkerton and allowed him to pursue the investigation? Instead, what he did, he would have seen as a fair exchange. If he allowed you to go to Richmond, that would have also ended his usefulness there and he would have remained here. Instead, you killed him."

"You do me an injustice, Lieutenant, I am no killer. This was not something I had ever done before, nor would I ever have done so had I not been forced into such a dreadful position."

Had it not been for what Dougherty had learned from Doctor Brownson, he might even then have believed him. Instead he revealed the last link in the chain of evidence.

"Do you remember Joseph Fuller?" Dougherty asked. For a moment his eyes were puzzled and then Dougherty saw in them the light of recognition. "I am sure that I will have little trouble establishing the fact that you were in Philadelphia in December of 1860. It was Joseph Fuller who discovered your true identity."

"My true identity? What sort of nonsense is this?"

"Not nonsense at all. I already told you how I was impressed by your ability to make use of the obvious. The motto above your gate is a perfect example. Without it I could never have deciphered the message you sent to your Confederate doctor friend, the same message which brought Arthur Elgin here for you to kill him. When I deciphered the message, I saw that you had signed it 'Galen' and that was the name of the man who killed Joseph Fuller. You are no novice at this. Fuller was not the first, was he? I have been told that there were at least two others. You are far too adept at it to be a novice. Seeing the ease and ingenuity with which you kill, I think that you have begun to like it. Even your oath as a doctor has meant nothing to you."

Dougherty had no idea what response to expect from him, but even at this juncture Naylor was perfectly calm, polite, even self-righteous.

"Regardless of what you may think, I am a loyal son of the state of Virginia and everything I have done springs from nothing but the deepest patriotism. Allow me at least that much consideration. I suppose I have little choice now but to allow you to turn me in, but first can we not, like civilized men, enjoy one last cigar together?"

As he spoke he turned, opened a drawer on the left side of the desk, and began to reach in. He acted with such coolness that, had Dougherty not been standing, he might well have thought that he was reaching for a pair of cigars. From his vantage point, however, he saw that the drawer contained something else. His hand was already on the polished walnut stock of the revolver. Dougherty drew forth his own and cocked it before Naylor could reach his.

"Please don't force me to shoot you," Dougherty said. "I have no desire to do that, and I certainly would not want to do something to cause such great pain to your wife."

He was really not sure what he would do if Naylor resisted. He had never shot anyone in his life and hoped never to do so.

Behind him, the door opened and Althea said, "Thank you, Lieutenant, for your kindness."

His first instinct was to turn in that direction, but he had sense enough not to. Instead, he motioned with his gun for Naylor to step away from the desk. Once he had done so, Dougherty turned slightly in her direction. Her lips did not quiver. Her hands did not shake. Her voice was not sad. Her magnificent violet eyes were no longer red rimmed, but clear and well in focus. Her aim was perfectly accurate.

"Thank you, my dear," Naylor said as she shot Dougherty.

Epilogue

Away with him! Away with him!
He speaks Latin.
William Shakespeare (1546-1616)
Henry IV, Part 1, Act 4, sc. 7 (1592)

Dougherty lay slumped against a wall, his head propped up, tilted to the left. His throat hurt, and something was lodged in his mouth. Slowly he lifted his hand and, with a tentative finger, felt inside his left cheek. The light was dim, but as he removed the finger and held it before his eyes, he realized that what he had felt was a large bolus of clotted blood. Bit by bit he removed it and only then became aware of the pain. His throat, his jaw, the back of his neck — all were painful and swollen. He groaned, and the sound was grotesque — hoarse and harsh. He tried to call for help, but produced only a weak croak no one could have heard, much less understood.

It took no little time and a great deal of effort to sit up fully. He looked about. He was still in Naylor's office. With agonizing slowness he struggled to his feet and leaned against the wall until he thought he could risk walking.

He left the office, leaning against the walls as he moved, and found his way to the front door. There was no sound in the house, just dead silence. His hat was hung on the rack behind the door, and he put it on, never thinking how incongruous it was to be worried about a hat, when he had been shot and should be seeking medical help. Once outside he realized that much of the afternoon was gone, and he was going to be late reporting to Major Briggs. The horse was where he had left it, patiently waiting. His foot slipped from the stirrup on the first few tries, each slip a source of agony, until he finally hoisted himelf aboard. The patient mount stayed still until he got into the saddle. He turned him in the direction of Keedysville. Much as he wished to get there quickly, he could not trust himself to remain on the horse if it moved faster than a walk.

He had just passed beneath the motto and turned toward the pike, when he heard a horse coming full gallop toward him. He thought of Naylor and his wife and reached for his gun. He did not have it. It must still be on the floor where he had fallen. Then, around the bend in front of him, he saw a sight that lifted his spirits as little else could have. It was Sean McBrien, coming at great speed, more the cavalryman than the medical steward. He slowed as he caught sight of Dougherty, and his expression changed to one of horror as he got close enough to see his face. The blood had flowed from the wound in his neck and from his mouth and was caked on his chin and his uniform.

"Sir, what's happened to ye?" he said. "Are ye all right? Fer Heaven's sake, Lieutenant, don't ye have the sense ye were born with? Why did ye not take me with ye? Don't ye know better than to be going off trying to solve mysteries on yer own? Not that ye can't solve them, but I think ye need someone with ye when it comes to bringing the solution home."

"We need to find Doctor Naylor and his wife. He killed Elgin, and his wife was in it with him." Dougherty's voice was weak — each word a new burst of pain that made him see flashes of light.

"I'm already aware of the Doctor's guilt," McBrien said. "Yer telegram from Doctor Brownson arrived, and since ye weren't there, I took the liberty of opening it. All it said was, 'Doctor Oliver Naylor is the name,' and it was signed, 'Brownson.' I'd already got yer note telling me where ye'd gone, and when I learned that Doctor Naylor had left the hospital and I realized that ye'd been gone a long time, I headed here as fast as I could. Are ye well enough, sir, to ride to the hospital?"

"I am," Dougherty said, "but we have to find the Naylors. Their house is deserted, and I am certain that they left me for dead and have gone to Virginia."

It was all he could do to say that much. His head spun, his eyes did not focus. He held tight to the saddle, and McBrien reached over to steady him. When he saw that Dougherty was back in control, he took the reins and led his horse toward Keedysville. The trip was endless.

At times he was groggy and fearful of losing consciousness, but each time his head cleared and they went on.

At the hospital, McBrien got him safely off the horse and helped him inside, where Doctor Briggs awaited them. He began to reprimand Dougherty, then saw the blood.

"Lay him down on the floor, McBrien," he said and bent to examine the wound on the right side of his neck. With a finger he probed beneath his jaw from right to left. When he touched the left jaw, Dougherty groaned and his eyes teared. He heard Briggs say, "Get the instruments ready for surgery." Then the dimness came again, and he lost consciousness.

Later he recalled moments of fretful wakefulness, which never attained to full consciousness. Time after time he sank back into an uneasy sleep filled with dreams devoid of all logic. Then he awoke, remembering nothing of the dreams apart from the fact that he did not like them. On the other hand, he awoke to something that he liked very much indeed — the flashing green eyes of Miss Genevieve Collingwood. She watched him, staring into his eyes with such intensity that he was afraid he might be in his last moments. He blinked things into better focus and tried to speak, but what came was a raspy scratch. He attempted to clear his throat and felt such exquisite pain that all he could do was groan.

"Please don't try to speak, James," she said.

James? Never before had she addressed him by his Christian name. He liked it.

"Major Briggs said that your throat would be sore for some time to come, and he does not wish you to attempt to speak for a while. He is sure that the harm will not be permanent, but he said that the outcome will depend to a large extent on your willingness to be a good patient. I will go now and get some fresh water for you. Sipping it may help."

He hated to have her leave, especially since it meant having her loose her grasp of his hand, which he discovered she had been holding as he slept. He did not long think of it. Almost immediately he drifted off. When he next awoke, he knew that he was in the hospital, lying among the wounded who had until then been his patients but were now his fellow sufferers. The sun shone through the east windows, as it had when he had first awakened. Miss Collingwood was back, his right hand clasped gently in both of hers.

"Lieutenant Dougherty, you are awake again. You look better already. Don't try to speak, but do see if you can sip some of this water."

Not "James," he noticed. Probably a sign that she thought he was recovering. He had a passing hope that it not be too quick a process. He tried to move and found it painful.

"Lie still," she said, and slipped her arm beneath his head to lift him up a little, just enough to place water into his mouth with a spoon. It felt wonderful on his lips and tongue, but was dreadfully painful to swallow. After a few tries, he shook his head to indicate that he was not ready for more. The movement made him moan. She lowered his head onto the pillow.

"There is no hurry," she said, "little by little is best. I can place a cloth in the water and squeeze it slowly onto your lips and the water can find its own way into your throat."

That whole morning passed in fitful spurts of sleep and wakefulness, each waking period graced by her presence. Even when he did not immediately see her, she was at his side in seconds. She must have gone about her duties with one eye on his every move. Her presence made up for the pain. He was visited that day by both Steward McBrien and Major Briggs, although he could not converse at any length with either. McBrien, he could tell, was concerned about him, although his words were as bright and cheerful as ever. "It's glad I am to see ye, sir" he said, "ye'll be fine and on the mend in no time at'all, sir. So says yer physician."

His physician, of course, was Major Briggs, who looked at him with his disconcerting squint.

"Awake, are you? It's about time. Never in my years in the army have I found a subordinate officer so adept at finding excuses to avoid taking his appointed duties. I suppose you'd best stay in bed. You'll be little good for anything else for a while. Keep trying to swallow. You need liquids and the effort to swallow will begin to ease the pain. If it gets too bad, let me know and we can find some laudanum for you."

It was on October 3 that the hospital received its most unexpected visitor. President Lincoln came to view the battlefield and to urge McClellan to move against Lee. He took advantage of his visit to see the wounded and to express the gratitude of the nation. Dougherty did not talk to him, but he saw him. He was the same man Dougherty had seen a year and a half earlier, when war was at hand and everyone was still convinced that it would be a matter of no more than days before it ended. He was the same man, but he had aged as the country had aged in the intervening months. His face, even in Philadelphia, had been gaunt. At Keedysville there were shadows about his eyes — eyes filled with an inexpressible sadness. The cheeks were sunken, each line of normal aging now exaggerated, etched deep. To see him was to see the ravages of war, and it filled Dougherty's heart with sorrow, even while Lincoln's indomitable spirit renewed everyone's courage.

By the next day Dougherty could swallow, and his voice was back. He could only whisper, but he knew he was on the mend. Major Briggs came again to see him.

"Well, Lieutenant, it looks as though you may remain with us after all... Unless, of course, you discover one more wandering Major who cannot dispense with your services. Have you diagnosed your own case yet? I suppose you have. It's one of the reasons that I hate to doctor a doctor; they always love to have their own opinions."

"I am happy to accept your diagnosis, sir," Dougherty whispered, the sound of his voice gruff and his throat hurting with each word. But at least he was speaking.

"You were shot," he said, "a diagnosis with which hardly anyone could disagree; not too taxing for an old army surgeon to discover. The bullet, fortunately for you, did not do nearly so much damage as it might have. It was a small caliber ball, possibly from the sort of toy pistol a lady might carry in a reticule. You might try to keep better company in future. She must not have been as adept at loading the gun as she was at aiming it. I suspect that either the powder was inferior or the gun had not been sufficiently charged. The ball caused damage, but it did not much tear the muscles and did not even pass clean through you. It lodged just under the skin of the left jaw. I cut it out with ease, and there will not even be enough of a scar to mar your manly good looks. The damage on the right side is a little more severe, but it was on the neck, and will not be so noticeable. You can always grow a beard. Not that it seems to make much difference to your nurse, who has hovered about as though you were the most important case in the hospital."

"What damage did it do?" Dougherty asked.

"It entered on the right an inch or so behind the ramus of the jaw and must have been fired from just a little behind you and on that side. The ball passed through the anterior edge of the sterno-cleido mastoid muscle, continued across the front of the throat and in something of a slightly upward direction. As I told you, it lodged on the opposite side, no more than an inch in front of the angle of the jaw and just beneath it."

He moved to stand directly in front of Dougherty, and told him to look at him, to roll his eyes left and right and up and down. He did the "hmmming" that any good doctor, Dougherty included, does when examining a patient, and Dougherty realized, for the first time, just how disconcerting that can be to the patient. Was it a good "hmm" or a bad "hmm"? Was it a knowing "hmm" or a "hmm" intended to disguise utter ignorance?

"There is a little ptosis on the right side, now almost negligible, I would say, and the pupil of that eye is still slightly less dilated than the other. I suspect that you are having some headaches and are likely to have some more when you try to get up and about. However, I think that you can rely on the fact that those symptoms will go away. In fact, the ptosis today is not nearly so pronounced as it was just yesterday. Miss Collingwood has been observing it most assiduously for me and has seen improvement."

That was what she had been doing? Observing his ptosis? That was why she had peered into his eyes so intently? To see if his eyelid drooped? Dougherty had hoped she had reasons other than that. Briggs must have seen something in his expression.

"Of course, I sometimes see her looking into your eyes, and I wonder if ptosis is truly her main concern... Ah, well, no matter... Who can account for tastes, especially in the young? There has probably been a bruise to the cervical sympathetic nerve, but I doubt that it was cut. If it had been, the symptoms would have been worse. There you have it. That is my diagnosis, and I rejoice that your throat is too sore to allow for argument. If you want my prognosis, I would offer the opinion that within a few weeks — even worse, maybe a few days — I will once again have to put up with you as a medical officer under my command."

It was also on that day that McBrien came, and he and Genevieve Collingwood sat down at the bedside and told him what had happened to Doctor Naylor and the beautiful Althea.

"This was the way of it, sir," he said, "When I brought ye here to the hospital, Major Briggs himself insisted on operating on ye, and a nice bit of slicing he did. He has a fine hand, swift and sure, and he seemed intent on taking special care of yerself.

"Once we was finished, there was nothing more to be done fer yerself but to wait, and I knew ye'd skin me alive if I done nothing about the Naylors. I guessed that they'd head to the river and cross at the ford once dark come on. I headed in that direction. The three miles from here to Sharpsburg seemed like ten, but that was only me own impatience. In Sharpsburg I run across our friend, Captain Sandrow. I told him what'd happened, and he got a few men and came along with me. The ford is three miles past Sharpsburg. It was getting dark and I was afraid they might be over the river before we ever got there. We spoke to some sentries, and sure enough they'd passed Naylor and his wife through late in the afternoon, him having a pass signed by our friend, Major E.J. Allen. He had to be headed fer the ford. He was in his buggy, and we were on horseback, so we made up fer lost time by heading across the fields. Without Captain Sandrow I'd never have found the place so fast. Even then we almost missed him.

"When we got to the ford, it was dark. At first we seen nothing. Then the troopers started to poke around the sides of the road, and one of them found the buggy with some cut branches to hide it. The horse was gone and I guess it'll find its own way home, if somebody don't adopt it first. We dismounted and went to the riverbank. There was a half moon and the night was clear, but sound carries over the water at night, so we heard the oars before we seen them. We went fer the horses. We were no sooner in the water, not galloping, ye know, but going slower so as to be able to hear where they were when from the other side a voice calls out, 'Who goes there?' and one of our men, a little in front of us, hollers, 'Watch out boys, I think it's the reb cavalry.' That was all it took. About ten shots come at us from the other side, but not one of them hit us. The Naylors weren't as lucky. We heard a splash, and then Mrs. Naylor cried out, 'Don't shoot! We're friends! Help my husband! He's in the river!' There was enough shooting by that time to slow us down, seeing as how there wasn't enough light to be sure we weren't running into a trap. Before we got to the other side, the boat was ashore and we heard horses riding away through the woods when we come out of the river. We'd no chance of finding them, so we turned round and come back. At daylight we rode downstream all along the bank and we found Naylor. He was shot in the heart and I'd guess he was dead when he hit the water. His wife got clean away."

It was not in Dougherty's heart to feel triumphant. He thought of the beautiful Althea and of the talents of her husband and, even though they were enemies, he could not bring himself to wish her harm. Naylor had killed Elgin and may well have thought of that as an act of war, but Dougherty was convinced that Arthur Elgin had never been a threat to Naylor's life — and he was just as convinced that Naylor knew that.

"Sir," said McBrien, "in all the activity of the last few days, I never did ask ye if ye'd found the secret to the code. Did ye ever learn what the message meant?"

Dougherty asked him if he would be good enough to fetch his notebook. When he brought it, he showed him what he had done, although the explanation came out slowly. His throat hurt and it took many a drink of water to urge him along.

"When I dropped the notebook and found the little packet of black earth that we had combed from Doctor Elgin's hair, it made me think of the Naylors' conservatory and the dirt I had seen there. Suddenly, in my mind's eye, I could see the flat boxes of plants with their jagged edged leaves and I realized that they were strawberries. The solutions had been under my nose and Doctor Naylor seemed to take a certain pleasure in urging me to look at them. He had made a point of my coming to see the conservatory in the daylight.

"That made me wonder if the key to the code might be just as blatantly displayed... and what was more likely than the motto above the entrance to Willowbrook Hall, *Ut languores curarent*? I applied it to the message, but the result made no sense."

He opened the notebook and showed them what his efforts had produced.

```
NELAG TNISS OPERI NEVNO CSETR
APSUT ICREX EMAUQ ETNAT AGOCM
UILEO RPTUE RANIT SEFTI CIDES
TETIC SONGO CAINM OROIN UINTI
NEVNI SILAI CEPSI SSUIR ALPME
XE
```

"I was ready to give up, when my eye caught one particular configuration of letters in the third column of the second row — 'EMAUQ,' and I thought how much easier it would have been to solve the code, if only I had the combination of 'QU' rather than 'UQ,' and that made me wonder if it was written backwards! What would I get if I took the letters after the Q? I began reading, and I found, 'quamexercitus.' I took the few letters before the Q and what I discovered was, 'antequam exercitus,' the Latin words for, 'before the army.' I reversed the whole message and it said: 'Exemplar iussi specialis invenit N. Iunior. Omnia cognoscit et se dicit festinare ut proelium cogat antequam exercitus partes convenire possint. Galen.'"

"What does it mean?" Genevieve asked.

"'The Young N[apoleon] has found a copy of the special order. He knows everything and says that he is hurrying to force a battle before the parts of the army can be brought together. Galen,' — an alias which was one more indication that the sender was a physician."

"How could Doctor Naylor have known that General McClellan had a copy of the order?" Miss Collingwood asked.

"Ah, sure that's easy enough explained," said McBrien, "It's been the talk of the army fer a few days. When Little Mac first got Lee's general order, there were some civilians from Frederick in his headquarters, and he made the mistake of telling them that he had what he needed to whip Bobby Lee. A few of them were sympathetic to the South. I think that Naylor might'a been there with the others. I'd have not a doubt that the word was sent back to Lee in more ways than one, and Doctor Naylor was one of the people who relayed it."

"I am sure that you are right," Dougherty said, "and it is this note, sent to his doctor friend from North Carolina, that was found by Doctor Elgin and that led directly to his death."

Like so much of war, it was a dreadful waste. The news was of little use to Lee, since he had already planned to regroup his army, and had full confidence that McClellan would give him more than enough time to do so, and he did. It was an absolutely useless secret by the time Doctor Elgin found the coded message, and that became the occasion of a brutal murder and, ultimately, of the death of Doctor Naylor and the grief of his wife. In spite of what they had done, Dougherty could feel only sorrow for them and for the others involved.

It was a few days later, and Dougherty was feeling much better, when McBrien arrived to say that he had been to Willowbrook Hall. He handed Dougherty his pistol.

He had gone there, having received another anonymous note, and discovered that John C. Babcock and Thomas Hanson had arrived before him. Hanson was all for forcing him to leave at once; but Mr. Babcock, who seemed not the least bit surprised to see McBrien there, allowed him to accompany them into the house. That was how he had come to have Dougherty's revolver; but he had also acquired some interesting information.

Doctor Naylor really had been an agent of Pinkerton, but he was also in the employ of the Confederate secret service, and it was there that his true loyalties lay. He supplied Pinkerton with information, including numbers and dispositions of Lee's troops, but his numbers were vastly inflated and his information on troop movements was always outdated, of little real value. He knew that the inflated numbers would play right into McClellan's excessive caution and would justify his endless demands for more and more reinforcements.

McClellan finally did begin to move. On November 7, a bitterly cold and snowy day, he was at Rectortown, Virginia, where he received news he could not have wanted to hear. Lincoln had finally come to the limit of his patience with McClellan's "slows." He had replaced him with General Ambrose E. Burnside. When McClellan went, so did Pinkerton. The General's parting message to the Army of the Potomac was quite moving.

> In parting from you I cannot express the love and gratitude I bear for you. As an Army you have grown up under my care. In you I have never found doubt or coldness. The battles you have fought under my command will proudly live in our Nation's history. The glory you have achieved, our mutual perils and fatigues, the graves of our comrades fallen in battle and by disease, the broken forms of those whom wounds and sickness have disabled — the strongest associations which can exist among men, unite us still by an indissoluble tie. Farewell!

By the time this happened Dougherty was back with the regiment in Rectortown to witness the sadness of the soldiers as McClellan took his leave. Dougherty could not share that sadness. He had become disillusioned with the man.

The death of Arthur Elgin was consigned to historical oblivion. For reasons of "national security" Allan Pinkerton had confiscated any drawings or photographs of the body in the possession of Frank Schell and Alexander Gardner. Nothing of the case would ever find its way into the annals of the medical museum in Washington. No report was ever made of any items found at the house of Doctor Naylor. Dougherty was ordered to be silent about his part in the case. The body of Doctor Arthur Elgin was consigned to an unmarked grave. Years later, when members of his family sought to have his remains returned to Virginia, they were totally unsuccessful in their endeavor. It was as if he had never existed.

Yet Dougherty did not leave Sharpsburg unhappy. McClellan took his fond farewell of the Army of the Potomac, but Dougherty took a much fonder farewell of Miss Genevieve Collingwood and had no doubt at all that his fondness was reciprocated. With the blessing of her parents, they pledged to correspond and Jen was true to her word, writing to him within days of their departure. Dougherty fully intended to survive and return to the care of his nurse.

Thanks

Although neither of them is still alive, I must begin by thanking my parents, Edmund L. and Rose M. Mulligan. Both were constant readers — my father of histories and historical novels and my mother of mysteries — and I was well into both areas before I was finished with grade school. My years of teaching at Mount Saint Mary's Seminary in Emmitsburg, Maryland, furthered the historical part, since I found myself so near to Gettysburg, Antietam and other Civil War sites. At the same time, I was teaching courses in medical ethics and that got me involved in a new hobby: The history of Nineteenth Century medicine, with some special attention to forensic medicine. I put all of it to good use in writing this book.

I must also thank a number of others who read various versions of the manuscript, commented upon it, proofread it, or encouraged me in the error of my ways in spending my time so frivolously. Among those people are: Harry W. Buchanan IV, M.D., Alice Holland, Cait Kokolus, Maria A. Loch, Eugene and Alice Mulligan, Edmund and Martha Mulligan, Mary Mulligan, Elizabeth M. Nagel, Mary Reiter, Vicki Sefranek and Karen Siegfried.

I offer special thanks to Maria A. Loch for patiently typing and retyping the various versions of the manuscript.

HISTORICAL NOTE

This book is a work of fiction, but it takes place within historical events, and I have tried to be faithful to that history. The following play parts in the story.

BEAVER MEADOW VS. BEAVER MEADOWS: Beaver Meadows in Carbon County, Pennsylvania, is where I was born. Although it jars me to refer to it in the book as Beaver Meadow (without the final "s"), that is it what it was called on the official maps of the Nineteenth Century.

JEFFERSON MEDICAL COLLEGE: Medical education in the United States in the early Nineteenth Century was a hit or miss affair. Physicians learned mainly by apprenticeship or were self-taught. Medical schools had a two year curriculum without clinical practice. Jefferson was a notable exception, making use of clinical practice under well educated, practicing physicians.

In 1824 Doctor George McClellan, the General's father, founded Jefferson in his home. Popular with students, he was often at odds with his colleagues, so in 1839 the Board of the College replaced McClellan with Joseph Pancoast as head of surgery. In 1841 the Board established the "Famous Faculty" of 1841-1856: Robley Dunglison (Institutes of Medicine and Medical Jurisprudence), Joseph Pancoast (Anatomy), John Kearsley Mitchell (Medicine), Robert M. Huston (Materia Medica), Thomas Dent Mütter (Surgery), Charles D. Meigs (Obstetrics and Diseases of Women and Children) and Franklin Bache (Chemistry). Dunglison was a pioneer in forensic medicine. In 1856, for reasons of health, Mütter resigned and was replaced by Surgeon Samuel D. Gross, immortalized in Thomas Eakins' "The Gross Clinic."

PHILADELPHIA: Until 1854 Philadelphia was bounded by the Delaware and Schuylkill Rivers to east and west, and Vine and South Streets to north and south. Beyond those boundaries were seven communities, each with its own police force. A criminal could escape a jurisdiction simply by crossing a street. Consolidation in 1854 created one city with 23 wards, each with a police station connected by telegraph to City Hall and policemen patrolled regular beats. In 1856 Richard Vaux, a Quaker, was elected mayor through a political alliance with Lewis C. Cassidy's Irish faction of the Democratic Party, and suddenly there were Irish policemen.

Mrs. Kiley lived in the Fifth Ward, an area still fairly prosperous, but already declining as the waterfront expanded. Dougherty is from Carbon County and would not have seen an African American until he came to Philadelphia. Even there African Ameicans were only 4% of the population, but in the Fifth Ward African Americans were 20%, most of them servants for white families. They could not use public transportation, so those who worked there would have lived in outbuildings or in the area's side streets.

There have also been some name changes. What Doctor Dougherty knew as Prune Street is now Locust, High Street is now Market, and State House is now called Independence Hall.

MEDICAL THEORY AND PRACTICE: In the 1860's there was no concept of germs and no notion of antisepsis, apart from carbolic acid to control odors in hospital wards. Anaesthesia was used, with both ether and chloroform available.

Medical theory included "heroic" measures, which purposely aggravated symptoms on the ground that this accomplishes more quickly what the body is attempting to do to rid itself of disease. Thus, diarrhea (which was epidemic in the military camps) was treated with rhubarb pills, castor oil and sulphate of magnesia — all laxatives!

Mercurials and antimonials were common. Calomel (mercurous chloride) and Blue Mass (a mercury based concoction) were used for diarrhea, with side effects such as profuse salivation, bleeding gums and loss of teeth or hair; and it did not always cure the diarrhea. Surgeon General Hammond was forced from the service by a dispute over his effort to curtail the use of mercurials in the military, even though their risks were well known. Taylor writes this about calomel: "This substance, now called chloride of mercury, although commonly regarded as a mild medicine, is capable of destroying life, even in comparatively small doses. Several cases have already been referred to, in which excessive salivation, gangrene of the salivary organs, and death, have followed from the medicinal dose of a few grains" (Alfred S. Taylor, M.D., F.R.S., *Medical Jurisprudence*, 4th American edition, Edward Hartshorne, M.D., editor, Blanchard and Lea, Philadelphia, 1856, p. 95).

The rain on the morning of September 17, 1862, left many soldiers with colds and their immobility after surgery, led to pneumonia. That was treated with diaphoretics (also called sudorifics) to increase perspiration. Muriate of ammonia was one such substance. Digitalis (foxglove) was used as a diuretic or for pulse regulation, but its overuse could result in convulsions or death. Aconite (monkshood or wolfsbane) and veratrum viride (extract of American hellbore) were quite toxic and are not used today.

THE LOST ORDER: Lee's Special Orders, No. 191, issued September 9, 1862, divided his army and sent it in various directions. On September 13, Private Barton W. Mitchell and Sergeant John M. Bloss of the Twenty-seventh Indiana, setting up camp on a space formerly occupied by the Confederates, found a piece of paper wrapped around three cigars. While looking for a light, Bloss read the paper and realized its importance. It was a full copy of Special Orders No. 191. It was taken to McClellan and he boasted that if he could not whip Bobby Lee with that piece of paper, he would resign. He spoke in front of some merchants from Frederick, some of whom tried to warn Lee. McClellan still moved too slowly and attacked only after the Confederates had reassembled near Sharpsburg.

DOCTOR JOHN HILL BRINTON: Doctor Brinton was McClellan's cousin. In 1850 he earned the A.B. from the University of Pennsylvania, and the A.M. in 1852, the same year in which he earned his M.D. from Jefferson Medical College. He was then 20. He studied in Vienna and Paris, tutored by Pierre Louis, an advocate of disease classification by clinical observation and post-mortem examination. Brinton returned to Philadelphia, set up a practice and took a position lecturing in surgery at Jefferson. In 1861 he entered the army. He was at the battlefield of Antietam as described in the story and the written order given him by Surgeon General Hammond is contained in his memoirs. He also tells of Sir William Muir and the innkeeper's wife and speaks of the "rigor of instantaneous death," about which he wrote an article for Hay's *American Journal of the Medical Societies* in January, 1871. He mentions the dead horse photographed by Gardner and Gibson, as does Oliver Wendell Holmes who saw it when searching for his wounded son, Oliver Wendell Holmes, Jr., future Supreme Court Justice.

WILLIAM H. ASPINWALL: The letter on General McClellan's desk, causing Dougherty's concerns about the General's loyalty was sent September 26, 1862, and reads as follows:

My dear Sir:

I am very anxious to know how you and men like you regard the recent Proclamations of the Presdt inaugurating servile war, emancipating the slaves & at one stroke of the pen changing our free institutions into a despotism — for such I regard as the natural effect of the last Proclamation suspending the Habeas Corpus throughout the land. I shall probably be in this vicinity for some days &, if you regard the matter as gravely as I do, would be glad to communicate with you. In haste I am sincerely yours,

Geo. B. McClellan

William H. Aspinwall of New York was McClellan's political ally and intervened with General Winfield Scott on April 21, 1861, to urge Governor Dennison of Ohio to give McClellan military command of Cincinnati. He supported McClellan's bid for the presidency in 1864. He visited McClellan at Sharpsburg, arriving on the same day on which Lincoln left for Washington.

JOHN C. BABCOCK: John C. Babcock was 25 years old at the battle of Antietam, having enlisted in an Illinois regiment. He was soon detached for service with Pinkerton. He was an architect and became a skilled cartographer for Pinkerton. He did his own reconnaissance, and took special pride in his horse, "Gimlet," a handsome animal with the look of a racehorse. Pinkerton left the Secret Service when McClellan was removed from command. General Ambrose E. Burnside then hired Babcock to serve in his intelligence operations. Babcock continued to be employed as a civilian by the Secret Service for the duration of the war.

THE BUCKSHOTS: The letter from Dougherty's mother refers to "buckshots" and "Archball." Archbald is near Scranton and the incidents described in the letter really happened. The Buckshots may have been precursors to the Molly Maguires. The problems in the coal regions of Pennsylvania during the Civil War may make a good story in themselves.

THE VICKSBURG SQUARE: This code was used by Confederates throughout the war. It was a simplified version of a more difficult "autokey" code developed in the Sixteenth Century by Blaise de Vigenère. It was used in the Civil War as described in the story, although the refinements of writing in reverse and the use of Latin are my own inventions — either of which would have been no problem for an educated physician of the time.

Some Further Reading

The reader who has enjoyed this story may also find the following books of some interest:

Adams, George Worthington, *Doctors in Blue*, Louisiana State University Press, 1952, 1996.

Billings, John D., *Hardtack & Coffee or The Unwritten Story of Army Life*, George M. Smith & Co., Boston, 1887. Reprinted by Bison Press, University of Nebraska, Lincoln, 1993.

Brinton, John H., *Personal Memoirs of John H. Brinton, Civil War Surgeon, 1861-1865*, Southern Illinois University Press, 1996.

Fishel, Edwin C., *The Secret War for the Union*, Houghton Mifflin Company, New York, 1996.

Frassanito, William A., *Antietam: The Photographic Legacy of America's Bloodiest Day*, Charles Scribner's Sons, N.Y., 1978.

Kernek, Clyde B., M.D., *Field Surgeon at Gettysburg*, Guild Press of Indiana, 1993, 1994².

Letterman, Jonathan, M.D., *Medical Recollections of the Army of the Potomac*, New York, 1866, reprinted by Bohemian Brigade Publishers, Knoxville, TN, 1994. This edition also contains: Clements, Lt. Col. Bennett A., "Memoir of Jonathan Letterman, M.D.," in *Journal of the Military Service Institution of the United States*, Vol. IV, Nr. XV, September, 1883.

Murfin, James V., *The Gleam of Bayonets*, Bonanza Books, 1965.

Priest, John Michael, *Antietam: The Soldier's Battle*, Oxford University Press, 1993, White Mane Publishing Company, 1989.

Priest, John Michael, *Before Antietam: The Battle for South Mountain*, Oxford University Press, New York, 1992.

Sears, Stephen W., *Landscape Turned Red*, Ticknor and Field, 1983.

Sears, Stephen W., ed., *The Civil War Papers of George B. McClellan*, Da Capo Press, New York, 1992.

Smith, Stephen, M.D., *Hand-book of Surgical Operations*, Bailliere Brothers, N.Y., 1862, reprinted by Norman Publishing, San Francisco, 1990.

Taylor, Albert S., M.D., F.R.S., *Medical Jurisprudence*, Fourth American from the Fifth and Improved London Edition, Edward Hartshorne, M.D., editor, Blanchard & Lea, Philadelphia, 1856.

Wiley, Bell Irvin, *Billy Yank: The Common Soldier of the Union*, Lousiana State University Press, 1952.

Woodward, Joseph Janvier, M.D., *Outlines of the Chief Camp Diseases of the United States Army as Observed During the Present War*, Lippincott, Philadelphia, 1863, reprinted by Norman Publishing, San Francisco, 1992.

Characters

The following is a list of characters named in this book:

Historical Characters

Musician Solomon Aarons
Major E.J. Allen (Allan Pinkerton)
William H. Aspinwall
John C. Babcock
Surgeon William Beaumont
Miss Lydia Bidlack
Major John Hill Brinton
Musician Timothy Carr
Father William Corby
Major John Devereux
General William H. French
Alexander Gardner
James F. Gibson
Surgeon Charles Goldsborough
Miss Hall
General Henry W. Halleck
Surgeon Patrick Heany
Mayor Alexander Henry
General D.H. Hill
General Joseph Hooker
Surgeon Anson Hurd
General Thomas J. Jackson
Major John J. Key
Colonel Thomas Key
General Robert E. Lee
Doctor Rensselaer Leonard
President Abraham Lincoln
General Joseph F.K. Mansfield
General George B. McClellan
Father Hugh McMahon
Assistant Surgeon Bernard A. McNeill
General George G. Meade
Principal Musician Patrick Moran
General (later Sir) William Muir
Lieutenant Colonel Dennis O'Kane
Colonel Joshua T. Owen
Allan Pinkerton
General John Pope
Philip Pry
Samuel Pry
General Israel B. Richardson
Frank Schell
General John Sedgwick
Steward Richard Sheridan
George Smalley
General Edwin V. Sumner
Edward "Ned" Thornton

Senator Henry Wilson
Surgeon Joseph Janvier
  Woodward

Fictional Characters
Lily Barstow
Mrs. Birmensen
Major Jeremiah Briggs
Doctor Carl Gustavus
  Brownson
Mr. and Mrs. Collingwood
Genevieve Collingwood
Constable Delaney
Corporal Jonathan Darby
Private William Dolan
Doctor James V. Dougherty
Doctor Arthur Elgin
Randolph Elgin
Sister Elizabeth

Joseph Fuller
Steward Gilbert
Trooper Gormley
Thomas Hanson
Doctor and Mrs. Holbrun
Benedicta Holbrun
Caroline Holbrun
Mrs. Martha Kiley
Sister Mary Agnes
Steward Sean McBrien
Mrs. Althea Naylor
Doctor Oliver Naylor
Captain George Sandrow
Constable Thompson
Tully
Maggie Warden
Private Carl Wentz
Trooper Williams

CPSIA information can be obtained at www.ICGtesting.com
Printed in the USA
LVOW132145030812

292910LV00007B/38/P

9 781475 101188